Praise for The Hunt

"The story is bona fide creepy, and as it builds to its cliff-hanger ending (which delivers quite a good twist), readers will be torn between hoping Gene can maintain the ruse and that he will take on the bloodsuckers already. As revolutions go, this one is well worth keeping on your radar." —*Booklist*

"In this terrifying and inventive adventure, Fukuda turns the vampire novel inside out. . . . With an exciting premise fueled by an underlying paranoia, fear of discovery, and social claustrophobia, this thriller lives up to its potential while laying groundwork for future books." —*Publishers Weekly*

"Take the overwhelming aloneness of *I Am Legend,* add in the hunt of *The Hunger Games,* and you'll see why this combustible combo results in a tense moment-to-moment calculation of Gene's chances at survival." —*Justine Magazine*

"Fukuda takes the feeling of isolation that dominates adolescence and builds a world around it in a novel where the tension rarely slackens. He turns up the violence a notch from *The Hunger Games* with language that is as graphic as it is eloquent. Readers will hanker for answers as they'll discover a kindred spirit in Gene, who so eloquently describes the feeling of being an island in the middle of a vast ocean." —*Maximum Shelf*

"I was blown away from the first chapter all the way to the end. Fukuda did an excellent job turning the world of vampirism upside down. Wonderful descriptions, great imagination, and very tight characters. If you love vampire worlds, then read this book. You will not want to put this one down!"
—*Night Owl Reviews* (Reviewer Top Pick)

"The dialogue is authentic and intense, the setting is grim and frightening, and the narration is superbly executed—lending an immediacy to the action as it unfolds. A fine piece of work." —*The Examiner*

"*The Hunt* is utterly disturbing, dark, twisted, but incredibly fascinating at the same time. It was a ride like nothing else I've read before. Gene was a smart and sharp hero I loved to follow! And the ending was incredible with a cliff-hanger that will leave you hanging and wanting more—right now! If you are up for a thrilling ride then go and get *The Hunt*!" —*Bewitched Bookworms*

"*The Hunt* was fast-paced and awesome, propelling me forward with each new twist. It was dark, gritty, and intense. Gene was a dynamic character, while the surrounding characters were insanely creepy. They were ruthless, and it was perfect. And the ending? Just right!" —*The Passionate Bookworm*

"Action-packed, heart-pounding, page-flipping action. I'm thoroughly in love. *The Hunt* is a riveting, thrilling read—definitely one of my favorite books of 2012 so far. I can't wait to get my hands on a sequel, even if I have to wait a year for it." —*YA Reads*

"This book was hard to put down. I kept thinking about it when I wasn't reading it! I just love this new world Mr. Fukuda created." —*Milk and Cookies*

"Holy. Crap. This book is creeptastic! Some parts gave me shivers and others had me gasping and screaming out loud. I loved every minute of *The Hunt*! I couldn't put it down. It's horrific, terrifying, gruesome, and inspiring. A story of survival, loss, and sacrifice that had me reading late into the night and early into the morning. If you haven't already added *The Hunt* to your TBR I highly recommend it." —*Paperblog*

"Great book. *The Hunt* is at once intriguing and frightening. It's twisted and dark with just enough hope that it kept me on my toes and turning the pages. I can't wait to see what happens in the series because it should be interesting!" —*I'm Loving Books*

"Andrew Fukuda has given us a vampire version of *The Hunger Games* . . . one of the creepiest novels I have ever read. Gene is a beautiful character. Seeing his feelings really made this story for me . . . a must-read." —*I Heart YA Books*

"I fell in love with this book. I'm just going to say all the huge cliché things right now, because they express my sentiments exactly . . . 'I couldn't stop turning the pages,' 'I was up reading all night,' 'I didn't want the story to end,' and 'I CANNOT WAIT TO READ THE SEQUEL!' " —*Taming the Bookshelf*

"Very unique. This book is a standout. Andrew Fukuda has some good and original ideas. This series will only get better with each sequel." —*Poetry to Prose*

"The action never stopped! Brilliantly written, the author weaves the story of Gene and his lonely, isolated life with his desperate fight to blend in that is literally a fight for survival. The book ends with an interesting puzzler, meaning much more to come in the next installment. Highly recommended." —*YA Lit Ramblings*

"Andrew Fukuda has the amazing ability to successfully create an alternate reality where . . . in one of the most action-packed endings that I have read recently, it all comes down to one thing: surviving. With a last line that will leave you stunned, you will immediately want to hunt down Andrew Fukuda and demand to know what happens next. This book definitely deserves four stars!" —*The Book Vortex*

"*The Hunt* gripped me from page one. Completely refreshing. The world Fukuda creates is fascinating and creative. I ended up loving it—creeped out, a little scared, holding my breath. A book I finished in one sitting. *The Hunt* is violent, intense, and absolutely captivating. I highly recommend this. I will definitely be reading the sequels!" —*Rex Robot Reviews*

"One of the best vampire books I've ever read! This is a breath of fresh air within the genre. . . . Definitely makes my best of 2012 so far list. If you're looking for something fresh to read within the paranormal and dystopian genres, *The Hunt* is for you."—*Birth of a New Witch*

"*The Hunt* is fast-paced and exciting. Andrew Fukuda does a wonderful job of blending traditional vampire lore with cool and new ideas. He did a good job of bringing the story to an end, while at the same time leaving the reader begging for more after an amazing cliff-hanger. Even if you aren't a fan of vampire stories, you should give this a try. *The Hunt* is definitely unique." —*Karin's Book Nook*

"If *The Hunger Games* were taken over by vampires, this would be the result. A perfect blend of horror and YA fantasy, *The Hunt* sets a whole new bar for vampire novels. With incredible suspense, drama, ethical dilemmas, and a bit of romance—it's completely riveting. I loved every minute of this fast-paced thrill ride. Don't miss this one." —SciFiChick.com

"*The Hunt* is a fascinating thriller starring two fabulous protagonists. The story line is fast-paced and filled with chilling action. Fans will appreciate joining Gene as he tries to avoid becoming the prey of *The Hunt*." —*Alternate Worlds*

"I must say. You're a clever one, Mr. Fukuda. Kudos. I found myself reading this everywhere I was. It keeps you in your seat and *demands* you stay there. With the constant threat of heart-pumping danger and imminent death, the characters only grow closer and stronger." —*Teen Librarian's Toolbox*

"Andrew Fukuda managed to surprise me. I can't wait to see how it continues in the next book." —*Fighting Dreamer*

"With his propulsive plot and highly developed characters, readers will find it impossible to resist the vivid world Andrew Fukuda has created in this stunning standout debut." —*RJ Does Books*

"Fast-paced, horrifying, and delicious! *The Hunt* is a brilliant new series . . . steeped in horror and riddled with tension and fear that left me spent and wanting more." —*Kimba the Caffeinated Book Reviewer*

"From page one, Fukuda draws the reader into a fast-paced, suspenseful narrative of suspicious coincidences, unanswered questions, and building action. . . . In addition to fans of vampire fiction, this book will appeal to readers who enjoy survivalist stories, action, and adventure." —*VOYA*

"Full of suspense and intrigue . . . the combination of postapocalyptic/dystopian setting and vampires is fresh and gripping. The characters are well developed, and Fukuda captures Gene's struggle to determine his sense of worth and identity after leaving his vampire life behind." —*School Library Journal*

Also by Andrew Fukuda

The Hunt

THE PREY

ANDREW FUKUDA

St. Martin's Griffin
New York

This is a work of fi ction. All of the characters, organizations, and events portrayed in this novel are either products of the author's imagination or are used fictitiously.

 For information, address St. Martin's Press, 175 Fifth Avenue, New York, N.Y. 10010.

www.stmartins.com

The Library of Congress has cataloged the hardcover edition as follows:

Fukuda, Andrew.
The prey / Andrew Fukuda.—1st ed.
p. cm.
ISBN 978-1-250-00511-3 (hardcover)
ISBN 978-1-250-02075-8 (e-book)
1. Juvenile Fiction / Action & Adventure / Survival Stories. 2. Juvenile Fiction / Science Fiction. I. Title.

2013002667

ISBN 978-1-250-00530-4(tr ade paperback)

St. Martin's Griffi n books may be purchased for educational, business, or promotional use. For information on bulk purchases, please contact Macmillan Corporate and Premium Sales Department at 1-800-221-7945, extension 5442, or write specialmarkets@macmillan.com.

First St. Martin's GriffinEdition:September2013

P1

For Obaachan

THE PREY

1

WE THOUGHT WE were finally free of them but we were wrong. That very night, they come at us.

We hear the pack of hunters mere minutes before they reach the riverbank: gritty cries flung into the night sky, coarse and sharp like glass shards crushed underfoot. The horse, nostrils flaring and eyes rolling back, rises from the ground with a start. Muscles fused together, it gallops away with ears pulled back, the whites of its eyes shining like demented moons, into the vast darkness of the land.

We grab our bags, the six of us, flee to the docked boat on legs that judder under us. The anchoring ropes are taut, and our shaking fingers are unable to loosen them. Ben trying to quiet his own whimpers, Epap already standing on the boat frozen with fear, head tilted toward the sound of their approach. Tufts of his hair stick up like surrendering arms, mussed from a slumber into which he was never supposed to slip.

Sissy hacks away at the ropes. Sparks fly off the blade as her strokes become swifter, more urgent with every passing second. She stops suddenly, blade held aloft. She's staring into the distance. She sees them: ten silver dots, racing toward us down a distant meadow before disappearing behind the rise of a closer hill. The hairs on my neck freeze into icicles, snap and break in the wind.

They reappear, ten mercury beads cresting the hill with unflinching purpose. *Silver dots, mercury beads*, such quaint terms, my futile attempt to render the horrific into the innocuous, into jewelry accessories. But these are people. These are hunters. Coming to sink fangs into my flesh, to ravage me, to devour and savage my organs.

I grab the younger boys, push them aboard the boat. Sissy is hacking at the last rope, trying to ignore the wails screeching toward us, slippery and wet with saliva. I grab a pole, ready to start pushing off as soon as Sissy's cut the rope. With only seconds to spare, she saws through the rope, and I push the boat into the river's current. Sissy leaps on. The river wraps around us, draws us away from the bank.

The hunters gather on the riverbank, ten-strong, grotesque spillages of melted flesh and matted hair. I don't recognize a single one of them—no sign of Crimson Lips, Abs, Gaunt Man, the Director—but the desire in their eyes is all too familiar. It is the impulse more powerful than lust, an all-consuming desire to devour and consume heper flesh and blood. Three hunters leap headlong into the swift river in a futile effort to reach us. Their heads bob once, twice, then sink harmlessly away.

For hours the remaining hunters follow us along the banks. We try not to look at them, affixing our eyes on the river and the wooden planks of the deck. But there's no escaping their screams: full of unrequited lust, a keening despair. The four Dome boys—Ben, David, Jacob, and Epap—huddle in the cabin for most of the night. Sissy and I stay at the stern, guiding the boat with the long poles, keeping well away from the bank. As dawn approaches, the cloudy sky grows lighter in slow degrees. The remaining hunters, instead of becoming more languid with the approach of sunrise and the inevitability of death, only scream louder, their rage intensifying.

The sun rises slowly and glows dully from behind black clouds. A filtered, diffused burn. So the hunters die gradually, in degrees, horrendously. It takes almost an hour before the last bubbled scream gurgles away and there is nothing left of them to see or hear or smell.

Sissy speaks for the first time in hours. "I thought we'd journeyed far enough. Thought we'd seen the last of them." It is only morning, and her voice is already spent.

"It's been sunny," I say. "Until the storm yesterday." The rain and clouds had turned the day as dark as night and allowed the hunters to set off hours before dusk and reach us.

Sissy's jaw juts out. "Better not rain today, then," she says and walks into the cabin to check on the boys.

The river surges forward with propulsive insistence. I stare down its length until it fades into the distant darkness. I don't know what lies ahead, and the uncertainty numbs me with fear. A raindrop lands on my forehead, then another, and another, until rainwater lines down my neck and along my goose-pimpled arms like protruding veins. I gaze up. Dark, turgid clouds shift, then rip open. Rain buckets down in dark, slanted bands. The skies are coated as black as a murder of crows at midnight.

The hunt has only begun. The hunt will never end.

2

WE SIT IN the cabin huddled together, trying to stay out of the rain. Our sodden clothes cling to our thin frames and concaved stomachs like mottled leathery skin. Every so often, someone will—driven by the illogic of hunger—open the food bag and find it (again) empty. All the berries and charred prairie dog meat long devoured.

With the heavy rain, the river current has picked up. We work shorter shifts steering the boat, our strength depleting quickly now. In the early afternoon, Sissy and I work together. Two hours later, we're wiped out. We collapse in the cabin while Epap and Jacob take over.

I am exhausted but unable to sleep. A wind gusts across the river, rippling the surface already dappled by pelting rain. I rub my face, trying to chafe warmth into my cheeks. On the other side of the cabin, eyes closed, Sissy is curled on her side, her head resting atop her clasped hands. Her face, relaxed in sleep, is soft, the outlines stenciled in.

"You've been staring at me for the past few minutes," she whispers, eyes still closed. I startle. Her lips curl upward in a faint smile.

"Next time just wake me. You could sear through steel walls with that stare of yours."

I scratch my wrists.

Her eyes peel open; she sits up. Thick brown hair flops across her face, as tousled as the blanket she now lays gently over Ben snoring next to her. She yawns, extends her arms high above her head, her back arching. She walks over, stepping around a stockpile of sticks we'd brought aboard, and plops down next to me.

"The current's strong," I say. "Maybe too strong. I'm worried."

"No, it's a good thing. Means more separation between us and them."

Only a few days have passed since we escaped from the Heper Institute. We were chased by a mob ravenous for our blood and flesh. By the hundreds they poured out of the Institute, banquet guests driven by bloodlust. Against such a horde, the six of us had virtually no chance of survival. Our only hope lay frailly and solely in the Scientist's journal, a cryptic notebook that suggested an escape by boat down this river. The river, by luck, we found; the boat, by greater miracle, we also found. But the reason why we've been led down this river by the Scientist: that, we have not found.

"It also means less distance between us and him," she says as if reading my thoughts. She looks at me with steady eyes that are soft and knowing. I turn my eyes away.

Yesterday, when I'd come upon Epap's portrait of my father, it was the first time I'd seen my father's face in years: the deep-set eyes, the strong chiseled jawline, the thin lips, the stony expression that, even in a drawing, hinted at a deeper grace and sadness.

Now I think of the secrets those eye must have held, the agenda never uttered by those lips. On that very last day, my father had run into our home, sweating profusely, deathly pale. I saw the twin punctures in his neck. He had gone to such lengths to fake his turning. When he ran outdoors moments before sunrise, I thought he was running to his death to save me.

When he was only running to his freedom and killing me.

I pick up two thin branches from the stockpile and start filing them against one another as if sharpening knives. "You think he left this boat for you, don't you?" I say. "That he planned this whole elaborate escape for you. You want my two cents? The boat wasn't meant for you. It was meant for him, and for him alone. It was *his* escape vehicle. Only he wasn't bright enough to find it. Or maybe he built it himself but was hunted down before he could escape."

She stares at the sticks, then at me. "You're wrong. The Scientist promised us—almost every day—that he would one day lead us out of the dome. He spoke of a wonderful place where there was no danger or fear, where there was safety and warmth and countless numbers of other humans. The Land of Milk and Honey, Fruit and Sunshine. That's what he called it. Sometimes he described it as the Promised Land. And whenever he spoke of escape, he spoke of it as *our* escape."

"That was a big promise."

She presses her lips together. "It was. But it was what we needed. You have to understand—we were born in the dome, all of us. And we honestly thought we'd end up dying in it after a long, harsh life of captivity. It was a miserable existence. The Scientist—well, he showed up out of nowhere. And with this one promise, he changed our outlook, our lives. He gave us hope. The boys—especially Jacob—were transformed. Hope does that to you." She smiles. "We don't even know what milk and honey look or taste like."

"You put a lot of faith in one man's promise."

She looks at me. "You don't know him the way we do."

I almost flinch at her words that cut deep. But I'm able to control myself. A life of training will make you an expert at hiding emotion.

"Don't you want to find him?" she asks. "Aren't you the slightest bit curious where he might have gone?"

The sticks in my hands stop moving. Truth is, I've thought of little else.

Moonlight reflected by the river stipples across her face. "Tell me, Gene," she whispers, looking into my eyes.

I pause, her words—*You don't know him the way we do*—still ringing in my ears. The things I could tell her. That the man they know as *the Scientist* is the same man I have called *Father*; that I have lived with him, played with him, conversed with him, explored the metropolis with him, been told stories by him. I know that when he slept, his hardened face fell away to expose the face of a little boy, and that he snored only softly, his huge barrel chest rising and falling, rising and falling, his hands lying lax at his sides. That my years with him were more than theirs, and deeper. That I have been *loved* by him with a father's love, and that bond is greater than any other.

Instead, I rub the sticks harder against one another.

"You have the weight of the world on your shoulders, Gene," she says quietly.

I cross my legs under me, not speaking.

"Secrets," she whispers, "they will eat you up inside." She gets up and joins the others.

Later in the day, the rain stops. Sunshine breaks through a partial break in the clouds and the boys shout with jubilation. Jacob declares all is now perfect: they now have sunshine *and* speed. "Take that, you hunters!" he brazenly yells. The other hepers, laughing, egg him on. "Take that! Eat my dust!" Their laughter soars into the bluing skies.

But I do not share in their joy. Because every gained inch away from the hunters is another inch widening the chasm between Ashley June and me.

She has come to me in these last few days, unannounced through the most random of objects: the shape of the clouds, the silhouette of the ever-nearing eastern mountains. Every second that passes, every ripple of water left in our wake, and I feel the noose around her neck pulled tighter. Guilt pricks me. She is alone in the Heper Institute after sacrificing herself for me. Holding out for me, for a rescue I was unable to execute. By now she must know I am not returning. That I have failed her.

The boys are shouting, giddiness wrapped around their words, shiny and glossy. They are yelling about the Scientist, about the Promised Land.

The sound of footsteps running on the floorboards. It's Ben.

"Come join us on the deck, Gene!" he says, a bright smile on his face. "It's so much warmer in the sunshine than in the cabin."

I tell him I need to stay out of the sun.

"C'mon, c'mon," he says, pulling on my arms.

But I snap them back. "I can't. I'm not used to the sun. My skin is burning up as it is. I'm not darkened like you hep—" And I'm only just able to stop myself.

His face falls. Then he slips away, into the bright glare of sunlight, leaving me alone in the cold shade of the damp cabin.

Over the next hour, sun columns pierce through the clouds. The land opens itself up, its soaked colors bleeding into the terrain. The verdant green of the meadows, the deep blue hue of the river. All afternoon, I hear their voices slipping through cracks in the cabin walls. Even in the close proximity of the boat, they feel a thousand miles from me.

Sun pours down, its hazy texture like grains of salt falling into the open wounds of my conscience.

Late afternoon. Like dogs bathing in the sunshine, they're sprawled around the deck, soaking in the rays, napping. Their energies depleted, stomachs caved in and growling even as they sleep. It's my shift again at the stern. I drink in the sound of water lapping under the wooden boards, a rhythmic, hollow sound that is strangely comforting. The undulating bob of the boat prods me into sleepiness.

Epap is awake. He's hunched over, scribbling something, completely immersed in a drawing. Curiosity gets the better of me and I amble over, unnoticed.

He's sketching an image of Sissy. In the drawing, she's standing on a rock at the edge of a waterfall, one arm raised and staring ahead, her arm as slim as the horizon is long. The waterfall sparkles as if bejeweled by thousands of rubies and diamonds. She's wearing a sleeveless silk gown, her chest bustier and waist narrower than in reality. In the drawing, someone is standing behind her. It takes a moment before I realize who it's supposed to be. Epap, in a muscle T-shirt, his arms rippling cords of bunched muscles, his washboard abs reflecting moonlight. One hand is placed on Sissy's waist, the other placed farther down, lighting on her right thigh with an overwrought tenderness. Sissy is reaching back and grabbing the back of his head with a passionate fist, her fingers intertwined in the strands of his wavy hair.

"Wow, that's quite a feat of imagination," I say.

"Wha—!" he exclaims, slamming the sketchbook shut. "You little snoop!"

"What's going on?" Sissy murmurs, her eyes blinking with sleep.

"Take it easy," I say. "When you're done with your, um, drawings, mind giving me help with the steering? The current's gotten strong."

I head to the bow, angling the rudder pole until the boat slowly rights itself. From inside the cabin, Epap is barking about something.

After a few minutes, it's David, not Epap, who comes out to lend a hand.

Whoa, he mouths, seeing the river. "We're going really fast." He grabs the other pole.

Epap is speaking to Sissy at the stern, his arms spread wide for balance. She shakes her head in response, pointing at the sun-columned but still overcast skies. Epap edges closer to her, his hands waving excitedly. They continue speaking, intensely, but I can't hear a word over the roar of the river. I walk over.

"—river," he's saying to her.

"What are you talking about?" I say as I approach them.

Epap shoots me a disagreeable look. "It's nothing."

I face Sissy. "What about the river?"

"The river is wet!" Epap sneers. "Now start minding your own business!"

"You're thinking of docking, aren't you?" I say to Sissy. "To hunt for food."

Sissy doesn't answer, only stares at the river, her jaw clenched.

"Let me tell you," I say, "that's a wrong move. That's a mistake."

"Nobody asked for your opinion," Epap says, positioning himself between me and Sissy.

"Getting off this boat is a big mistake, Sissy," I say, stepping around Epap. His back bristles with annoyance. "Didn't we learn anything from last night? There's—"

"What part of 'mind your own business' do you not understand?" Epap snarls. "In fact, just go get the rope lines ready. We'll need to anchor this boat down once we land."

"Are you out of your mind? They want to eat us—"

Epap's head flies around, raw disdain swimming in his eyes. "Oh, really, figured that one out yourself, did you?"

"Listen! They might still be out there—"

"Not anymore, they aren't," Epap says. "Don't you know anything about them? I'm surprised how little you know considering you've lived in their midst your whole life. Hello, the sun burns them up. And hello, the sun is shining down now."

"It's not enough sun. The hunters, they're clever, they improvise, they have technology, they have determination. You underestimate them at your own peril."

"The only thing out there is food," Epap yells back. "There's wildlife running everywhere, it's like a petting zoo out there. Must have seen at least three prairie dogs already. Now, just leave the decision making to Sissy and me."

"Epap," Sissy says. She shakes her head. "I don't know. Maybe it's too risky."

A wounded expression crosses his face. "But Sissy, I don't understand. You just agreed to go hunting for food." His eyes are equal parts confused and incredulous. "You know how hungry we are. Think of poor Ben."

"Of course. But let's be levelheaded about this, okay?"

"No, Sissy, you just agreed with me. That we should dock and go hunting."

"I'm trying to be careful—"

"Is it because of him?" Epap says, jabbing a finger at me. "Just because he said we shouldn't dock, and suddenly you're agreeing with him?"

"Stop."

"Because of him?"

"Epap! I'm not saying we stay off the land for good. But let's wait for the skies to clear. For the sun to really scorch the land. If we have to wait until tomorrow, then we wait. An extra day of hunger isn't going to kill us. But rashly and prematurely going on land just might."

Epap turns his back to her, anger fuming off his narrow shoulders.

"Why're you so quick to get on his good side? I can't believe you're siding with him!"

"I'm not siding with anyone. I'm siding with reason. With what's best for all of us."

"What's best for *you*! You want him to think well of you, that's why you're siding with him!"

"Okay, I'm done arguing," she says and walks away.

Epap glares at her back. He's still got anger to burn. "See what you've done?" he says to me. "You think you're so smart, don't you? You think you're such a tough guy. *Oh, look at me, I survived for years living in their midst. Oh, look at my swagger*. You know, you're just ridiculous to me."

Don't be baited, walk away, I tell myself.

"Did you want to be one of them?" Epap says in a low voice. "Were you ashamed of who you are?"

I stop in my tracks.

"Because I've seen the way you look at us. I've seen the smugness on your face," he says, his lips twisting into a snarl. "You look down on us. It pains you to have to associate with us. Deep down, you look up to *them,* don't you? Deep down, you probably want to *be* one of them."

"Epap, drop it," Sissy says. She's turned around again, watching us carefully.

"You have no idea," I say to Epap, my voice tight.

"Come again?" he says, a silly grin on his face.

"You have no idea what they are. If you did, you'd never have said something so stupid."

"I have no idea? Really? I mean, really? *I* have no idea?" He glares at me with naked derision. "You're the one who has no idea. But then again, why would you? You've rubbed shoulders with them, been buddies with them all your life. You've never seen them rip your parents to shreds. You've never seen them tear the limbs off your sister or brother right in front of you. You don't know them the way we do."

"I know them better than you think," I say. My voice is low and even-keeled, but bunched, ready to be unleashed at a split second's notice. "Trust me on that one. I mean, what do you really know of them? They've been little more than your doting nannies, feeding you, clothing you, baking you birthday cakes—"

Epap comes at me, his finger pointing like a talon. "Why you—"

Sissy pulls his arm down. "Enough, Epap!"

"There you go again," he cries. "Why are you always so quick to side with him? *Enough Epap, stop Epap.* What is he to you? Why do you . . . oh, forget it!" He tears his arm away from her. "You want to go hungry together, go ahead. But if we get sick, if we starve, it's on you, don't you forget that."

"Quit with the melodrama, Epap." Her chest heaves up and down.

He casts his eyes away, doesn't say anything. Then suddenly leaps at me, his momentum catching me and sending our bodies crashing hard against the deck. The wooden boards drum hollow on our impact.

A curious, deep thump rumbles beneath me. As if I've jarred something loose under the boat.

Epap is cursing and swinging on top of me, and it's all I can do to deflect his blows. Then Sissy is prying him off me, her face a furious red.

"We've got enough to deal with!" she shouts. "We need to focus on fighting *them,* not each other!"

Epap spins around, stares at the riverbank. He runs a hand through his hair, his breathing ragged. But I'm not paying attention to him. All my focus is on the deck under me. I knock on it. The same hollow thump reverberates back. I knock the deck a yard away, and a thump of a different timbre sounds back.

"What is it?" David asks. Now they're all turning to look at me.

I thump the deck with all my might. And I hear it again, the sound of dislodgment. Of something secreted under the boat, hidden from unwanted eyes. A lump suddenly forms in my throat as I realize something.

"Gene?" Sissy says. "What's going on?"

I look at her with dazed eyes.

"Gene?"

"I think something is under this boat," I say. And now everyone's staring at me. "It's been under our noses this whole time."

Ben studies the deck, confused. "Where? I don't see anything."

"The only place a hunter wouldn't think—wouldn't dare—look," I say. "Underwater."

Diving into the river is like cracking through the face of a mirror. And as welcoming; it's all shards of cold that slash and cut my bare skin. My lungs contract to the size of marbles. I surface, gasping for air. The current is a beast. Although a rope is looped around my chest in the off chance—not so off, I now realize—that I might get swept away, it offers little comfort. I immediately grab the side of the boat. I allow myself a few seconds to get used to the cold, then duck under.

For grip, I wedge my fingers between the wooden planks of the deck. My legs go flying with the current, pulling me parallel with the boat. I'm like a flag flailing in high wind. Sunlight pours between the planks, thin slats of light cutting downward in the murky waters. It's eerily quiet down here, just a deep mournful humming broken up by the occasional swishing sound. My eyes dart around, trying to find something, anything, out of the ordinary.

There. A boxed compartment, jutting from the boat's dead center. Carefully, I allow my body to drift toward it until I'm wrapping my arms around it, thankful for the support. A metal latch, rusted over, hangs on the underside. It doesn't give on my initial pull. I yank it and the whole underside swings open.

A large slab of stone tumbles out, hitting me on the back of the head. The pain is numbing and disorienting. I make a quick, blind grab for the tablet as it slides down my body. But I'm too late. The tablet slides down my legs, bounces off my left shin, and fades into the murky depths.

Lungs bursting, I spin around until I'm crouched upside down, feet planted on the underside of the boat. It's now or never. One chance to make a dive for the tablet before it descends past the point of retrieval. I kick off the bottom of the boat. My body missiles downward, into darkness, into the cold.

A fraction of a second before the rope looped around me pulls taut, my fingertips touch stone. I grab it. Then I'm bounced up as if on a bungee cord, the force of it almost dislodging the tablet from my hands. I cradle the tablet against my bare chest, feel grooved lettering engraved into it.

I surface out of the water in a spray of white, my body reduced to one gigantic mouth gasping for air. Epap and David see the tablet and pry it from my tired arms. They leave me in the water, clinging to the side, barely able to hang on.

By the time I heave myself onboard, my body flopping wet and heavy, they've all huddled around the tablet. Heads pressed together and angled, they're reading the words chiseled into stone:

STAY ON THE RIVER.

—*The Scientist*

Their mouths are cracking open. A chorus of giggles and laughter leaks, then bays out. They are all smiles and astonishment and delirium.

"I told you! I told you! I told you!" Ben is shouting, slapping everyone on the back. "He'd planned this all along!"

Sissy is standing, hands clasped to her mouth, her eyebrows arched high, tears brimming in her eyes.

"I *knew* he'd come through for us!" Jacob shouts. "The Promised Land! He's leading us to the Promised Land. Of Milk and Honey, Fruit and Sunshine!"

Sissy's face breaks into a smile that almost feels like physical warmth. Her eyes close in relief. "How did you know the tablet was under us, Gene?" she asks.

I pause before speaking. My father would often play treasure-hunt games when I was a toddler, leaving me clues around the house. I remember how flustered I'd become, unable to find the clues I knew were there. He'd force me to slow down, take deep breaths, survey the scene with equanimity. He'd say: *You're looking but not seeing. The answer is right under your nose.* And almost inevitably, once I calmed down, I'd find the clue wedged between cracks in the floor, laid between the pages of a book I'd been holding the whole time, or placed in my very own pocket.

But I don't tell them any of this. "I was just lucky, I guess," I answer. I start to shiver, the wind gusting blades of ice into my body. I'm only wearing underwear, having taken off my clothes before diving in.

One of the hepers says something; a burst of communal laughter follows. Sissy rejoins them, clapping her hands. So much emotion gushing off of them.

I walk into the cabin where I've left my clothes in a pile. I strip off my underwear, wring it with shivering hands and arms. I can still hear them guffawing, their eruptions of laughter hee-hawing back and forth. I don't understand why they have to so demonstrably display what they're feeling. Can't they simply feel their emotions without needing to project them? Maybe captivity has stunted them, rendered them incapable of intuiting another's emotions unless it's spelled out for them in a vomit of colors.

They start giggling now, talking about the Scientist this, the Scientist that. This is the confirmation they've been looking for. The sign that the Scientist never left them, or betrayed them, that he is in fact waiting for them at the end of this path. For *them*.

And not for me.

Me, he abandoned in a metropolis of monsters. To fend for myself. A boy who cried himself to sleep and wet himself in bed for months afterward. But for *them* he created an elaborate escape plan involving a journal (clearly meant for them to find), and a boat to lead them to the Land of Milk and Honey, Fruit and Sunshine.

I hear another giggle, then another, their laughter like taunting jabs. I am about to tell them to shut up when I realize they have, in fact, fallen into a silence that is as sudden as it is eerie. I glance through the cracks in the cabin wall. I can't make out very much, just David and Jacob raising up the stone tablet. Quickly, I slip into my dry clothes and walk out of the cabin.

They've stood the tablet up on its base and gathered behind it. Water is still dripping out of the grooved letters and down the face of the tablet, forming a puddle on the deck. I read the words again.

STAY ON THE RIVER.
—*The Scientist*

But the Dome hepers are looking not at the front of the tablet but the back. Their eyes, seeing something I cannot, are wide with shock as they travel up the tablet, past the top rim, and fall on mine.

"What?" I say.

Slowly, they turn the tablet around for me to read.

Four words. Four words that will become as indelibly etched in my mind as they are permanently chiseled into the stone tablet.

DON'T LET GENE DIE.

The first words in years from my father for me, about me. A whisper from the past, growing into a breeze, then gusting into a blaze. A skein of electricity jolts through my body and I feel the crackling of ice thawing in my marrow. And though it is a surge of light and hope and strength that flows through me, all I can do is collapse to my knees.

Jacob and David are the first to reach me, and they're picking me up. I feel their hands clapping me on my back, their voices loud but no longer jarring, their bodies pressing against me but somehow no longer intrusive. Their arms sling over my back as they hold me up, wonderment spreading across their faces. Smiles break out, and their eyes are warm with welcome. Sissy's eyes clench shut as she presses her balled hands to her lips in excitement. When she opens her eyes to look at me, they are hot and tender.

"I knew it," she says. "It's no accident that you're here, Gene. You were always meant to be with us. To be a part of us."

I don't say anything, only feel river water dripping down my body. A wind picks up and my body shivers. She wraps her arms around me and gives me a hug. I'm still wet but she doesn't mind.

"Don't be a stranger anymore," she whispers into my ear, so softly, the words can only be meant for me, and she pulls me in closer one last time before we separate. Her face and the front of her chest are damp as she throws the blanket Ben has just brought over across my shoulders. Sunshine pours down on the boat, on the river, on the land, on us.

3

WHEN I WAS in second grade, on the night I was almost eaten alive, I sat alone in the corner of the cafeteria. It was early for lunch, and the relative emptiness of the cafeteria would be a large reason for my survival that night. In commemoration of the Ruler's Birthday, special synthetic steaks that were particularly bloody and flesh-textured were served up for lunch. Everyone ate with zest, teeth ripping into the steaks, blood oozing down chins and into dripping cups.

I bit into the faux meat and felt the ooze of blood seep out like water from a sponge. It was hard to ignore the gamy texture. I had long overcome the gagging reflex that biting into bloody synthetic meats used to induce, but this new, commemorative meat was especially noxious. I breathed in deep, controlled inhales, careful not to let my nostrils flare. I closed my eyes in fake delight, and bit into the chunk of meat one more time.

I felt a prick of pain in my upper gum that almost made me wince. I paused, my teeth still sunk into the meat. Blood collected in the cavity of my mouth. I let it flow out. Down my chin. Into the dripping cup. Took another bite. This time, the pain shot out in a bright flare, radiating around my skull. It took everything to stifle a cry. Teeth still sunk into meat, I kept my eyes closed, as in bliss, willing the gathering tears to dissipate from behind my eyelids.

And it was from behind the black curtain of closed eyes that I first heard the eruption of hissing and neck-snapping. Building in volume, stemming from all four corners of the cafeteria. I waited a few more agonizing seconds until certain my eyes had dried before opening them.

Students were twitching with excitement, saliva now mixing with the blood pouring down their chins. A few were attacking their steaks with renewed fervor, mistakenly believing that the tantalizing aroma stemmed from the meat in hand. Others, the older students, were lifting their noses into the air and sniffing. They were detecting something else altogether.

I bit into the meat again, not fully comprehending what was going on. I was only in second grade, after all. I was only a young boy, a little runt. Again, a jolting stab of pain in my gums. Blood sopped out, collecting in my mouth. But something was different about the blood.

It was warm.

I did not understand. I pushed the overflow of blood out of my mouth, felt the warmth even more keenly on the skin of my chin.

And almost instantly, everyone in the cafeteria stopped eating. Hisses broke out, loud and inquisitive. A few students leapt up on their chairs, their necks snapping instinctively.

I moved my tongue across the upper row of teeth. Starting from the back tooth, moving from tooth to tooth, over the rough crevices, over the pointed tip of the fake fangs I inserted every dusk. My tongue slid over my two front teeth, over the first, then—

Where my other front tooth should have been, there was a gap.

My tooth had fallen out.

I stood up. Half the cafeteria was standing or crouching on

their seats now. Even the kitchen staff, on the other end of the cafeteria, stopped working. Only the table of kindergarten students, mistakenly believing the aroma to be from the faux meat, kept on eating, eyes wild, jaws chomping.

I grabbed my dripping cup. Pretended to drink from it, but behind the cover of the chalice, I pressed my lips together, forming a tight seal. I let the blood pour over my chin, down my neck, onto my clothes. To cover over the heper blood as much as possible.

I put the cup down, walked slowly, casually out. When I felt a set of eyes fall on me, I bent over to do my laces, pretending I had all the time in the world and not a single concern. I walked out, one step at a time, sucking at the gap in my teeth, sucking my own blood down my throat, not wanting a single drop to escape my mouth, swallowing and swallowing and swallowing.

I forced myself to walk down the hallway. I willed myself not to cry. I almost lost control over my bladder and that would surely have meant my demise. But I controlled it all. Seven years old, clenching my eyes, my bladder, my face. Refusing fear, refusing emotion to make the faintest dint on my face. My father had taught me well.

My classroom was empty—everyone was at lunch—and after I closed the door behind me, I almost faltered. Almost gave in to the fear and the panic, almost let the tears and blood and urine come seeping out in a deluge of surrender and fear. But I gathered myself and lifted up my deskscreen. Still sucking and swallowing the blood, making sure that none of it dribbled outside my lips, I typed in my father's e-mail address. My fingers shook as I pressed each key. It was a simple message, a message he'd taught me to use in times of emergency.

A blank e-mail. No message.

It meant only one thing.

I hit SEND then picked up my bag. I exited the classroom, heard the growing commotion in the cafeteria. Shouts and yells. I swallowed and swallowed and hoped it was enough.

My father would be receiving the e-mail now. And I knew no matter what he was doing, no matter how busy he might be in that glass skyscraper, he would drop everything. On the spot. And come for me.

I made myself walk slowly, as if merely strolling outside. I avoided the front gate where traffic was heavy. I walked through the soccer field, the baseball diamond, then onto the street. A few midnight pedestrians turned their heads my way as they strolled past, their noses twitching. But I kept swallowing, and my eyes, brimming with frightened tears, were hidden behind my shades.

Only when I got home, thirty minutes later, only after I locked the door and lowered the shutters, did I fall to my knees, all strength and self-will clipped. I curled around my knees, and hugged my legs for they were my only comfort, and I pretended they were another warm-blooded person giving me solace.

And that is how my father found me fifteen minutes later when he flew into the house, quickly locking the door behind him. He gathered my quivering body into his, drawing me with his thick, muscular arms into his warm fold. And he did not speak as I sobbed into his shirt, dampening the front. He only stroked my hair back, and after a minute told me it was fine, told me I had done well, that he was proud of me, that I was a good boy.

But he had to leave me, a few hours later. After the moon had set and the sun had risen, he opened the front door and went out into the empty, sunlit streets. To my school. It was my tooth. He had to find it. If it were found in some isolated corner of the cafeteria, or next to a table leg, suspicions, still nascent and therefore likely to simply die away as all crazy heper rumors eventually did, would be confirmed. And if that happened, they would quickly put two and two together, and come for me within minutes, within seconds, they would race for me, they would eat and consume me.

But when my father returned hours later, minutes before the arrival of dusk, he came back empty-handed. He could not find my tooth. He was fatigued and his face fought fear, but he told me not to worry. Perhaps I had simply swallowed the tooth, he'd said, and the tooth was safely disposed of inside me.

I started to cry; I thought it was okay, I was home, he'd let me cry earlier. But he reprimanded me. "No more crying now. No more tears," he said. "You have to leave for school soon, your absence might draw attention." I managed to stop crying, but could not quell the trembling that quaked through me. I thought he would scold me again, but instead, he took me in his arms and hugged me tightly, as if to absorb the vibrations into his own body. I felt safe in his arms.

"I wish we'd just turn," I said into his chest.

He stiffened immediately.

I went on. "Why don't we do that, Daddy? I'm tired of being fake, hiding all the time. Why don't we just turn? It'd be simple, I could find a way to bring home some of their saliva." I was suddenly so lost in my own words, I did not register the anger in his face. "All we'd have to do is dab the saliva into a small cut on our skin. And then it will all be over, all this hiding and pretending. We can just become normal, like everyone else. We could do it together, Daddy."

"No!" he said, and this word was like a shout rammed into my head, the echo of which would never stop resonating. "No." He cupped my face with his large hands, brought his eyes level with mine. "Never say such a thing. Never think such a thing. Ever again."

I nodded, more with fear than understanding.

"Never forget who you are, Gene." His hands pressed tighter against the sides of my face. I don't think he was aware of the force with which he held me. "You're perfect the way you are. You are more precious than the sum of all the people out there." And he spoke more words, promises and oaths and vows to never leave me, and eventually his voice softened, the timbral tone soothing me, coursing through my body until it seemed like his voice melded with the DNA of my molecules. He held me tightly in his arms until I stilled.

My missing tooth was never found. Probably, I'd swallowed it. But for weeks and months and even years afterward, I lived in this constant fear that somewhere out there, in some forgotten hole or crevice or crack, lay my tooth, dull and yellow, about to be discovered. Like my own excruciating existence: discarded and hidden, eventually to be discovered.

And yet. Although I lived in a tiny crack between two worlds, in my father's arms was a universe of solace that was as high and wide and deep as love itself. And that day in his arms, I made a vow that would fuse so seamlessly into the core of my being that I'd forget ever consciously making it; until a decade later, when, floating on a boat down a river and seeing my name carved into a stone tablet, I would suddenly remember and commit myself anew to this vow: my father was my world and if he ever disappeared, I would search for him to the ends of this fractured earth.

4

NIGHT FALLS. AND with it, the day's celebratory mood. The land blackens into a gloaming and the river, once smooth as plates of armor, is fraught with an urgent undertow. White splashes kick up against the river's edge, ephemeral ghosts. Nobody utters the word *hunter* but the fear it generates is ever present in the tense lines grooved into our foreheads, in eyes that nervously scan the land, in tense backs that will not lie down to sleep this night. Although we have not eaten in days, our bodies have adapted to the lack of nourishment by tapping into inner reserves. But very soon—two days, at most—these reserves will be depleted, and we will start breaking down.

Sissy is sharpening her daggers, eyes fixed on the riverbank. Epap paces back and forth, the Scientist's journal in hand, occasionally flipping through the pages. When it happens, it is sudden.

"Sissy . . ." David whispers, eyes saucer-wide.

There are three of them. Sprinting in tight formation, a mile behind us, racing along the bank. They are on all fours, their bodies cheetah-like, legs and arms extending out to the ground, grabbing it, thrusting it under them in a blur with every leap and kick. The lead runner drops off, rejoining the line at the back of the formation. A new lead runner takes its place in the front. I see what they're doing: drafting off one another in a paceline, all the better to cut down on drag and exploit the lead runner's slipstream. Running in a paceline will mean improving their net group speed by at least 10 percent—a significant advantage in a journey encompassing hundreds of miles.

In seconds, they are sprinting alongside us. They are a tapestry of horror. Their skin, partially melted in the daylight like warm plastic in an oven, has, with the arrival of night, petrified into solid, pulled-back folds. Splattered randomly about their bodies are splotches of hair, tufting out in ugly streaks. No, not hair; these are remnants of their SunCloaks now melded into the soft pliability of half-melted skin. They've become ragged stray animals, foaming at the mouth, diseased skin dripping off bones, skinned paws pounding the ground. Their eyeballs swivel around to gaze—with longing and devotion—at us.

The third hunter looks vaguely familiar. Somewhere behind all the melted folds of flesh is a face I almost recognize. A large bag is strapped on its back—on all their backs, in fact—bulging with what looks like heavy equipment and bundles of rope. There must be at least a ton of gear on them. Their staggering strength is horrendous and awesome.

And then they sprint past us.

"Sissy?" Jacob utters.

Not even a single look thrown back at us. Their loping pale bodies disappear over the crest of a short hill. They reappear on the rise of the next hill, but much farther away, smaller, their collective speed, if anything, even faster now.

"Sissy? What're they doing?" David's face is ridden with fear. He stares off into the distance where they have disappeared. "Why did they race off?"

Sissy turns to me, confused and anxious. "Do you know?"

I shake my head. Nothing about this makes sense.

"I don't like this," Sissy whispers, and for the first time in days, a genuine fear shifts in her eyes. "They're getting craftier and stronger. They're getting more innovative, more determined by the day."

She's right. This is the first time they've hunted prey with smarts and determination to match. They've become craftier out of necessity.

Sissy taps against her thigh. Frustration seethes in her eyes.

"We have to dock, Sissy!" Epap shouts. "If they're in front of us, we can't simply allow ourselves to drift toward them."

She stares down the river. "It could be a trap. There might be another group of hunters behind us anticipating we'd pull over. Let's not get outsmarted here."

"I don't think that's their game plan," I say. "That's not how they operate. When it comes to hunting hepers, they're irresistibly selfish. Altruism for the benefit of another group doesn't enter into their thinking. If there is another group behind us, then the group that just passed us doesn't stand to benefit at all." I gaze into the river ahead of us. "No, I think there's only one group. The one that sprinted ahead."

"And they're setting a trap?" Sissy asks.

"I think so." I grimace. "I don't know."

"Then what are we waiting for?" Epap says. "Let's dock now." He starts moving for the pole.

"Wait!" Sissy says. "Maybe that's what they're hoping we'll do. Maybe they've circled around and are secretly trailing us even now from behind those hills. Maybe tricking us into docking *is* the trap they've laid; they're just waiting for us to stupidly self-remove the only barrier we have between us and them: the river. We dock, and they'll be on us in ten seconds flat."

"What do we do, Sissy?" David asks.

A steely determination glints in her eyes. "We stay on the river. If they've laid a trap ahead, we charge through. Whatever they have for us, we fight. But we don't wait for them, twiddling our thumbs. We chase our fate, whatever it is." She looks at me. "That's how *I* operate."

For almost an hour, we see nothing. The boat flows down the surging river, every second fraught with tension, an eternity of uncertainty. I'm at the stern, eyes peeled, searching. The river froths white against the banks up ahead where it narrows. *Don't let up,* I keep telling myself, *not even for one sec—*

The boat is suddenly stopped in its tracks as if we've hit a cement wall. We're thrown forward and sprawl all over the deck. I'm almost tossed overboard—only a quick grab at the boat's edge keeps me from plunging into the river. Sissy is the first on her feet, and she's swinging her body around, trying to get a sense of the situation.

I see what's stopped us. A rope spanning the entire width of the river, now pulled taut by the boat. The contraption the hunters had been carrying must be a harpoon. They used it to shoot the rope right across a narrow river bend.

"I think my ribs are cracked," Epap says, gritting his teeth. His hands fold gingerly before his chest as if cradling an invisible baby. "I can't breathe, it hurts even to breathe—"

"Sissy!" I shout. "Give me your dagger! We've got to cut the rope!"

The sound of feet pounding the boards, then Sissy slides feetfirst toward me, splashing up water. She stares into the river, sees the rope. Horror dawns across her face. She's about to reach down to slice the rope when she pauses.

"Cut it, Sissy!"

"What if they're hiding in the water?"

"They can't swim underwater!"

"Then where are they?"

"I don't kno—"

Something splashes in the river a few feet from us, sending up a huge spray.

"What was that?" Jacob cries.

Then another loud splash, closer to the boat this time.

"Are they in the water?!" Jacob says, moving away from the splashes. "Is that them?"

"No!" I shout, "they can't swim!"

"Then what—"

A *thrack* explodes next to my foot, sending up shredded wood chips from the deck. A large iron-cast grappling hook—black as night with four razor-sharp claws—is embedded halfway into the deck. The grappling hook is attached to a rope that extends all the way to the riverbank. And that's where I see them. The hunters. They're partially hidden behind a grassy knoll but the rope is like an arrow pointing right at them.

I fasten my hands around the grappling hook. A slippery emission coats it—their saliva—and I jerk my arms back. "Don't touch the hooks!" I yell at the top of my voice. "Their saliva is all over them!"

"Now's not the time to be delicate!" Sissy shouts back. "We have to pry them off!"

I stare back at her, dumbfounded by her ignorance. It's possible she simply doesn't know: if the hunters' saliva gets into an open cut or sore and into our bloodstream, it will all be over. The turning will begin. I rip off my shirt, wrap it around one of the claws. "Don't let it touch your skin!" I yell. "Use your shirts!" But I can't wrench the claw free—it's too deeply embedded into the wood.

Another grappling hook smashes into the deck on my right, narrowly missing David's head.

The hunters spill out of the shadows, pulling at the grappling-hook ropes, their strength churlish and brutal. The boat lists toward the riverbank with discomfiting speed.

"Sissy! Cut the rope!" But she can't hear me; she's trying to pull the other grappling hook out. That one is embedded even more deeply—she's not getting it out. I reach for her belt, grab a dagger, and then I'm reaching over into the water at the stern. But when I touch the harpoon rope that's pressed against the boat, my heart sinks. It's made of a hard synthetic material I instinctively know is resistant to cutting. It'll take fifteen minutes to cut through with this knife. I try to shove the rope downward, hoping to dislodge the boat that way. But the rope is pressed too tightly into the wood.

By now the boat's been pulled halfway to the bank, close enough to see a hunter—hissing, ankle-deep in the river—making a throwing motion. A grappling hook soars into the night sky.

"Watch out!" I shout.

Ben is focused on dislodging the first grappling hook; he doesn't see this one in the air arcing down toward his head. Epap, still cradling his ribs, leaps up and pulls Ben away just as the hook smashes into the very spot he was kneeling. They fall to the ground, in front of the cabin, Epap's body flopping to the deck. He's been knocked out; I see an ugly gash down the side of his face where a hook must have struck him. Blood gushes out.

The hunters scream with ecstasy into the night.

The rope line falls right on top of Epap, and now I'm diving at him, shoving him roughly aside before the line can pull taut and pin him painfully against the deck, or, worse yet, sever a limb. Three grappling-hook lines are hauling us in now. And with such force, the far length of the boat lifts a foot off the water. The boat, listing at an angle, ripples faster yet toward the bank as if powered by a sideways motor.

Sissy is hacking away at one of the grappling-hook lines, but she gives up. They're made of the same synthetic material as the harpoon rope. Her eyes focus with intensity, a hundred calculations made in seconds, a dozen options considered and discarded until there is only one remaining. She grabs David and Jacob roughly, pushes them into the cabin where Ben and I are still sprawled. Epap is still knocked out, his chest rising and falling with shallow rapidness.

"Listen to me," she says. Water drips off her face. "I'm swimming for the bank. I'll dive off this side of the cabin and swim underwater so they don't see me. In the meantime, you all distract them. Keep pulling on those hooks."

"Sissy, no!" Ben cries.

"It's the only play we have left."

"There's got to be something else—"

She grabs Ben's arms, hard enough to make him wince. "There isn't, Ben."

"Then let me go," I say. "I'm a strong swimmer, I can make it."

"No," she says, sheathing her dagger into her belt.

"We both go, then," I insist.

"No," she says, snatching the dagger out of my hand. She snaps it securely into her belt.

"Sissy—"

And she stares at me with a fierce look that is somehow both anger *and* wonder. She holds my gaze a beat longer than necessary. "*Don't let Gene die*," she finally whispers, and just like that, she whisks past me, dives into the river with barely a splash.

David starts to cry. I pull him up, him and Jacob, and Ben, too, knowing all three will need each other. "Listen to me, boys," I say with as much conviction as I can muster. "Sissy gave you a job to do. Get those damn hooks off our boat. Use your shirts, no skin contact. Do you understand?" Jacob nods, and I gently cup David's face with two hands. His skin is too thin. He wasn't meant for a world like this. I stare courage into his eyes. He nods.

"Go!" I say, and push them out to the deck. They scamper off, each to a hook.

And then I am leaping off the boat, diving into the river.

Cold, black liquidness. The current whips me downstream. I fight against it, resisting the swirling eddies that almost spin me around. Get spun down here, and you'll be forever disoriented. I stroke hard, forsaking fine-tuned navigation, simply wanting to propel myself forward before my lungs give out.

The bank comes at me like a vicious slap. Sharp rocks cut into my hands, jamming my fingers. I pull myself out, wet clothes weighing me down. Force myself forward, on my feet. I see the boat. Farther than I'd have thought. The current carried me almost fifty meters downstream. A warm liquid spreads down my hand. Even before I see it, I know what it is. My blood pouring out from the gashes.

Howls break out, high-pitched enough to shatter the stars, shake the moon. They smell my blood.

The three grappling-hook lines suddenly go limp, and the listed side of the boat falls back into the water with a splash. The hunters have let go. They're coming for me.

"Sissy! Where are you?"

"Over here. Come quickly."

She's standing by a pile of equipment dumped on the ground. More ropes, grappling hooks, a loaded harpoon gun. The hunters must have placed extra equipment here earlier for insurance. In case we were somehow able to break free from the first trap, they'd simply race down and set up another.

"They're coming, Sissy."

"I know."

I pick up the harpoon gun. Try to, anyway. It weighs a ton. I won't be able to carry it, much less use it. Not alone, anyway. "Sissy, help me with this gun. Together we can lift it."

She doesn't answer.

I look up. She's gone.

More howls squeal toward me, disconcertingly close. I race up over the crest of the hill, and there, standing halfway down, looking diminished in the moonlight is Sissy. She's gripping a dagger in one very white, clenched hand. Two hunters streak toward her. Hours of anaerobic exertion have burnished away their body fat. Their rib cages poke through their gaunt chests, and membranous skin flaps on their bony frames like bleached clothes hanging on a laundry line. The third hunter is nowhere to be seen.

Sissy doesn't move. They're twenty seconds away, and she's biding her time, trying to find the best angle to fling daggers. But she doesn't understand them the way I do. I know their tactics.

"Sissy," I say, running to her. "Take them out now."

"No," she whispers. "Too far."

"They're going to split soon. One left, one right, they'll come at us from opposite ends. To disorient you. To blindside you. You'll be aiming for one while the other is leaping on your back. Now, Sissy!"

She believes me. In a blur, she flings out the dagger, east of the incoming hunters. As they continue sprinting, their heads turn to watch the rotating, blinking blade. They follow its slow, languorous arc over the river then back toward them.

And in the last moment, as it curls around at them, they leap over the flying dagger.

They turn back to face us again, a victorious yowl screeching out of them. They know. They've been told about Sissy's daggers.

But there's something they don't know.

That's not the only dagger in the air.

While their eyes had followed the first dagger's trajectory, she'd flung out the second.

One of the hunters is viciously flung to the side, as by an invisible leash quickly pulled taut. The second dagger has impaled its neck: the hunter's melted, cheesy skin offers little resistance, and the blade penetrates until almost the whole hilt is embedded. The hunter lies on its back, legs and arms scrabbling the air like an upside-down turtle. It struggles to get up, can't. The blade has punctured its windpipe.

The other hunter screams into the air. Not with fear. Not with sorrow over its downed compatriot. But with glee. It will now have a larger share of the hepers. It comes at Sissy with a manic salivary giddiness.

Sissy reaches down to her belt. Only three daggers left. She flings the first to her right. All eyes—including the hunter's—swivel to follow it. But she's faked us out. The blade is still in her hand. And then it is not. She's flung it in a boomerang arc, in the other direction of her fake throw.

But she's not pausing to watch her handiwork. She's flinging the other dagger straight ahead right between the eyes of the hunter. Two daggers now, both slashing through the night air toward the hunter whose head is turned away, still trying to locate the arc of the dagger never thrown. It doesn't have a clue. It's going to be a double direct hit.

But this time, there's something *we* don't know.

The hunter knows. It's always known the first throw was feigned.

In the last second, it drops its body to the ground, skidding on its side. The two blades clash together, right above its head. There's an explosion of sparks. The hunter squeals from the flash of light. But that's the only pain it feels. And even now it is standing up, eyes fixing on us. It brings up its wrist, rakes it with long, deep gashes. Its eyes dance with mirth and glee.

There's only one dagger left.

The hunter charges at us. It is only seconds away.

Sissy thrusts her arm back, readying to throw the last dagger in hand. But she makes a rare mistake. A fatal mistake. As she pulls her arm back, the dagger slips out of her grasp. It flies behind us, soaring up into the sky.

The hunter screams with delight. It is the closest sound to laughter I've ever heard one of them make. It is an obscene, perverse sound.

Sissy turns around as the dagger sails into the sky. Her movement is deliberate, purposeful, as if every microsecond that has passed and that is about to pass is part of a coordinated plan. The dagger is easy to spot. It's perfectly silhouetted within the circumference of the bright full moon.

I'm not the only one watching the dagger. The hunter is keenly tracking the dagger's upward path, its head rising. The full glare of moonlight catches the hunter by surprise, hitting it flush in the face. The hunter squints, then clenches its eyes with a yelp. It's momentarily blinded.

And now I understand.

The dagger reaches its apex then suddenly boomerangs diagonally back down toward us. Right at my face.

Sissy leaps in the air, snatches the blade out of the air. In the same movement, while still airborne, she flings the dagger at the hunter. The blade flashes past me, an inch from my head. The hunter's eyes are still rammed shut; it never sees it coming.

The dagger bludgeons into the side of its head, right through the soft depression of the temple. The blade pierces true and deep, inflicting unseen but necessary damage within the skull and eye sockets. Eyeball juice squirts out from between the clenched eyelids. The hunter drops to the ground, wracked with spasms. It tries to dislodge the dagger but, in its pain-fueled panic, ends up only inflicting further damage. Its arms slash wildly, legs kicking at blades of grass.

Sissy is in a semicrouch after landing from her throw. I place my hands on her upper arms. They're quivering with minute tremors along her slender but toned triceps. They feel like the most lonesome, bravest arms I've ever touched.

"Come, I'll help you," I say.

"There's still one more out there." She straightens her back, her body at first leaning against mine, then she starts running.

"Sissy! Where are you going?"

She runs fifty meters out, bends to pick up two daggers. She quickly sheathes them, and sprints back, glancing at the downed, groaning hunters. At the daggers protruding from them. She wants her daggers back. But she knows better than to tempt fate.

A single baleful howl sounds from a boulder to our left. The third hunter, crouching in the moonlight. It has been silently observing us this whole time, studying us, learning our tactics.

Sissy backpedals until she's beside me. "This one's different. More dangerous."

It climbs down, sleek and feline, its paws padding around the rocky, dimpled surface. I recognize it. Her. It's Crimson Lips. One of the lottery hunters. Her face is distorted now, as if viewed behind a glazed window, her usually rouged lips pulled back and melded into her cheeks. Yet even now with a body that has the constitution of porridge and melted plastic, her movement is graced with a fluidity that is savage and sexual.

"Get behind me," Sissy whispers. "I'll take it out with the daggers."

"Daggers won't work. Not with this one. She's been observing and studying; she knows all your tricks now."

Sissy grips and regrips the daggers.

"Keep walking backward," I whisper. "I have a plan."

Crimson Lips jumps off the boulder, starts moving toward us in a crouched-down, slow-motion crawl. Her legs and arms move in parallel tandem, left leg with left arm, right leg with right arm, the legs stepping on the very spot on the ground just vacated by the arms.

"What's the plan?" Sissy asks.

"The harpoon."

Sissy shakes her head. "It's too heavy."

"Not if we both lift it. Now!" I say, spinning and running for the pile of equipment I'd seen earlier. Sissy matches me stride for stride. We slide on each side of the pile, the dewy grass allowing us to skid easily. Crimson Lips bounds toward us.

"Help me!" Sissy is hoisting her side of the harpoon. I grab the other and together we lift it. It's the weight of three large men. I place two fingers on the trigger; Sissy's fingers are already there, and I lay mine atop hers.

Crimson Lips, on seeing the harpoon, skids to a stop.

"That's right, back off!" Sissy shouts.

Crimson Lips's head cocks to the side. She darts to the side, then torpedoes right at us, an ear-splitting scream issuing out.

Sissy and I squeeze the trigger.

It takes every ounce of strength in our combined four fingers. The harpoon tenses, then violently snaps, spasming as the projectile explodes out. Our aim isn't perfect, but it's good enough. Crimson Lips lifts her hand—a useless blocking reflex—and the sharp spearhead slices through her fingers. I see two stumps—the index and middle fingers?—flung in the air as the spearhead impales her left shoulder. Crimson Lips is spun around, collapses to the ground. Her pain-torched scream is horrific.

"C'mon, let's go!" Sissy shouts, and she's grabbing my hand, pulling me along. We make a wide arc around Crimson Lips as she squirms on her side, trying to pull out the spearhead. Without success. Weighed down and weakening, she grimaces with pain. Our eyes meet.

"Your designation is *Gene*?" Crimson Lips says.

I freeze in my tracks. The sound of my name on her lips chills me to the core.

"That's the word she kept uttering," Crimson Lips says.

"Who?" I say, stepping back toward her. And already, I know.

"Closer," Crimson Lips says, her voice lower, huskier. "Come closer, Gene."

Sissy pulls at my arm. "No, Gene! It's just trying to delay us. There might be others on their way."

Crimson Lips's eyes fasten on mine. "The girl you left behind at the Heper Institute," she says, her head slanting lopsidedly. "When it was finally over, she kept murmuring *Gene, Gene, Gene.*"

Blood drains from my face. *When it was finally over*. I blink hard, the earth reels on its axis—

Sissy smacks me in the face. "We have to leave. Now!" And she is pulling me along by the arm, forcing me to run with her.

Crimson Lips's screams follow us all the way to the boat. The boys have flung off all three grappling hooks but the boat is still being held up by the harpoon rope. We follow the line and locate the harpoon gun, anchored between two boulders.

"Help me, Gene," she says. "Hey, snap out of it, what's the matter with you?" She starts kicking the harpoon gun on one side, hoping to upend it slantways between the boulders.

From the deck of the boat, David is yelling at us. "The hunter's coming back!"

That's all the incentive she needs. She delivers a powerful kick, dislodging the harpoon from horizontal to vertical. It disappears between the crack.

We leap into the river, swim after the boat. The sting of the cold water snaps me out of my daze, and I swim hard, stroking and kicking with fury. The boys pull us up, and we flop onto the deck, unable to do more than gaze at the stars above; they are so stationary, it hardly seems like we're moving at all. Only by the fading screams of the hunter do I know we are once more on the move.

Epap comes to, groaning aloud. The boys rush over to him, but I'm already up on my feet, pushing them aside.

"Stay away from him, don't touch him!" I say.

"What's the matter?" Sissy says.

"He might be infected. He might be turning."

By their blank stares, I know they have no idea what I'm talking about. "He got hit on the head by one of the grappling hooks. Those hooks were covered with their saliva." I lean Epap gently back down to the deck, start carefully checking his vitals. "One measly droplet of their saliva gets into you, and you'll turn. Transform. You'll become one of them."

Their eyes swing nervously over to Epap. He's staring at me, eyes agog with fear and bewilderment.

"You haven't heard of it because turnings are very rare. Most of the time, we don't survive attacks, we just get devoured."

"How long is this . . . turning process?" Sissy asks, worry etched into her face.

"It's quick. Ranging anywhere from a couple of minutes to several hours. It depends on how much saliva was passed. If you're infected by the saliva of more than one person, the whole process is exponentially speeded up." I examine Epap's skin, looking for any cuts or gashes. "I think you're okay, Epap. You're not showing any symptoms. They always appear immediately."

"Like?" he asks nervously.

"Cold skin, shivering, profuse sweating, rapid heartbeats. But you're fine. You lucked out."

Ben throws himself at Epap, hugging him.

"Stay away from me," Epap says, sitting up. "We don't know for sure if I'm safe."

"You're fine," I say. And the boys rush him, knocking him back down. In the midst of their tangle of arms, I see Epap's face break into a smile. An arm shoots out from the pile—Jacob's arm?—and grabs my hand. Before I know it, I'm pulled in, my body flung into the tent of their sobs of relief.

The boat pitches forward, gaining speed in the fast current. In front of us, the hulking silhouette of the eastern mountains looms ever closer.

5

HOURS LATER, I'M still awake. I move to the stern, away from their loud snores in the cabin and from Sissy steering at the bow. I need to be alone. Nothing moves in the moonlit plains; it is as still as a black-and-white photograph. The river is all sinewy muscles now, tendons rippling along its length, flowing quickly. It seethes forward, eager and angry in equal turns.

I am thinking of Ashley June.

Crimson Lips's words reverberate in my head, even hours later. *When it was finally over . . .*

The last I time I saw Ashley June, she was on a monitor screen at the Heper Institute, hunched over the kitchen workstation, furiously writing a note. I still have that note in my pocket, damp and sodden, fraying at the edges. She had risked her life, fled into the bowels of the Institute, for the smallest possibility that I'd return and rescue her.

I've studied that note countless times. I know the shape of every letter, every curl and dot. I take it out now, the paper damp, her handwriting blurred with moisture.

I'm @ Intro. Will wait 4 U.
Never Forget

One last time, I run my finger over her handwriting. A wind blows, cold and harsh, and I already know what I will do next. I close my eyes, unable to look as I rip off a small piece from the corner of the paper. I release the ripped piece into the wind. It whips away, fluttering like a tiny moth as it disappears into the night. I rip off another piece; and another; and another. And as the moon rises higher, I release a hundred million of these pieces into the wind, the paper in my hand diminishing. Until there remains only a piece the size of a small fingernail clipping, so small I cannot tear it any further. For a long time I hold on to this piece. Then with a silent shout of grief, I release it, and it is gone, and there is nothing left in my hand.

6

I'M SHAKEN AWAKE. David's pale face looms over me.

"What is it?" I say. The sky is dark, it is still night. "More hunters?"

David shakes his head. "No. Something else."

"Epap? Is he okay?"

"He's fine." David pauses. "It's something . . . We don't know exactly . . ."

I'm on my feet immediately. The current is fiercer now, a torrent, as if the river's patience has suddenly and decisively snapped. Sprays of water, kicked up like geysers, smack down on the deck, leaving the imprint of splayed hands. The sky is as dark and chaotic as the river, clotted scabs of black.

Everyone's looking at me, fear written all over their wide eyes and pinched lips.

"The current's fast because of all the recent rain," I say, trying to calm their wrangled nerves. "But I wouldn't get too spooked over it."

"We lost the steering poles. The current ripped them out of our hands."

"What?"

"But that's not why we woke you," David says. "Can you hear that sound?"

At first, I hear nothing beyond the slap of water against the boat. But gradually, I discern a faint hiss, like static over the radio, distant but unsettling. I shut my eyes, concentrating. "Ahead of us. Farther down the river."

"I first heard it about ten minutes ago," Epap says quietly. "It was on and off, fluctuating. But now. Listen to it. It's getting louder. Closer."

I stare ahead as far as possible. Which, in this darkness, is only about fifty meters. Even the riverbanks have disappeared from sight. Fear like a dirty fingernail scrapes along my spine.

"I think that sound is a waterfall," Epap says. "The Scientist taught us that waterfalls make a hissing sound as you approach them from afar." He turns to me, his face dotted with spray from the river. "What do you think, Gene?"

"I don't know the first thing about waterfalls. Before now, I thought they belonged only in fantasy novels." I stare into the darkness ahead. The hissing has become more like a sizzling sound. Louder, more ominous.

"I think this boat is headed right for a waterfall," Epap says. "We need to get ready to swim for the riverbank." He looks at me and I nod back. "I'll untie the rope off the anchor point," he says.

Over the next fifteen minutes, the river's fury intensifies. We get spun like an out-of-control carousel. Raindrops fall as if flung down in fury. And that ever-present hissing gains volume. We gather around Epap. He loops the rope around our bodies, tying us securely with tight knots. We squint against the spray of water and cold wind, trying to keep balance on the bobbing, spinning boat.

"Look at me," Epap says. "Everyone. Look at me. We need to jump off this boat, swim to shore—"

"Epap, I don't know!" Jacob says. "The river's flowing too fast! We might get swept away, separated, pulled under!"

"We have no choice!" he shouts back. "Everyone hold onto this rope. If you get pulled under, if you get swept away, just hold onto this rope!"

"We'll still get swept away!" Jacob shouts, shaking his head.

"No!" Sissy barks back. "Epap's right. We have to jump."

With one loop of the rope circled around our chests and wound tight under our armpits, we tiptoe to the edge. Sissy turns to me, her mouth right at my ear. "You and me. We have to stick tight together." She checks my rope, pulling it taut, with wet, white knuckles bulging from her hand. "The others. They can't really swim. David and Jacob, a little bit. But Ben and Epap will be dead weight. Do you understand?"

I nod. The speed of the boat is now terrifying. For a heart-stopping second, the boat goes airborne before pummeling back down.

"Everyone on my count!" Sissy shouts. "Remember: Don't let go of the rope. Kick with your legs, don't use your arms. Your hands never let go of the rope, understood? Never let go!"

I stare into the river, the water a swirling madness. It's not going to work; we're going to get swept away. Jacob is right. The current's too strong now.

"Three . . ." Sissy shouts.

As soon as we hit the water, we're going to get sucked underneath, then pulled in six different directions by deadly undercurrents. It's a dark, watery death hole we're leaping into.

"Two . . ."

Next to me, Jacob stiffens suddenly, as if realizing something.

"One!" Sissy's knees bend, preparing to leap into the black river. Down the line, the others are gray smudges readying to leap.

I bend my knees, jump—

"STOP!" Jacob shouts, thrusting his body away from the edge.

The rope pulls taut, catching me midair. I'm wrenched back, an *oomph* escaping my mouth, then I'm crashing on the deck. Seconds later, like delayed echoes, comes the sound of the others hitting the deck.

"Jacob!" Sissy yells. "What are you doing?"

"We're supposed to go over the waterfall!" he shouts. "We're supposed to stay on the river!"

"What are you talking about?" Sissy yells, rain smacking her face.

"Look, the hunters can't swim!" Jacob shouts. His eyes are brimming with excitement. "They drown easily in water. That's what the Scientist told us. Remember? He said a panic reflex kicks in if the water goes above their jawline. They freeze up, drown within seconds."

"So what?" Sissy says.

"So think about it. For them, a waterfall is certain death. They would never venture farther than this, it's suicide. But that's not—not necessarily—the case for us. We swim. We *can* survive a waterfall. It's like a keyhole that only we can fit into. It's the bridge to freedom only we can cross. That's why the tablet instructs us to stay on the river."

"I don't know," Sissy says.

Jacob is not deterred. "I think that's why the Scientist taught us about waterfalls. To prepare us for this. But remember, he always described them in a scenic, beautiful way. Like it's a gateway to paradise." His arms flail excitedly about, and suddenly I'm remembering the sketch Epap was working on yesterday. It *was* a beautifully rendered waterfall, an oasis of beauty. "We're meant to go over the river," Jacob says. "And down the falls."

"You're not thinking straight, Jacob," Sissy says. "That's a *waterfall* ahead of us!"

"I know, I know, I know," he says, eyes squeezing shut. His hands clench and unclench. "But we're supposed to stay on the boat! I know this."

"What are you talking about?"

"Stay on the river!" Jacob shouts. "That's what the tablet says! That's what the Scientist wants us to do. Stay on. Keep heading down."

"Within reason!" Sissy says. "That's a waterfall coming! What you're suggesting is sheer lunacy."

"Please, Sissy?" Jacob says, his eyes pleading. "Let's not deviate one bit. Let's do exactly what the Scientist instructed us to do. Stay on the river and not get off. Because it's what gets us to the Promised Land. To the milk. The honey. Fruit and sunshine. To streets filled with other humans, sports stadiums, playgrounds, amusement parks with thousands of kids milling about. We stick to his instructions, we get there." He shakes his head violently side to side, tears coming out. "It's all worth taking a chance for. Please, Sissy?"

Sissy bites her lower lip, stares ahead at the river, her face racked with concentration. She looks at Jacob. "We always stick together, don't we?" she says to them.

"Always, Sissy," Jacob says, his voice thick with emotion.

"So whatever I decide, we're all in, agreed?" she says. He nods. "You trust me, then?"

"I do."

She draws in a deep breath. "We're getting off this boat. Now."

Jacob's shoulders slump.

Lightning suddenly streaks across the sky, silhouetting the eastern mountains, a hunched, black colossus, so close now I smell the musk of a mahogany forest. For a millisecond, I see the river. Bands of water slide forward with terrifying speed and eagerness. It is a raging beast now, surging and frothing with anger straight into the mountain. Not around it, or through a steep narrow pass. But somehow right into the very heart of darkness.

I put my hand on Sissy's arm and shake my head. "It's too late, Sissy. The river's a grave now. We'll surely drown."

Her eyes narrow against the wind and rain, her lower jaw jutting out with frustration. She knows I'm right. There's nothing more to say. River water mixes with the cutting wind, drenching our faces. We stare forward, wondering what awaits us.

Five minutes later, the rain suddenly stops and the temperature plunges. The night becomes darker, black ink dousing us. The river roars in our ears now, an echoic tenor that rumbles.

We've entered something. A cavernous black tunnel. Inside the eastern mountains.

"Can't see anything, can't see anything," David murmurs next to me. "We're in the mountain, we're in the mountain, somehow we're *inside* the mountain."

I close my eyes. Open them. It makes no difference: just the same impenetrable black then black then black then black until the disorientation almost causes a physical panic. Everything is blacker, faster, wetter, louder now. The roar of the waterfall is deafening.

"Get ready, everyone!" Sissy shouts. We're crouching together, arms linked, the rope connecting us. "Get on one knee! Stay low on one knee! Be ready to leap outward—"

Her voice is drowned out. I pull myself up on one knee, lifting Ben up next to me. I feel a mist of fine spray on my face. We must be mere moments from going over.

"When we go over, jump as far from the boat as you can!" I shout, not knowing if they can hear me over the din. "Curl your body into a ball, don't let go of the rope. No matter how far we fall, don't let go of the rope!" I look over to see if anyone's heard me. But I can't see a thing. I only feel the tension of their bodies, the fear pouring off them in droves.

Then we're at the waterfall. The roar is deafening.

I open my mouth to scream but even fear has fled away.

The boat tilts forward and in that instant before we plummet over the precipice and the sick vacant falling sensation hits, all I want to do is grab Sissy's hand; and somehow in the darkness we find each other's hands and our grip is fierce and untidy and blood-warm human. And then the waterfall is here, then it is not, and then we are falling down a throat of blackness.

We fall for what seems like forever.

7

THE WATER HITS us—just when I'd given up on ever hitting bottom—with the concussive force of a concrete sidewalk.

And then I'm in a world of murky underwater darkness, the swirl of bubbles, the deafening churn of water smashing water. The rope looped around my chest pulls taut as metal, whiplashing my head backward. An arm claws across my face; somebody's leg kicks out at me. I don't know which way is up, which way is down.

Follow the bubbles up, I tell myself. I do, kicking hard. I feel the tug of rope against my chest. They're all under me. I'm pulling up the whole chain of bodies myself.

Then I'm breaking surface, from liquid black to empty black, stroking and kicking furiously. There are no shapes to be seen, only black-gray silhouettes. I push forward, reaching for a blackness that is darker than the surroundings. My hand hits something solid, and it is the feel of salvation. I grab it with two hands, and hoist myself up. I'm on a rock.

I spin around, start pulling the rope toward me. And like a miracle, they surface, one by one, sputtering, crying, cursing, coughing.

Alive.

8

THAT NIGHT, WE lie in a crumpled heap on that hard limestone rock. We have no idea how large or small it is, nor the inclination to find out. We are only too glad to be alive as we huddle together, sobs of relief racking our bodies.

"We wait till morning," Sissy says. "Wait for the light."

Nobody says anything. Not then, not for the next few hours. But I know what we're thinking: What if Sissy has it all wrong? What if morning doesn't bring light? What if in this womb of darkness, morning offers no reprieve from the unremitting black?

"Whoa," David says, the first to wake up. Turns out, we're on not an isolated rock, but the actual bedrock surrounding the plunge pool of the waterfall. Around us, countless shafts of sunlight shoot down from hidden openings in the ceiling. These shafts are so defined, they are like physical columns holding up the massive cave. And *massive* is too gentle a term: the cave is a behemoth. More sunbeams form, shooting down hundreds of meters in every direction, exposing the cavernous lay of the interior.

The waterfall itself is not nearly as tall as it had *felt* while plummeting down its length last night. It kicks up a huge spray that moistens thick layers of moss on the underside of the waterfall's overhanging rocks. Although there is no sign of the boat, a few of our bags are afloat and pressed up against the side of the plunge pool.

"Check those out!" Ben says, pointing up.

Stalactites cone down from the ceiling hundreds of meters above us, hanging like fanged teeth, sunlight glazing them reddish orange. Interspersed between the stalactites, vines dangle down like stringy food caught between teeth. Huge towers of calcite lift off the cave floor at leaning angles, and ferns and palms rope themselves around the base of these towers. Thinner stalagmites rise fifty meters tall, but it is the sheer gargantuan size of the cave that bedazzles us the most.

"You could fit a city in here," I yell, wanting to be heard above the din of the waterfall. "Skyscrapers twenty, thirty stories tall. Whole city blocks a mile long." Nobody responds; nobody hears me. I move away from the waterfall where it's quieter.

The others follow and we gather in a large column of sunlight. The warmth is glorious. The sunlight bleaches our skin, makes us glow with a nuclear effervescence.

"Now what?" Epap asks. All heads turn to Sissy.

"We explore," she says.

"Is this it?" Ben asks. "Is this the Land of Milk and Honey, Fruit and Sunshine?"

"I hope not," Epap says, shaking his head. "This place is the dumps. I'd take the Dome over this, actually. I haven't seen any milk, honey, or fruit. There's sunshine, drips of it, anyway, but we had more back at the Dome."

"This is what we'll do," Sissy says. "We break up into two groups. We look for a clue, a sign, anything. The Scientist must have left us something." She looks around, then hikes into the depths of the cave, Ben and Jacob in tow.

"All right, you two," Epap says to David and me. "Let's go this way. Eyes peeled, guys." We head off perpendicular to Sissy's direction, along the bank, following the river.

Hours later, there's nothing to show for our efforts. The terrain makes walking difficult, with loose rocks seemingly designed to sprain our ankles scattered everywhere. David, Epap, and I proceed slowly, not wanting to miss anything, but we spend most of the time with eyes fixed in a narrow cone of vision on the ground, negotiating around stones and slippery moss. And though we're heading toward what we hope is the cave's exit, after two hours, there's still literally no light at the end of the tunnel. If there even is an end. The river plunges down into a succession of large bowls at three different tiers, the descent steep and treacherous. Several times, we have to sidetrack considerable distances to get around huge boulders. We slip often on moss-laced rocks, our hands flailing wildly, grabbing at towers cloaked with flowstone and at tall rocks with scalloped surfaces. Eventually, our path is completely impeded by a wall of fluted limestone, massive and algae-skinned, ten stories high. The river snakes through a relatively narrow opening and into another tiered series of waterfalls. We head back, bodies hunched over with fatigue, starvation, and discouragement.

The other three are sitting in a column of sunlight near the waterfall when we return. Judging from their drooped shoulders and dour faces, they haven't fared much better. They hand us our share of lunch: a few berries they'd found that we scarf up eagerly.

"So much for the Land of Milk and Honey, Fruit and Sunshine," Epap says. "No food, no milk, no honey. Not even any wood to burn."

"We should head outside," Jacob says. "Follow the river out."

"We just did that," I reply. "Tried to, anyway. It's farther and more difficult than you think."

"It's our only move," Jacob says, glancing at the waterfall. "We can't backtrack—we'd have to climb up the sides of this waterfall, and they're way too steep and slippery. But we can't just stay here, either. We need food. We should leave now."

"No." Sissy says this without looking at us. "We stay here."

"Sissy—" Jacob begins to say.

"Look! I'm staying," she snaps. "You go if you want. I'm staying."

Jacob clams up, hurt shooting into his eyes. "I only meant—"

"I'm not arguing with you, with any of you! There're only two things we need to do, okay? Find some kind of sign left by the Scientist, and keep Gene alive. Is that simple enough for you to understand? This is our life distilled down to its rawest elements right now. Find a sign, keep him alive. Two things, people."

We sit stunned by her outburst. She walks away, her chest heaving, disappearing behind a large boulder.

I follow her. She's staring into the waterfall, arms crossed against her chest.

"Hey," I say, as gently as I can. I step through a short narrow pathway between two boulders.

She doesn't reply, only bites her lower lip, just half of it; the other half loops out in a fat curl. Her eyelids shut halfway, and a tear spills out that trails down over her cheekbone. She doesn't turn away as I thought she might. Her hand rises—to wipe the tear away, I think—but stops in front of her lips. She half-cups her mouth, her fingers quivering, her lips collapsing. Now she turns away from me, just as I see her face breaking.

The pressure has gotten to her. The burden of all their lives carried squarely on her shoulders alone.

I place my hand on her. She doesn't move away as I thought she might, but leans into my hand, the curve of her shoulder fitting perfectly into the cup of my hand. Her flesh is soft, but there is a fierceness in it, too, in the thin coat of hard muscle and the solid protrusion of jutting shoulder bone. She turns and looks at me with a fierce intensity. It is the kind of attention my father taught me to always avoid. Eye contact meant you were at the center of a person's attention; get out of it, fade out of it, move away.

But I cannot look away. I never realized how aquiline and beautiful her eyes are.

"I feel like I'm failing everyone, Gene."

"You're being ridiculous. We'd all be dead by now if it weren't for you." I move closer to her until I can feel heat thrumming off her body. "I'm with you, Sissy. I want to find him as much as you do. If not more."

For a moment, something swims across her eyes that is yielding and soft.

It's too much for me. I flick my eyes away.

We don't speak for a few seconds. Then she shakes her head. "I feel like I'm missing something obvious," she says. "Something he's left behind. A clue, a sign. Something right under my nose. Like the games he used to play with me."

A strange jealousy rises in me. So he had played the same game with her. I thought I was the only one.

"Everything okay, Sissy?" It's Epap on the other side of the narrow passageway. Sissy pulls away from me as Epap slides between the boulders.

"Is everything okay?" he asks again, peering intently at her.

She wipes quickly at her tearstained cheek. "Fine," she murmurs and brushes past him. She slips through the narrow passageway.

Left alone with me, Epap gives me a sharp look. I tuck my head down, walk by him. When I return to the group, Sissy is already sitting next to Jacob, ruffling his hair, smiling. Jacob laughs.

We're too tired to move. The beams of sunshine have held up so far, but there's no telling how much longer they'll last.

An hour passes; a few of us drift off to sleep.

Sissy suddenly sits up. "Oh, so stupid!" she says, smacking her forehead.

"Sissy?" Epap says.

She doesn't reply, only walks toward the waterfall. She steps carefully on the wet bedrock around the perimeter of the plunge pool. One slip into the pool so close to the waterfall, and she might find herself pinned underwater by a deadly undertow.

The other boys are waking up now. "What's she doing?" Ben asks.

Pressed up against the wall to the side of the waterfall, Sissy pauses. Then she steps forward and disappears into the curtain of water.

"Sissy!" Ben shouts, and in the next second we're all rushing over to the waterfall. Ben is beside himself with worry and it takes two of us to hold him back. We peer anxiously through the heavy sheets of crashing water.

"There!" Jacob yells, pointing to the side of the waterfall where the curtain of water is thinner and frayed.

She is a hazy blur behind the cascading sheet of water. Her arms stick out first, then her head, hunched down against the pummeling water. When she's pushed through, she's completely drenched. But she's smiling with the widest, most sparkly grin. "You guys coming in or not?"

"Huh?" Epap says.

"C'mon, don't be so scared," she teases. "I found a cavern back here."

"Hold on, Sissy," I say. "How do you know we're supposed to go in there?"

"Just a guess," she says, laughing loosely. "And maybe because I found a whole set of dry clothes *and* a rope ladder leading away."

It's dark in the cavern. Only a single hazy column of sunlight illuminates the interior. Our clothes are soaked through, and already we're starting to shiver.

"About those dry clothes you mentioned . . ." I say through chattering teeth. Sissy smiles, takes us to a basket hidden in the shadows. There's enough clothes for a dozen people of varying sizes.

"How did you think to look behind the waterfall?" I ask her as we change into the dry clothes.

She slips on a pair of wool socks. "If you're trying to keep hunters from discovering the Land of Milk and Honey, a waterfall would just about be the most effective lock and bolt. No hunter—assuming it could even survive the waterfall—would ever think to look back here. The Scientist is smart like that." There's a twinkle in her eye. "Try to keep up with me, okay?" she says with a smile.

After we've changed, she gathers us in the column of sunlight and points up. For a moment, I don't see anything unusual. Just the single beam shining down like a spotlight from a ceiling overrun with dangling vines. Then I see it: lost among the vines, barely noticeable, a rope ladder.

It's inside the column of sunlight. In the one place hunters would never think—or dare—to glance up. Yet another lock and bolt.

Using Epap's clasped hands as a foothold, Sissy hoists herself up. She's able to grab the lowest rung on the ladder, then swing her feet upward, flipping upside down, her ankles twisting and securing themselves around higher rungs. Her body dangling down, arms outreached, she grabs Ben, now sitting on Epap's shoulders. It's not easy, but Sissy is able to heave him up. And in like fashion, we launch ourselves onto the ladder and start ascending, without an inkling of how long and arduous a climb it'll turn out to be. Had we known, we'd not have set off at so quick a pace.

Only half an hour later, our excitement flagging, our exhaustion gaining, the tubelike walls close in on us. Claustrophobia comes thick and fast. I, being broad shouldered, feel it most keenly. My elbows jab the jagged walls, and even my deltoids get scuffed up. It's such a tight fit, we're tempted to jettison our bags. In one particularly narrow spot, I get stuck; even with my arms raised above my head, I can't squeeze through the funnel. Epap has to push from below, his hands on my buttocks, a supremely awkward moment.

Sunlight in this narrow, vertical tunnel is short-lived, lasting only a half hour longer. The light recedes upward on one side of the tunnel, curved and slow at first; then, with a sudden acceleration of speed, it catapults up and away. Visibility gone, we're plunged into a heavy grayness. And with the dark comes a precipitous drop in temperature. It's a strange sensation; the increasing darkness and cold make it feel as if we're descending into the earth, and not climbing upward, out of it.

"Sissy, can you see an opening from where you are?" Epap asks from below me.

"All I see is a dot of light. A pinprick. Too small to be able to accurately judge distance. But it looks really far away."

After a few hours of climbing, we take a long break. We loop our limbs in and out of the ropes, securing ourselves. Arms ready to drop off, hands rubbed raw by the coarse ropes, we carefully pass the remaining berries up and down. Ben, above me, can't still his arms. "They keep shaking," he tells me, "I can't make them stop." His elbows are sandpapered into bloody gashes.

Our bodies are broken, our spirits are down.

Ten minutes later, we start climbing again. After only five seconds, all the searing pain rushes back. It doesn't feel like we'd rested at all.

9

NIGHTTIME. FRIGID AIR flows down the narrow well. I'm sick. My head is clogged with phlegm. Heat hums off my forehead, melting the ice on the walls into rivulets, like the inside of my drippy nose. We're paired off, Ben with Sissy, Jacob with me below them, and David and Epap below us. Jacob snores away in front of me, on the other side of the rope ladder, secured by rope, my arms slinked under his armpits. Our bodies are further secured in place by our snug fit against the walls of the well.

"You okay?" Sissy whispers. A long moment of silence passes. "Psst. Gene. You awake?"

"I am. Thought you were talking to Ben."

"Nah. He's knocked out. Like a baby. How's Jacob?"

"Fast asleep. Epap and David, too."

"That's good. Are they secure enough?"

"Yeah. Checked them twice."

"Good," she says. "Good." The rope creaks slightly as she adjusts her position. "Tomorrow we'll be out of here."

"Think so?"

"Pretty sure," she whispers. "I know something you don't."

"Tell me."

"Snowflakes."

"Naw. Really?"

"Yeah. Started about ten minutes ago. Just a few flakes. Felt them on my face, prickling my nose. We must be closer to the top than we think. Snow can't drift too far down."

"I haven't seen or felt anything."

"I think I'm blocking most of it."

"Yeah, your hippo butt *is* kind of blocking the way."

"Ha ha, so funny."

"I mean, from down here, your hip is so big, it's, like, caused this total and complete eclipse."

She doesn't say anything.

"Any bigger, it'd cut off air circulation," I add.

The rope ladder shakes a little. Finally, she busts out, unable to contain herself. "Stop," she pleads, giggling. "You should talk. Your butt is so huge down there, it's like its own entity."

"That's Jacob you're looking at."

"I said stop," she says, laughing quietly.

We fall into an easy silence. Ben and Epap snore in rhythm with Jacob's breathy puffs on my shoulder.

"Hey," Sissy whispers a few minutes later.

"Yeah?"

"I think we're getting more light."

"It's morning already?"

"No. The light's silvery. Must be moonlight."

She's silent for a few minutes. When I glance upward, all I see is darkness.

"It's really coming down now," she says.

"The light or snow?"

"Both. Hold on." The rope shifts slightly as she moves into a different position. "Okay, now look up, tell me if you can see anything."

I see the silhouette of her legs pushing against the wall, allowing a faint rim of silver light to filter through. Through that small opening, snowflakes drift down. One lands on my cheekbone. It pricks my skin; I touch it, feel a small dab of water. Minutes pass. More flakes fall through, dreamily, like silver shavings of the moon. A weight lifts off my chest. The space around me expands, slows. The world purer, the angles cleaner.

"Hey, can you tell me something?" Sissy asks. Her voice is as soft as moonlight.

"Go ahead."

"When we were attacked at the river, one of the hunters mentioned a girl." She pauses.

For a long time, I'm quiet.

"I'm sorry," she says, "I didn't mean to pry."

"No, it's not that. Just trying to find the words."

"I shouldn't have, it's your—"

"Her name was Ashley June. Like me, she survived in the metropolis by pretending to be one of them." The words flow out quickly as if pent up for too long. "We'd known each other many years without realizing we were both the same. Until a few days ago, that is, while we were both at the Institute. When our true natures were discovered, she gave her life to save me."

"I'm so sorry, Gene. I don't know what to say."

"I didn't want to leave her. I tried to go back for her. But I had no choice, there was nothing I could do. There were too many of them; it would have been suicide to go back . . ."

"And that's the truth," Sissy says softly. "There was nothing you could do. I was there, Gene. I saw the waves of people coming out for us. You did the only thing you could have done, which was to flee."

Jacob moans loudly in my ear. I realize I've been squeezing him too tightly. I ease my grip around his chest.

After a long moment, Sissy says gently, "There was nothing you could do, Gene."

"I know."

"I'm truly sorry."

We're quiet for a long time after that. The rope creaks, stills.

"Sissy."

"Yeah?"

"I'm going to tell you something now. Okay?"

A pause. "What is it?" she says.

"It's about the Scientist."

"Go on."

"I've been keeping something from you."

"I think I know what it is," she says after a moment.

"No, I don't think so. Not this."

"He's your father, right?"

My jaw goes slack, dropping down to the bottom of the well. "How did you . . . *what*?!"

"Shh . . . you'll wake the others," she says.

"Did he tell you about me?"

"No. He never did."

"Then how did you—"

"It's the way you move. So much like him. How you sit on the ground, one leg stretched out, the other bent, your chin resting on your kneecap. The color and shape of your eyes. The expression on your face when you're deep in thought. Even the way you speak."

"Do the others suspect?"

"Ha. They guessed it the second we first saw you."

"No way."

She laughs a little. "We might have led sheltered lives, but we're not blind to the obvious." The rope sways a little as she shifts position. "Do you think . . . he's above us?"

"You mean in heaven?"

"No. Above, as in wherever this well opens up to."

"He better be. Nothing means more to me than finding him." I pause, surprised myself by this unexpected disclosure. But it's true. Ever since finding the tablet, since seeing my name engraved in stone, I can think of little else. I glance up, then softly say, "I'd walk to the ends of this world to find him, Sissy."

She's quiet, as if waiting for me to continue.

"Can you tell me something?" she asks.

"What's that?"

She hesitates. "Tell me what it was like. Your life together. Did you have any siblings? Was your mother alive? Were you a happy family? Tell me about your life in the midst of all those monsters."

A minute passes in silence.

"My sister and mother died when I was young. They went out one morning with my father and, hours later, only my father returned. They were eaten. People talked about it for years, about the extraordinary, miraculous discovery of a heper girl and mother right there on the city streets at the crack of dusk. They spoke of how the girl's legs were broken when she was hit by a carriage, how her mother stupidly stayed by her side, refusing to leave her. And of how, when the mob reached them, the mother covered the girl with her own body. It was over in seconds. The eating, anyway."

The rope creaks. "I'm sorry, Gene. We don't have to talk about this anymore."

I think that's the end of the conversation. But I surprise myself when I start speaking again. At first, the words come out halting and uncertain, one word, two words, a sentence. Then something catches, a momentum builds, and thoughts and memories flow out of me. Until it no longer feels like I'm pushing words out, but like an outpouring, a catharsis, a confession. And when I finish, my voice fading, she doesn't say anything. I fear she has fallen asleep.

Then she whispers: "I wish I could hold your hand."

Snowflakes descend softly past my face, blinking out of view as they drift downward into the darkness beneath my feet.

10

Sissy is right. We surface the next day, the opening to the vertical tunnel surprisingly close.

Minutes after the chamber fills with sunlight, jolting us awake, we start climbing. Our arms and legs are cold and stiff, but the light gushing down butters us warm, lubricating our joints. Soon we forget about our blistered hands and bleeding fingers and concentrate on grabbing the next rung. And the next. Until, like newborn babies, we pour through the opening and into a clearing, gasping in the fresh mountain air, our eyes squinting against the sunlight.

We're in the palm of a verdant valley, sheer granite cliffs rising on all sides like craggy fingers. A light haze hovers low inside the valley, filtering in and out of the dark woods that encircle us. Trees emerge from the fog like individual minions of the hinterland coming out to greet us. Or warn us away.

Towering over everything is the mountain peak. It lofts up high and arrogant, its face craggy and gnarled, as if squinting angrily at the brightness of the sun. Or at us, walking on its broad shoulders. Halfway up, a distant waterfall spouts out of a sheer wall, ribboning down thousands of meters, fraying into a mist at the bottom. A faint rainbow arches within the sprays.

Exposed in the open as we now are, the cold temperature slices into our bones. The breeze, though slight, slips through our clothing and porous skin, frosts our rib cages. Another coughing fit seizes me, and I double over, phlegm ripping up my pipes like thumbtacks in acid. I touch my forehead. Hot as a branding iron shooting off blasts and flares. The ground slants, shifts, the mountain and sky spinning around me, my own private avalanche.

"To the woods," I say, "away from this wind."

"Hold on," Sissy says. She kneels down at the opening of the tunnel and starts studying the circumference.

"What are you doing?" Ben asks.

"Over here, look," she says, pointing to the only portion of the lip where the grass is matted down. "Whoever's been using this tunnel has been coming and going in this direction. We head off in the same direction through the woods, I say."

The woods are a nest of warmth. The wind dies almost as soon as we set foot among the trees. A delicious aroma of vanilla butterscotch causes our stomachs to rumble. We stumble around before finding, amidst a bed of pine needles on the ground, the faintest trimmings of a path. We follow it, our excitement building.

But after only fifteen minutes, we stop to catch our breaths, leaning against a lichen-dabbled tree. We're unaccustomed to the thin mountain air. A jay lights upon the branches high above us, its black head jerking snappily from side to side. It calls out with a grating, scolding *skareek, skareek* as if chiding us for our lack of vigor. Chilled quickly, we move on but at a more deliberate pace. Twenty minutes later, we stop.

"The trail just died on us," Sissy says, looking around with worried eyes.

"We should find a place for tonight, yes? Get a fire going?" Epap says, teeth chattering.

"We have to hurry," Sissy says. "Because this cold means business."

"You and me forage for wood, Ben and Gene stay here—"

"No," Sissy says, cutting Epap off. "We do everything together now. We don't separate, not for a second, you hear? This forest wants to tear us apart, I sense it."

We all do. We walk clustered together, arm sometimes brushing against arm, shoulders bumping. We don't mind.

And then, just as the forest is threatening to condense into the blackness of thick tar, we break into a clearing. The curtain of trees and darkness falls away. On the far side of the clearing, the land completely drops off, plummeting down a sheer cliff. From where we stand, I can see glacial lakes and meadows in the valley far below. But my eyes are quickly distracted by something else.

In the middle of the clearing, bathed in sunlight, is a log cabin.

11

THE CABIN WINDOWS are shuttered, black lids tamped against the window frames. The front door is painted black and shut so tightly it looks to be hermetically sealed.

Sissy steps forward into the clearing, her shoes stepping into the plush snow.

"Sissy!" Epap whispers.

She turns around, signals for us to stay. As the boys retreat into the woods, I catch up with her.

"You're going about this the wrong way," I whisper.

She stops. "How's that?"

"Don't walk up to the front door—"

"Oh please. It's not like I was going to knock."

"Don't even go up to the front porch. It's likely to creak." She doesn't respond but I know she's listening. "I'll take the right side, you take the left. After five minutes, if we hear nothing, we'll meet around the back. Only if the back's clear, we try the front door."

She nods and splits off.

The snow is encrusted hard on the ground and I'm careful to step slowly into it. Once at the side of the house, I slide cautiously toward the shuttered windows. I wait for a long time before placing my ear against the shutters. Not a sound.

The cabin feels empty.

After five minutes, I step carefully to the back of the cabin. Sissy is already there, ear pressed against the shuttered window. She holds up her hands, shaking her head. *No one inside*. She raises her eyebrows. *Shall we go in?*

The front porch creaks under our weight despite our efforts to tread softly. At the door, Sissy takes hold of the knob, flinches at the cold, then grips it firmly. Her hand turns, and the door swings open with surprising quiet.

We step in, swiftly close the door behind us. Best to cut off the light streaming in as quickly as possible. Let sleeping dogs lie, if there are any. We step into a dark, narrow hallway, and wait for our eyes to adapt to the darkness. We wait for sounds we do not want to hear: skittering, scratching, hissing. But there is only silence.

Shapes emerge only gradually. We tiptoe into the room to our immediate left, the floorboards creaking under our boots. Our eyes scan the ceiling first; at the first hint of anyone sleeping up there, we'll backtrack immediately out of the cabin and race away. But it's empty, just a few crossbeams. A bare table and large storage closet furnish the otherwise empty room.

We venture cautiously to the room across the hallway. The ceiling is similarly clear of any sleeping, dangling bodies. A wooden stool sits in the corner, its circular seat like an open eye staring at us. It's a tumbledown room, bereft of any other furniture, tinged with the smell of mold. Long eaves above us, oddly ominous. *Something bad was done in this room*, I think to myself, and shiver. We slink out.

There's only one room remaining, located at the very end of the hall. Sissy is two paces ahead of me and her head snaps back as she enters the room. Her face lights up with hope.

It's a bed. A flimsy mattress sitting on a narrow frame, a small blanket tousled against the pillow like shed snakeskin.

I walk to the windows, find a lever for the shutters. The shutters grate noisily upward. Daylight pours in, brighter than I remembered even though thick clouds now completely coat the sky. I now see a curious contraption hung against the far wall of the room. It looks like some kind of humongous kite, a monstrous moth nailed into the wood.

Sissy is at the bed, inspecting the mattress.

"What do you think?" I ask.

"I think this place has been empty for quite some time." She sniffs, trying to detect lingering odors. "We bunker down here tonight. Hunt some game, build a fire, replenish our energy reserves, get a full night's sleep. At first light tomorrow we'll look around, see if we find anything else."

"What if this is it? The Land of Milk and Honey."

She walks to the window, stares out. "Then it is."

I look at the bed. "Then where is *he*?"

12

LATER AT NIGHT. They are asleep in the bedroom: the boys squeezed on the mattress, feet dangling, Sissy curled into a wooden chair. I walk down the hallway, into one of the other rooms. We'd debated after dinner—a pair of hunted marmots cooked over fire—whether to close the shutters. In the end, we opted—the claustrophobic black tunnel apparently still affecting us—to risk keeping them open. I'm glad we did. The wintry landscape, cast in a silvery moonlit hue, is soothing. Even the looming mountain peak bestows a regal calm.

I wrap a parka jacket tightly around me, appreciating the warmth. It's one of a number of clothing items we'd found stashed away in a wooden chest. Ben found the chest under the bed, and he'd shouted with glee when it opened to coats lined with rabbit fur, scarves, wool socks, and gloves. And an odd-looking vest, weighed down by hooks and carabiners attached top to bottom.

The house creaks constantly, the wooden beams shifting in the dropping temperatures. The noise—cracking loudly at times—frightened Ben as he settled into bed for the night.

Everything is okay, Ben, I can still hear Sissy's voice in my head, *everything is just fine.*

Perhaps she's right. Perhaps this is it. The end, the destination, the Promised Land. This cabin, this clearing, this mountain. And any moment now, my father will come hiking out of the woods and into this cabin.

Footsteps in the hallway. The sound startles me; as I spin around, my fingers scrape across the splintery windowsill. A stab of pain and I flinch my hand away. Warm beads of blood prick out of my finger.

It's Epap. He peers drowsily into the room, moonlight hitting him flush in the face. I'm hidden in the shadows; he doesn't see me. His face folds in puzzlement. He's about to turn away when he sees something outside the window.

The whole structure of his face collapses, his pallor washing out. He drops into a crouch.

"Epap?" I say, stepping out from the shadows.

He jumps at the sound of my voice. But instead of scolding me, he presses his index finger against his lips. Then flicks his chin in the direction of the window. Staying low, I sidle over to him.

Somebody is standing in the clearing outside.

A dark lithe figure cut in the white snow. A girl.

Staring right at us.

13

SHE IS AS stationary as we are.

A young girl; I put her at thirteen or fourteen. She looks like a wood elf with her pixie-cut bleach-white hair and waifish figure. A black scarf is cinched around her neck, dark like the shell of a black scorpion. She's expressionless as her eyes swivel from Epap to me and back to Epap again.

"No sudden moves," I whisper to Epap, trying to keep my lips as still as possible.

"The shutters, we need to close them."

"No time. She'll be on us in two seconds. If we give her a reason."

We stay very, very still.

"What now?" Epap asks.

"I don't know."

She takes a step toward us. Pauses. Lifts an arm, slowly, until a finger points directly at me. Then descends down again.

"I'm going out to her," I say.

"No!"

"Have to. This cabin offers as much protection as a paper lantern. If she wants us, she'll have us."

"No—"

"She doesn't know what we are. Otherwise she'd be at us already. I go out, lure her in. Then we pounce on her."

"That's not going to—"

"It's the only play we have. Now go wake Sissy. *Quietly*." I push through the front door.

I have lived among them my whole life. I know their mannerisms, can ape them down to their smallest nuances. I walk out calmly, without betraying a trace of fear. As I step off the front porch, I pause at the rim of darkness before stepping into the moonlight, my eyes half-lidded for effect. I let my steps flow smoothly, gliding through the snow, trying not to kick up any puffs of snow. I layer on my face an expression as bland as the moon. My arms hang at my sides without swinging.

And then I remember.

The blood on my hand.

She twitches spasmodically. She is looking at me anew with fervent interest. Her arms crook, her head tilts to the side, her eyes narrowing then widening.

She takes a step toward me, then another, and another, until her legs become a blur.

She comes at me, face beaming brightly, knifing through the snow, through the night air, like a whispered curse.

I steady myself, readying for the pounce. At my neck. They always go for the neck first.

From behind me, through the open door, I hear Epap—"Sissy, wake up wake up wake up!"—his voice as distant as the stars.

And the girl—

Something's off.

She's still running. Hasn't even covered half the distance yet. Her arms still pumping the air, instead of pawing the ground on all fours. Her chest is heaving from exertion, clouds of snow kicking up around her.

And then it hits me all at once. I study her even as she draws closer, my suspicions being confirmed.

But not yet. There's one last test. And it's an all or nothing.

I raise my finger, the one dappled in blood.

Her eyes flick to my hand, halting there for one endless second. Then shift back to my face, unmoved.

She's not one of them. She's one of us.

"Hey!" I shout, not sure what to say next. "Hey!"

And still she keeps running at me. From behind, I hear the clocking of feet on floorboards, drawing closer.

I spin around, arms raised high. Sissy is sprinting down the hallway; I see her dim shadow, one arm raised, the glint of a dagger about to be unleashed. "Sissy, wait!"

But I'm too late. As she clears the threshold, one foot planting on the front porch, she hurls the dagger. Because I'm standing in the direct path, she has to throw it off to the side, boomeranging the dagger toward the target.

I don't wait—there's no time. The boomerang trajectory has bought me three seconds.

I leap forward, start tearing toward the girl. She's coming at me, I'm going at her. I hear a whirring sound, fading, then growing stronger.

The dagger. It's arcing back toward her. Toward us.

I fling my body at the girl, my arm catching her across the chest. We go crashing into the snow. Not a microsecond later, the dagger sails over us.

I don't waste any time. "Sissy! No!"

Sissy's arm is already rearing back, another dagger perched in her hand.

"She's like us! *She's like us!*" I yell.

The dagger, gripped above Sissy's head, freezes. Then slowly drifts down. The boys emerge from the darkness of the cabin. Their eyes wide, their foreheads creased with confusion.

The girl gets up, dusting off snow. "Where's the Origin?" She stares at me, then at the others. Her eyes are a piercing ice blue, bereft of even an iota of warmth.

We stare back at her, speechless.

"The Origin, where is the Origin?"

Finally, after another moment of silence, Ben speaks. "What are you talking about?"

And now it is her turn to look at us with utter confusion. "The Origin. You're supposed to have the Origin."

Finally, Ben asks the question weighing on all of us.

"Who are you?"

14

ONLY AFTER WE'RE back inside the cabin, standing awkwardly around the table, does she tell us.

"Clair," she says. "Like the air."

Sissy, regarding her with undisguised suspicion, asks. "Do you live here? Is this your home?"

The girl shakes her head. "Nayden, nark," she says.

We stare at her. "Excuse me?" Sissy says.

But Clair disregards her, turns to me. "Do you have the Origin?"

"What are you talking about?" I say. "What's this about the Origin?"

The girl's small chin quivers. She blinks, runs out of the room. She heads down the hallway, her eyes scanning about, and into the bedroom. By the time we catch up, she is upending Epap's bag, spilling items of clothing and his sketchbook onto the bed.

"Hey, what do you think you're doing?" Sissy demands, snatching the bag out of her hands.

"Tell me where the Origin is!" the girl says.

"We don't know what you're talking about!" Epap says.

"You do! Krugman said you were coming. Said you'd have the Origin."

"*Who* said this?" Epap asks. "Who's Krugman?"

They continue to pepper the girl with questions. But not me. My heart in my throat, I grab the sketchbook off the bed, flip the pages to the portrait of my father. I thrust the page in front of the girl.

"Is this who?" I shout. Everyone stops speaking, turns to me. "Is this Krugman?"

The girl peers at the drawing. Her eyes widen as if with recognition. But she only says, "No, it is not him."

My heart falls.

"This man who told you about us," Sissy says. "Krugman. Does he live here?"

She shakes her head. "He lives far away."

"Then take us to him," I say.

"Show me the Origin first." The girl's voice, though light and airy, hints of stubbornness within. "Then I will take you to him."

"Take us to him first," I say, "and then we'll show it to you." Ben looks at me quizzically.

She pauses. "Okay," she replies, but with suspicion in her eyes. "We leave at sunrise."

"Nayden, nark," I say. "We leave now."

Clair studies my face. There are thoughts going on behind her perceptive eyes, mysterious and indecipherable. For a brief second, something like recognition seems to shine in them. "Okay. Get your things. It's a ways."

We're filled with questions as we follow her, but the exertion required to keep up makes it nearly impossible to talk. I can see why she wanted to wait until sunrise. The journey is much longer than I'd anticipated. We hike in darkness past a gurgling stream, then out of the forest. Ascending, we leave the tree line far below, and traverse across a seemingly endless stretch of barren granite. We're *hours* on these undulating granite domes, their surprisingly smooth surface shimmering under the moonlight like a crowd of bald heads. The view is glorious up here, with waterfalls cascading out of the sheer cliffs and lush coniferous forests cushioning the valley floor, but I'm too fatigued to appreciate it. And sick. My head spins, hot with fever, even as the cold wind shoots shivers through my body. The high altitude does me no favors, either, making me light-headed and dizzy.

At one point, the path hits a steep mountain face. There's a pair of metal cables drilled into the granite face, which we use to ascend. We pause halfway up to catch our breaths. From our vertigo-inducing vantage point, I see the distant Nede River, gleaming like a silver thread far below us, impossibly small and insignificant. We push on, reaching the top in a state of utter exhaustion. Clair seems unaffected; she stands impatiently while the rest of us suck air. She kicks at loose rocks, her eyes roaming over the satchel bags worn between us. No doubt looking for the Origin, whatever that might be.

Finally, with dawn approaching and our legs shellacked from a long descent, Clair cuts a sudden left, whisking through a narrow slit between large boulders. When we exit the other side, it's as if we've stepped onto a wholly different planet.

Instead of the harsh wind of the mountain face, the tranquility of a redwood forest greets us. We step gladly into it, the green of the grass underfoot, the proud brown of the redwood trees, a dotting here and there of a burst of chrysanthemum flowers. A gentle brooking sound grows louder; when we eventually come across its source—a mountain stream—Clair tells us to drink. The water is amazing: sweet and filled with a crystalline freshness. Our thirst slaked, we push on with eagerness, our feet moving at a faster clip.

"Almost there now," Clair says.

The sun is breaking through the trees now. More color, more shapes, all of it suffused with warmth and color. Unseen birds chirp in the high trees above us. Rounding a bend, Clair cups her mouth and belts out a yodel. It's unlike anything we've heard before; Ben can't stop staring at her.

"I'm giving the Mission a heads-up," Clair says. "Letting them know I've found you."

" 'The Mission'?" I say.

She doesn't answer. We walk for another ten, fifteen minutes.

And then. The forest suddenly collapses away. We stop in our tracks.

A fortress wall rises above us, several stories high. It is constructed out of huge boulders held together by a fibrous slapdash of concrete, metal, and tree trunks. The dawn sun creeps over the eaves of the mountaintops, and the fortress's state of disrepair becomes obvious. Only a tower at the corner of the fortress appears to be well-maintained, armored with smooth, dark steel plates. Circling the circumference of this corner tower is a large window, the glass lit up. "That's Krugman's office," Clair says, pointing.

Clair leads us through the opened gates—two hulking metallic slabs six inches thick and the height of three people. Judging from the level of rust on the ground tracks, the gates haven't been closed in quite some time. For years, possibly. Clair brings her hands to her face again, and the same yodel ululates out.

We step through, and now we're inside the walls.

"Whoa," Ben says softly, as if afraid of bursting a mirage.

There is a whole village community inside. Dawn light spreads across the commune, the burnished red light bathing thatch-roofed cottages. The cottages glow with a soft hue, plush as cushions, internally lit by roaring fireplaces. Smoke lifts serenely out of tall ornamental chimneys. A window opens from a nearby cottage; I see the appearance of a head, quickly joined by another.

A brook bubbles in front of us, the water crystal clear. Arching over the brook is a cobblestone bridge, embedded with hand-hewn stones that glimmer in the dawn light, like warm eyes twinkling at us.

More windows open. Heads large and small appear in the window frames. Doors open wide, filling with bodies that spill out.

Ben grabs Sissy's hand. "Sissy?" he whispers with excitement.

She smiles, squeezes his hand. "I think everything is going to be okay now."

The people pour out of their homes like colorful goldfish, their clothing bright and cheerful. Neither ambling nor hasty, they make their way toward us, hobbling curiously side to side, their eyes glistening.

"How many people?" Epap asks.

"A couple hundred of us," Clair answers.

We stop at the foot of the cobblestone bridge; across the other side, the gaggle of villagers do the same. For a minute, we stare at one another. Their faces are rotund and healthy. Many are still in their pajamas, their hair bed-headed. A pink warmth emanates off their cheeks.

A large man steps forward from out of the crowd, his ample stomach lolling about his waist. My heart freezes—but only for a second. Clearly, this bulky, towering man is not my father. The man surveys us for a second, then bends backward, arms crooked at his side, and bellows out a laugh. It's a hearty roar, full-throated and joyous. He approaches us, his form rising higher as he walks along the arc of the bridge. Halfway across, at the bridge's apex, he spreads his arms wide, his face beaming.

"Welcome to the Mission," he says, his voice deep and sonorous. "We've been expecting you." He stops a few steps from us, his presence overpowering, his charisma dripping down on us like raindrops off an umbrella. His large silhouette blocks out the rising sun; in his shadow, the temperature drops a notch. But only for a moment. He quickly shifts position as if realizing. Beaming down at us, his smiling face wavers. He's trying to figure out who's the leader of this group. His eyes bypass Epap, slide past Sissy, linger on me, shift back to Epap, then, finally, settle on me. He reasserts his smile. "The name's Krugman. My extreme pleasure in meeting you. My delectable, indescribable delight!" His hand reaches down and swallows mine, beefy and muscular. But the skin is soft, smooth, effeminate.

"Shall we?" he says, moving to the side, his arm swinging slowly to indicate the way. The bridge arches like a rainbow before us, splashing down in a sea of smiles.

Cautiously at first, then with building excitement, we start to cross the bridge. Sissy and the boys, having lived in a dome their whole lives, have never entered a crowd before, and wariness causes them to pause at the apex of the bridge. From here, we catch a whiff of succulent food odors the likes of which I've never smelled before. Our stomachs grumble.

"This has to be it!" Ben cries. "It just has to be. The Land of Milk and Honey, Fruit and Sunshine." He tugs at Sissy's sleeve. "This *is* the place, isn't it? Where the Scientist promised to bring us?"

She doesn't say anything but her eyes glimmer wetly.

"It is, isn't it?" David urges her.

At last, she gives a nod, barely detectable. "Maybe. We still need to be—"

But that's all David and Jacob need to hear. Immediately, they're grabbing our hands, pulling us across the bridge.

The crowd parts to allow us through, but only slightly. As we push through, the villagers reach out to touch us, their eager hands patting us on our backs and shoulders, their heads nodding and even bouncing with excitement, their teeth shining with a whitened cleanliness. Every which way we look, there are welcoming eyes and affirming nods. At one point, Ben tugs my arm. He's all smiles now, tears tracking down his cheeks; he's saying something but I can't hear for all the clamor about us. I bend down and catch a phrase—"Land of Milk and Honey, Fruit and Sunshine, we must"—before his words are swallowed up.

And I think he's right. As the sun rises above us, gaining in warmth, spreading its light over the mountain, over the village, over the crowds of smiling people, as I hear the sound of affirming laughter so loud as to vibrate my bones, as I catch Sissy smiling at me with the purity of the bluest sky, I feel a sensation unlike anything I've ever felt before.

It feels like a homecoming.

15

KRUGMAN LEADS US through the village on the main path paved with bricks and flagstones. He's an enthusiastic guide, occasionally taking the time to teach us the names of new sights and sounds. Closer up, it's clear that the cottages are well constructed, built on stone foundations with half-timbering in the upper stories. Wildflowers placed in small ceramic vases adorn windowsills, a colorful array of lilies, lupines, geraniums, marigolds, and mignonettes. Everything is neat, clean, bright, orderly. Faces—virtually all of them young girls—peer at us through the tall mullioned windows. More girls follow us, a few of the older ones staring at me, whispering to one another.

Epap has been a bobblehead since we arrived. He's never seen another girl besides Sissy, and the onslaught of females is a sensory overload for him. He gawks at them, his eyes wide and dazed, a nervous smirk pulling at his mouth.

Krugman introduces the buildings: the storehouses, the clinic, the carpentry cottage, the maternity ward, the garment chalet. Each is slightly larger than the residential cottages. As we leave the northern end of the village, the cottages suddenly drop off, the flagstone-and-brick path ceding to the natural dirt and soil of farmland. A smell rises in the air: blood and meat and animal dung. Several small cottages sit in the middle of the farmland: the butchery shacks, Krugman says without looking. We pass more farmlands, aligned with neat rows of what Krugman tells us are corn and potatoes and cabbage heads, and an array of apple, pear, and plum trees. A few figures move between these rows, small as ants.

As Krugman circles back through rows of blackberry bushes and a field of rye, a glacial lake suddenly merges into view unannounced. The lake water is crystal clear; multihued stones by the shore shimmer through the shallow water. A mountain breeze gusts, rippling the mirrorlike surface, distorting the upside-down reflection of mountains, clouds, and sky. A few boats are tied to a small dock that's made out of driftwood logs. By this time, our stomachs are rumbling with hunger, louder than ever. Krugman smiles at the sound and leads us back to the village square, cutting across a swath of grassy meadows.

We're taken to a large dining hall inside of which are lined rows of empty tables and benches. Young girls bring out plates of food from the kitchen, stealing curious glances at us as they whisper the name of each dish. We scarf the food down. Even though I'm coughing up a storm, I can't hold back. My eyes are watering, my nose is running and dripping into the dishes, and my head is spinning around like drunken mosquito. But I can't stop stuffing my face. Porridge and scrambled eggs and bacon and rolls of bread. These are the names of the dishes uttered as they're placed before us. The villagers remain outside, their faces squeezed in the window frames observing us. All so pretty and young.

And that's when it first hits me. An oddity. Almost everyone here is female and young.

I study the youthful faces squeezed into window frames. Toddlers, prepubescent youth, teenagers, predominantly female. There's only a scattering of young boys, none older than seven or eight years.

The interior of the dining hall is a study in contrast. Instead of young girls, about a dozen older men stand around the perimeter of the room, balding, paunch-bellied, in their forties and fifties. None of them come close to resembling my father. These men are doughy and bearded whereas my father was muscularly cut and clean-shaven. In the far corner, two particularly paunchy men stand on each side of Krugman. All cheeriness seems to have left him. His eyes and mouth are level and somber, his thick arms folded across his chest. He says something—just a word or two—and one of the men leaves his side and heads outside.

That is when I notice the painted portraits. About a dozen, spread along the length of the wall and interspersed by tall windows. Magnificent oil paintings of men, dignified and posed, hung high and framed with hand-carved wooden frames. I casually gaze at a few of them before turning my attention back to my plate of food.

I freeze.

With my heart suddenly hammering away, I push my chair back and stand up. Nobody seems to notice, not Sissy or the boys, who are too busy scarfing down food and drink.

It is the slowest walk, it is the longest walk. One foot in front of the other, my eyes fixed on a single portrait hidden in the shadows. The dining hall suddenly grows quiet; everyone is watching me as I make my way to the portrait, trancelike.

I cough, hacking up a lungful of phlegm. But I keep walking, and the portrait looms closer, the face seeming, in my feverish state, to float toward me. And as it does, the darkness around it dissipates like tendrils of mist unfurling off a mountain peak. A face emerges, staring at me with familiar eyes that are kind and authoritative, the sunken cheeks brooding and muscular. Large cheekbones on a chiseled face, the hair now gray, the crow's-feet at the corners of each eye more pronounced.

My father.

Footsteps behind me, heavy, stopping a few meters away. "Do you know him?" Krugman asks.

I ignore the question with my own. "Who is he?"

"He is Elder Joseph."

Joseph. Joseph. I run the name in my mind as if the very incantation will conjure up memories. Nothing. My head spins, feverishly, throbbing.

"Where is he?" Sissy asks. She is standing behind me, her face ashen. Behind her, the boys are half standing, half sitting at the table, their eyes fixed on the painting.

"How do you know him?" Krugman asks.

And I ask the only question that matters, the question that I have asked and wondered for years in unbroken silence and unremitting darkness. "Where is he?"

Krugman's voice is gravelly and sullen. "He's no longer with us."

"Where is he?" And this time, it's Sissy who's asking, her voice urgent, fear tingeing her words.

Krugman turns slowly to her, his massive bulk shifting like a continent. "He died. In a tragic . . . incident," Krugman says.

I take a step back. But I do not feel my feet moving. I do not feel them touching anything.

A pain shoots into my head, piercing, as if a section of my skull has been removed and a plank of splintery wood run against my exposed brain. The room suddenly brightens with a red light that blinks hypnotically. My collapse is a maddeningly slow spiral in which I see their faces, white smears and moons, swirling about in a world gone empty.

16

MY FATHER WOKE me with a shake on the shoulder.

"What is it?" I asked. I was not afraid; there was a look of excitement on his face.

"We're going out," he answered.

"We are? Why?"

"Come on," he urged.

"Do we have to, Daddy? I don't want to go out into the sun."

"Just come," he said, and of course I did. Dutifully, I put on my shoes, applied lotion over my arms and face, pulled the hat low so that the brim broke hard off my eyebrows. We pocketed our fangs. Just in case. The daylight, as we opened the door, was like acid pouring into our eyes.

We walked the streets without our shades. These were the little tricks you learned, over the years. Don't wear shades in the daytime; they might leave tan lines on your face. Don't wear a watch for the same reason. All these rules, sacrosanct in every regard. But this day, for whatever reason, my father broke an important rule: if it can be helped, avoid going outside on a cloudless day when the sun shines down unobstructed. I stared at my father, wondering. But he said nothing.

We walked in the shadow of skyscrapers when we could, hugging the side of the towering buildings. The streets were empty, of course, silence seeped into the concrete sidewalks and chrome buildings and the unlocked entrances of cafés and shops and delicatessens. The fountain pool in front of the large Convention Center sat flat and unbroken, a perfect mirror of the blue sky.

My father walked through the revolving doors of the Domain Building, the tallest skyscraper in the city at sixty-four stories. The Ministry of Science and the Academy of Historical Conjecture were both housed in this skyscraper. It was here in this single building that my father worked for as long as I could remember. I followed him through the revolving doors, and into the fifty-nine-story atrium. Sunlight poured into the spacious, airy glass lobby, refracting in a blinding array of rainbow-tinted beams.

"Over here," he said, standing by the glass elevator. A glass elevator shaft rose up the length of the atrium, all the way to the top. Although no one else was around, in the building or even in the city for that matter, we spoke in hushed tones.

"What are we doing here, Daddy?" I asked.

"It's a surprise. Something I've been planning for a few weeks now."

The elevator door opened and my father punched in a combination for the top-floor button. The executive-level floor where access was restricted to the select few who had security clearance. I looked at him in surprise and he gazed back, scratching his wrist. The elevator pulled up quickly, and I had to swallow to pop the pressure in my ears.

We flew past the many floors filled with lecture halls and scientific laboratories and conference rooms and ubiquitous government cubicles. Past the mysterious forty-fifth floor that had been closed for decades. Finally, the elevator dinged and we came to a stop. The doors opened. Immediately, an even brighter gush of sunlight rushed in, flooding our eyes. My father's hands touched my shoulders, prodding me forward, into the scathing light. I inched forward.

The light was not unexpected. I'd been up to the top floor at least a dozen times over the years, my father proud to show off his workplace. That is where I take my lunch break, he'd say (on the stairs, alone, Daddy?), that is where the brooms and mop and vacuum cleaner are stored, that is where I wash the towels, that is where I store the cleaning supplies, that is the trash chute. He knew every square inch; stepping out of the elevator into blinding light, he moved without hesitation, taking my arm gently and heading left.

Our shoes squeaked on the translucent floors. Glistening gleams of sunlight reflected off metal beams, refracted through the windows surrounding us. Proof positive of my father's janitorial diligence and professionalism. He wore an expression of pride as we walked down the hallway, sunlight splashing everywhere like wading in a pool of diamonds. This floor, housing the most secretive archives and documents, was the most secure location in the city: the highest elevation point soaring above all others, surrounded around and below and above by a moat of acidic sunlight during the daytime. It was impenetrable to everyone. But us.

The only darkened area on the whole floor was a small closet-like shaft tucked away in the northeast corner. Called the Panic Room, it was sectioned off with walls that were a translucent gray, made of a special glass that neutralized the toxicity of sunlight. The Panic Room was designed as a safety precaution in the extremely unlikely event that someone might be inadvertently locked in the top floor at dawn. At the press of an interior button, the floor of the Panic Room would open into a chute that dropped ten floors. It was sometimes referred to as the most private, solitary, and safe space in the whole metropolis during the day, not that anyone had ever had need to test it.

There were only eight office suites on this floor, each separated by glass partitions and furnished with desks and chairs made of Plexiglas. It was like being in a fishbowl; you could stand at the end of the floor and see clear through to the other end. At night, the occupants of each office—and what they were doing—were visible to all. A transparent government, people quipped. Top level and very senior governmental officials worked on this floor, their nights spent gazing at the city spread below them as they stared at their desk monitors, taking in the spinning numbers ticker-taping before them, their heads swiveling from right to left, sometimes in synchrony. They spoke with cool detachment to one another as they made one important decision after another. Their only break from this dreary monotony was lunchtime, when my father would serve them slabs of raw meat that sat in puddles of blood.

Something quick I have to do, my father would say whenever we were here in the daytime. And I'd watch him move quickly from one office suite to the next, turning on the deskscreens, riffling through files, occasionally scribbling a few hurried notes into his notebook. Watching his stooped back, his nervousness as he turned on the deskscreens, I knew he was up to something illegal. The kind of illegal that, if he were caught, would lead directly and swiftly to the execution squad.

But on this day, my father did not sneak into any of the office suites or ask me to wait by the reception desk. We walked across the elevator lobby and up a stairwell. The walls hovered in on us, darkness again draping around me, and I was not prepared for the sudden wide open space that greeted me after my father opened the top door. I felt flung into the skies.

My father's body moved with an excited charge now, an uncharacteristic eagerness about his walk as he led me toward the edge. I could see the office suites directly below us, through the glass ceiling upon which I trod.

"Daddy?"

"Okay, stop here." We were only ten feet from the edge, close enough for me to view the street far below. "Close your eyes."

"Daddy?"

"Just close your eyes." His footsteps led away from me.

I closed my eyes. It was my father, and there was no fear in me. A minute later, I heard his approaching footsteps.

"Okay, open your eyes now."

I did. In his arms was a large, winged contraption, covered in sleek, metallic panels. My father's eyes were shining bright, watching my reaction. "What is it?" I asked.

"A plane. Remember I told you what a plane was?"

I stared at it, puzzled.

"The thing that flies in the sky? Remember?" He was disappointed.

"But it's not flying right now. Is it dead?" I asked.

"No, silly. It's remote controlled," he said, showing the control he held in his hand, a square panel with long antennae. "Here, hold the plane high above your head. No, put your hands here, on the wings. That's right, now hoist it up high. No matter what, don't let go. Ready?"

"Ready."

And he flicked a switch on his control. Immediately, the plane started to thrum in my fingers, resuscitated and alive, a winged bat struggling to wriggle free. "You should see your face," he said, scratching his wrist with two free fingers.

"Do I let it go?"

"No, hold on to it. When I say *now,* give it as mighty a heave as you can. Diagonal, up into the sky, hard as you can, okay?"

"Okay."

Calmly, he waited, until the vibrating thrum soon began to fatigue my arms. Just as I was about to put my arms down, he said, "Get ready!"

And I felt the wind pick up from behind, lifting the bangs of my hair, then filling my shirt like a balloon. My father waited. Then the wind gusted, flapping my clothes, threatening to rip the plane out of my hands.

"Now!" my father shouted, and I threw the plane up into the skies. The plane flew out, wobbly, the wings madly keening. I thought it would fumble and fall for sure. But instead it steadied and sailed.

"Whoa! Daddy, it's flying!"

He nodded back at me, his fingers making minute adjustments on the knobs. His lips quivered faintly, unconsciously. I stared at him. It was the closest I ever saw him smile.

The plane rose high in the sky, oscillating wider and wider. My father placed the control in my hands. I almost dropped it, not with surprise but fear. He wrapped his hands around mine.

"Push this button," my father said.

"What does it do?"

"Puts the plane on autopilot."

We watched as the plane grew smaller and smaller in the distance, twinkling like a star in the sunlit sky.

"Where is it going, Daddy?"

He pointed. "There."

"The eastern mountains?"

He nodded. And then he spoke words that frightened me. "Don't forget this moment."

"Okay," I said.

But he wasn't satisfied. "Don't ever forget where the plane is going. I want you to remember this, okay?"

"Okay." I looked up at him. "Where is it going?"

There was a silence so protracted I thought he hadn't heard me. But then he whispered a word so softly I don't think I was meant to hear. "Home."

For a moment, it appeared he was going to say something more.

Not just another word or sentence, but a whole torrent of thoughts uncontrollably spilling out. A fear clutched my heart. Because for all my curiosity, I found myself not wanting to know, not wanting to hear the stench of confessions too long unspoken, of secrets too carefully guarded. *I don't want this,* I thought to myself, *I don't want this at all.*

But my father closed his eyes, and when he opened them, eyelids flying upward, resolve had settled in them.

"Remember where this plane is going, okay?" he said.

It did not seem remarkable to me that day, the direction of the plane. As if my father had only willy-nilly chosen that heading, or allowed the random wind to determine the plane's course. But later, years later, I realized it must have been deliberate. Any other heading, and the plane would have eventually crashed in the endless desert. But only eastward would the plane have found a different end: into the green of mountain meadows, the blue of glacial lakes, the white of that mountain's snow suffused with the red glow of dawn's light.

17

. . . DIM VOICES, THEN silence. A coarse blanket placed gently over my shivering, freezing body, which I grab with burning hands. I fade out . . .

. . . I surface out of a gray heat, a sheen of sweat soaking into my clothes. Even in my feverish state, I sense the passage of time: the heft of nights and days gone by, the rise and fall of moons and suns. On my burning forehead, a cold compress is daubed once, twice, sizzling on contact. Soft voices murmur out of the darkness before subsiding into silence. A cool hand slides into mine, refreshing and lovely, like smooth marble. I grip it tightly as I descend back into the fevered pit of heat and cold . . .

Hours—days?—later, I'm able to open my eyes. The room—flattened into a two-dimensional canvas—ripples like a wind-gusted flag. A face looms toward me. It is Ashley June, her skin sick and pale. But the color of her hair is off. Then the face morphs into the contours of Sissy's face. Her brown eyes peer with concern into mine. The room tilts and I clamp my eyelids down. From next to me comes the soft sound of water gently splashing. A wet towel is pressed against my burning forehead. The world careens into black . . .

. . . My eyes crack open, crusty with residue. A day, a night has passed since they last opened. And almost immediately, I start to collapse into the dark chamber again. But not before I see Sissy, staring out the window unaware of my awakening, her face awash in moonlight and taut with tension. And fear. Something is wrong. I slip away . . .

I awaken. It feels like a rebirth: for the first time in days my mind is lucid, my body reclaimed though weak. I touch my forehead. It is cool and dry. The fever has broken. I breathe in, feel the rattle of phlegm lodged in my windpipes.

Sunlight sprinkles through the sheer curtains. I'm in a small room, wood paneled and made more spacious by a large alcove. Sitting in a leather armchair, fast asleep, is Sissy. Her mouth is parted, the blanket rising and falling ever so slightly.

I struggle to sit up, my strength whittled away.

"Easy does it, nice and slow," Sissy says at my side in a blink, her hand under my head as she lowers me back down.

"How long?" I caw. My voice, rough and raspy, does not sound like my own.

"You've been out three days. You were touch and go for the first two days, burning up. Honestly, we didn't think you'd pull through. Here, drink some." She holds a bowl to my lips. "The fever broke last night."

"I got it." But the bowl weighs a ton, and I almost spill it. Sissy cups my hands with her own, steadies the bowl. I take a few gulps, then lean back into the pillow. A wave of warmth courses through my body.

Sissy looks exhausted, her hair a frazzled mess, a few strands pressed into her cheek as if stenciled in. Large bags under her eyes, with tension roped taut across her face. There's something wrong.

"Is it morning or afternoon?" I ask.

The question catches her. "I dunno. I've lost track," she says, and peers out the window. "Looks like afternoon." She studies the windows on the other side of the room. "Yeah, that side's west, so it's afternoon."

"Where is everyone? The boys?"

"Out and about."

"Are they okay?"

She nods. "And then some. They've really taken to this place." She attempts a smile, but her lips are lined with tension. "They're loving it here. They couldn't be happier."

"So this really is it, then? The Land of Milk and Honey?"

She nods, falls quiet.

"Sissy, what's wrong?"

"No, nothing. It's great. Fruit and sunshine. The Promised Land." But she is no longer looking me in the eye.

"Just tell me," I urge her gently.

She bites her lower lip, shifts in her chair. In a hushed voice, she says, "There's something off about this place."

I sit up. "What do you mean?" Phlegm gets caught in my chest, and I start hacking away. She slides next to me and lightly pounds my back. "Sissy, tell me."

She shakes her head. "You need to rest."

I grip her hand. "Just tell me."

She hesitates. "It's hard to put my finger on it. Nothing really big, just a bunch of small things."

"The boys have noticed it, too? Epap?"

A stab of frustration lights her eyes. "There's too much food, too many fun distractions here. I brought it up with Epap yesterday and he didn't have the faintest. Told me to knock it off, to stop being paranoid. To relax and enjoy this place. But I can't. Something's off-kilter."

Just then, the sound of footsteps approach from outside the door. The door bangs open. A tall man, slightly hunched as if embarrassed by his height, stumbles in. Sissy stiffens.

"What are you doing here?" he snaps at her. "This is not good. This is *not* good!"

"What's the matter?" I say.

The man's eyes swing toward me. "You're awake!" he says, swaying.

"I am."

He blinks long and hard. "I'm Elder Northrumpton. I've been taking care of you." His voice is slurred, his eyes bloodshot. Even from the bed, I can smell fumes of alcohol pouring out of his mouth. He stumbles over to the windows, fumbles with the latch. Leaning out, he belts out a yodel, his hands cupped to the sides of his mouth. Even his yodel is slurred. Then he turns back around.

"Please get ready," he says to me. "Supper is in a few minutes. A group of girls will escort you over to the banquet hall shortly." He points to a cupboard. "A set of warm clothes, fitted for you. I'll give you some privacy to change. But hurry."

"He should stay in bed," Sissy says. "He's weak. Surely we can bring food to him."

The elder's eyebrows knot together with irritation. "He is to dine with the rest of us in the banquet hall," he answers. "Grand Elder Krugman will be most pleased to see Gene up and about. Most pleased at the quality of care I've given him." His licks his lips. His attention shifts to Sissy. "And what are you doing in this room? You're not supposed to be here."

Sissy tenses but doesn't say anything.

"Let's go. Now." He walks out of the room, leaving the door open. No sound of footsteps accompany his exit. He's stopped right outside the door, waiting in the hallway for Sissy to follow.

Sissy leans over to me, her eyes sharp. "Listen, you have to know something," she whispers quickly.

"What?"

"It's about your fa—" She gazes at the door. "—about the Scientist."

And at those words, the air in the room is sucked out. I remember now: Krugman's fat lips opening, the noxious odor of his breath in my nose, his words in my ears: *He died. In a tragic . . . incident.*

My father. Dead.

Again. The second time in my life I must grieve him, miss him, feel abandoned by him. Feel the emptiness in the world left by him.

It's suddenly hard to breathe.

Sissy's hand slides into mine; the soft touch is familiar. I now realize it was her hand that held mine over the past few nights and days, a cool salve on my burning skin. It was she who nursed me back to health.

"What is it? What about him?" I say.

A floorboard in the hallway creaks; the elder suddenly reappears in the doorway. "Now!" he barks. Sissy stands to leave, but I grip her hand. I need to know.

She pauses, seeing my earnestness, then grabs the damp cloth and makes a show of dabbing my brow one last time. As she does, she bends over until her lips are right against my ear.

"It was a suicide," she whispers. "They said he hung himself in that log cabin."

What?

"I'm really sorry," she whispers.

A loud creak as the elder starts moving toward us. "Let's talk later," Sissy says quickly, squeezing my hand as she leaves. Their footsteps thump away on the floorboards. I am left alone in a plunging silence.

Suicide doesn't make sense. My father valued life. He instilled in me from an early age its very sanctity. During the hellish existence we lived in the metropolis, he refused the easier path that death offered; instead, he daily fought to survive yet another day. *Living* was dogma to him. And if he fought to stay alive in that wretched metropolis for so many years, why would he so soon commit suicide *here*, in the Promised Land?

A chorus of girls' voices suddenly ambles through the windows, interrupting my thoughts.

The wind chimes are clinking
The sunshine off the spoons glinting
Tell us all, tell us one
Time to eat, a supper sublime.

Their voices warble in a seamless blend. I pull the curtains back from the window and they're right there. In two rows of ten, making a semicircle, facing me. Serenading me. Their faces, scrubbed and sparkling, as if gleaned straight from the crisp mountain air. They gaze up at me on the second floor with earnest smiles.

I pull away from the window, lean out of sight against the wall. Their voices continue to sweep in; I want to close the windows. The darkness in me at war with the bright sunshine outside, the smiles and harmony.

Three songs later, I hobble outside. Sunlight tingles my face pleasantly. This, along with the cool mountain air blowing dust out of my bones, gives me an uptick in optimism. Sissy is standing off to the side, arms crossed over her chest. I'd assumed the choir would stop singing once I came out, but they continue even after I beckon them to stop. Their round, cherubic faces blush with embarrassment whenever our eyes meet, but that doesn't stop them from staring at me.

Their eyes wide, their mouths opened, they look to be in a perpetual stance of astonishment.

The doctor sniffs. "It's all about beauty and peace and harmony here. That's the essence of the Mission."

After the last song, the choir disbands around us. A girl approaches me. "Please, we'd like you to join us for supper."

"Yeah, I think I got that," I reply, trying to sound good-natured and appreciative. Her cheeks bloom crimson.

"This way, then," she says.

The group of girls escort Sissy and me down the cobblestone street in a tight crescent moon formation. Every one of them is smiling with exuberance, their white teeth glowing under the sunlight. As we make our way toward the main square, their bodies waddle and sway, most curiously.

"That's how they walk," Sissy says next to me. "I asked them about it, but they brushed it off. Like they do with all my questions." She lowers her voice. "I think it has something to do with their feet. They're puny."

She's right. Their shoes, poking from under their frocked dresses, are mere nubs.

More girls line the street, many of them chubby-cheeked and potbellied. And then it hits me that what I had earlier taken for flabbiness is actually something else: they're pregnant. In fact, once I start paying attention, every which way I look, girls in various stages of pregnancy are waddling about with roly-poly bellies. It's got to be at least one in every three. All of them smiling, mouths stretched wide to expose twin rows of gleaming, shiny teeth.

"You okay?" Sissy asks, looking sideways at me.

"Yeah," I say. I shake my head, clearing my thoughts. "Where's the gang?"

"Probably at the dining hall already. They've been eating nonstop since we got here. They have the bulging bellies to prove it."

Like everyone else here, I'm about to say, but then we're already entering the banquet hall.

What immediately strikes me is how crowded the banquet hall is compared to the first time. Four long tables stretch down the length of the hall, each flanked by long oak benches. Each table is packed with village girls and a sprinkling of toddler boys from one end to the other. The hall is crowded but orderly and quiet. Sunlight pours in through the tall windows that rise up to the rafters; slabs of light pour through them, cutting diagonally across the dining hall.

I'm ushered to the front of the hall and onto a stage. The boys are sitting around a table set there. Sissy's right; they've all put on the pounds. Faces rounder, a languid, rested look about them. They're happy to see me; Ben, David, and Jacob run over to give me a hug.

"Ben!" I exclaim as we sit down. "Your cheeks! They're the size of balloons!"

Everyone at the table laughs. Jacob joins in the fun. "It's like all ten pounds Ben's gained here went straight to—and only to—his cheeks." He reaches over and good-naturedly pinches Ben's cheek.

"How many days have we been here?" I ask. "Three days or three months? Look at the weight you guys have put on!"

Ben tilts his head back and smiles. "Can't blame us," he says, laughing. "The food here is ridiculous."

Ours is not the only table on the stage. Another table—this one sturdy and with legs so regal and thick, they seem grown out of the stage itself—sits at the front edge. On top of a heavily starched tablecloth, silver cutlery sparkles beside gleaming plates.

"The senior elders sit at that table," Jacob says, his eyes watching the kitchen doors.

As if on cue, a group of elders enters the hall. Immediately, every person stands, heads bent down in deference. The elders saunter in, their rotund bellies lolling over their belts. Krugman is the last to enter; only after he sits down do the elders, then the rest of us follow suit. It's all done with surprising quiet. Even the benches scrape against the floorboards with a minimum of noise. And then we're all sitting perfectly still, nobody moving. At last, Krugman, grasping a mug, stands up.

It's now I notice that Sissy's not with us. Now that I think about it, she vanished from my side shortly after we entered the dining hall.

"We are once again assembled here today in celebration of the arrival of our stalwart travelers. Long have they journeyed and many are the dangers they have overcome to reach us. Such a miraculous arrival calls for celebration, many times over. For our brothers, once so lost, are now found."

There is loud applause as Krugman pauses. He gazes fondly at the five of us.

I lean over to Epap. "Where's Sissy?" I whisper.

"Shh," he says, barely turning to me, his eyes remaining fixed on Krugman.

"Those of us," Krugman continues, "who have been fortunate to converse with them can attest to this: they are kind, intelligent, thoughtful, sensitive souls who are warriors in their own right. We welcome them as one would a family member: with warm, extended arms, embracing them joyously into the community of the Mission. And our joy is made complete today," he says, his voice rising dramatically. "For Gene, fearless leader of the company of new friends, has fully recovered from the most debilitating of illnesses. We give due thanks to Elder Northrumpton for his expertise and persistence in restoring Gene to full health. I am happy to say that young Gene will be moving out of the clinic to reside at an as yet undecided cottage."

Elder Northrumpton bows his head in acknowledgment.

"Let us pray," Krugman says. Heads bow as one. "Great Provider, this day we give you thanks for the abundance of food and drink and mirth and sunshine you so faithfully provide each and every day. We give thanks for the bestowment of health upon our new brother, Gene. We pray that in your wisdom and timing, you will deliver the Origin into our trustworthy care. Great is your faithfulness, great is your mercy, great is your kindness, great is your protection over this beloved community." He nods at a girl standing by the kitchen doors, and almost instantly a river of dishes flows out, the server girls waddling side to side.

"Where's Sissy?" I ask Jacob, sitting on my other side.

He's only half listening as he watches the food being brought in. "Sitting with all the other girls on the main floor," he murmurs disinterestedly. "Girls aren't allowed on the stage."

"You should have insisted that Sissy . . ."

But he's no longer listening. He's turned away from me, is leaning over to David, pointing at the first dishes heading our way.

I scan the rows of girls. There. In the back, lost among the sea of girls. Sissy is sitting in the middle of a row, as quiet as the others. Our eyes meet but for a second. Then a row of serving girls walks to my table, blocking my view of her.

The food, brought quickly to our table and almost as quickly devoured, is amazing. Served piping hot, steam still rising from them, they have exotic names, announced by our server as she sets the plates before us. The boys attack the dishes when they've been barely set down.

"Epap!" I say. "We should get Sissy up here with us."

He shakes his head, his cheeks bulging. "She's fine. Girls eat on the floor. It's in the bylaws," he says, his words jumbling out of his full mouth. He stuffs his face with even more food, unable to keep up with the pace of food streaming out of the kitchen. And soon enough, I'm doing likewise. I'm famished, I realize, a good sign that I really am over my illness. Dishes roll out of the kitchen, hot, charred, the meat of squirrel and rabbit and pig and cow, all accompanied by the most decadent sauces of mouthwatering succor.

"Where does all this food come from?" I ask to no one in particular, and no one bothers to answer. After two courses of dessert, we lean back in our chairs, gorged and sated. A bell rings from the back of the hall; at once all cutlery is put down. Benches scrape back and the villagers rise as one. Only the elders remain seated, still eating.

A girl shuffles to the center of the hall.

"A reading of the bylaws," she proclaims in a clear, loud voice. "Number one."

"Remain together in groups of three or more," booms everyone else in unison. "Solitariness is not permitted."

"Number two," the tall girl yells.

"Smile always with the joy of the Provider," shout the girls.

"Number three."

"Obey the elders as unto the Provider himself."

They remain standing as another elder, still chewing, stands up. "We have wonderful news. We celebrate today the birthdays of Cassie, Fiona, and Sandy. Cassie and Fiona will be sleeping in the tavern facilities tonight; Sandy will be napping there this afternoon."

There is no response from the girls.

The elder sits down. At that, the villagers are led out row by row. A large blackboard stands by the exit doors. As each girl walks past the board, she slows to read it.

"What's that?" I ask.

"It's their daily assignment," Epap says. "Every day, each villager is assigned to a different cottage for a specific task: sewing, maternity care, cooking, whatever. The elders say it's good to become adept at all things. The daily assignments are completely randomized. You never know who you'll be working with, or sleeping next to. Because you sleep in the same cottage you worked in that day. You work in the fabrics cottage, you sleep there that night. Helps foster a sense of community. Mixes things up."

After supper, Krugman and a handful of elders take me on a tour. Epap and the other boys, already familiar with the layout of the Mission, scamper off. Sissy is nowhere to be seen. When I ask about her, the elders merely shrug their shoulders. Unlike the village girls, the elders are sure-footed, their strides long and natural, their boots striking the flagstone and brick path with strident confidence.

"We pride ourselves on two things in this village," Krugman remarks, his pudgy arms swinging back and forth. "Food and singing." As if on cue, one of the elders lets loose a gargantuan burp, foul and wet, the stink of rotten eggs and sour milk. It drifts wetly through us.

"That's not the singing part," one of the elders says, snorting out laughter as the other elders laugh their approval.

"This here," Krugman says a minute later, "is the culinary section of the village. You only need to sniff to know you're here. You could gain weight just by breathing in these sweet smells." He takes in the cottages. "Come, let's take a peep into one."

We enter the nearest cottage, the bakery. The aroma of baking bread, donuts, and croissants fills the air. I'm first into the cottage, and in the second before the girls inside become aware of our entrance, I catch their expressions. Dour, grim, as if all color has been sucked away, leaving the washed-out kitchen a somber gray. And then the girls are smiling, their voices trilling, a light switched on.

"Welcome! What a wonderful surprise!" a nearby girl says with upturned lips and sprightliness in her movements.

"Prepare treats for our esteemed guests, on the double!" Krugman shouts stridently. Motes of flour blow from his mouth like a frosty winter breath.

We are given samples of cupcakes, soufflés, all delectable. As we leave, the girls bow down, hands clasped in front of them, thanking us for the visit. Everyone is smiling.

"Where do you get all this food?" I ask Krugman as we make our way down the street. We walk past a group of girls carrying buckets, water sloshing inside, smiling bright and bowing as we pass. "All the ingredients the girls were using," I continue when Krugman doesn't answer. "I've seen very little farmland, so where does it all come from?"

Krugman gazes at me, mirth gushing from his eyes, as if sheer happiness alone is answer enough.

"It has to come from somewhere—" I start to say.

"The Good Provider is faithful," Krugman says. "His provisions are new every morning, new every morning."

"I don't think—"

"Ahh, we've arrived at our next stop! The singing sector!" Krugman bellows, turning away from me. Two elders are staring at me. Their eyes burn with a corrosive friendliness.

"These cottages here," Krugman pronounces, "are the apple of my eye. This is where we train our choir. Only the most musically gifted are permitted to train here. Listen, can you not hear them?" He pushes the door open, and the music comes to an instant stop.

"Elder Krugman, we're so glad you've deigned to visit us," the girl seated at the piano says. By the protrusion of her stomach, she looks to be at least seven months pregnant.

Krugman smiles. "I've been telling our guest about what a special group you are. I trust you will not disappoint him in days to come."

"Certainly not."

More pleasantries are exchanged. Their voices trilling, their faces plastered with sunny sweet smiles.

And it is that way in every cottage we visit: the carpentry cottage, the woodwork barn, the fabric and design cottages where girls learn knitting, crochet, embroidery, macramé, cross-stitching. We are greeted with bowed heads and stilted exchanges. Even the girls we pass on the main street act with the same petrified friendliness, teeth exposed, smiling to the ground. Only the babies in the maternity ward—there are rows and rows of occupied cribs—veer away from the scripted small talk, their cries and screams shrill with displeasure.

The tour ends upon night's arrival. The glow of dusk, settling like a purple film of dust upon the mountains, is erased by the descent of night. Almost all the elders drop out of the tour, citing a meeting, and head off to the tavern. I'm left with only a pair of junior elders, silent and glum. Streetlamps blink on.

"We'll take you to your new lodging cottage," they say.

"Where my friends are?"

They shake their heads. "There's no room for you in that cottage. We've been instructed to take you elsewhere. You'll like it. It's recently built, a brand new cottage, no one else in it. Lots of privacy."

"I'd prefer to stay with my friends. I don't see why I have to be all alone."

"Come now. You won't be the only one who's alone. The girl, what's her name, the little pip-squeak—Sissy—she's out on the farms."

I stop. "She's not with the boys?"

"She has big feet. Girls with big feet are not permitted to sleep in the town vicinity. Big feeters must sleep off the town premises, on the farm. It's in the bylaws."

"Speak of the devil," the other elder says. "There she is."

Sissy is with a group of ten girls. An elder looms right behind Sissy, gazing at her backside with eerie focus. His rotund arms fall out of his sleeveless vest like hairy globs of lard.

"Hey, Sissy," I say.

"Hey," she replies quickly. "Gene." There's a plaintive quality to her voice. Then the elder coaxes Sissy forward. The group proceeds down the cobblestone path. I watch as they blink into darkness before reappearing, smaller and diminished, in the cone of the next streetlamp. At the last streetlamp, Sissy turns to look at me. Her face is small and pale. She is mouthing words to me. *Come to me.* And then she falls out of the light and into a darkness that swallows her whole.

18

ASHLEY JUNE COMES to me in my sleep. It is a strange dream that skirts the hazy line of a full-blown nightmare. I am back at the Heper Institute, in the isolated library where I stayed. The musty stench of dust, moldy books, and yellowed pages fills the air. Ashley June emerges from the darkness in a crinoline hooped wedding dress. She descends from the ceiling, her face iridescent white and unspeakably sad. Her eyes are preternaturally large, brimming with black eyeliner and tears. But she is not crying as she takes my hand. No, she does not take my hand, but my wrist, and this is the first sign that something is very wrong.

We glide along the brick path toward the Institute. On each side, rows of staffers stand watching us, their faces somber and disinterested, their bodies slouched over with fatigue. As if they have been waiting for a very long time for us to pass through. No one speaks. Even the wind that kicks up ghouls of sand in the desert plains is silent. Then we are entering the main building of the Heper Institute. In the foyer, as we step on the carpet (the touch of the silk on my bare feet is seductive and the threads seem to individually stroke themselves against my soles), the hunters are there to greet us with silent acknowledgment. They are hanging upside down, scratching their wrists unhurriedly, their bodies swaying slightly like carcasses hung in the breeze. Their wounds from our last violent encounter gape at me, thigh wounds and cratered holes in their chests and heads. Crimson Lips hangs still impaled by the harpoon. Her lips are bright red as they whisper, over and over, *Gene, Gene, Gene*. All the time, Ashley June holds my wrist, not my hand, her fingertips shockingly sharp, scratching my skin. As if all of this is so very funny, a long, drawn-out joke. But eyeliner is now streaking down from the corner of her expressionless, dry eyes.

She guides me down the stairs, both of us gliding down with ease. The wintry chill intensifies, the blackness concentrating until it feels like we are pushing through cold black gel. Ashley June's wedding dress, glowing white, is like a white flame falling into a dark well.

At the Introduction, she ties me to a post. She is meticulous but bored as she fastens rope around my wrists and ankles, securing me. I am not afraid, not in the least. She is here with me. She examines the knots, then flows away from me, drifting like an apparition to the manhole lid that leads to her chambers, the Pit. The manhole cover lifts up as she draws closer. She disappears inside, like a genie back into a bottle. The light from her dress is swallowed up, the cover rims shut, and the arena plunges into an impenetrable blackness.

And now I am afraid.

I pull against my restraints and to my surprise they fall away like strands of melting lard. I try to find the manhole cover, but I am blind in the darkness. I stretch my arms before me, fingers spiked outward.

Ashley June.

But then things muddy in my mind. I fumble her name.

June Ashley.

No, no, I think, shaking my head. *Ash Junely. Ash July. Come to me, help me.*

And then I am somehow in her chambers, inside the Pit. I know it by the proximity of the wet walls, my presence like a thick dry tongue inside a tiny mouth. "July Ash!" I cry. "July Ash!"

She emerges from the darkness; her face is all I see. But it is the face of someone else, and I am momentarily confused. Then I realize it is her, but the image is ever shifting and evolving, the eyes shrinking and angling, the cheekbones enlarging and drooping down her cheeks, the bridge of her nose widening then thinning, the color of her eyes like a prism shifting from green to yellow to black. It is her. Then it is Frilly Dress. Then it is Abs. Then it is Crimson Lips.

She speaks. *Gene, Gene, Gene,* whispered over and over, at first with urgency and fear, then subsiding with a resignation that blurs her enunciation. *Gene-Gee-Ge* . . . Until it no longer sounds even like Ashley June but an amalgam of all the voices of the village girls, at first smiling and sonorous, then infused with an energy that builds into a frenzy, like an audience chanting. Faster and faster, louder and louder, the voice splintering and building into a fevered pitch.

I shake my head, trying to clear it. But the darkness of the Pit has oozed into the folds of my brains. I no longer understand, no longer remember. And that is the horror of the moment, what finally snaps me out of the nightmare.

I can no longer remember her face. I can no longer remember the sound of her voice.

19

I WAKE WITH a shout. The aftertaste of the nightmare lines my cranium like acidic rust. For a moment, I think the fever has returned but my forehead is dry and cool to the touch. I close my eyes and try to fall back to sleep. But sleep has fled, chased away by the nightmare, and will not return this night.

Come to me, Sissy had mouthed to me.

The stars are out in full force. Nothing moves, not a sound leaks from the surrounding cottages as I walk down the cobblestone path. I pass the dining hall, the kitchen, smells of charred meat still lingering in the night air. Right outside the infirmary, I step on larger cobblestones embedded in the path, wide as tree trunks. Earlier I'd seen Ben skipping on them as if he were fording a river, arms stretched out for balance, his laughter breaking out with giddy delight.

A scream rips through the night like a laceration.

So close, I jump out of my skin. Before I can recover, a door to the infirmary opens right in front of me. I slide up against the wall, squeezing into a sliver of shadow.

A dark figure, hooded and hunched, closes the door, passes

quickly in front of me. I smell the odor of odd body fluids streaming off it. It's holding something in its arms, inside a sling of sorts. And then it is gone. But not before I see a short pale leg sticking out of the sling. A newborn's curled leg, its pudgy toes small as tadpoles, steaming in the cold night air. I hear a faint, muffled cry from within the sling.

The hunched figure heads down the path with haste, the baby's crying already at a wane.

I follow them at a careful distance. The hooded figure veers off the path and heads toward an oddly shaped, windowless building set back from the other cottages. This building is lopsided and tilted, arching high on one side and falling down smooth as a playground slide.

In a splash of moonlight, the person suddenly spins around, his pale face swiveling toward me.

I recognize him: one of Krugman's henchmen with heavy-lidded eyes, an aquiline nose, and pock-filled jowls.

I duck behind a cottage, hoping the shadows keep me from detection. The sound of steps comes toward me, soft and swift. I hold my breath, not daring to peer around, not daring to move. The footsteps pause. After a moment, they recommence but away from me, the sound diminishing.

When I peer around the corner, the street is empty. The elder gone. I listen for the cries of the newborn baby, but the street offers no sound. I walk slowly through the stillness, staying in the shadows. All is quiet, all is empty.

Despite the chill in the air, my back is slick with sweat.

Minutes later, even after I've left the street of cottages and am walking across the meadows for the farm, I feel on edge. My strides are nervous and quick and the fronts of my boots become damp with night dew. Halfway across, I glance back. Other than the silver line of my own footsteps in the meadows, there's no sign of anyone else. To my right lies the glacial lake, dappled with moonlit sparkles.

The farm is quiet. I'm not familiar with the layout and find myself in the chicken pen. Only a few chickens are awake, their herky-jerky heads jabbing away at empty air, the rank smell of feathers filling my nostrils. I head toward a small cottage where I think Sissy might be lodged. But I reverse course as soon as I hear the sound of pigs rooting and snorting inside.

There's an isolated cottage that abuts the pastures, and I head there. A few cows stand in those pastures, mere silhouettes, their presence oddly calm and pacifying. Frosty breaths flow gently out of their nostrils like smoke from a winter night's chimney.

Before I'm even halfway there, the front door flies open and Sissy comes sprinting out of the cottage. She doesn't slow down as she draws closer but leaps into my arms and gives me a fierce hug.

"Damn, it's good to see you," she says, her mouth right by my ear. "Once they moved you, I had no idea which cottage to sneak into. Where have they put you?"

"What's the matter?"

She only shakes her head. "Nothing. Just wanted to see you. I fell into a habit, I guess, of checking on you every night. Making sure you weren't dead." She pulls her head back, thumps my chest a few times with her fist. "What took you so long to get here? I've been waiting for hours!"

"I'm sorry. Guess I'm still recovering and need the rest."

She pulls me gently by the arm toward the woods. "Let's talk. But not here," she says glancing back at the cottage.

We walk in a comfortable silence on the silvered grass toward the woods. Her hand slips into my palm, her fingers interlacing with mine. Her skin is cool, smooth, soft. It's still a jolt for me, the feel of another's skin on mine. After a moment's hesitation, I squeeze her hand back. She gives me a sideways smile, her ponytailed hair swaying.

Inside the woods, darkness and silence enfold us like a dome. There's nowhere to sit, so we stand beside a tall redwood tree. We face each other, our bodies pressed close for warmth. And something else. Our faces so near that our frosted breaths merge into one.

A small bead of moisture sits on her eyelash. I want to reach out and touch it.

"Are you okay?" I ask.

She bites her lip, nods.

"I can't believe they separated you from the boys. Put you out here in the boondocks."

"It's in their bylaws."

"Their precious bylaws! Didn't the boys want you to stay with them?"

"Of course. And they were insistent."

"Then why—"

"The elders were more insistent. And I didn't want to cause a stir or get on their bad side. Remember, this all happened mere hours after we first got here, and I wasn't sure what I was dealing with. I thought it was better to play along at the time. So I told Epap and the boys that it was okay."

"I can't believe Epap didn't—"

"No, I made it happen. I insisted."

"Still, he could have fought harder for you."

She shakes her head slightly. "Go easy on him. On all the boys. After spending their entire lives in a dome, a little losing of their heads is to be expected." She smiles. "They've been plied with food, drink, entertainment. And Epap's been surrounded by more female attention than he can handle. They're all completely besotted with this place."

"I'm not buying it, Sissy. After everything you've done for them, after you single-handedly brought them here without so much as a paper cut, you'd think they'd show a little more loyalty to you."

She squeezes my hand. "Hardly single-handedly," she says.

"Well," I say, flicking my eyes downward as the heat of a blush rises to my cheeks. "I only pitched in, you did the brunt of the work."

She frowns. "I was referring to your father. Everything he did: the map, the boat, the tablet."

"Ah, yes, my father," I say. "Of course."

She giggles. A strange sound, like a slippage, a spill. Her hand reaches up and brushes my hair. "Did you think I was talking about you?" Her mouth widens into a smile.

"No, of course I knew you were talking about my father."

And then the mood changes. Maybe it's the sadness that enters my eyes, or the sudden sag of my shoulders, but her smile disappears. She strokes my hair, but softer, slower now.

"I'm sorry about your father," she says.

"It's tough for both of us."

"But doubly so for you. He was your father." Her breath clouds between us. "They said they found him in the log cabin. No suicide letter." She shakes her head slightly. "I didn't believe it at first. Couldn't. That's totally not like him at all."

"What would drive my father to do such a thing?" I gaze at the distant lights of the village. "What is it about this place?"

She grips my hand tighter. "Gene, there's *so* much that's off here."

I nod slowly. "I've noticed. I mean, what's with those dainty feet, all the pregnant girls? The elders walking around like peacocks? All those bylaws and precepts. And where are all the teenage boys, the adult women?"

"You don't know the half of it," she says excitedly. "You've been mostly unconscious, blissfully unaware. There were times I wanted to slap you awake, just to have someone to talk to."

"How about Epap, the boys? Haven't they noticed anything?"

She shakes her head with frustration. "The boys—including, no, especially, Epap—have been useless. *Useless*. They're too taken in by this place, completely oblivious." She grits her teeth. "And when I brought this up to Epap, he accused me of being paranoid."

I nod, remembering she'd mentioned this earlier today. "I can't believe he accused *you* of being paranoid. You're like the most levelheaded person I know."

She lets out a laugh, and I can hear her insides unknotting with relief. "Oh Gene," she says, "sometimes they even had me second-guessing myself. Honestly, I spent a lot of time wondering if all this really is weird, or just a normal I'm not accustomed to. I mean, I've spent my whole life in a glass dome, what do I know of the real world?" She shakes her head, then starts thumping me on the chest. "Don't ever get sick again! Don't ever leave me alone like that!"

The sound of wind flutes through the woods, shifting the branches. A drop of water, collected in the cup of a leaf, falls from above. It lands on Sissy's temple, slides down along her jawline. I wipe at it, my fingers brushing wet against her soft skin.

She is still thumping my chest, but her hand moves slower now, distracted. Until it halts halfway, left hanging in the air between us. I gaze into her eyes. They were once merely brown; but now they seem to burst with the color of the woods about us, the color of chestnut and orchard and cypress.

I move my hand from the side of her face, and gently cup her fist. She is about to say something.

And then I am averting my eyes, releasing her hand.

After a moment, she lowers her arm. We stand without moving, without speaking.

"You said I don't know the half of it," I finally say.

"What?"

"About this village. What else have you seen?"

She looks about. "Oh, right." She laughs, not with humor but as if she's clearing her throat or changing the conversation topic. "Come this way. I stumbled on something really weird the other night. I'm not sure what to make of it."

She leads me through the trees, occasionally bending low to duck under low-hanging branches. We stop when we come upon a sudden clearing. Before us is a steep embankment that serrates the forest cleanly into two.

"Up here," she says, climbing the embankment.

We crest the embankment, our boots dislodging and rattling loose pebbles and small stones. Two narrow metal rails lie stretched on top of the embankment, running perfectly parallel to one another about a child's body length apart. They seem endless, running the entire length of the embankment and disappearing into twin bookends of darkness. Wooden planks lie perpendicular to and between the metal rails, connecting them like rungs of a downed ladder.

Something colder than ice freezes in me.

I stoop, grab hold of one of the rails. Cold knifes into my skin as I stare down the rail's length, my eyes trailing its gradual fade into the darkness.

"Do you know what it is?" Sissy asks. "Is it a track for some weird sport?"

I stand up, gaze down the length of the rails in the opposite direction until they disappear. My neck stiffens with dawning fear. "It's something called a 'train track.' I read about them as a kid. In fairytale picture books."

" '*Train* track'?" She stares at the tracks. "What's a *train*?"

"Something big," I say quietly. "A locomotive used for travel. Over vast, unimaginable distances, hundreds of miles, even. On these metal beams. With incredible speed." I am trying to hide my emotion, but my shaking voice is giving my fear away.

"*Hundreds* of miles?" Sissy takes a step toward me, her face paling. "What's a *train track* doing here?"

"I don't know."

She looks at the distant cottages of the Mission.

"Gene," she whispers, her eyes wide. "What is this place? Where are we?"

20

DESPITE BEING UP most of the night, I'm up at the crack of dawn. I'm in my own room, but not in my bed. Sissy lies there, adrift in slumber, her face lax on my pillow. But her body seems tense, even in sleep, as if the memory of the last few hours—and probably, for her, the last few *days*—has seeped into her restive mind.

She wanted to stay with me, she'd told me last night at the train tracks. I asked if that might get us in trouble. Wouldn't her absence at the farm be noted, wasn't it against the bylaws—

"Screw the bylaws," she'd replied. Truth is, I didn't want to be alone, either. Back in my cottage, by the time I got the fire going—we were chilled to the bone—she'd fallen asleep. Quickly, as if for the first time in days.

Not wanting to wake her, I sit up quietly on the sofa and stare at the dead embers in the fireplace. The windows to my left face east, and the curtain is rimmed with a burnt orange. There's no sluggishness in my mind or body, only adrenaline. Within a minute, I'm flinging on my jacket and stepping outside.

Warm sunshine butters down, gaining in strength as I make my way along the still-empty streets. The mountain peak, rising up behind the village, is largely stripped of snow, only the uppermost tip covered in white. I take in a lungful of clean air.

The path winds around the village in a horseshoe manner that doesn't quite make a full circle. As I come to the end of the path, my attention is diverted to a brook gurgling on my left. A well-trod path leads down to the bank where sits a large wooden deck crossed with laundry lines. Scrubbing boards and buckets are stacked neatly underneath a sitting bench. I could use a drink of water. I head down.

The water is cool, clear, cold. After drinking enough to slake my thirst, I douse my face and hair. Drops of water line down my back, stinging and energizing. I feel my thoughts crystallize, alertness sharpen.

Across the river, someone is standing. Watching me.

"Hey, Clair," I say, startled. "Clair like the air."

She doesn't answer, only continues to stare at me. "You shouldn't be out here," she finally says. Her voice cuts crisply through the still air. "It's against the bylaws."

"Nor should you," I say. "Come over here," I urge her, motioning with my hand.

For a second, she pauses. Then she relents, leaping from rock to rock across the brook, her boots hardly getting wet.

"Hey," I say, realizing something after she's crossed over, "how did you do that?"

She's confused. "I used the stepping stones. You saw me—"

"No. I mean, you're not like the other girls. You're not hobbling or waddling. You're like . . . normal."

"You mean ugly."

"What?"

"I have ugly man feet. Just say it."

I stare down at her boots, stained darker brown by the water. "I don't see how—"

"Yes, yes, I know. They're huge. They're man feet. I get it. So they haven't been beautified into lotus feet yet. You don't have to stare." Her lips turn down in revulsion. "But my time is coming. I was supposed to have my procedure last year. But then I got assigned."

"Assigned to what? What are you talking about?"

"I'm a wood collector. I need to have man feet to forage the forest, gather wood. That's my assignment."

"That's why you were so far away from the village. At the cabin."

Her eyes open in alarm; she looks quickly around. "Broadcast that to the whole world, why don't you?" She steps closer to me. "Please don't tell anyone, okay? I'm not supposed to stray that far away. Not anymore, anyway."

"The log cabin. That's where the Scientist—Elder Joseph—retreated to, wasn't it, where he lived?"

She nods, her eyes dropping.

"Why did he live there? So far from the Mission?"

"I must go now."

"No, please. You're like the only person I can talk to here. What happened to the Scientist?"

Her eyes narrow with suspicion. "He died. Suicide by hanging." She studies me carefully. "Haven't you been told?"

"It wasn't a suicide. It wasn't, was it?"

Her face goes dark, her eyes recede into their sockets. "I have to go now," she says. "We're breaking the first bylaw. 'Remain together in groups of three or more. Solitariness is not permit—' "

"I know what the bylaws state. Forget them for a second, will you?" I step toward her, soften my tone. "I've got the creeps about this place. You can tell me, Clair. What happened to the Scientist?"

For a moment, a light flickers in her eyes.

"He didn't die by suicide, did he?" I say with urgency.

Something in her relents. Her posture softens and she opens her mouth to speak—

The sound of singing issues behind us, rhapsodizing about sunshine and grace and a bright new beautiful day. A line of village girls, arms weighed down with full baskets of laundry, appears from around a bend. The girls stop in surprise on seeing me standing on the deck.

I turn back around. Clair's gone. I scan the woods, trying to catch movement. "Clair?"

But she's disappeared.

Frustrated, I walk past the line of laundry girls. They stoop low, heads bowed, lips pulled back to expose teeth in what's supposed to be a smile. So fake, even my put-on smiles look more sincere. *Good morning,* they chime. *Good morning. Good morning.*

A few of them have already rolled up their sleeves, readying to dip clothes into the stream. I see the flash of skin, then an ugly puckered scar on the inside of one's forearm. A thick protruding scab in the shape of an X, thick pale pink bands, like intersecting leeches. I'm ready to ignore it and move on. But then I see the same scar on another girl, except she has two such scars on her arm.

I stop. Stare at the scars. Realize what they are. Realize what's been done to the girls.

They've been branded.

The girl sees me staring, and quickly rolls her sleeve down to cover the scars. But only her left sleeve; she doesn't touch her rolled right sleeve still bunched over her elbow. The skin on her right forearm is also marked. Not with branded scars, but with a curious tattoo:

☺

"What's your name?" I say to her.

She flinches at the sound of my voice. For a moment she freezes; they all freeze. "Good morning, sir?" she says, her mouth smiling to the ground, her voice withering with fear.

"What's your name?" I ask, as gently as I can.

"We're not supposed to speak to you," she says. She's cringing.

"Why not?" I say, trying to keep my voice steady. "Just your name. That's all. What's your name?"

"Debby," she mumbles after a pause.

"Debby," I repeat, and she jumps at the sound of her name coming from my mouth. "What's that?" I ask, pointing.

She peeks up, sees me indicating the tattoo mark on her arm. "It's my Merit Mark," she says, casting her eyes back to the ground.

"What's a Merit Mark?" I ask.

But she doesn't answer. Strands of her loosened hair tremble in the wind.

"What's the matter?" I say. "Why won't you—"

"Leave her alone."

There's an audible gasp. All heads quickly stoop lower. Except the girl who spoke. Her eyes are on mine. There is fear in them. But there is also something hard as stone that does not wilt. But only for a second. Then she lowers her head, stares hard at the ground.

I look at this girl closely. She is the tallest of the group, but also the thinnest. A splattering of freckles splash across her nose and cheeks. But that's not what is most distinctive about her. It's her left forearm. She has *four* Xs branded into her skin. Brutal, ugly, like metal instruments burrowed into her skin.

And then her eyes rise up again to meet mine. Without shyness. Or shame.

Instead, there is a careful, cautious speck of . . . hope.

"What are those?" I ask, pointing at the brands on her arm.

"They're called Demerit Designations."

I glance at her right forearm. It's clean, void of any smiley face tattoos.

"Why do you have these . . . *Demerit Designations*? What do they mean?"

And all she says is: "Please." Her voice is soft but sturdy.

"What?" I say.

"If I answer your questions," she says, "I break the bylaws. And if I break the bylaws, we all do. That's written in the precepts. *Guilty by association*. We'll all get disciplined, not only me." And her eyes come up to meet mine again. There is an urgent pleading in them. "Some of us stand to lose a lot with one more demerit." Her voice lowers. "So please. Please let us be about our business. Please leave us be."

I take a step back, not sure of what to do next.

She shuffles forward. "Come girls," she says, and they all follow her onto the wooden deck, their feet clocking hollowly on the planks.

I walk up the path, confused. So many questions, half-formed in my mind, the answers to which I know I won't receive. The colors of the village greet my eyes, the bright flowery dresses of yet more village girls making their way down the path, the bright red splash of bricked chimneys, the gaudy yellow of window frames.

Before I turn the bend, I look back at the deck. All the girls are now stooped over, pulling laundry out of their baskets and scrubbing clothes in the river. Only the girl with freckles is standing. Her head is turned sideways but I can tell she is watching me, carefully, from the corner of her eyes. Then she, too, kneels down and tends to the laundry.

My morning is spent ambling around as if on a casual, relaxed stroll. In fact, my eyes are peeled for . . . I'm not sure. Something. Anything that seems out of sorts. But it's all the same—groups of girls settling into their daily chores, carrying bags of flour to the kitchen, watching over the play of a group of toddlers in a playground, hammering away at new cabinetry in the woodwork barn, carrying bottles of milk in the maternity ward to row after row of babies howling in their cribs. When my legs tire, I sit down in the village square and watch all the activity from a bench. Basking in the warm sunlight, I hear the occasional squawk of a low-flying eagle, the chatter of children, the clatter of dishes coming from the kitchen. It's easy to be lulled into the provincial pace, the warm colors, the honeyed aromas drifting from the kitchen. I can almost understand how Epap and the boys could so easily have the wool pulled over their enchanted eyes.

My thoughts drift to my father. Every cobblestone I step on in this village, I wonder how many times he'd stepped on it; every doorknob I turn, every fork I use, I wonder how many times his fingers touched them. His fingerprints are everywhere here. But invisible. His presence seems to be floating around the streets, his eyes on me, as if he's trying to tell me something.

By the time Sissy finds me, I'm drowsy and, despite everything, almost content. She's edgy, sitting next to me with a razor-sharp posture.

"I can't find the boys," she says with irritation.

"Did you check the dining hall?" I mumble. "That's where you're likely to find Ben."

"He's not there." She sighs. "It's been like this the whole week. Every day they're off discovering some new activity in yet another nook and cranny. I can't keep track of them. Gene, I feel like I'm losing them."

"They're fine."

"I know." Then in a lower voice: "Are they? Are we?"

I sit up, blinking my eyes into sharpness. "We should ask someone where they are."

Sissy snorts. "Good luck with that. The girls here don't answer my questions. They don't even look at me. Except to shoot me the evil eye when they think I'm not looking, probably because I'm breaking one of their precious bylaws again."

Right then, we hear Epap shouting with excitement. His lanky body bounds up the path. "Sissy! You've got to see this, you have simply got to see this!" His feet kick up a cloud of dust as he brakes in front of us.

"What is it?" Sissy says. "Calm down."

"No calming down over this, let me tell you," he says, panting excitedly. He ignores me, not so much as a glance, as his hand clamps down on Sissy's wrist. "C'mon," he says, turning and pulling her along.

Sissy pulls her hand away. "I don't think so."

Epap turns back, a hurt expression ripping through his face. He shoots a quick look at me, then gazes back at Sissy. "You really need to see this."

"What?"

"Seriously, it's amazing. I saw a class of young kids on a field trip. I tagged along. You won't believe what I saw."

"Okay, I'll come, just don't wrench my arm out of the socket."

He shrugs his shoulders, starts walking. Every so often, he glances back to make sure Sissy's still following. He takes us along the meandering path, past the schoolhouse.

"Where are you taking us?" I ask.

He ignores me, walking faster toward the oddly shaped building I recognize from last night. The dark building toward which the elder had carried the bundled newborn. "Epap, what is this building?" I ask, but he doesn't answer.

About twenty young children are queued outside the closed double doors. Two older girls—the teachers?—converse quietly with an elder. All heads turn to us as we arrive.

"You won't believe what's in here," Epap says, wetting his lips.

The elder turns to us as we approach. "Is this a maternity ward?" I ask him.

"Come again?"

"Aren't newborn babies brought here?"

His face stiffens. "Nothing of the sort. The maternity ward is way back there," he chuffs, pointing back in the general direction of the village square. "This is the Vastnarium."

"The 'Vastnarium'? I saw a newborn being carried here last night."

His eyes snap to mine. "We don't discuss births. It's against the precepts." He turns away.

I frown. I'm about to ask him another question when the double doors swing open. A stream of schoolchildren, blinking in the light, pours out. Their faces are pale, frightened pictures of alarm, as if they've just viewed a horror movie they had no business watching.

"Epap," I say, "what is this place?"

But he's too excited, too preoccupied with sidling next to Sissy to listen to me.

The young elder speaks to another elder inside, whispering in hushed tones, occasionally glancing at us. Finally, they nod in agreement, and we're all corralled in, walking in single file.

The iron-plated doors close behind us, plunging us into darkness. A metallic hum slides across the door, then there's silence. We're in, we're locked in now.

"Do not be afraid, do not be afraid," Epap whispers somewhere in the darkness, his voice giddy with excitement. "Sissy, this is going to be amazing."

One of the teachers speaks. "In a moment, the next set of doors will open. It will open up to the small auditorium. Walk carefully; it's even darker inside there. Sit down on the second row. I will hand you a GlowBurn as you enter; don't snap it until I say so." With a clang, the doors open. We all tread in. Something is handed to me and I grab at it. It's soft, about a foot long, feels like a plastic tube. This must be a GlowBurn.

We shuffle in, walk along the length of a curved bench, sit down. A dark shape looms toward me. "Come with me, you three," the teacher says to us. "We have special VIP seats for such esteemed guests as yourselves. Usually only the eldership is permitted to sit there, but for you we'll make an exception." Sissy, Epap, and I get up, move to the front row. The VIP bench is wider and cushioned with a velvet pillow.

The teacher's voice comes from behind. "Welcome to your bimonthly visit to the Vastnarium. As always, the purpose of this visit is to remind ourselves of the cruel world that we are called to watch over, to reignite in us a sense of purpose and mission. To make real that which might regress to the merely abstract and theoretical."

Next to me, Epap is bouncing up and down with excitement.

"Now," the teacher says, "take your GlowBurns. Snap them, then throw them twenty meters in front of you." Instantly, from the row behind, a clatter of snaps cracks the dark. A nimbus of green light breaks out. Not a second later, rotating blades of green light fly over our heads, smacking against a glass wall in front of us. The sticks smash on impact, splattering a glowing green fluid. The fluid drips down, illuminating the glass wall. And what lies within the walls, within the sealed glass chamber.

The chamber encompasses an area roughly the size of a classroom. A petite young girl stands inside, her body willowy and sylphlike, long raven hair falling over one half of her face. Her eyes are feline-shaped, awesome in intensity, her lips small. She lifts her head slowly, as if with great reluctance. She stares with only mild interest at the row of students but when she sees the three of us sitting in the VIP seats, her head cocks viciously sideways. She stares intently at us.

"What's going on?" Sissy asks, her voice urgent. "Why is that girl inside?"

Epap can barely contain himself. He slides closer to Sissy, his mouth widening in a toothy grin. "What makes you think it's a girl? What makes you think it's even human?" He inhales, once, twice, wetly, quickly. "It's one of them. A 'dusker.' That's what they call them here. Fitting name, don't you think, since they only come out at dusk. Wish we'd thought of it. All those years being gawked at by them at night, it would have been nice to have a name to yell back at them."

Sissy flinches back, her face collapsing in shock. Her hands grab the front edge of the bench. I see the bones of her hands jutting out with tension as she stares at the imprisoned girl. The *dusker* girl. I whisper the word, "Dusker."

What is it doing here? How did it get here?

Epap snaps his GlowBurn. The green light illuminates his suddenly serious face. He leaps to his feet, throws the stick with all his might. It splatters dead center. He raises his hands aloft in celebration, then notices the GlowBurn still sitting in my suddenly slack hands. He snatches it, snaps and throws it with a shout. The stick smacks into the glass directly in front of the girl. She does not blink. She's still staring at us. At me.

Behind us, everyone is quiet. Not a sound from the group of young children.

Epap finally sits down. "Just wait for what's coming next," he says, breathing hard.

Boots *clip-clop* down the center aisle. A teacher walks down, her arms wrapped around a tightly capped plastic jar that's filled to the brim with a dark liquid sloshing inside. The dusker girl suddenly goes erect, its back bent, eyes fixed on that jar. "We must never forget, never stop fearing," the teacher whispers, "the insatiable hunger and thirst duskers have for our flesh and blood. Watch and learn, little children."

The teacher stands in front of a tiny glass slot, the dimensions of which are so small, they'd barely accommodate even a small fist. She pauses. The dusker, as if by some previous agreement, moves to the opposite side of the chamber, eyes fixed on the jar. The teacher waits until the dusker crouches on all fours, then places the jar into the tiny slot and shuts the door. The teacher bolts the door and the corresponding slot door swings open on the inside of the chamber. Instantly, the dusker girl springs forward, sprinting across the short length of the chamber. It doesn't slow down but simply flies into the wall with a force that would have concussed a dozen heads. The dusker grabs for the open slot even as it drops to the ground, its arms and legs grappling as if each limb were a separate entity in direct competition with the other.

A young girl screams from the row behind me. Then another tearful cry, the sound of sobbing now spreading down the line of schoolchildren.

The dusker rips open the lid with her teeth, then pours the liquid down its throat. Within seconds, it's downed the liquid, its tongue flicking out to lick the blood dribbling down the sides of its mouth. The dusker girl looks at me again. A surprising sadness fills its eyes, an expression of shame courses off its face. It turns around and retreats to the far corner. Into the only part of the chamber still hidden over in shadows.

"And that was only pig blood," the teacher whispers over the children's sobs. "On the rare occasion, when it's fed human blood, it is that much more frenzied, that much more manic."

Human blood? I think, chilled at the thought.

The teacher walks over to where the dusker is hunkered. She snaps another GlowBurn, holds it toward the dusker. "See how the light of the GlowBurn bothers it," she says as the dusker scampers away, arms shielding its eyes. "Duskers are averse to almost every light we know. They cower before even the light of a full moon."

"How did you get this dusker?" Sissy asks, her voice tense.

"No questions," the teacher says. "We don't permit questions in the Vastnarium."

"Why not?"

A pause. "That's just the way it is." This time, it's not the teacher who speaks. The voice is masculine. The elder. Standing by the doors, recessed in the shadows.

"I just want to know—"

"Carry on," the elder directs the teacher, his voice loud and dismissive.

Epap leans over to Sissy. "This is the best part," he whispers excitedly.

The other teacher walks down the aisle, lugging a heavy burlap sack that is dripping with blood. She walks along one side of the glass chamber and by a door that I notice for the first time. For a reason: it's barely visible, no more than a rectangular outline etched into the glass, a thin metal handle on the outside. An electronic key lock stands in front of it, on the outside.

I jolt in my seat. "No way! Tell me you're not going to open that door."

The teacher stops lugging the sack for a second. "Of course not. Don't be ridiculous." She starts pulling the sack again, past the door.

"Does that door even work, then?" I ask.

"Huh?" the teacher says, huffing with exertion.

"That door. With the keypad."

"It's secure, don't worry. Always locked. Only the top-level elders know the combination."

"What's it used for? Isn't it way too risky to—"

"No questions!" The elder's voice booms loudly like a slammed door.

The teacher lugs the sack to the far corner. The dusker, observing, cocks its head and rushes over to a tiny square pool of water on the ground pressed right up against the glass. I hadn't noticed this small pool before. Its watery surface is flat as a mirror, an exact square with sides no wider than three feet. The dusker stops right in front of it, kicked dirt falling into and rippling the surface of the pool.

"Duskers love human flesh," the teachers says, "but they will also ravage any kind of animal flesh. Today, we have pig flesh."

And that's when I notice yet another square pool of water. This one is on the outside of the glass chamber, right by the feet of the teacher, identically dimensioned as the inside pool. It lies on the other side of the glass as if the two pools are perfect mirror images of one another. The teacher lifts the sack directly over this outside square pool, drops it with a splash. To my surprise, the sack is swallowed up, altogether disappearing, before bobbing back up like a cork.

"This is actually a U-shaped well," the teacher explains to Sissy and me, "with one vertical shaft descending on the inside of the glass chamber, and the other vertical shaft descending here on the outside. These two very narrow shafts drop ten meters down where they join underground, forming a U. The openings, as you can see, are here at my feet, and"—she takes a glance inside—"at the dusker's feet. This U-shaped well is completely filled with water. Because duskers can't swim—they could drown in a puddle, stupid things—it's perfectly safe. In fact, so averse are duskers to water, many speculate that this U-shaped well is the most secure portion of the chamber. In my book, it's absolutely genius, so simple yet brilliant. It enables us to feed the dusker larger items—like these chunks of pig flesh—that don't fit through the tiny slot."

The teacher grabs a long pole from under a row of seats, and plunges it into the well. She uses the pole to push the sack down the well. When the pole is almost fully submerged, she leans it at an angle toward the glass, jiggles it. Satisfied, she pulls the pole back up. "I've pushed the sack over to the other shaft. It's floating up the vertical shaft on the inside now. All we need to do is wait. Shouldn't be long now."

The dusker is on all fours as it stares intently into the watery opening, its chin almost touching the water. Its body hums with anticipation; strands of saliva drool into the water. The light begins to fade and the teacher snaps a few more GlowBurns. The dusker flinches against the light but does not otherwise move. It has thrown its long raven hair over its head in a way that obscures its face. As if to hide in shame. Then its hips rise into the air as its head dips even closer to the water. In a blink, it plunges an arm into the water, all the way to its armpit, its face twisted to the side an inch above the water surface.

Then the bag is grabbed out of the water, and the dusker girl is ripping through the hessian sack material. Sprays of drool and droplets of water fling in the air and splatter against the glass. The dusker snarls and plunges her face into the cold wet meat.

And suddenly Sissy is on her feet and walking out. The elder by the exit doors tries to stop her but she brushes his arm aside. I hear doors slamming open, see a surge of light tide in and out. By the time I catch up with her, she's lifting her head to the sky, taking in deep gulps of breath, eyes squinting against the brilliant light.

But then Epap is pushing past me, rushing to her side.

"Sissy, what's the matter?" he asks.

She turns from him. "Leave me alone!"

"What's the matter?" He's genuinely confused. His eyes dart between Sissy and the Vastnarium. And then at me. "What did you do to her? Did you touch her? In the dark?"

"What are you talking about?" I say.

"No, seriously. Did you touch her?"

"Stop it, Epap!" Her voice is loud but resigned. "Nobody touched me."

"Sissy?" he says.

She doesn't answer, starts to walk away, her legs uncharacteristically wobbly. Epap jogs up to her, places his hands uncertainly on her shoulders. She squirms out of his frail hold, swipes his thin arms away.

That sets him off. "What is it, Sissy?"

She spins toward him. "How could you do that to me? Why did you take me in there?"

"What?"

"How could you possibly think that'd be something I'd want to see?"

"No, no, you don't understand. It was perfectly safe. That glass is like the Dome glass. It's impenetrable. And the door is securely locked. As for the well, you heard the teacher, it's full of water; duskers can't get through that. I'd never put you in harm's way, Sissy, you know that—"

Rage burns off her face. "That's not what I'm talking about!"

"Sissy! I don't understand, Sissy." He runs a hand through his hair. "I thought you'd like it. Why wouldn't you? After all they've put us through, it's like *take that you chumps, see how you like being in a glass prison! See how you like being gawked at like animals!*" And now he's almost shouting. "Why wouldn't you like that?"

With a shake of her head, she walks over to me, and pulls me along by the elbow. "Will you come with me?" she says softly. "We need to get to the bottom of all this."

Epap is bewildered. He doesn't know what to do with his dangling arms, or his flopping head, or the bits of himself crashing to the ground. His eyes fall on Sissy's hand on me, and when his eyes flick up to meet mine they are sharp with a pained clarity.

"What is it about him?" he says, jabbing a thumb in my direction. He strides after us when she doesn't answer. "What is it about him that has you turned on? He only has to whistle a tune and you're instantly panting for him." Epap grabs her elbow, spins her around, tearing her hand away from my arm. Sissy crooks her arm back, is about to launch a fist at his face. Break his nose, black him out.

But she holds back. Her clenched fists tremble at her side.

Epap is undaunted. "Look at who the Mission girls are clamoring after. Look at who they're shooting eyes at. Look at who they're blushing over. It's me, Sissy! Me! Not him! Haven't you seen them, Sissy? Haven't you seen the way they follow me, talk about me, look at me? Because maybe you should. Then you'll stop taking me for granted. Then you'll start to *really* see me."

Sissy glares at him, her jawline hard.

"What must I do, Sissy? All those years—our whole lives—together, do they count for nothing? This new guy comes sauntering in and instantly you're swooning over him. What does he have that I don't? I twist and turn and bend over backwards for you, and you burn me in return. You *burn* me, Sissy." He takes a step closer, crowding her space. But she doesn't move, holds her ground. "Don't you realize what I can give you? They all want me, but it's you *I* want—you I'm willing to give everything."

A short pause, a softening in her expression. She takes a step toward him—his eyes momentarily brighten—then past him.

His face falls.

"I'm sorry, Epap," she says.

She takes my elbow, gently pulls me along. Together we walk away. She never looks back.

21

"WHERE ARE WE going?" I ask Sissy as we head briskly down the street.

"I'm getting to the bottom of this, Gene."

"Tell me what you have in mind."

"I'm going to Krugman. I'm getting answers out of him."

Ten strides later, I say, "Sissy, we need to tread lightly."

She stops. Her eyes are on fire. "We both know something is terribly off about this village. The captive dusker. The train tracks." She shakes her head. "Something about this place led your father to suicide, for crying out loud! The time to tread carefully is over!"

"And I know that, Sissy! But give us a little more time to dig deeper on our own. Disclosing our suspicions to Krugman at this point isn't the best move."

She kicks at the ground. "You're forgetting something. While this is all new to you, I've been up and about for five days now. And I'm done snooping, playing detective. No more pussyfooting." She runs her hand through her hair. "Truth? I'll go at it alone if I have to. But I'd really prefer having you with me, Gene."

I see the intensity in her eyes. She may be right. Confrontation might be the only way to get answers. I think about the laundry girls this morning, their tattoos and brandings. Their unwillingness to speak. I nod at her. Gladness wells in her eyes.

"Where's Krugman?" Sissy asks a group of village girls as we pass them. They shake their heads, faces smiling blankly.

"Where's Grand Elder Krugman?" I ask another group of girls. They bow, shake their heads, refusing to meet my eyes.

"It's useless!" Sissy says in frustration.

"Hey you!" I shout at an elder through an open window. He's leaning back on his chair inside, feet propped up on the table and a mug in hand.

He blinks, his eyes foggy. Frothy ale spills down the side of his mug. "What?"

"Tell me where Krugman is!" I shout, knowing I'm creating a scene. Through the window I see the other patrons—all elders in what looks to be the tavern—staring at me, their eyes watery and amused.

"It's not for you to ask," the man replies.

"It's urgent. I need to speak to him." I walk up to the window.

"Well, don't we all." His words are slurred. Inside, the tavern is crowded with elders in varying stages of inebriation. The beer mugs, wineglasses, whisky tumblers gripped with thick, bloated fingers. Fumes of alcohol mix with the smog of tobacco smoke, adding to the foul odor chuting out their slack mouths.

I pull away from the window. As I disappear from sight, they think I've given up and left. A comment is murmured, followed by a rumble of laughter. Sissy and I surprise them when we barge through the swinging front doors seconds later. Their smirks and smiles die on their faces.

"I said I need to see Krugman. Where is he?"

An elder at the bar turns his shoulders square with mine. "What's the problem? Maybe I can help you." He says it with a prissy, overeager voice that I realize is in jest. The round of laughter that breaks out confirms my suspicion.

But not before I see an elder with nervous eyes and an overeager laugh glance toward the back of the bar. At a closed door.

"Is he in there?" I say, pointing at the door.

And just like that, the laughter dies. Air is sucked out of the pub, tension rises in its stead. "He is, isn't he?" And already I'm taking a step toward the door, Sissy right behind me.

Instantly, the men stand as one, their drunkenness cast aside as if it were always a choice, chairs and stools scraped across the floorboards. They dispense with words as they move swiftly to block our way. One of them puts his arm out, sending it thudding into my chest.

"Far enough now, pretty boy," he says.

"He's in there. I need to talk to him."

"Can't."

"Then tell him to come out."

"No. You need to—"

"Krugman!" I yell. "Krugman! I need to speak with you. Right now!"

The other men waste no time. In a blink, they're enclosing around me, grabbing the back of my neck, my arms, shoulders—

"Is this all really necessary?" Krugman asks, opening the door and walking out. He shuts the door, his fingertips stroking the Artemis wood panels. His voice is soft, casually toned as he buttons his pants, tucks in his shirt. His eyes are clear and mellow, placated. "Really, you'd think an avalanche was headed this way." He peers at the elders. "There isn't, is there?"

"No, no," a man says. "Just a young boy with his lass having a meltdown over nothing."

"Tell me why you've got one of them—a dusker—in this village," Sissy says next to me.

"Oh, I see you've had a chance to visit the Vastnarium," Krugman says. "I was going to personally take you there myself, but looks like that won't be necessary anymore. And please, I'd prefer almost any term over *village*. Makes the Mission sound so . . . provincial."

"What's a dusker doing here?" I say.

Krugman nods to someone at the bar. Moments later, two tumblers of whisky are brought over. Krugman takes one in each hand. "Were you not paying attention during the Vastnarium presentation? The dusker serves an educational purpose. It reminds our children, in as visceral a way as possible, of the dangers that lurk in the Vast past the safety of our walls. Really, you ought to pay more attention." He extends his arm to me, offering a drink.

I ignore his invitation. "I was paying attention. And now you need to pay attention to me." Krugman's eyes widen. "I've lived in 'the world out there,'" I continue. "I know firsthand what they're capable of. They'll stop at nothing for human blood. By keeping a dusker here, you've only brought the danger home."

"The dusker is securely imprisoned," Krugman says, agitation in his voice. "If you knew anything about that glass, you'd know there's no getting out of it. It's unbreakable. See, that glass—"

"I'm familiar with that glass technology. And all too familiar with duskers. That dusker girl might look weak and docile while imprisoned but it is plotting and conniving to break out as we speak. Trust me on this one: it will find a way out."

Something in Krugman suddenly hardens. His chest lifts, stiffens in place, then collapses down. But when he turns his gaze upon me again, he's smiling gently, chin pulled down. A fat black mole appears on one of the fatty chin folds, a perfectly centered, upside-down cyclopean eye. A few strands of hair spill out of it like water out of a spouted can. "The Mission is run like a well-oiled engine. The citizens live busy, fulfilling lives. What is more, they are happy. You see the way they smile, you hear the way they sing. Their happiness, in fact, is of the utmost importance to us. The *utmost*. We make it our duty to ensure that they have a magical, blissful childhood. Every need, every want provided for. In abundance."

His eyes fill with a mix of mirth and hatred.

"Your every need, since you arrived, we've met. Food, medical care, clothing, entertainment." His mouth stretches into a sneer. "But perhaps you have other needs to which we have neglected to attend?"

"I don't think I understand," I say.

"Well, of course you don't," he says, and winks at me. "You've enjoyed the food here, no doubt. You've enjoyed the lodging here, equally without doubt. Perhaps," he says, smirking at the other elders, "you should also enjoy the girls, if you want. That could be easily arranged."

A few of the men snicker. It sounds like *titter, titter*.

"Your comrade in arms, Epap, has availed himself of the girls here. And there's more than enough to go around. I'm sure you've seen how many pretty ones we have here. We keep the . . . less appealing ones out on the farm, out of harm's way."

"Out of sight, out of mind," an elder offers, to the sound of more guffaws.

"See," Krugman says after a moment, "this is the part where you laugh along with us. Where we slap you on the back, take you by the shoulders, lead you to the viewing room."

"I don't know what you're talking about," I say.

"The little thing is uninitiated." The elder who says this, a tall man with squirrely eyes, taps his fingers atop his protruding stomach. The other men laugh along with him.

"The lad is a little uptight, poor thing," Krugman says. "Repression has wound him up. Really, we should have been more considerate of his needs. Shall we, then? Head to the viewing room? Girls in abundance there."

Sissy speaks behind me. "I don't think so. But speaking of abundance . . . how *do* you have so much food? Where do you get all the supplies from? And what of the medicine, the tools, the dining silver, the glass—"

"You have questions, I see," Krugman says, regarding us with cool, assessing eyes. For a protracted moment, no one speaks. Then he smiles with his engaging charisma again. "And you will not be satisfied until you have answers," he says, in a not-unfriendly tone. "Like little cats, you two. Two curious little cats. Meowing away like street cats in heat."

One of the elders smiles, his lips parting crooked.

Krugman sniffs, studies the fortress wall. "Come then," he says, pointing outside, "I'd be more than happy to comply. But let's go to my office, shall we? It's in the corner tower of the wall. Not too far, a short walk from here."

Right then, the closed door behind Krugman opens. A young girl starts walking out, her hair disheveled, pressed up on one side. She startles at the sight of all the men, pulls the blanket tighter around her body, quickly over the slight slip of shoulder skin. Her head shoots down, she mumbles an apology, then slides back inside, closing the door.

Nobody says anything. Then Krugman turns back around, facing everyone, his expression beaming. "Well," he says, his vinegary breath fanning toward me. "She's certainly been 'initiated.' "

The roar of laughter in the tavern shakes the floorboards. And even after we exit the tavern and head toward Krugman's office, the trill of laughter follows us. On each side of the street, doe-eyed girls stop and bow.

22

AS KRUGMAN AND his two henchmen, along with Sissy and I, cross the cobbled town square, Krugman points above us. A long cable stretches from the roof of a nearby cottage out toward the fortress wall. "That cable line supplies my office with power," Krugman says. "For all my toys and gadgets I keep there. Easiest way to find my office is to look up. The power cable will lead you right there."

It does. Right out of the cluster of cottages, off the cobblestone path, into the meadows. All the way to Krugman's office located in the corner tower of the fortress wall.

We climb up a tight spiral staircase inside the wall, the metal clanging under our boots as we corkscrew upward. At the top, we're led down a long corridor and into his office. It's impressive. Floor-to-ceiling windows span the diameter of the office and frame an impressive, panoramic view. The sharp, crisp tone of the interior is softened by the blending of traditional furniture. Rustic oak bookshelves line one side of the office, the shelves curiously empty of books but filled instead with framed pictures—clearly drawn by children—of rainbows and sunsets and ponies. On the other side of the office is a large flagstone fireplace. An oval carpet, wheat-colored with floral borders, lies in front of a fireplace. Above the fireplace hangs a framed painting of lush green meadows and blue lakes and flowers and a blazing hot yolk of a sun.

A girl—barely thirteen years old—steps forward. She serves each of the elders with a tumbler of whisky.

"Have a seat," Krugman says, indicating an odd-looking sofa chair. We hesitate. "It's called a chaise longue," he says, noticing me studying it. "That's the classic pronunciation, but of course, you wouldn't know that. Look at that handwoven sea-grass base. The subtle creaking sound when you sit or lie on it, how it converts into a bed, just enough room for two to snuggle. The pared-down cushions, the organic aesthetics. Love it." He smiles. "But you didn't come here to ask about office décor, did you? Come, what questions burden you?"

Sissy and I look at each other. I start to speak, stop. I'm not sure how to begin.

Krugman, noting my struggle, smiles congenially. His chin presses inward, folding into a double chin. His black mole pops out, its hair fanning out like rat whiskers. He smiles, settles into his high-backed leather chair. "Here we are," he says. "Have at me. With whatever ails you."

I clear my throat. "First off, we want to thank you for everything. Your hospitality has been amazing, the welcome more than we could have ever dreamed. The food, the singing, the—"

"Where do the train tracks lead to?" Sissy says.

Krugman's eyes swivel slowly around with relish, eyelids closing languidly before opening. They clamp down on Sissy like wet gums. It is almost as if he has been waiting for this very moment when he can finally stare at her unabated.

Sissy is unfazed by his look. "And that's just to start with. Tell us why you were hardly surprised by our arrival. If I were living here and six travelers materialized out of nowhere, I'd be beyond myself with shock. Instead, it almost seemed like you were expecting us. Tell us why."

"I can. It might take—"

"And tell us more about this village. Where do you get all the food? All the supplies. This furniture. The glass. The freaking piano. Up here in the mountain, you should be barely scraping by. Instead, you're living in the lap of luxury. You might have impressed Epap and the others with this place, but to me, it all begs more suspicion than awe."

"And tell us about the Scientist, about Elder Joseph," I say. "How did he die? Who was he? When—"

Krugman smiles as if—

". . . there's something humorous about our questions?" Sissy says tersely, glaring at him.

Krugman leans back and bellows out laughter that jiggles his whole belly. The cyclopean mole on his chin peers out at us again. "Nayden nark, nayden nark," he says, his eyes moistening. "I don't think that at all. It's just that the two of you are such a charming pair, the way you keep finishing each other's thoughts. So cute." He nods at the server. She walks past the two henchmen, leaving immediately.

"Fact is," Krugman says as the office door swings shut, "I've been meaning to have this conversation with you. With Gene anyway. As the eldest male in the group, he's the de jure leader, no?" He gets up from his chair, turns his back to us.

"It'll be easier," he says, "if I start at the very beginning. I don't know how much you know, so let's assume you know nothing." For a long time, he stares outside. "This might be difficult for you to . . . accept. If at any moment you'd rather I—"

"We're ready," Sissy says. "Just tell us already."

He slants his body sideways, staring outside. And that is how he speaks, not at us, but outside. "We call them *duskers*—the things that want to eat you, drink your blood." Krugman turns to us. "But I see you've already been told. What do you call them? I'm rather curious, actually."

"Nothing," I say. "I mean, they're just . . . people. We are the abnormalities, the freaks. The hepers." I spit the last word out contemptuously.

"I'm about to tell you something that is going to, well, astound you, for lack of a better word. I'm sorry it's coming at you all at once, but I'm afraid there's no other way about it." And now he angles himself back toward the window, keeping his eyes fixed on the distant mountains.

"Centuries ago, for reasons too complex to get into, the world was being torn apart by schism and faction between warring nations. The major superpowers—called America, China, India—were amassing mind-boggling arsenals of nuclear, cyber, and biochemical weapons. Smaller nations, afraid of being left out, were forced to pick sides and fall in line. In a world saturated with nuclear, cyber, and biochemical arms, and stacked to the rim with every arsenal of counterattack, it became clear: nobody was going to pull the trigger. To do so would be to commit catastrophic suicide, to annihilate the whole world in hours, if not minutes. Everyone would lose, there would be no victor.

"And so ensued a different kind of arms race, the objective of which was not to amass the most weapons, but to build a new kind of weapon. A secret weapon so unconventional and unanticipated that it would both take out the unsuspecting enemy nations and allow an actual victor to emerge from the rubble. But what was this weapon? What would it look like, what would it be?"

One of the elders walks to Krugman, whisky bottle in hand. He refills Krugman's tumbler. Krugman's fingers whiten against the glass. He throws his head back, gulps his drink down.

He continues. "A small group of renegade scientists in a little island country named Sri Lanka tried to engineer a new kind of weapon. They called themselves the Ceylonites, a grandiose name for what was nothing more than a band of postgrad engineering students with too much time on their hands, too much school debt to repay, and who, during a global depression, could not turn down an entrepreneurial opportunity of a lifetime. To develop military arms: not nuclear, not cyber, not biochemical. But genetic."

He gives off a shrill laugh, high-pitched, the kind that is not itself convinced of the underlying humor. "A genetic weapon. In short, a genetically mutated supersoldier. Resistant to nuclear fallout. Resistant to every form of biochemical warfare known to man. And, being fully fleshed and free of computer chips, resistant to cyberattack. And not just resistant, but resilient. A supersoldier capable of attacking not through the well-protected channels of the sky, air, and cybernet, but through boots on the ground. What nation maintained defense systems against a land campaign anymore? All land defenses had long fallen into disuse, crumbling Maginot Lines as sturdy and useful as the cobwebs that filled them. But a land campaign by resilient supersoldiers would be brutal, surprising, devastating. What if such a supersoldier could be genetically engineered?"

Krugman pours himself another shot. He swirls the whisky in his hand, seeming not to notice the few drops that spill out. "What if, indeed? We shall never know. The financiers got cold feet and pulled the plug on the whole operation. But one fringe fanatic member of the Ceylonites, a twenty-seven-year-old man by the name of Ashane Alagaratnam, was obsessed with the experiments; even after financing fell through and the lab shut down, he stole supplies and equipment from the compound. Disavowed by the Ceylonite leadership, Alagaratnam continued his research in his hideaway, makeshift lab. The fool.

"The authorities eventually caught on, arrested all those involved. Except for Alagaratnam. By that time, he was on the lam, had gone dark, was off the grid. We know scant little about what happened over the next few years. But what we do know: he eventually ran out of money until he didn't have enough finances to purchase even test mice. And so he used the only test mouse he could afford."

"He used himself," I whisper.

Krugman nods. "Something went wrong. Horribly wrong. Only he didn't know it. The changes being wrought in him, they gestated under his skin, hidden from view. So he kept on experimenting on himself, oblivious to what he was unleashing inside. When the symptoms broke out, they did so slowly at first. Heightened sensitivity to sunlight, a growing disdain for vegetables coupled with a newfound relish for all meats, the rarer and bloodier the better. Then one day . . ."

"His symptoms became more obvious," Sissy ventures.

Krugman laughs, his eyes briefly clenching shut. "To say they became more obvious . . . that's putting it mildly. *Cataclysmic* is more like it. Alagaratnam kept a video journal, now a preserved historical artifact. You can see his rapid disintegration on-screen. The symptoms gushed out over the course of only a few hours. What started out as a zit-sized mark on his face, ended up a . . . cataclysmic explosion of nightmarish proportions mere hours later." He takes another swig, chugs it.

"The saving grace was that this all took place on the small island nation of Sri Lanka. Obviously, that island nation was devastated, the whole population transmuted within a week. But at least the outbreak was contained. Outbound planes were immediately shot down, boats easily sunk. And that's all we had to do to contain it. Watch the skies, monitor the seas. Let the sunlight kill the hideously transformed. Eventually, the transmuted people ventured outside only after dusk. That's how they got their name, duskers. These weren't zombie savages incapable of reflection and self-awareness, or brutes filled with hedonistic, prurient tendencies. But for their lust for human blood and flesh, they were otherwise . . . civil. Intelligent. They knew who they were, spoke and thought with self-reflection. When food whittled away—when there were no more humans, no more animals to feed on—they didn't turn to cannibalism. They simply starved to death. Or ran, in group suicidal pacts, into the blazing sun."

"And so that's how it ended?" I ask.

Krugman's eyes squeeze shut again, and his whole body starts jiggling up and down. No sound escapes his mouth. A line of tears streaks out, coursing down his chubby cheeks. The strands of hair on his mole lick up the tears.

"Really? That's how it ended? I mean, really? Then how did all those duskers end up out there? Then why are we, centuries later, still dealing with them?" His laughter suddenly stops on a dime. "You can't stop a contagion," he says, his voice beginning to slur.

"What happened next?" Sissy asks.

"To this day," he says, wiping at his tears, "we don't know how the contagion leaked. Not with certainty, anyway. Some have speculated that a bird—with a smidgen of dusker saliva on its feathers—must have flown undetected from Sri Lanka to India. And then perhaps a kindhearted child picked up the wounded bird, and the dot of saliva rubbed against . . . a paper cut? Who knows?"

He runs his finger along the rim of the tumbler. "Things looked desperate for a while. Whole continents were taken over by the duskers, the world population left huddling in forgotten corners of the globe. The South Pole, with its twenty-four hours of sunlight, was initially very popular. That is, until the summer ended and the season of unceasing night began." His lips press together. "All over the world, these were very dark times. When the demise of humankind seemed inevitable and imminent."

"What happened then?" I say. "To humankind."

"A miracle. Historical accounts are sketchy, but a game changer came out of nowhere."

"A game changer?" I say.

"Actually, more like a destiny changer. Felt that way, anyway. On this little island off the coast of China called Cheung Chau. A young woman by the name of Jenny Shen, working alone and hidden in an otherwise abandoned island village, heroically found an antidote. I don't have time to go into the details, but suffice it to say that the antidote was successful. Over the course of many decades, the tide turned. Eventually, we had the duskers on the run. Ultimately, ninety-nine-point-nine-nine percent of the duskers were wiped out."

"What about the remaining hundredth of one percent?" Sissy asks.

Krugman pauses. "They were immune to the antidote. For whatever reason, instead of killing them, the antidote only made the few stronger, stouter. Faster. Scarier. But this pesky group was small enough in number that we were eventually able to round them all up, encage them. They were about two weeks from orders of extermination when bleeding-heart liberals and the religious right joined hands." He spits out the next few words. "They made strange bedfellows, let me tell you. With a unified, formidable voice, they urged that if humans were indeed the more enlightened species, then we could not subject duskers to execution. The liberal left championed the duskers' inalienable rights. The evangelical right claimed that the duskers possessed souls capable of redemption, souls that could be saved. Blah, blah, blah. The fools, both camps. And the general public, too, for buying into it.

"The short end of it all is that the remaining duskers—two hundred and seventy-three of them—had their executions commuted and were instead sentenced to exile. After some debate, the international tribunals elected to throw the duskers into the desert. Into an abandoned city in the desert, to be exact, a perfect prison with already-constructed homes and hotels and buildings sitting empty. We erased their memories, then threw them out there. Gave them some raw materials to work with. We felt certain that the hundreds of miles of desert under a scorching sun made for an uncrossable buffer between them and us. And it has: it's proven to be the thickest prison bar, the securest prison facility ever. A veritable moat of acid, an impassable galaxy between us and them."

His tongue snakes out, licking his blubbery lips. "The only problem was we didn't anticipate them being so . . ." He sighs, heavily, spittle spraying off his lips. "We sent them out there to eventually go extinct, to die on their own terms in their own time, in a way that didn't upset the bleeding hearts or religious right. But we didn't know how resilient these duskers would be. Ultimately, they're plucky at heart, resourceful survivors, and that's what they've done. Survive. Actually, over the centuries, they've done more than survive. They've thrived. They've perpetuated their own species. Like a pack of rats. Built up a whole metropolis, developed their own technology. To the extent that now all we can do is keep an eye on them, and stay completely out of sight. Those duskers catch a whiff of us, they get the slightest inkling, and they'll be crossing the desert to devour us, come hell or sunlight."

Krugman stares down at the tumbler. He sets it down, picks up the whisky bottle, and drinks straight out of it. His eyes flush watery and bloodshot. "And that, my ladies and gentlemen, is why we're here. Why the Mission is here. To be the watchful eyes of humanity. An outpost to keep a lookout for duskers. Because these duskers are frisky as a pack of dogs in heat, let me tell you. Now, centuries later, there're close to five million of them, if our estimations are anywhere near accurate. And so we keep watch over them. Make sure they aren't developing technology that would enable them to traverse the desert." He sniffs. "You should be happy to know that after centuries of observation, it appears the duskers don't have the slightest inclination to stray. They really do hate the sunlight."

I glance over at Sissy. Like me, she's shocked, barely able to register this deluge of information. Her mouth slack, her skin pale, she turns her head. Our eyes meet like arms reaching out, clasping.

I speak, my voice wrung out. "Tell me how Elder Joseph fits into all this."

Krugman pauses for a long time. I think he's going to end the meeting; he's tottering with indecision. Then he speaks, softly, as to himself. "He was a brilliant scientist, one of the keenest minds I've ever worked with. Young, brash, prodigious. We enjoyed a level of simpatico, he and I, in the early years."

"The early years?" I say.

"Before he . . ." Krugman shakes his head. "Before he went off the deep end. Although even back then, there were signs of his instability. He worked obsessively in his laboratory, with a dedication that bordered on obsession. He came to believe that a cure could be derived for duskers. Some kind of curative concoction that would reverse—yes, reverse—the mutations in the dusker genetic code sequence. Something he called the Origin." Krugman's eyes flash toward us for a second. "But the Scientist needed to better understand the physiology of the duskers, had to collect samples. And so he arrived at a conclusion that proved to be his eventual undoing: that he needed to go into the duskers' metropolis.

"It was a ludicrous notion, of course, and I think deep down he knew it. For years, he stalled, trying to find some other way to concoct the Origin. But in the end, he realized there was no other option. He needed to venture into the duskers' metropolis. And not alone. He'd have to collect a ton of samples; he'd have to take a team in with him. Sounds crazy, sounds like no one would sign up for it. But he had a way with words, and a charisma that dripped and oozed. He played on their religious sentiment, arguing that it was our spiritual duty to do this. That it was all for the good of the duskers' souls. Before long, he convinced a group of about thirty—thirty!—to go with him. Across the desert and into the hornets' nest."

"When?"

"What, two, three decades ago? They snuck into the dusker city, intending to stay for a couple of weeks at most. But they severely underestimated the . . . tenacity of the duskers. The unimaginable happened. Or the utterly predictable, depends how you see it, I suppose. Our people got separated, then devoured within days, if not hours. Communication lines were completely compromised, transportation channels destroyed. They were pushed into hiding and when food resources ran out, they were left with only one option: infiltrate and merge into society, pretend to be a dusker. And years, decades passed, without a word from them. Frankly, we thought they were all dead.

"And then, a few years ago, Elder Joseph came back. Like a phantom made flesh and blood again. Walked right out of those woods, through the gates, and into the Mission. A miracle dropped from the skies. Or a curse. Because he was a broken man, eyes wild, given to fanciful notions. He insisted on staying here at the outpost, on continuing his research in the laboratory. He declined every offer to be honorably discharged and returned to the Civilization."

Sissy's head cocks right at this. "Wait," she says. "What do you mean?"

Krugman is puzzled. "He wanted to stay. What option—"

"No, no," Sissy says, shaking her head. "The part about returning to civilization."

"Well," Krugman says, confused, "this isn't the Civilization. The Mission is just an outpost, like I said. Haven't you been listening? There's a whole wide world out there, ninety-nine-point-nine-nine-nine-nine percent of the rest of the globe, filled with our people, our cities, our civilization. We've had to rebuild ever since the dusker uprising, and we're not anywhere close to our pre-dusker days, but we're slowly getting there."

Sissy and I stand dumbfounded.

"What did you think was out there?" he asks. His face is brittle with bewilderment, his glassy eyes probing us.

"I thought the earth was filled with peop—with duskers," I say. "I didn't think there were many of us left, perhaps only a scattering in isolated pockets." In fact, until three weeks ago, I'd thought I was the last of our kind. Until, that is, I encountered the group in the Dome. Until Ashley June revealed herself. Until the Director disclosed—perhaps inadvertently—the existence of hundreds more like us imprisoned like cattle at the Ruler's Palace.

Krugman stares wide-eyed at us. "Come here," he says, beckoning with his arm. Whisky spills out of the bottle. "Come to the window. Let me show you something."

He jabs the window. "Over there," he says, "in the distance. Just off the ridgeline, there where the land drops into the deep ravine."

We see it. A double-leaf bascule bridge, the two lifted halves standing sky-high and upright like sentries posted on opposite sides of the deep ravine. "About once a fortnight," Krugman says, "our supplies arrive. By train. Food, furniture, crops, medicine. That's what you wanted to know, isn't it? It all comes by train. We lower the halves of the bridge. The train crosses. We unload it at the station. Then we send the train back, takes about four days each way. A little shorter on the way back to the Civilization on account of the steep descent from the mountain. The train positively flies down. And it's all self-automated. Quite a marvel how simple it is: push a few buttons, and away it goes, the bridge lowering, the train disappearing down the mountain. Doors remain locked until they reach the destination points, be it here or the Civilization. Usually, we send the train back with a list of any supply needs beyond the usual requirements. And, on special occasions, the train leaves here with a passenger. Or two."

Sissy and I turn to look at him.

He nods, a dull glint in his eyes. "For those who have served well, those who have been commendable in their service of the Mission, a reward awaits them in the form of an honorable discharge. For the select few, they get to ride the train back to the Civilization, where they will be opulently compensated with a government stipend to last them for the rest of their lives. But it has to be earned."

"With Merit Marks," I say, realizing.

Krugman, with an expression of mild surprise and faint respect, nods. "You don't miss much. Yes, Merit Marks. Earn five Merit Marks, and you've earned your ticket back to the Civilization. Mind you, it usually takes at least a decade of service."

"How do you get one of these Merit Marks?" I ask.

"Oh, many are the ways, I suppose. Unflinching adherence to the bylaws, love for the eldership and citizenry of the Mission, giving birth to a healthy child. Demonstrated diligence to daily duties over a decade of service. That sort of thing."

"And what about a Demerit Designation?" I ask. "How do you get one of those?"

The room falls quiet. "Ah, yes. Demerit Designations. Quite simply, disobedience to the bylaws will earn you a Demerit Designation. Or two. Depends on the level of transgression. But come now, that is not what we're about here at the Mission. We'd much rather focus on the positives, the Merit Marks—"

"Let me guess," I say, recalling the girls with brandings and tattoos on their left and right arms. "One Demerit Designation subtracts against the total Merit Marks. One branding scar nullifies one smiley face. Makes it that much more difficult to get to five." *And what happens when you get to five Demerit Designations?* I'm thinking to ask when Krugman interrupts my thoughts.

"Subtraction, I suppose, yes. But we here at the Mission prefer to see it as *addition by subtraction.* Keeps enthusiasm up, morale up, incentivizes the citizenry." Krugman smiles, puts his hands on my shoulders, squeezes reassuringly. "I can see what this is about. You're worried about"—he flicks his chin at Sissy—"your girl here. About her many transgressions. Look, don't worry. We're not going to hold it against her. In fact, don't even worry about Demerit Designations or Merit Marks. You've all been fast-tracked. You're not going to have to wait: not a decade, not a year, not a month or a fortnight, even. See, a train is scheduled to arrive here later tonight. It'll take us several hours to unload the supplies. And then, if all goes well, all six of you will embark the train late tomorrow and journey to the Civilization. To your well-deserved oasis."

Sissy puts her fingers on the window, presses her palm against it. She shakes her head. "Sorry, this is all coming at us so fast."

"I understand."

For a minute, we stare at the bridge, trying to digest all this paradigm-shattering information. "Why have you decided to fast-track us?" Sissy asks.

Krugman laughs, shoots a knowing glance at the other elders. "As if I have a say in it!" He opens a drawer in his desk, takes out an envelope, a thick royal red wax seal broken across the opening. He slips out a single piece of paper with embossed letterhead and hands it to me. "A letter from the headquarters in the Civilization. Go ahead, read it for her."

I don't bother to correct Krugman's misassumption that Sissy is illiterate. Instead, I unfold the paper, stare at the cursive handwriting. Sissy leans in to read.

The Civilization has recently received credible intelligence that a group of six young people, ranging between the ages of five and seventeen, have escaped from dusker imprisonment. Our agents have informed us that they are likely headed toward the Mission. Should they reach said destination, they are to be treated with the utmost care and hospitality. They are to board the very next train and be brought back to the Civilization. It is imperative that they return with "the Origin."

Yours, the Civilization.

"We received that letter only a few weeks ago," Krugman says. "That's why we weren't completely astonished when you appeared at our doorstep. We were expecting you, see."

Sissy flips the paper over. It's blank. She looks up at Krugman. "So we'll be getting on this train tomorrow," Sissy says, her voice edged with suspicion. "And you were going to tell us this, when?"

Krugman laughs, a cough of mirth. But inside that explosion of sound, I detect his irritation. "Why, when young Gene recovered. That's when. We weren't about to get your hopes up only to be forced to dash them if he wasn't well enough to make the journey. Remember, he was barely hanging on just a couple of nights ago. But look now," he says, looking at me, "he's the very picture of health and vitality, isn't he? So, you'll be leaving us tomorrow with both our blessings and, no doubt, the fondest of memories."

For a minute, the only sound is the *tick-tock tick-tock* of the grandfather clock.

"What about the Scientist?" I say. "Why wasn't he sent back to the Civilization? You'd think he would have received the same treatment as us. Why wasn't he fast-tracked?"

The air tenses. In the window's reflection, I see Krugman's henchmen—silent this whole time—stiffen. Krugman says, "The simple answer is: we never received a directive from the Civilization."

"And the long answer is?" Sissy says.

Krugman laughs loudly, a guffaw. "The long answer is: it's complicated."

"Then give us the long answer," I say. "Tell us everything. Tell us why he committed suicide."

Krugman sniffs with irritation. "You have to understand something. When Elder Joseph returned, he wasn't altogether in his right mind. He proved to be . . . uncooperative."

"How so?"

"He clammed up. Refused to talk about his life among the duskers. No one had ever lived in the dusker metropolis and lived to tell the tale. He was there for over two decades; he should have been a storehouse of information. But he refused to talk about his time there. And very oddly, when it came time for him to return to the Civilization by train, he refused to go. Outright refused, locked himself in this lab, in fact. When pressed, all he would say was he had to wait for the Origin."

"And what did he say about the Origin? Didn't you think to ask?"

Krugman smiles ambiguously. "Of course we did. He only said that it was a cure. That in the years living with the duskers, he'd been able to gain daily access to laboratories and top-secret scientific documents. Posed as a janitor at the highest-security building in the metropolis, apparently. Anyway, with access to all that information and equipment, he'd been able to concoct a formula. For the Origin. The cure that would reverse the genetic effects on the duskers, completely retransform duskers back to humanity."

"Reverse the effects?" I say.

"That's what Elder Joseph said. If he's to be believed."

"This cure, the Origin," Sissy whispers, just as overwhelmed as I am. "He didn't have it on him, then?"

Krugman shakes his head. "He wasn't able to bring it with him, but claimed it would one day surely arrive. He became like a raving prophet, every day prophesying with staff and rod about the coming of the young ones carrying the Origin. *Blessed are the young feet of those who come bearing the Origin,* he kept chanting. When he wasn't working in the laboratory facility we have here, he was on the fortress wall, keeping watch through the night. Frankly, toward the end, he lost it. He had to be isolated in a cabin about half a day's hike from here."

I nod, remembering the cabin from a few days ago. "How long was he there?"

"Not long. A couple of months at the most. We'd check on him every few days. One afternoon, we found him hanging from the crossbeams." Krugman gazes somberly at us. "You wanted to know. So there you have it, the unvarnished truth. Hurts, doesn't it, truth?"

"But what drove him to kill himself?" I ask.

Krugman's glassy eyes flash with sudden clarity. He gazes out the window; when he looks at me again, his face has tightened. "Have you noticed something?"

"What's that?"

"This conversation. It's been a little one-sided. Frankly, I'm getting a little tired of hearing the sound of my own voice. I'd like to do a little more listening now. And for you to do a little more talking."

Sissy and I glance at each other, confused. "About what?" Sissy asks.

"The Origin." He sniffs. "I'd thought Elder Joseph was completely off his rocker when ranting about it, but then you six suddenly appear quite out of the blue, just as he'd predicted. And then the Civilization apparently not only gets wind of this *Origin* theory but actually seems inclined to believe it. So. Tell me. What is it? And more importantly, where is it? I'd like to see it, please."

"I'm sorry," I say. "We don't know what it is. We don't have it. And that's the truth."

Krugman smiles to himself. "I can understand why you'd want to be circumspect about it, even cagey, but I mean, we're friends now, are we not? Even family, perhaps, no?"

"We don't have it," Sissy says. "We're not being cagey."

He pulls in his chin; the mole crowns. "Know what I also believe?" Krugman says, a drip of excitement enlivening his voice. "I believe in quid pro quo, in tit for tat. Do you understand what these terms mean?"

I shake my head.

"It means a fair exchange. I give you something, you give me something. I've given you information, answers to your questions. Now, in return, quid for my quo, you give me something. Understand? A little tit for my tat. See? I give you hospitality, now you give me the Origin." His voice, growing more excited as he speaks, shakes with building emotion. "It is only fair—"

"We don't have it," Sissy interrupts, and Krugman's body flinches. "We simply don't have an inkling what it is, this Origin. We'd never heard of the thing until we arrived here."

Krugman regards her for a long time. Then he gives the smallest of nods, and the two henchmen behind us move toward the door. "Very well, then. They will escort you back to your cottage."

We turn to leave, Sissy in front of me. She stops. The door is still closed, the two henchmen standing directly in front of it. They are smiling, arms folded across their barrel chests.

"One more thing," Krugman says, his voice jangling.

23

A FAVOR I need to ask you," Krugman says, inspecting then removing grime from under a fingernail.

"Go ahead," Sissy says. "What is it?"

"Let me search you."

Sissy's arms go taut. "Come again?"

"Listen," I say. "We already told you we don't have the Origin."

"I don't believe you," he says with clinical detachment. But his eyes, as they swing up to meet mine, are anything but detached. They are cauldrons of hurt pride and brimming anger. Something too long restrained is unleashing in him.

"Look here," Sissy says. "Whether you believe us or not doesn't change the fact that we don't have the Origin. You could search us from head to toe, and you'd—"

"Really?" Krugman says, a sinister glint reflecting in his eyes. "How funny you should mention that. I was just about to suggest the very idea myself. From head to toe."

Sissy's brows knit together in confusion. She throws me a glance. *What's going on?*

Behind us, the floorboards creak. One of the henchmen steps

toward Sissy. "Remove your clothes. All of them. We need to examine your skin."

I stare at the men, then at Krugman again. "Tell them to move away from the door, Krugman."

"No," he says softly. His eyes lilt over to Sissy, softly, with sickening tenderness. "We have reason to believe the Origin might be a typographic sort of clue, imprinted on your skin somewhere. Some kind of lettering. Perhaps an equation or a code of sorts. Take off your clothes."

"I don't think so," I say before Sissy can respond. "We'll be leaving now."

"And you will," the other henchman says with a low rumble. "*You* will. But she stays. She's the only one we still need to search." A faint smile touches his eyes. "We've already examined the four boys. And you, we checked you out while you were sick and out like a light. You're all clean." His eyes flick toward Sissy again. He starts reaching up to her.

"Don't you touch me," she says.

There's no sound but the tick-tocking of the grandfather clock, now jarringly loud.

"See, that's the thing with girls with big man-sized feet," Krugman says from behind us, his voice a slithering coo. "When their feet haven't been beautified, when the foot glands haven't been broken. Left undestroyed, these glands secrete male hormones into a girl. Turn her from a princess into an opinionated ox. One who fails to understand her place in society, who mistakenly thinks she can walk like a male, talk like a male, have opinions like a male. Say no to a male. 'Like a gold ring in a pig's snout is a girl with big feet.' "

"Look at those gargantuan man feet," one of the henchmen jeers. "Can we even be sure she's really a girl?"

A protracted pause. Thoughts churning, options weighed, indiscretions considered.

"Sometimes," the henchman whispers, "you can't be too sure about these things."

"Maybe we should find out," the other says, catching on. His close-set eyes creep down Sissy's body. "There are ways of"—his mouth droops, an upside-down smile—"ascertaining fact. Of *uncovering* the truth."

They start to move toward her.

I fly in, without elegance. But with the strength of conviction. I shove the men backward, and their ample backsides slap hard against the door. They bounce off, their fury bringing crimson to their cheeks. One of them is swinging his arm back, readying to piston it out at me, but Sissy leaps at him, driving her elbow into his sternum. He doubles over, spittle and curses flying out.

I don't know what would have happened next if Krugman didn't start to laugh. Not just any kind of laughter. This is an uproarious upheaval of his guts, a bellowing that rattles our rib cages. He collapses into his office chair, his laughter soon falling into aftershock mode, a low rumbling from the pit of his stomach.

"You guys," he says between laughs. "I said tit for tat, not tête-à-tête." He laughs at his improvised humor. "No more private conversations, okay!" Krugman's face beams. "Teatime is over!"

The back of Sissy's hand touches mine. Then we are sliding skin over skin, until we're holding hands, our cold palms fitting perfectly.

Krugman is smiling, his beard rising and bunching up at the cheeks as if a pair of mice have burrowed themselves in there. "Come," he finally says, his thumbs crooked behind his belt. "This is not what the Mission is about. We're about sunshine and smiles and happy faces. Not fracture and violence."

"Could have fooled me," Sissy says, her voice low.

"You shrill little harpy," one of the elders shouts. "You disobedient wench, we ought to feed you to the—"

"Enough," Krugman says. His voice is soft. His eyes still dance with humor, but the wetness seems acidic now. "I'm afraid this is all my fault. I've forgotten how tired you must be, and how on edge, too, after all you've been through. Please, pardon my lapse." He widens the smile on his face. "Shall we let bygones be bygones? Water under the bridge? Let all things past, pass? That sort of thing?"

I nod. Warily. "We'd like to leave now."

"As you wish," Krugman says. He motions the other elders to step aside. As we brush between the henchmen, through a parted sea of lard, Krugman mumbles something.

"What's that?" Sissy says.

"Nothing," he murmurs.

On the cobblestone path, we walk past smiling groups of girls, their teeth perfectly white, standing off to the side. Black clouds have drifted across the skies, brusque and meaning business. Within minutes, cold, driving rain drums down in slantwise bands. Sissy and I walk quickly, side by side; our hands have never let go, and they form a small cove of warmth against the soaking cold. I don't tell her what Krugman mumbled as we left. Mostly because I don't quite know what to make of it, if it really is the veiled threat I suspect it is. *All good things*, he'd whispered as we left, *come to those who wait.*

24

BY THE TIME we reach my cottage, we're soaked through. Sissy grabs my satchel bag off the sofa and upheaves its contents onto the bed. Scraps of food, Epap's sketchbook, the Scientist's journal, and small trinkets fall onto the duvet.

"See anything that might be the Origin?" she asks.

"I'm sure they've been through the bag already," I say. "And besides, aren't they under the notion that the Origin is something engraved on our skin? That it has to do with lettering or something?"

She picks up the Scientist's journal, leafs through it, then tosses it onto the bed in frustration. She's beginning to shiver. We're both freezing. I walk over to the fireplace; my trembling fingers try to get a fire going.

"L-l-look," Sissy says, chattering. She's pointing at the coffee table. A tray of food has been laid atop it and, judging from the steam still rising from the earthenware bowls of soup, it was delivered very recently. "You get your own room with a fireplace and hot shower, *and* room service as well?"

I touch the loaf of bread on the tray. Still warm. "Look, why don't you have some? It might take a while to get this fire going. The soup will help warm you up."

She agrees, sitting on the sofa and slurping the soup down. Her nose pinches up.

"Something the matter?" I ask.

She shakes her head. "Just really salty. But good. And hot."

I busy myself at the hearth, picking out a few branches stacked on the side. But the kindling is slightly damp and I'm having a hard go at it. Sissy slurps down the last of the soup but she's still shivering.

"Sissy, go take a hot shower. It'll help warm you up."

She's too cold to disagree. She gets up and I give her a set of clothes from the dresser. "They're too big for you, but better dry and big than wet and cold."

She closes the bathroom door. I take the opportunity to change into dry clothes myself, casting off my cold sodden clothes. A few minutes later, I have a hearty fire blazing away. I sit back on the sofa, easing my cold bones into the soft give of the cushions. The flames lick and dance their light across the room, transforming the walls into a firestorm of red and orange. From the bathroom, I hear the far-off sound of water splashing.

Despite the fire and set of dry clothes, I'm still cold. I gather the duvet from the bed, place it over my legs. I stare into the fire. The meandering flames are like my own disoriented, shifting thoughts. I have some soup, but it's lukewarm now, and too salty. I set it down after finishing half of it and stare out the window.

A darkness has ripened in the village, dissolving the trails of smoke rising from the chimneys, swallowing whole the thatched roofs. A few minutes later and night has absorbed the winding paths outside our front door. An occasional whistle of wind peals into the village, muffled by thickening clouds that float hidden in the dark skies. Raindrops speckle the window like small gashes.

My thoughts are preoccupied with what Krugman just told us.

A different kind of cold—more unsettling, disturbing—seeps into my bones.

Sissy walks in, her face cleansed, her hair damp.

She stands directly in front of the fireplace for a few minutes, running her fingers through her damp hair. Light from the fire gilds the loose strands, setting them ablaze.

"That shower really helped," she says. "Thanks." The firelight dances across her freshly scrubbed skin. "But it's made me really sleepy. I was almost nodding off in there." She sits next to me. For a few minutes, as the warmth of the fire spreads over us, we sit in silence. She cradles her legs under her hips, pulls the duvet over her lap.

"Pretty crazy past two days," I say.

"Pretty crazy last hour." She eases back into the cushioning, cracks her knuckles. "I was just getting used to this village, all these other humans around. And now I learn there's a whole world of us. My mind's trying to wrap itself around all this . . . but it's like grabbing for purchase in quicksand."

I nod. "It's a lot to get used to."

The fire snaps, kicking up a plume of sparks.

"What is it?" she says. "You're hiding something from me."

I shift my body sideways so I'm facing her. "Krugman might be lying, Sissy."

She doesn't say anything, but her eyes swim over my face.

"Krugman says the train goes to the Civilization. And maybe it does. But . . ."

"We don't know anything about the Civilization," she finishes.

"Other than what he tells us. He says it's a paradise, that it's an incredible place. But what if it's not? What if there's . . ."

"What?"

I take her hands into mine. I feel the warmth of skin, the beat of her pulse on my fingertips. I suddenly don't want to say what I know I have to; I simply want to stretch this quiet moment into an hour, a day, a year, a decade, to be alone with her without the interference of the world. But she lifts her eyes expectantly to mine, and I speak.

"What if the train leads straight to the duskers?"

Her face barely shifts, but her hand in mine tightens.

"When I was at the Heper Institute, the Director let slip something about the Ruler's Palace. He said it was a place where hundreds of hepers were secretly housed. Kept in underground pens, like cattle. To be consumed at the Ruler's behest." I stare into the fire, then back at Sissy's whitening face. "What if those train tracks lead to the Ruler's Palace?"

"We're the cattle?" She glances at the emptied bowl of soup, the half-eaten loaf. "And that's why they're fattening us up?"

I grit my teeth. "I don't know. Maybe I'm being paranoid. Maybe the Civilization is everything they've said it is. A paradise. The final destination to which my father's been leading us all along." I exhale with frustration. "This place is strange, no doubt about it. But what do I know about weird? Or about normal, for that matter? I mean, I've lived my whole life masquerading as a dusker in a dusker world. What do I know of the human world?"

I stare out the window. The sky is smeared over with black clouds. Rain falls, bringing more darkness down with it. The outside world begins to dissolve into a black husk, enclosing us in this small room of flickering firelight. "I've lived my whole life caught in a crack between two worlds. And I don't belong to or know either one."

"Don't look to me for help, Gene." She's trying to be light about it, but a heaviness sits upon her words. "I'm just like you," she says. "I've lived in a glass dome my whole life. I don't know anything about either world, human or dusker."

I grip her hand tighter. "You have your instincts, Sissy. You are the most intuitive and grounded person I've ever known. Trust what your gut is telling you."

She doesn't say anything for a long time. With her other hand, she smooths the wrinkles of the duvet with hard, pressing strokes. "We need to figure out where that train takes us, Gene. I won't let the boys get on until we find out. And I won't let you get on, either."

She holds my stare. The firelight flickers in her eyes. They seem uncharacteristically glazed and heavy-lidded. "We don't have much time," I say. "Less than two days."

"I know," she says, her words slightly slurred, as if dragged down by fatigue. "We're missing something, aren't we? An obvious clue, something really blatant."

Minutes pass in a comfortable quiet. The sound of rain falling on the roof is drumlike and hypnotic, lulling my body into a strange slackening. The window is now reflective, and I catch our mirrored reflections in the glass, burnished-red firelight curling over us. For the first time in days, I see my face. It seems older now, the edges harder. I'm beginning to resemble my father even more.

A numbness settles on me. It doesn't seem to fit the moment: in light of the paradigm-shattering news, and with the dilemma of whether we should board the train hovering over us, we should be pacing back and forth, our voices agitated and excited. Instead, we're both slouched on the sofa, drifting away.

"Somehow it all comes down to my father," I say, trying to awaken myself through conversation. "Find out what happened to him, and we find out where those train tracks lead. He's the key to all of this."

I think she's going to say something in response. But when I turn to her, I see her eyelids have become further weighed down with tiredness, her head drooped to the side. She blinks hard, tries to stifle a yawn. "Hey," she murmurs, staring at her empty bowl. "What was in that soup?" A wetness gleams in her eyes. She settles deeper into the sofa as if fusing with the leather.

Neither of us speak. The fire crackles and hisses. A heavy weight pushes me down, gently, but with insistence, into the sofa. It's all I can do to resist that nudging pressure, to keep from crashing. The room starts to darken and swim, gray waves drifting to black puddles. I stare at Sissy's emptied bowl of soup, and at mine, half-empty, the rims blurring. An alarm begins to ring in me, but it is far-off and muted.

"Gene?" Sissy mumbles softly.

"Yeah?"

She slides deeper into the sofa, her body slipping across the smooth leather to rest against me. Her soft flesh melds against the contours of my side. We feel like a perfect fit.

"What is it?" I ask.

For a long time, she doesn't say anything and I think she's finally drifted away. But then words murmur out, soft as the wings of a butterfly. "Don't leave me, promise?" And her eyes close at that, her head slipping across the back of the sofa and down against my shoulder. I feel the flesh of her forehead against my neck, smooth and warm, the pulse of her neck against my collarbone.

Her lips part and small breaths puff gently out. She's asleep now. I touch her face softly, my fingertips tracing her cheekbones, the tawny fur of her eyebrows. I touch her bangs, push them from her forehead.

Firelight flickers about the room like frenzied snakes. They are the color of Ashley June's hair: a fiery, jealous red, swirling madly. All I can do is close my eyes against this assault of guilt. I caress Sissy's arm, draped across my chest, back and forth, back and forth. Every stroke feels like a betrayal, a betrayal, a betrayal.

Slumber pulls me down with a swiftness that is a mercy.

25

I WAKE TO the sound of fat raindrops pelting the windowpane. It is pitch black outside now. The fire has been reduced to glowing embers and the room has turned cold. On the floor, cast aside like shed skin, lies the crumpled duvet.

Sissy is gone.

I place my hand on the still-indented sag in the sofa where she'd fallen asleep. The leather, cold. I stand up, the floorboards creaking in lockstep with my aching bones. The room spins, lurching backward then forward. Stumbling toward the bathroom, my legs kick into the coffee table, upending the earthenware bowls.

Cold water helps. I douse cupped handfuls into my hair, so much that when I raise my head, freezing rivulets course down my neck, chest, back. Alertness—and alarm—knife into me.

"Sissy!" I shout into the dark hallway outside the room, then again, louder, on the street outside. The downpour has driven everyone indoors; the streets are deserted. The ground has turned muddy with the rain, and imprinted in the sludge are large duck-footed boot prints. Too large to belong to the lotus feet of village girls, these must belong to adult men. Elders. At least three of them, by the look of it.

I follow the trail of boot prints. But it vanishes once I hit the cobblestone path. I glance up and down the street.

"Sissy!" I yell. Only the splatter of rain on cobblestone and thatched roofs answers my cry. I run toward the village square, through a murky gray. Usually the hub of activity, it is now emptied of movement, noise, even color, all vibrancy washed away. The cottage windows are shuttered like eyes shut tight.

"Sissy!" I shout again, now cupping my mouth. "Sissy!"

A door to one of the cottages swings open. A figure steps out, stands under a small awning. It's Epap. His shirt, as if hurriedly put on, is unbuttoned halfway down. "What's happened?" he says with a brooding glare. "Where's Sissy?"

"She's missing! Help me find her!"

It's hard to read his expression. In the shadows he studies me, unwilling to step into the rain.

"Epap?"

He shakes his head, once, twice, blinking slowly. He slinks back into the cottage, a retreat that betrays the grudge he's still harboring against Sissy. I turn around, furious and disappointed in him. I'd hoped for more.

But then he's flying out the door, putting on a hoodie, his feet splashing urgently through puddles of mud. He's flung the hood over his head by the time he reaches me.

"Tell me what's happened," he demands. His eyes are stirring with concern.

"She pissed off the elders. And now they've taken her somewhere."

His eyes swing to mine, searching for truth. "That's crazy. Why would you think something like that?"

"They spiked the soup, knocked her out. I didn't drink as much so—Look! Are you just going to ask me questions or are you going to help me find her? I think she's in serious trouble."

"Overreact much?" he snaps back, shaking his head. "They've been nothing but good to us. Why don't you just relax and quit with the paranoia already?" One side of his mouth droops down. "What, you think just because Sissy's not with you, it must necessarily mean she's been abducted? It couldn't be because, oh, I don't know, because she simply doesn't want to be with you?" He flings his arms into the rain, snorts. "You got me out into this lousy weather for *this*?"

I don't have time to explain or for drama. I pivot around, considering which direction to take off.

Epap grabs my elbow. I turn, about to yank my arm away. But the look in his eyes stops me. "Wait," he says. He exhales with deep frustration. "You really think something's wrong?"

I nod.

"How do you know this?"

"Epap, are you with me or not? I'm not going to waste time explaining."

Something in him relents. "Let's go find her," he says.

And when I take off, he's right there beside me, our legs spinning in tandem, mud splashing like tiny explosions at our feet.

But the empty streets and darkened cottages yield nothing. "Where is everyone?" Epap says, panting hard next to me when we stop. He leans against a cottage wall, doubled over and grabbing at his knees.

"C'mon," I say, also trying to catch my breath. "Let's keep looking."

He nods, pushing off the wall. "Hold on," he says and flicks his chin to our right.

A village girl, hooded, scurries out of a cottage. She surveys the empty street, then starts waddling toward us as fast as her lotus feet can manage.

Epap and I glance at one another, then hurry over to the girl. She stops, waits for us to reach her, nervously scans the street. As she grabs my arm and leads us into a narrow alleyway, her sleeve catches on mine, and is pushed up her arm. Four branding marks on the inside of her forearm. She pulls down her hood from her head. It's the girl with freckles.

"It's too late," she whispers. "Go back to your cottages."

"Where is she?" I demand. "Where have they taken her?"

"It's over. You have nothing to gain by looking for her. But a lot to lose. For your own good—and hers—go back."

"Is she okay? Has she been hurt?" Epap says, stepping forward.

"She'll be returned in due time."

I grab the girl's arm, gently but firmly. She's skinny and beneath the slight layer of flesh, her bone is hard and rigid. Intelligence swims in her eyes. "You came out here to help us," I say. "So help us. Where is she?"

She hesitates. Then she whispers: "It's already too late. But go to the clinic. You know where it is, yes?"

"The clinic?" Epap says. "I know where it is but why on earth do we have to go there?"

She pulls her arm away. "You're too late." She waddles away, disappearing into the same cottage from which she'd emerged earlier.

Epap's face is scrunched together in confusion and growing panic. "The clinic?" He turns to me. "Gene, what's going on?"

I don't answer even though an awful suspicion spills into me. I take off, running harder than I have all night.

We're completely winded by the time we reach the clinic but we waste little time. Epap bursts through the clinic door, leading with his shoulder. He sees something: his back stiffens like a puppet whose strings are suddenly jerked upward.

Sissy is in the middle of the otherwise empty room, laying in a contraption that resembles a dentist's chair. But one with straps and constraints. Her arms and legs are splayed ungracefully apart, her eyes closed, mouth slack.

A faint odor of burnt flesh lingers in the air.

"Sissy!" Epap shouts as he rushes to her side. Her left sleeve is pushed up, exposing the soft underside of her forearm. In the middle of her smooth flesh, like a separate entity iron-pressed on, sits an X-shaped bulge of pus-oozing flesh. She's been branded.

We don't say anything, only move quickly to unstrap her from the constraints. Her breathing is quick and shallow, her lips murmuring nonsensically. Tenderly, Epap rolls her sleeve higher to keep the coarse wool from chafing the fresh burn. I move to pick her up but he shoves me aside. He lifts her with a strength and grace that belies his thin arms, cradling her securely against his chest. His eyes close with partial relief, and his lips begin to move against her hair.

"I've got you, you're safe now, Sissy," he whispers. As he hoists her up to get a better grip under her legs, her head bangs up against his nose. He doesn't yell or cry out in pain; he only holds her with greater tenderness against himself until the wave of pain subsides.

A jab of unexpected jealousy strikes my heart.

Epap rushes out into the rain. It's coming down with the force of a waterfall, drenching us completely in seconds. Despite the added weight, he's running with a speed that's difficult to keep up with. Or sustain.

"Epap!" I grab his arm to make him stop. "Where are you headed?"

"Back to my cottage." He tries to pull his arm away.

"No." I find his eyes. "Your cottage is on the other side of the village. Ten minutes away. Sissy shouldn't be out in this rain for that long. Not in her condition. Bring her to my room. It's much closer."

His arms are beginning to tremble. Adrenaline has run its course and he's completely drained. He nods, quickly. "Take us there."

But I pause. A thought occurs to me. "We have to get the boys," I say.

Epap understands immediately. It's not safe for them to be alone. An attack against one of us is an attack against all of us.

"Give me Sissy," I say. "You get the boys, Epap. You know where they are. I don't."

He shoots me a wary look. "No," he says, "I'll carry her—"

"All around the village?" I say. I put my hand on his shoulder. "I'll get her back safely. I promise you this." He stares at me, indecision rippling on his face. "Sissy will want the boys when she awakes. Go get them."

That convinces him. He shifts Sissy into my arms. I did not realize how much I have wanted this: the sideways collapse of her head to nestle against my chest, the slight give of her flesh against mine. It takes everything in me to resist the urge to embrace her more tightly, to plunge my face into her hair and draw in her musk.

Epap is staring at me with suspicion. I tell him the location of my cottage and then we're off, running in opposite directions. And I am suddenly tireless, as if drawing life force from Sissy, and my feet gather speed and urgency under me. I smash into falling raindrops, breaking them apart into a thousand million particles of mist.

26

Back in the room, I work quickly. I lay Sissy down on the sofa, and she curls into it, arms shivering, blue lips muttering delirium. I pick the duvet off the floor and wrap it around her in a tight cocoon, laying her branded forearm on top. It's not nearly enough; her body quakes with a deep-seated cold.

I slide quickly over to the fireplace. Some of the embers are still glowing, and in only a matter of minutes I have a fire blazing away. She's still trembling. A film of yellow mucous oozes out of her branding wound, the skin around it a vicious red.

"Oh, Sissy," I whisper through gritted teeth. I brush her damp hair back from her temple. Before this moment, I didn't know fury and tenderness could coexist in the same heartbeat.

The boys arrive only minutes later, their feet pounding up the steps and along the hallway. They burst through the door, their faces pale, their hair windswept and damp.

"How is she?" Jacob says. They gather around the sofa, stroking her hair, not quite knowing what to do. David gasps when he sees her branded skin. Ben starts to cry.

"Get a damp towel from the bathroom," Epap tells Ben, giving him something to do. "We need to keep that wound cool." Ben scampers off. Epap pulls the duvet back, then glares at me. "You idiot! Her clothes are soaking wet. No wonder she's still freezing."

"Well, what was I supposed to do? Undress her?"

Epap doesn't answer. He turns his attention to directing the younger boys. He points to the chest of drawers, and Jacob is up on his feet, pulling out a set of dry clothes. David runs to the bathroom to retrieve a towel. "And put socks on her feet, too," Epap tells them as they start to unbutton and peel off her sodden clothes.

Epap and I walk out to the hallway, closing the door behind us. He rubs the back of his neck.

"They drugged the food," I tell him. "It knocked out both Sissy and me. That's when they took her."

He nods. I'm expecting rancor, and perhaps accusation, but his voice is surprisingly soft-toned. "Are you okay?" he asks.

"I'm fine," I say after a few seconds.

Epap nods, walks across the hallway, and leans against the wall. He rests his head back, closes his eyes.

"They wanted to search her," I say, "and she said no. A strip search, Epap."

Epap's eyes snap open. "What?"

"They wanted to remove all her clothes. To examine her skin."

He blinks. "Why?"

"They think the Origin might be an inscription or something tattooed on us. An equation, a formula, maybe. Something to do with lettering."

He mouths a silent *what?* He turns to me. "But why only her? Why not you or me, or the boys?"

"They've already examined us. Me when I was sick. And you guys probably when you were bathing in the bathhouse."

Epap's eyes turn inward, widening with realization. "They had the girls wash us. And towel us down. Every inch of us."

"You didn't protest? Or complain?"

His face turns crimson, his eyes fall to the ground. "No, I mean, what was there to complain about? We thought it was good hospitality."

I scoff at his answer, but silently. I pull back the curtains on the hallway window. Nothing moves out there but dark sheets of rain. "You've really had the wool pulled over your eyes," I say. "You have no idea, do you? About this place."

He folds his arms across his chest. "I know about the branding. It's not what you think. Just takes a little getting used to. As with all their other . . . quirks. These quirks . . . they're like beer froth. You just gotta get past it to get to the good stuff."

"They branded *Sissy,* Epap. That's not a quirk I could ever get used to. That's not froth."

The floor creaks under Epap as he shifts his feet. He doesn't say anything. Behind the door, we hear the boys speaking in hushed tones as they finish changing Sissy. A long minute later, Epap asks, "What do you think we should do next? Are we in danger? Should we leave?"

I shrug. "I should be the one asking questions. I've been sick and unconscious for days, you ought to know this village better. But you've been so busy cozying up with the elders, ignoring the 'froth.' You know squat about this place."

He paces a short way down the hall, comes back. "That's unfair."

"I'll tell you what's unfair. Leaving Sissy all alone at the farm. That's what you and the boys did. You deserted her. She led you safely to this village, through the Vast, up the mountain, protecting you guys from dusker attack after attack. And what did you do in return? As soon as you set one foot in this place, you dropped her like a sack of potatoes. Off you went, running around, carousing with—"

"Enough!"

"—all the local girls, not giving a moment's thought for Sissy."

"Sissy can fend for herself! She doesn't need hand-holding—"

"It's not about that! It's about sticking together, it's about—"

"I said enough! I don't need a lecture from *you* about loyalty!" His face is filled with anger. But it's not directed at me. His clenched fists thump against his side. Self-hate and guilt tighten his shoulders.

"You left her alone," I say, softer now. "You shouldn't have done that. The younger boys, okay, I can understand them getting caught up with everything here, losing their heads. But you. You should have been more collected. And you should *never* have left Sissy to fend for herself, Epap. What were you thinking, going off with all those girls? You did it to make her jealous, didn't you?" I say, my voice rising with accusation.

His lips tighten. He paces down the hallway again, with small, tight strides. He stares disconsolately at his boots. When he walks back, it's with slower, meditative strides. He leans against the wall and kicks backward, his heel smacking against the wall.

"I didn't do it to make her jealous," he says quietly. "Spending all that time with the village girls, hanging around with them, it wasn't to play the jealousy game. I'd never do something so . . . juvenile."

"Why'd you do it, then?"

His eyes mist over, and he turns them downward. "To prove to *myself* that I could get along fine without her. That I didn't need her. That in the company of other girls, I would forget her." He sniffs. "And in the beginning, I thought I would. All that female attention, it was intoxicating, see. But I was wrong." He stares down at his hands, exhales angrily through his nose. "And you're right, I should never have neglected her. I totally dropped the ball on that one."

His eyes rise to mine and they are balanced and steady and filled with resolve. "I'm better than that. I'll make good. I will."

I give a quick nod, our eyes never breaking contact. It's taken over a week, but Epap and I have finally had our first real interaction.

"Something's got you spooked about this place," he says. His eyes turn hard with self-reproach. "What have I been missing?"

"There are things I just learned. And which you definitely should know." I flick my chin toward the room. "But let's go inside. I want the boys to hear this, too."

Movement. Outside the window, a line of gray figures trundling in the rain toward us.

"Hold on," I say. "Someone's coming."

It's a trio of village girls. They bring medicinal ointments and bandages. Kneeling before the still-unconscious Sissy, they work with practiced efficiency. A pungent cream is lathered onto the branded skin. It's wiped off after a few minutes, and a different yellowish cream is layered on, less thickly. A bandage is placed around the burnt skin, but not on top of it.

"Apply a new coating every hour," the lead girl says. She has hard eyes that sit upon soft, chubby cheeks, and her hair is done up in braided ponytails. She gets up to leave. The others follow suit, the floorboards creaking under their collective weight.

One of the other girls, with a high-pitched, wavering voice, speaks. "The elders wish to express their displeasure. Your removal of this girl from the clinic was a major indiscretion. Grand Elder Krugman, however, has decided no further discipline is necessary. Enough punishment has been meted out tonight. *Justice has been rendered, orderliness has been restored.*" The last sentence is intoned like a chant.

"However," the third girl says, her face thin and flat, "the eldership further wishes to convey their desire that you each return to your abodes. All sleeping arrangements are strictly enforced. We will escort the boys to the cottage, and carry the girl back down to the farm."

The boys look at each other.

"No," Epap says. "That is not happening. We're all staying here. From now on, we're together."

"The eldership is insistent."

"As am I," Epap says.

The girls, unaccustomed to challenging males face-to-face, wilt easily and quickly. One of them adjusts her dress. "I know what you are thinking," she says. "That what happened tonight to your friend Sissy is an awful thing."

"And it isn't?" I say.

The girl peels back her sleeve. She has three brandings on her forearm. "I was once wild and undisciplined. I did not appreciate how my unruliness was a cancer to the Mission's harmony. But I've matured. And now, I can honestly tell you that since I've learned to place the Mission before self, I've found the peace and joy I'd been seeking in all the wrong places. I'm happier than I've ever thought possible, especially knowing one day I will achieve the highest of joys, my ticket to the Civilization."

She sees incredulity in my eyes. "The elders teach us—and I have come to see this is true—that this Mission will rise or fall depending on how well we sync with its harmony. That is why any deviance, no matter how small, must be dealt with swiftly and, unfortunately on rare occasions, drastically. But this is a peaceful, wonderful community. You must stop looking for a devil in every bush. Because you look needlessly."

"You've been branded three times," I say, pointing at her forearm. "What happens when you get five?"

She doesn't answer, only pulls her sleeve over her arm. Her left eyebrow twitches. "It is time for us to leave," she says. They pick up the medical baskets, waddle out of the room. I hear them tromping down the hallway.

Curiously, one of them has remained in the room. She is standing still. It's the girl with braided pigtails. She suddenly spins around, looks at me.

"Be very careful," she whispers urgently, her eyebrows pulled together into a single line of fear.

"What?" Epap says. Too loud.

The receding footsteps in the hallway stop. Then they start up again, but instead of fading, they get louder. They're returning. And quickly. Like fists raining down on a door, louder, louder.

"What's going on?" I whisper to the girl.

But it's too late. The girl hears the approach of the other two and quickly collects herself. "Will you at least let us bring you some food?" she asks loudly. The other girls are back at the door, gazing curiously at her.

"No," I answer. "Not after what happened earlier with the soup."

The girl waddles out of the room, her pigtails bouncing up and down.

The trio of girls clomp down the stairs. We hear the front door open and close. And then they are gone.

27

"SO THAT'S WHERE we are," I say to the boys. My voice is threadbare and hoarse after talking so long. "We need to decide what to do. Get on the train or not."

For the past hour, I've shared with them everything Krugman told Sissy and me in his office. About the world, the history of the duskers, the Scientist. And about the Origin. Every so often, to give them time to digest the information, I'd stop speaking and add more wood to the fire or check on Sissy's arm. I needed the time, too. Between almost getting into a fight in Krugman's office, being drugged, and searching for Sissy, I had yet to digest everything myself. When I shared my suspicions about the Civilization—that it might not be the Promised Land but instead the Ruler's Palace—my voice quivered, and I had to dig my fingers into my palm to keep them from trembling.

Epap puts his arm around Ben, who is now on the verge of tears. Nobody says anything as they sit on the rug between the fireplace and sofa on which Sissy still lies. Their faces are knotted into deep frowns. I spread a fresh coating of lotion on Sissy's burn. Her breathing is deeper, more rhythmic, her brow drier. The effects of whatever drug she ingested fading, she's coming to. Any minute now.

Outside, dusk—hidden behind the curtain of black rain—has segued imperceptibly into night.

"But we don't know, do we?" Jacob says. "Not for sure, right? The Civilization *could* be the Promised Land. The train *could* be the way to paradise."

"But remember what the girl with pigtails said," I say. "She warned us to be careful."

"But think about what the other girl said," Jacob says. "That we shouldn't go looking for a devil in every bush. Maybe this place really is the gateway to paradise."

Sissy groans in pain, eyes still closed.

"Look what these same people did to Sissy," I say. "How can you trust anything they say?"

Jacob gets off the floor, stands by the window. "Listen. I had this dream last night. About the Civilization." He pauses, hesitating. But then he starts speaking, and a warmth suffuses his cheeks. "It was so real. I saw outdoor stadiums full of humans watching sports in sunlight, just like in all those books we read. Outdoor markets with hundreds of different stalls, summer concerts on lush grass, city blocks filled with restaurants, tables spilling out onto the streets, humans sitting and eating . . . salads. And there were amusement parks with parades and magical castles and thrilling rides. Carousels full of laughing children, magical boat rides surrounded by singing puppets that the Scientist told us about. We can't *not* go there."

"C'mon, Jacob, that's just a dream. We can't make a decision based on something so fluffy," Epap scolds mildly.

"It's no more fluffy than your guesswork." He runs his hand through his hair. "All I'm trying to say is we don't know anything. Not for certain, anyway."

We fall quiet. I throw in another piece of wood and we gaze at the fire as if somewhere in the swirling light lies an answer.

"But we do know one thing for certain." It's Ben, his voice a high squeak. He is sitting hugging his bent legs, chin on kneecaps. He lifts his head off his knees with a smile. "The Origin. What it is."

We all turn to him.

"*Who* it is, actually," he says. He lifts his arm, his finger stretched out and pointing right at me. "You are the Origin," Ben says. "It's so obvious."

"Me? How do you figure that?" I say, wanting to scoff, but somehow unable to. A skein of goose bumps breaks out along my body. The boys are all staring at me with the same expression they wore a few days ago. On the boat when they'd turned over the tablet and read the engraved words—

"*Don't let Gene die,*" Ben says.

"*Don't let Gene die,*" Jacob repeats, slowly and thoughtfully, as if feeling out the texture of each syllable. His eyes, when they rise to meet mine, widen. "Ben's right. The Origin's not a thing. It's a person. It's you. You must be the Origin."

Wood crackles in the fireplace behind me.

"It kind of makes sense," Epap says, pulling on his lower lip. "I mean, we've searched high and low for it. Through all our belongings, clothes. We've scoured the pages of the Scientist's journal and come up empty every time. If the Origin was a *thing* in our possession we'd have found it by now." He glances at Sissy lying on the sofa. "You said the elders believe it has something to do with lettering, maybe words tattooed into our skin. But what if the lettering isn't something on our skin. But—"

"—in our name. In your name," Ben says, staring at me.

Gene.

"What if the Origin is in your genes?" Ben says. "Like genetics. All that DNA stuff the Scientist taught us."

They are staring at me as if I've suddenly grown five heads. "Naw," I say, shaking my head. "Not that simple." I frown, catch my reflection in the darkened window. "Is it?"

"Gene," Epap says, slowly rising to his feet. "Did your father ever mention anything to you?"

"About what?" I ask.

"Did he ever tell you why he named you *Gene*?" Epap asks. If he's mocking me or joking around, it's not showing in his voice or steely gaze.

"Hold on," I say. "You think I'm the Origin because . . . it's in my *genes*? You think the cure for the duskers is in my genetic code?"

Their wide eyes and gaping mouths are answer enough.

"C'mon now!" I snort. "Don't be ridiculous! Look here, a name's just a name! A sound. There isn't any special meaning attached to it!" I look at Epap. "You're going to tell me that Epap has some special significance? Or Ben does? Or Jacob?"

"Actually," Epap says, and his face is blooming with realization, "they do. All our names do. The Scientist said he christened us according to some aspect uniquely ours. Ben got his name after Big Ben, a mythical clock tower, because of his chubby arms and legs when he was a baby. He named Jacob after the biblical character because of how he walks with a slight limp. As for Sissy, he named her 'Sis' so Ben would remember they're siblings, half-siblings, anyway. Eventually, we just started calling her Sissy because of the way it rolled off the tongue. He named me Epap—"

"Okay, okay, I get it," I say. "He gave you cute names. I'm happy for you. But I can tell you this: he never explained my name to me. It was just a name. No special significance attached to it whatsoever."

But it's as if they haven't heard me. They're smiling, eyes wide with awe. "This whole time," Jacob says, his eyes glistening, "right in front of us. The Origin. The cure for the duskers, the salvation of humankind. The freakin' Origin."

I stand awkwardly before them, wanting to wave off their attention and unwarranted conclusions. The stiff leather on the sofa creaks.

"Well, there's hope for you dunderheads after all."

It's Sissy who's spoken. We turn to her. Her eyes are open, her head propped up on the sofa arm. She's trying to smile. "Maybe I should pass out more often," she says. "Remove myself from the picture. Apparently, it forces you guys to think on your own. Come up with some pretty good ideas."

"It was me, Sissy!" Ben shouts, smiling and running over to her. "*I* was the one who thought of it first!"

She kisses him on the cheek. "But of course you did. You're my brother, aren't you?"

Ben points at me proudly. "And he's the Origin."

28

Sissy is up for only a few minutes before she violently heaves into a basin. She wipes her mouth free of dangling vomit, tells us she feels better now that it's out of her system. The odor is foul, and I take the makeshift vomit basin outside. When I return, they're having a heated discussion.

"We should get on the train," Jacob is saying, one hand cupping the elbow of his other arm. "I really believe it's why the Scientist brought us to the Mission. This place, it's like a waiting room where we board a train to paradise. Okay, it's a weird waiting room, I'll grant you that much. It's filled with eccentric regulations and ruled with an iron fist. I get it. But it's a waiting room nonetheless." He sighs with frustration. "A week from today, we'll be eating at fancy digs or being paraded in luxury around town and laughing at these silly suspicions. This is the time to be celebrating, not second-guessing the Scientist. He brought us here to get on the train. I mean, how much more obvious can it be?"

"If that's the case, why didn't he board the train himself?" Epap says.

"He was waiting for us, for Gene—the Origin—to arrive. Probably, he wanted to board with us and personally escort us to the Civilization." He waves his arms in frustration. "He'd be rolling in his grave if he could hear us now."

"And you just made my next point for me. Because he *is* in a grave. If he was waiting for us, why did he kill himself?" Epap asks.

Jacob swallows hard. "I don't know," he says, his voice shaky. "Maybe he was expecting us to arrive much sooner. Months, years earlier. When we didn't show, maybe he thought he'd failed us and that he no longer deserved to go to the Civilization. But we can honor his life now by going where he'd strived for years to one day take us: the Civilization."

The room falls into a heavy silence.

"I don't know, Jacob," Sissy says quietly. "I'm sorry, but there's something unnerving about the Civilization. About the Scientist's suicide. I think we honor him best by staying alert and using our heads. We need to know more before boarding the train."

"And how long is that going to take? A week? A month? A year?" Jacob's eyes settle on Sissy's brand. "We can't stay here indefinitely."

Sissy notices Jacob staring at her brand, and half turns her arm. "We have food and shelter here," she says. "This mark they gave me tonight is nothing. A little scratch. Barely hurt at all." She gives him a reassuring smile. "We'll be fine here."

Jacob stares down at his feet, his eyes glistening over. "You know me, Sissy," he says, his voice shaking with emotion. "I'd never go against what you decide for us. If you say you need more time to investigate, then I believe you. But find out quickly, will you? And promise you won't keep us here a day longer than necessary?"

She walks over to him, pulls his head against her chest. His body, taut with tension, wilts with release. He puts his arm around her waist, his body quivering against hers. Tears stream out of his closed eyes. "Not a second longer, okay, big guy? You'll be the first to know. Hey, no more crying! You're too big for tears now."

Jacob nods, wipes the tears off his face.

"You're such a dunderhead, you know that?" Sissy says, ruffling his hair.

29

THEY SETTLE IN for the night, the three younger boys sharing the bed, Sissy on the sofa, Epap on the rug. I take a tall wooden stool out into the hallway, position it next to the window. I want to keep watch, I tell them, just in case.

I hear their voices murmuring in the room, their banter somber and low-key. Eventually, their voices turn to silence, then to light snores, their breathing synchronized even in the unconsciousness of sleep. I think to walk into the room, lie down on the bed. They will make room for me as they always have. But I stay rooted on the stool and gaze out the window. I need to be alone.

The rain, falling with the intensity of forty days and nights, comes to a sudden stop. After an hour, when even the runoff dripping off the eaves ceases, a clean silence overtakes the night. The clouds break but imperfectly; moonlight pours through the shredded skies in a fragmented, haphazard splash across the range of mountains.

Gene.

Gene.

Did he ever tell you why he named you Gene?

My thoughts are interrupted by the creak of floorboards. Sissy—pale and ashen like a ghost—floats down the dark stretch of the hallway. The duvet is wrapped around her shoulders like a shawl.

"Why don't you come back to the room?" she says quietly. She walks over when I don't answer. Our shoulders almost touch as she looks out the window. Her sleeve is rolled up; dark shadows cover her forearm.

I place my hands tenderly on her arm, draw her into the moonlight. The branding wound looks even worse now, the puckered skin oozing with discharge. "Oh, Sissy."

Her eyes harden, but they're different this time. With the boys, to veil her pain, her eyes were set like reflecting shields. But now I can see past the flinty hardness where lie pools of deep hurt and anger.

She tells me she does not remember very much. She only recalls the wooziness that beset her after drinking the soup, the sensation of being carried away, then nothing until she was back in my room. Where she found herself branded. "I'm sure they must have also searched me," she says, and even in her whisper I can hear the rage. "I don't know what's worse—knowing they did it, or not being able to remember it ever happened."

"I'm sorry. I tried to find you—we did, Epap and I. But . . ."

"We can't let this get to us," she says, quietly, but again I see the flash of rage in her eyes. "I mean, don't get me wrong: I want to kick the living hell out of them. But we can't afford to get sidetracked. Our number one priority," she says, turning to meet my gaze, "is to find out about that train. Running around with my own personal vendetta will only get in the way."

Beads of her condensed breath glimmer on the window. Her arm trembles slightly in my hands.

"You sure you're okay, Sissy?" I reach up to brush aside the hair covering her eyes. "Hey, maybe we should all just take off. Pack our bags and leave. Venture into the woods."

"No," she says. Very quietly. "Where would we go? How would we survive? Winter's coming. Besides, Jacob's right. Maybe the train really does take us to the Promised Land. We can't ditch that possibility too soon—it might be the best option we have."

We fall quiet. The clouds stretch thin then split apart, allowing more moonlight to illuminate the village. Gradually, Sissy's posture begins to relax, the expression on her face softens. She leans against me, our shoulders slightly touching. I'm suddenly all too aware of the give of her flesh against mine. I've been holding her arm this whole time; slowly, I pull my hands back. Her arm drifts down to her side.

"What is it?" she says.

I swallow. "Nothing." We gaze outside again. The sound of snoring drifts down the hallway.

"C'mon," she says, "we should get some rest. Come back to the room, there's plenty of space, it's warm." She puts her hand on my elbow. "Sleep will clear our heads. In the morning maybe we'll think of something."

I shake my head.

She stares intently at me. "So much the lone wolf, Gene."

"It's not that."

"What is it, then?"

"The answer's out there somewhere. In the village. Not in our heads." I push my hands into my parka pockets. "You told me once my father would play this hide-and-seek game with you. He played that game with me, too. All the time. He'd hide a prize but leave little clues around to help me find it."

Her eyes sparkle with the memories. *"The answer is right in front of you. Right under your nose."*

I nod. "I can't shake this feeling that somewhere in this village is a clue he's left for me. Right in front of me. Right under my nose. And I just need to find it." I turn to her. "There are answers out there. Waiting to be found."

She takes my hand gently. "I think I know where we should look."

30

We move swiftly through the moonlit streets. Deep puddles on the ground are transformed under the bright moonlight into gleaming pools of mercury. Full strength has returned to Sissy, and she walks easily beside me, her boots split-splatting on the wet path alongside mine. Cottages flank us on the narrow streets and we do not speak until we veer off the main street and onto a dirt path.

"This way," Sissy says when we're halfway between the village and the farmlands.

I wrap my parka tighter around me against the cold and follow her to an outcast building a hundred meters out, on the edge of the woods, rectangular and boxy. And drab. No windows and only a single metal door breaking up the bland concrete surface. Half of the building is awash in moonlight. The other half is hidden in the shadows of overhanging trees. "The Scientist's lab," she says as we draw closer to it. "I've already searched inside countless times when you were still sick. I knew the elders would have scoured every inch of the place, looking for the Origin. But I wanted to see for myself what the Scientist had been working on."

The air inside is musty, dank with the odor of mold. Sissy flips a switch and overhanging fluorescent lights flicker on. The lab is composed of about five large workstations, all of which are littered with test tubes, small experiment burners, cylinders, and beakers. Scattered on benches and even on the dirt-packed floor are open textbooks and notepads filled with scrawled handwriting I'd recognize anywhere. My father's.

"He must have slept here," Sissy says, pointing at a hammock hanging in the corner. "A lab rat, researching, investigating, studying around the clock."

I pick up a notebook. It's filled from front to back, top to bottom with nonsensical chemical equations and formulas. If there's any meaning to them, it's lost on me. They have no more meaning to me than the mad, delusional workings and scribbles of a man pushed over the edge.

"I went through all the notebooks," Sissy says. "And they're all the same. Filled with those equations. Do they mean anything to you?"

I shake my head. I walk along the wall, eyes searching. In a tall glass cabinet, endless rows of vials sit in racks, many half-filled with a translucent liquid. "What was he doing in here? What was he working on?"

Sissy's voice from the other end of the lab is echoic and distant. "I think he came up with the glowing green liquid inside the GlowBurns." She walks over to me, opens the glass cabinet, and removes two vials. She pours the contents of one vial onto the surface of a work bench, splattering the liquid into a small pool. Then she opens the other vial, pours its liquid content atop the pool. Instantly, the intermixed liquid begins to glow green.

"From what I've been able to gather from the notebooks," she says, "he was working on this liquid for a few years. It's an alternative-energy light source of some kind." She picks up a notebook and taps it on her thigh. "I've wondered if there was more to it. A hidden agenda."

I pick up another notebook. More equations, chemical formulas, nary a single sentence with subject, verb, object. Not an iota of a personal pronoun. "That's it? That's all he did in here? Worked on some stupid glowing liquid?" I pick up another notebook, flip through it, let it fall to the ground. "There's got to be more."

"I've been through all the notebooks, Gene. There's nothing but formulas and equations related to the glowing liquid."

I move between workbenches, eyes swiveling around, searching. Open a few drawers containing dirty beakers, flasks, grimy plastic goggles, metal rulers beginning to rust. "A sign, a clue, something. It's somewhere in here."

"Maybe," Sissy says. "It's a long shot, but if I missed something, I thought you might pick up on it."

I open glass cabinets, pushing aside cylinders and beakers, searching for an etching in the wood benches, a hole in the wall through which a sunbeam might form. But after an hour of searching, there's nothing but smoothness, blandness, emptiness. An empty shout of silence.

"Gene. We've looked through everything." She bites her lower lip. "There's nothing here."

And now I start shoving racks of test tubes off the benches, not caring when they break on the ground, not caring that they shatter into shards on the ground, and now I'm knocking over stools, kicking them out of my way. I'm pulling dusty parkas and scarves off wooden pegs. I'm looking for my name, written, etched, chiseled, on wood, on plastic, on glass, I'm looking for the letter *G,* the letter *E,* the letter *N*. I'm looking for my father.

"Gene."

I'm grabbing more notebooks, riffling through them, and they offer up nothing but more nonsensical equations and clouds of kicked-up dust that get into my eyes, making me blink, and the backs of my eyelids grate against my eyeballs, drawing wetness. So much time spent to write, so many letters penned. But never once the letters *G* and *E* and *N* used in combination.

"Gene."

And then I'm grabbing the covers of his notebooks, ripping them into two, the spines cracking as if filled with cartilage, throwing the torn halves at the glass cabinets. And then I'm switching off the light, scanning the dark, hoping for letters and words glowing in the dark, a secret message left for me. But there is nothing but a blank slab of darkness. And then I'm flinging open the door, needing air, eyes shut tighter than my own fists punching the metal frame, my racked body shuddering with an anger that feels like grief and despair both.

"Gene." And Sissy is next to me, stepping into the small column of bright clear moonlight beaming down on me. It is like a silver tent, and her hair is lit with a sepia haze.

She touches my face. Eyes fixed on mine, fingers lightly tracing my jawline. I feel every pore of her fingertip, feel the softness of her skin turn to the sharp edge of her fingernail as she grazes along my chin, down my neck, over my Adam's apple.

I press my face against the cold metal door frame. A clean hush falls on us. "There was this night, when I was seven. My father had to go look for a tooth I'd lost at school and he was gone for hours but it felt like forever. I was just a boy and I thought he'd been devoured for sure. But just when I'd given up hope, he came back and I made him promise that he would never leave me. And he told me he never would, he told me that even when it seemed like he was gone for the longest time, he would always come back. He promised he would never leave me."

I shake my head, let out a pent-up breath.

"Why did he promise only to later abandon me?" I say. "And why bring me here, only to desert me again? Not a single note. Not a single damn word. How difficult could it have been for him to write *Dear Gene*?"

Her hand strokes the side of my head, her fingers gliding through my hair, her skin grazing across the top of my ear.

"If it's true that I am the Origin, was I nothing more to him than a science project?"

"Gene," she whispers, her thumb brushing my cheekbones, spreading a dampness. She leans forward, slowly. Our lips touch, silently and softly, like two clouds touching in the sky, coalescing into the softest spot in the universe. I close my eyes.

And then the ground begins to rumble. Ever so slightly, a mere vibration.

We open our eyes, and it is as if my whole vision—and all that matters in the world—is her brown iris with radiating spokes of green. Her pupils, dilated and dark, enlarging, drawing me in. I feel her hands slip down my back.

And then I am grabbing her, drawing her toward me, and our bodies collide and our arms at last find their way around each other. We pull each other in tightly, and the rightness and wrongness of this pelts me until I don't know what to do but hold her even more forcefully. Our temples, pressed against each other, pound-pound-pound-pound in synchrony. The pulse at her temple is as light as a feather, and the strands of her hair touching my skin feel like soft fingers undoing knots within me.

And then the rumbling becomes more obvious, rattling even the glass beakers around us. She pulls her head away, and I feel landscapes of emptiness whoosh between us.

We pull apart. "What's going on?" she says.

We step outside. Beneath our feet, the ground hums ever so

slightly. But it's the sound that is drawing our interest: a metallic rattling, the expulsion of a loud hiss. From the other side of the woods.

"The train," Sissy says.

Something else catches our attention. In the distance, groups of farm girls are shuffling toward what must be the train station. Like black ants, emerging out of their holes, marching dutifully and silently through a meadow dotted with a million glistening raindrops.

31

SISSY AND I steal along the periphery of the woods where we won't be so easily seen. On the other side of the forested peninsula, we come upon a large clearing. Sitting in the middle is what looks to be a train station. Dozens of girls are already standing on the two platforms, busy at their tasks. Sissy and I crouch behind a large black spruce at the lip of the forest. Moonlight through the branches falls dappled on the ground.

A train sits between two platforms. Steam pours off the lead engine car still hot from the long journey; it hisses, clicking and clacking as it winds down. At least a dozen cars are strung behind the lead car like black links of a metal chain. Ribbed with arched steel bars, each car has the appearance of a large, hideous birdcage. The bars, too closely set for even a skinny child to squeeze through, still leave the interior fully exposed to the outside elements: rain, snow, wind. And, most crucially, sunlight. In other words, these train cars are built dusker-proof. Even the flooring is meshed steel. Any stowaway dusker catching a ride on this train would find little shelter from sunlight. Within minutes, it would be reduced to a sloppy puddle, dripping through the mesh floor, trailing along for miles between the train tracks.

All manner of items are stored in these cars, from cans and bottles and jars stored in large translucent plastic boxes, to tables and chairs stacked perfectly together like pieces of a jigsaw puzzle and wrapped with translucent plastic sheets. Bottles of wine and whisky and beer are encased in climate-controlled glass chests with air-ride suspensions.

"Look," I whisper. On the platform closest to us, a girl picks up a hose attached to some kind of generator. She widens her stance, bends low for support, and depresses a button.

A continuous jet of water shoots from the hose. The girl is pushed back a few steps by the powerful propulsion before righting her stance. As she starts hosing down the contents of the train car, she is joined by a dozen other girls on both platforms. Spread along the length of the train, each girl mans her own hose. It becomes immediately obvious: cleaning the plastic boxes and containers is a task of highest priority. Not a square inch is missed. Even the underside of each compartment is hosed down. A mist of spray cocoons around the train.

Small groups of elders walk down each platform, clipboards in hand. But if they mean to inventory the shipment, there's no apparent rush. They amble to the last car where a crowd of girls have gathered.

"Let's move in closer," Sissy whispers, and we scoot under cover of the trees, then glide along the meadows. Nobody notices us; all attention is fixed on the train. And on the last car in particular. The elders gathered there yell at the girls to stop spraying. The generator is turned off, and the jets of water sputter into drips. Gradually, the misty cloud enveloping the last car begins to dissipate. The ribbed car slowly emerges from the mist.

Sissy takes my hand, squeezing tight.

Inside the compartment, water dripping off the ribbed, metal bars, something moves.

Sissy and I are the only ones who tense with fear. Nobody on the platform shrieks or even flinches. A silhouette shifts, then shuffles to the edge. More shapes emerge inside the last car, moving incongruently with one another like the waves of a turbulent sea. As the hum of the generators dies down, sounds sift through: bleats and squawks and clucks and oinks of fear and fatigue and hunger.

I exhale sharply through my nose. A palpable relief fills my chest as I reach for Sissy's hand.

"What is it?" she says.

"It's livestock," I say. Her eyes sweep questioningly over me, trying to understand. "Duskers love to eat certain animals," I explain. "Like cows and chickens and pigs. Their appetite for these meats is nothing compared to their lust for our flesh, of course, but still. They've driven cows, chickens, and pigs to scarcity. Now, these meats are only available to the upper elite class on the rarest of occasions. The general population *never* gets to consume them; most make do on synthesized, artificial meat products. Sissy," I say with growing excitement, "duskers would never give up these livestock. Especially not for humans."

Realization flares in Sissy's eyes. "Which means whatever's at the other end of these tracks—"

"More than likely isn't duskers." I say, squeezing her hand. "It's got to be a place filled with our kind. The Civilization is the Promised Land! Jacob's right: we've been worrying over nothing."

Sissy's eyes sweep down the length of the tracks, following them as they disappear into the darkness.

I continue speaking. "I thought the meats we've been eating here were from the farm. Not shipped in. But now it makes sense.

At the rate we consume meat, there's no way the cattle could be self-sustaining. Most of the meat would have to be brought in."

But Sissy's head is turned away down the length of the train tracks. Her jawline ridges out, hard as a granite cliff face in moonlight. She looks at me out of the corner of her eyes, then down to her exposed forearm. At her branded flesh. "I don't know, Gene," she whispers, frowning. She bites her lower lip. "Call me overcautious but I still need more."

We quietly observe the activity on the platform. More elders arrive. There's laughter and smiles, their pleasure with the shipment obvious. Already, a few of them are opening the alcohol chests, uncorking a few bottles. I hear Krugman's laughter lifting into the night air seconds before his face glides into view. He's gripping two bottles by their necks like a man strangling a pair of geese.

The girls work en masse in a silent, coordinated movement: lines of them radiate out from the train station carrying containers, while other girls—empty-handed now—sweep in like a returning tide. They move slowly on account of their diminutive feet but their sheer numbers ensure that progress is steady. They will be finished unloading by dawn, noon at the latest. Then the train will be ready to make its return trip.

Sissy knows what this means. She has to make a decision soon. But her face is twisted with uncertainty.

"I have an idea, Sissy," I say. I shift position to face her as I place my hands on her shoulders. "I'll get on the train. But only me. You and the boys stay here. No, hear me out. I'll go to whatever is on the other end of these tracks. If it's everything we hope it is, if it is indeed the Promised Land, I'll return on the next train back and get you and the boys. Then we all leave here together."

"And if—"

"If I never make it back, you'll know not to go there."

She's still shaking her head but slower as I finish speaking. A brief hesitation ripples across her face—the plan makes sense, and she knows it. But then she stares straight into my eyes. "No way," she says.

"Sissy—"

"No. You don't get to play sacrificial hero."

"I'm not trying to play anything. Think it through, Sissy. With my plan, you and the boys stay together. Isn't that what you want?"

Her eyes waver for just a moment. "We stay together—that's what I want."

"The boys will be fine without me."

She places her hand on my cheek. "When I said *we stay together,* I meant you and me."

My hands slip off her shoulder. "Sissy . . ."

"I don't want to be without you," she says. A breeze flows across the meadows, blowing hair across her face. Her eyes, sharp and intense, catch mine through her windswept bangs. Moonlight swims silver in them. Then it is as if all sound vanishes, the breeze soughing through the grass, the voices on the train platform, the sound of livestock in the train, all fading away. As if the only sound left in the universe is her voice. "I don't want us to be apart," she whispers. "Not for a week. Not for a day. Not for a single hour, Gene."

My hand reaches out to brush aside strands of her hair. I tuck them behind her ear, and she leans her head into the palm of my hand, pressing her cheekbones against my skin. I pause, thinking.

She must feel the resolve stiffen in me, the contraction of my pupils. Because as soon as I pull my body away, she reaches up to stop me. But she's too late.

"Gene! No!"

I'm sprinting across the meadow for the platform. I hear her slicing through the grass giving chase. But I've gotten too big a lead on her. I bound up the stairs three at a time to the platform.

"Krugman!" I yell. He's halfway along the platform. I sprint toward him, crowds of girls parting before me.

"I'll get on the train," I tell him as I reach him. I'm gasping for air and trying to speak at the same time. "But it'll be just me. The others will stay here and await my return. Only then will we all leave together."

Sissy catches up seconds later. "Whatever he just told you," she says, "it's not going to happen." She turns to me now, and anger sizzles off her face. "You are *not* getting on this train alone."

"Just let me do this," I say.

Krugman starts laughing, uproariously, his leg stomping on the ground as if pixie dancing. The crowd of elders behind him glance at one another, then start smiling. A few guffaw loudly with Krugman.

"My, my," Krugman says, smacking his belly, "I'm caught in the middle of a lovers' spat! Who knew it'd be so much fun to watch. All so . . . *drama*!"

And then the smile snaps shut, his laughter coming to an abrupt end. The elders also stop smiling, dropping their lips to cover their teeth. Krugman stares at us, his bunched cheeks drooping into jowls. "Fact is, it's all neither here nor there. Because this discussion is academic. You're *all* getting on the train. You read the official Order from the Civilization—you are all to journey there. *All* of you. Discussion closed. Train should be ready to leave in several hours."

Sissy's next words are spoken quietly and with calm. But the elders jolt with every spoken syllable. "I don't think so," she says. "We're not getting on."

Krugman presses his chin inward, and scowls at Sissy. "And what has got your knickers in a twist?"

She speaks in a near whisper. "I guess it's out there now, so let me just say it. We have questions about the Civilization. We don't know if it's the place you've represented it to be."

"So I've gathered," Krugman says. He exhales slowly, phlegm in his throat combining with the stink of halitosis. "I'll try not to be offended by this apparent lack of trust in me. I'll try not to feel . . . betrayed—is that too strong a word? No, I don't think it is—by this misbegotten belief that I've somehow lied to you about the Civilization."

He spits to the ground, and the phlegm, large as bird poop, is acidic yellow, half-solid, and dotted with tiny bubbles. "After all I've done for you, after all I've provided for you, *this* is what I get in return? Not only ingratitude, but suspicion? Come now, what have I ever done to deserve this kind of distrust?"

"Take a wild guess," Sissy says, her words cutting into the thick, tense air.

Krugman smiles, then slowly bends forward to examine her forearm. A slight flick of his tongue at the corner of his lips. "I think it's getting infected," he says with a miniscule smirk.

She jerks her arm out of sight.

"I've treated you like guests in my home," he says. "But this is still *my* home. There are rules and regulations that *all*, even honored guests, must abide by. I'm sorry you chose to run afoul of these rules. But that was your choice."

He gazes at the girls with a look of fondness. Their heads downturn as his eyes fall on them, their postures closing inward like sleeping grass touched. "These bylaws and precepts that you have such narrow opinions on? They are nothing more than the blanket that bestows warmth and coziness to this community."

"I'm sorry, but I don't feel a lot of warmth or coziness here," Sissy retorts.

"My, my, aren't you full of interesting comments today." He snaps his fingers, and a girl approaches with tumblers of whisky on a tray. He downs a shot, wipes his mouth with the back of his hand, but roughly, smearing a trail of whisky on his cheek. "Let me give you a small suggestion. You've been through a lot, okay. You look tired. Why don't you just relax over the next few hours? Make the Mission your own veritable Shangri-la retreat. Until tomorrow when you—*all* of you—depart on this train for the Civilization. So in the meantime, just sit back, stop asking pesky questions, and simply enjoy the rest of your time here in this happy place."

"You say the Civilization is a paradise?" I say, stepping in front of Sissy. Krugman's demeanor is making me suspicious all over again. I'm feeling less optimistic by the second.

"Very much so," he says.

I pause. "Then I'm confused. Maybe you can help me with something."

"How so?"

"If the Civilization is such a wonderful place . . ."

"Yes?"

"Then I'm wondering why the Scientist chose not to go there. Why he chose never to board the train."

The leer on Krugman's face dies. The eyes of the elders behind Krugman swing toward me, their irises taking on the quality of cold steel.

Krugman stares at me for a long time. "We've been through this already. He was a disturbed man." His words come out not as a suggestion but as a threat daring me to disagree. "Our mistake was not forcing him back to the Civilization. The man needed professional treatment. He needed to be institutionalized."

"Really?"

"And besides, who can blame him for wanting to stay here at the Mission? Granted, it's not the Civilization, but it's not exactly the dumps, either, now is it? A close second, if I may say so myself. A pot of gold at the end of the rainbow, a ray of buttery sunshine. Where singing and smiles and joyful dispositions are de rigueur."

"Well, that begs another question," I say.

"Go ahead."

"If this village is such a ray of sunshine . . ."

"Yes?"

"Then why did the Scientist kill himself here?"

Silence.

"Careful, boy," one of the elders warns.

"No, I mean, you just said this place was the pot of gold at the end of the rainbow. That's exactly how you put it. So why do you think he decided to hang himself if this village really is so great?"

Krugman's words snap out quickly. "Like I said, who can explain the actions of a madman? But he was the exception. Everyone is happy here. Look around for yourself and tell me you don't see the smiling faces abounding."

"You mean the faces tattooed into their arms?" Sissy asks.

"Well, no, I wasn't referring to those ones. But we can go there. The girls wear their tattoos proudly; in fact, they love to flaunt their Marks of Merit. They're like trophies. It really feels like that for them. Notches on their belt marking their dream-come-true ticket to the Civilization."

"Seems like everyone wants out of here," Sissy says.

A cow in the last train car moos loudly.

"Seems like nobody particularly cares for this place. For its rules. For—"

"Enough." Krugman says.

"—the elders, the—"

A movement to my right, an elder taking one step forward, his finger pointing at Sissy. "She's gone too far! We should just feed her to the dus—"

"Enough!" Krugman's voice booms, jowls vibrating, jolting me. The flesh of his face loosens from his skull and his hairy mole bounces on his bobbing chin. The elders tense like a collective muscle around me, like a tightening noose. For a few moments, Krugman sighs heavily, as if with regret at his outburst. But when he whispers his next words, slowly, each word fraught with a menacing undertone, it's clear that regret is the last of his emotions.

"You will all get on the train tomorrow. There's nothing further to discuss."

"Oh, yes there is. There's plenty to discuss. But we'll discuss it privately among ourselves. Just the six of us. Come on," Sissy says to me. "Let's go. This conversation is over."

"It's over when we tell you it's over," barks a salt-and-pepper-bearded elder.

"Let me spell something out for you," Sissy says. "We're going back to the cottage now. And we're going to be left alone. We will decide for ourselves whether we get on that train or not. If we decide not to, don't worry, we'll get out of your precious village. We'll head on out, see what's out there. But we decide our own path. Until then, the six of us will be preparing and eating our own food."

"Now you just hold on—"

"C'mon Gene," Sissy says, pulling me along, "let's go." We start moving backward. "We don't want choirs with singsong voices coming to wake us up with a song. We don't want any food deliveries by smiling girls waving GlowBurns—"

"You're a piece of work, you know that?" Krugman shouts suddenly, in a volume and with a venom previously unheard. Something has finally snapped in him. It is as if a totally different person has taken over his body.

The group of village girls closest to us shuffles quickly away.

"You should know your place, girl!" Krugman's ears ring bright red. "You see any other girl interrupting me, you see any even speaking to me, even daring to look me in the eye? You've learned nothing," Krugman says, his voice lower but tense with rage. "One branding wasn't enough, was it?"

"If there's anyone who needs to be branded," Sissy retorts, "it's you."

Krugman's mouth drops open. His cheek fat wobbles sideways as if he's actually been slapped across his face. "You ugly, big-footed, opinionated wench," he whispers. "You don't speak to me like that in front of the elders and expect to get away with it. You don't speak to me like that in full view of all the girls and not face consequences." And he takes three quick steps toward Sissy, his fat-swollen hand raised.

I step in front of Sissy. "Enough!" I shout.

Krugman stops midstride. His eyes are lava pits of fury, the redness spreading into his cheeks. Nostrils flaring, his barreled chest heaves up and down. His stare knifes through me, trying to penetrate through to Sissy.

"I've been playing nice," he says. "Asking politely. That's clearly been the wrong approach. But I can be tough. Is that what you want?" he says, glaring at Sissy. "Because Daddy can play rough if you want."

And he suddenly leaps forward with frightening speed, bum-rushing me into the crowd of elders behind. Something hard smashes against the back of my head, and my body turns to mush. I collapse on the ground.

"Gene!" Sissy screams through my haze.

I hear the slap of skin and fight to regain consciousness. It's then I see Sissy picked up around the neck like a puppy. Dragged away, toward a train car, fat, hairy arms cinched around her neck like a choke leash.

"Take her!" Krugman yells to the other elders. "Lock her in the train!"

"Get your hands off her!" I shout, and I'm somehow back on my feet, charging forward. I grab at the man restraining Sissy and he's all blubber and liquid fat. I deck him in the face. I feel the crunch of bone, see flabs of fat wobble across his face. He crumples to the ground on one knee, dropping Sissy. He wipes his face and his hand comes away with a smear of blood from an opened gash.

"Now you've done it," he says and I feel a chill in my bones.

I kick him in the face, and he falls to the ground nose first.

A mob materializes in front of me. They are all arms and fists and kicking legs that pummel my midsection. I parry as many blows as I can, but there are too many of them. I get spun around, the air sucked out of me. My vision grays. Arms snake around me, and hands grip over my body, like the talons of a grappling hook.

From behind me, the clink of blades, a flash of sparks.

Sissy.

In her hands are a pair of daggers. One from her belt. The other from the secret compartment in her boot. She twirls the daggers, but it's not for show. That much is clear from the look on her face. She will do business with anyone who interferes. She will inject lifelong regret into anyone foolhardy enough not to move out of her way.

Krugman underestimates her. He suddenly lunges toward Sissy.

She leaps up, her right hand raised above her head. She swings that hand downward as Krugman flies at her; and just as I'm expecting the sickening squish of metal blade into fatty flesh, I hear a thudding *clunk*.

Sissy has crushed Krugman's skull with the handle of the dagger. She came down hilt—and not blade—first.

Krugman wavers, then his eyes roll up, whites showing. His eyelids snap shut and he collapses into a heap on the platform. His body wobbles back and forth. He groans.

Their leader dealt with, the elders quickly wilt.

Sissy and I make our way toward the stairs. The girls are looking at us with fright, but in a few, I detect a kind of awe in their eyes.

"He had it coming," Sissy says to them.

One of the elders speaks back, his gaunt face pockmarked like a peanut shell. "You're wrong. You're *dead* wrong. You'll see. Dead wrong."

The elders start to laugh. A snicker at first, then a jocular outburst, like a braying that sends shivers down my back.

"Keep moving," I whisper to Sissy, "just keep moving."

Back in the village square, the streets are deserted, not a soul in sight. Even the cottage windows are shuttered closed, doors shut. Echoes of male laughter from the train platform ring out in the distance, trailing us all the way back to my cottage.

32

We wait for dawn. Huddled around our packed bags in the room, ready to flee at the first hint of light. Sissy, Epap, and I have drawn up a plan: we'll follow the railway tracks. On foot. A journey that might take several weeks, if not months, but at least we'll be free and not trapped inside a train car. We can forage and hunt for food. And once we draw close enough to the destination, we should be able to view it from afar and decide whether to proceed or not. It is this ability to determine our own destiny that sells us on this plan.

Sissy wants to leave immediately but I talk her out of it. Darkness in the woods would be so dense, we'd be at the utter mercy of unseen dangers. Better to wait for light. And besides, we won't be able to cross the bridge until it lowers tomorrow. Best to hunker down for now, stay warm, conserve our energy. Sleep if possible.

Gathered in the hearth, we watch the fronds of fire. Ben complains of thirst. Grabbing a jug, Sissy and Epap steal out to the river, bring back enough water for everyone. No one's around, everything is quiet, they say. The night deepens, thick with menace. Not a light shines in the village, not even a speck of green light or the flickering waver of candlelight. The night air is thick with menace.

Fatigue eventually settles on us, nudging us to sleep. We decide on one-hour shifts. At the first sign of trouble, we'll run out together. Still wired from the fight at the train station, I volunteer for the first watch. It'll be hours before I can sleep, I think.

Alone now, the cottage has fallen quiet. Minutes pass; I think I hear the sound of faint snoring. My breath frosts the windowpanes, then dissolves away, only to reappear seconds later, an ephemeral phantom.

The sound of singing arrives gently and gradually. At first, I think one of the boys upstairs is singing. But as the voice gains force, lyrics emerging, I realize it's coming not from upstairs but outside.

I lean forward, peer through the frosted glass. It's pitch black outside—nothing to be seen. I crack the window open and the voice comes in clearer. Here in the Mission, there's nothing unusual about singing, but something about this is strikingly different.

For one, it's a solo. Stripped-down, almost naked in comparison to the usual choral singing. And something else. The voice is imbued with a haunted mournfulness, not the usual sprightly exuberance, and the lyrics are stripped of the usual saccharine optimism.

Lord and God of Power
Shield and sustain me this night.
Lord, God of Power
This night and every night.

My breath, frosting on the glass, quickens. I know this song.

It is a lullaby my mother used to sing to me.

The voice is completely off, of course. My mother's voice—the only thing I remember of her—was smooth and melodic, whereas this voice rattles like a dragged chain of metal links. But the melody is exactly the same. Even the lyrics, though I do not know them, fall into place like a lost key into a forgotten lock.

Within seconds, I'm out the door and in the cold air of night. The singing stops. But not before I see a faint haze of gray retreating away. I give chase.

He's fast. It has to be a *he*; the village girls, hampered by their lotus feet, couldn't come close to achieving this speed. "Hey, you! Wait!" I yell.

He doesn't look back, doesn't slow down. Instead, he picks up the pace. He ducks behind a cottage. By the time I reach it, he's nowhere to be found. It's all silent cottages and darkness. Then—there. His shadowy, wafer-thin figure cutting across the meadows, toward the fortress wall. Bleach-white hair glinting in the darkness. Now I know who it is.

"Clair," I shout.

She keeps moving forward. I'm on the coarse grass now, trying to keep pace. A few minutes later, she's reached the fortress wall. She disappears into the shadows like a stone dropped into a black lake. She's there, and then she's not.

When I reach the wall, I touch the cold black steel. Smooth. No grooves indicating an entryway. Then I see her footprints, little silvery splotches in the night dew, whisking beside the wall toward the corner tower. I race along, find a door. Pull it open, and then I'm inside the tower. Her boots *clomp-clomp* on the spiral staircase.

"Wait, Clair!" I yell, and my voice echoes back at me in diminishing waves, startling me. I climb the stairs, my boots thumping loudly on the metal steps.

She's not in the tower room. A door that opens outside to the top of the fortress wall is open. When I walk through, I see her standing outside halfway along the length of the wall, gazing out at the moon-splashed mountain ranges. She's waiting for me.

She doesn't turn around until I stop a few meters from her. And yet still, she waits, her breath gusting steadily, calmly.

Finally, she turns to me. Her eyes are shiny and wet.

"I knew it was you," she says. "You're just the way your father described you."

33

WHAT?" I STAMMER. Too many thoughts whirl in my head all at once. I step toward her on suddenly unsteady legs.

"From the moment I first I saw you," she says with a sad smile, "I knew it had to be you. His son."

"He told you about me?"

"I knew it couldn't be any of the other boys—too young. And the older boy—Epap—just didn't look the part. But you. That same determination coursing through your blood. That same look in your eyes, angry and sad at the same time."

"Clair! What are you talking about?" I grab her elbow. "How do you know so much?" She looks suddenly afraid, and I ease my grip.

"Do you have the Origin?" she asks. "I'll tell you everything, I promise, but please, tell me: Do you have the Origin?"

I let go of her arm. "I don't know. I'm not sure. But tell me what's going on here. Explain everything."

She gazes out at the dark meadows slanting downhill into a black precipice. Here and there, large boulders bulge through the landscape. "I don't have much time," she says. "We were followed. *You* were followed. You really riled up the eldership at the station tonight."

"They'll get over it."

"Trust me. They won't."

"Don't worry, okay? Nobody followed us. Stop imagining—"

"Nobody followed *me*. I was quiet as a mouse. But somebody followed *you*. You moved with all the subtlety of a roaring avalanche." She points toward a cluster of cottages. "Look over there. You can make out two people standing. Now coming this way."

She's right. I see two gray smears walking carefully off the path, heads stooped down. They're tracking us. "Hurry, then," I urge her.

She speaks without hesitation, her thoughts logical, her sentences flowing as if rehearsed. "He told me this song would draw out his son. A foolproof filter. And he was right." She smiles. "I practiced it in my head every day so I wouldn't forget."

"Why did you wait so long? I've been up and about for a couple of days already."

"I tried, believe me. But I couldn't exactly sing the song from the rooftops. The lyrics are subversive, the elders would have grilled me to death about it. No, I had to wait for the opportune time."

"Tonight."

"Less than ideal, with everyone on edge because of what happened at the station. But given your imminent departure for the Civilization tomorrow, I had little choice."

I look out to the meadows. The two men are bent over, examining the ground. They start toward the fortress wall.

"Hurry," I urge, "fill me in on everything."

She inhales deeply. "The Mission was built many decades ago—"

"Just cut to the chase. Pretend we're five minutes along in this conversation. Tell me what's going on."

She shakes her head. "It's not that simple. I need to tell you about—"

I exhale loudly in frustration. "Hurry. Please."

She sighs. "Tell me what you already know. We'll go from there."

"My father became a recluse here," I say, hurriedly. "He supposedly raved about a cure for the duskers—the Origin. Eventually, he had to be removed to a cabin, the one in which you found us. And that's where he committed suicide."

She doesn't answer, only stares in the direction of the two approaching figures. They're closer now. She grabs my arms and leads me quickly back to the tower room. She closes the door behind us and the room plunges into blackness. The crack of plastic snapping, then another. The room lights up green.

"Most of what you just said is true," Clair says, handing me a GlowBurn. "Your father found it hard to fit in again with the Mission community. He claimed things had changed for the worse, accused Krugman of running a—" She pauses, remembering. "—a 'totalitarian dictatorship.' The elders didn't know what to do with him. Some thought he was a cancer to village morale and wanted him returned to the Civilization. Others believed he still had value and might prove in time to be an asset. So they reached a compromise. He could stay, but away from the village. They let him stay in the cabin."

"All by himself?"

She nods. "They made me the gopher. I'd go down two times a week with medicine, supplies. That's why they didn't bind my feet but let them grow into man feet—so I'd be able to walk the many miles, climb the cabled ladder. I hated it, in the beginning, mostly because of how my feet got so big and ugly. The other girls were merciless with their taunts. *Man feet, man feet, man feet.*" She grimaces from the memory. "But then I came to enjoy the solitude of the hike. And eventually, his company. At first, he'd offer me a glass of water. Then later, he offered snacks; in time, we started having meals together. Over the months, we became close. He told me about his family, his wife, his children. About you. Where he used to work—"

"What did he say?" My voice, loud in this room.

"What?"

"About me, what did he say about me?" My words tumble out of my mouth, over each other, like unwieldy wooden blocks tumbling down a staircase.

"That you would come here someday. He was certain of it."

I shift on my feet. "Anything else?"

She throws her hands up in exasperation. "Stop interrupting! I need to say everything in sequence lest I forget some important detail—"

"No. Just get to it now. Tell me what else he said about me."

She draws in a lungful of air. "Very well."

From outside, the sound of voices, still distant, but drawing closer.

"He said you were a boy born with a mission. With a certain destiny."

"Me?"

"That you have a purpose, a calling. That your life has a significance greater than you could ever imagine." She pulls down her hood. "Why are you looking at me like that?"

"I don't know what you're talking about. My father never said anything about this. What mission?"

"I'm supposed to ease you into this gradually."

"Lately, nothing's been gradual or easy. Just tell me."

She steps toward me, her eyes locked on mine. "Do not be surprised, do not be afraid of what I'm about to tell you."

"What's my mission, Clair?"

"You're not to get on that train, Gene." Her eyes pinion mine. "Not tomorrow or the day after. Not ever. You are to go somewhere else."

I search her face for understanding. "What? Where?"

"To your father, Gene. He's still alive."

34

Her words slap me with a palpable force. My knees buckle under me.

"He's alive? Where is he?" I hear myself uttering. My words, a thousand miles away, lost in the swirl of thoughts churning through my mind.

She's about to say something, then shakes her head. "No time," she says quietly, as if to herself. "Come here." She walks to the other side of the room, moves aside a few empty cartons and boxes until a small door is revealed.

"No way," I stammer. "Tell me he's not in there."

"Of course not," she says. "Don't be ridiculous." She opens the door and walks in. I follow. A second later, I hear the snap of plastic, and then the room lights up with a green glow.

It's actually a long hallway, its length disappearing into the far shadows. Along the walls, like large pinned butterflies, hang several large contraptions, each resembling enormous kites with large wingspans.

"We're inside the fortress wall now," Clair says.

"What are these?"

"They're called 'hang gliders.' "

I touch the fabric of the nearest one. A synthetic plastic material.

"In the early days," Clair says, "when the Mission took its outpost duty seriously, people used to fly out on hang gliders to scout the land. Always under the cover of daylight. To keep an eye on the duskers. To make sure the duskers were staying in the city, that they weren't exploring or traveling across the desert."

I look at the dozens of hang gliders, shadowed along the wall from top to bottom. "Why did they stop?"

"The elders got too big and heavy to operate them. And they forbade further flying after a few girls, it's rumored, flew away and never returned. Now no one can operate them: the elders are too fat, the girls can't run for takeoff because of their feet. Not that anyone cares. Everyone's forgotten they ever existed."

I walk the length of the hallway with a GlowBurn, the rectangle of green light touching the walls around me, exposing more dust-coated hang gliders. "Are they still operable?"

She smirks. "You wouldn't get very far. They're almost all in disrepair. The operable ones are mostly gone—burnt to a crisp many years ago." She sees my frown. "They were burned in one huge pyre by order of the elders. This hallway—I think it was the repair room. They forgot about these ones."

Backtracking, I touch the large hang glider nearest the door. It has an especially long wingspan, its synthetic material brightly colored.

"This one looks new," I say.

Clair nods. "Relatively. It's the only one that I'm sure flies."

"My father?"

She runs her finger fondly across its span. "He constructed it. It was the training model. Two can fly at a time. We'd fly out together, your father and I. He taught me how to fly it."

"Did he fly a lot?"

"Yes. Secretly, of course, at night. The elders would never have permitted it. After he was banished to the cabin, he was free from their watchful eyes, and freer to fly. He kept another hang glider at the cabin."

I nod, remembering the hang glider on the cabin wall. "Where would he go?"

"Everywhere. Somewhere. I don't know."

I slide my finger over a hang glider. A thought occurs to me. "My father used a hang glider to escape," I say, excitement thrumming in me. "The elders couldn't allow his escape to be made known to the villagers. So they concocted a story about his suicide. I've nailed it, haven't I?"

Clair nods.

"So where did he go?"

But she shakes her head. "I can't tell you unless you do something."

"What do you mean?"

She folds her arms. "I can't tell you where he is or how to get to him unless you first show me the Origin."

"Are you kidding me? I have nothing for you. Only idle speculation, wild theories. Now tell me where my father is!"

"He made me swear not to tell you until you first produced the Origin. Because that's your mission, Gene. To take the Origin to your father."

I exhale loudly with frustration. "Okay, whatever then. You're looking at the Origin."

She's confused for a few seconds, glancing up and down my body. "Where . . ." Her voice drifts. She shakes her head, starts putting on her wool hat. "You're wasting my time. If all you're going to do is joke about this then—"

"No! I'm being serious."

"There's no way—"

"Clair! I'm telling you what I know," I say, waving my arms pleadingly. "Look here, I bet my father hinted that the Origin had to do with lettering or typography or something like that. He did, didn't he?"

She looks at me warily.

"*Gene*," I say. "It's so obvious, but everyone sees right through it. It's exactly the kind of clue my father would dangle in front of people. Obvious yet invisible at the same time."

"Stop it!"

"No. I'm serious. It's in my genes. It's me. I'm the Origin!"

She stares intently at me, my neck, my chest, my arms. I see her mouth *the Origin,* and her pale face whitens even more.

"Now tell me," I say. "Where's my father?"

A flare of annoyance fills her eyes. "I'm only supposed to tell you if I'm absolutely certain you have the Origin. And I'm not. But there's no time left for certainty."

"Understood. Now tell me where he is."

"East."

"East? There's nothing east of here." I glance around at the silent audience of hang gliders, at this odd, elfin girl with bleach-white hair standing before me. "You know what? Why should I believe you? Nothing you say makes sense. How do I know you're not making this up?"

"Your father said you might not believe. So he told me to show you something." She goes to a small wooden chest hidden in the shadows of the corner, lifts open the lid. When she turns around, she has a small model airplane in her hand.

My rib cage contracts, squeezing my lungs. I recognize the plane. It's the remote-controlled airplane my father flew from the rooftop of his workplace, the tallest skyscraper in the dusker metropolis. The plane is smaller than I remember, its faded chrome surface dented and pinged, but when I look closer, it's undeniable. It's the very same one.

"He told me that he'd programmed it to fly to a specific spot," she says. "He knew exactly where it would land. And years later, after he returned to the Mission, sure enough, he found this plane. Dented, smashed up, rusted over, entangled in treetops, but not a hundred meters from where it was supposed to land."

I turn the plane over in my hands. It's been repaired and spruced up, coated with varnish. And there's some writing. Across the underside of the two wings, the same unmistakable cursive handwriting I've come to know from reading my father's journals. Only four words.

"*Follow the river east*," I whisper.

"You need to go east," Clair says softly. "*We* will go east. By hang gliding. I will fly us there on this hang glider for two." Her eyes dart down with a curious guilty expression on her face. "We'll follow the river. It comes out the mountain on the other side. Then east the whole way."

"There's nothing there. It's all barren, empty land."

"Your father is there. In a place he described as the Land of Milk and Honey, Fruit and Sunshine."

All I can do is turn the plane over in my hands, touch the cool metal plates.

"It's your very purpose in life, Gene. That is what your father told me. Your whole life has come down to this: going east with the Origin. Nothing else matters. It's what you were born to do. Your mission."

Voices shout from outside. Closer to us, perhaps almost at the fortress wall.

She speaks at a hurried clip. "We need to leave tonight. But not now. Not with the elders right on top of us. Besides, I need to go back to my room, get the supply bag I've hidden. The journey will take a few days. We meet back here in an hour."

"What about my friends? I can't just leave them behind."

She hesitates, her eyes clouding over with the same guilty expression I'd caught on her face moments before. "Maybe only Sissy . . ." she begins to say, then shakes her head. "No, there's room only for you and me on the hang glider," she says nervously. An odd, peculiar glint in her eyes, of guilt and wrongdoing.

"We need to bring the others, too." I shake my head. "What am I saying? I have too many questions—"

"And there'll be plenty of time once we're up in the air." She pulls me through the door, leaves the fading GlowBurns behind as she shuts the door. In darkness, she places cartons and boxes in front, and slides over to a slit window. "They're coming up now." She turns to me. "I'm going through this window, then across the wall. You're too big, you won't squeeze through. You head down these stairs and bump into them. Just say you were exploring." She throws her hood over her head. "We leave tonight. Be back here in one hour. Don't tell anyone. Okay?"

"No. It's not okay."

But it's as if she doesn't hear. She props one foot on the slit window, stops. "Your father told me something. Sometimes, he flew to the dusker metropolis. It'd take a whole day to fly there and back. But he wanted to see you. Even if it had to be from afar, way up in the skies."

I grab her arm. "Why did you stay? If the Land of Milk and Honey really is out there, why haven't you already taken off yourself?"

She shakes off my arm and pulls herself through the window until she's crouching on the windowsill, half her body dangling outside. "Because your father asked me to stay. And wait for you." She looks me in the eye. "He was a good man. I'd do anything he asked." And then she's out the door, into the night, sprinting along the fortress wall.

35

THEY FIND ME coming down the spiral staircase, a pair of elders, faces red from either drunkenness or exertion. Or both. They have no words for me, only hands that try to grab my arms. I shake them off and after they realize I'm not trying to run off, they simply follow closely behind me. Not a single word is passed between us. And no sooner are we back on the cobblestone path than they suddenly disappear. One moment they're right beside me, the next they're gone.

Odd that they wouldn't escort me back to my cottage. I try not to think too much of it. But an uneasiness grows in me. I stop, listen for the sound of their fading footsteps. But there's only the thin whistle of wind.

A raindrop falls on my face. It's fat and pregnant with cold, nothing tentative about it. Within seconds, another drop, then another, splatters on my cheeks and forehead, until the rain falls heavy and full all around me.

But that is not why I'm suddenly cold. I look about. The rain curtains down a cascading wet darkness, full and thick. A TV static of flickering wet black and dark gray. Rain pitter-patters hard on the cobblestone, the sound of a thousand marbles clattering down.

I start moving. Back to my cottage. Quickly, with fear driving my feet forward on cobblestones that are slick and icy. At the village square, I stop and listen. Silence and stillness, only my heart thumping away. Something snaps in me, a conviction that drives my feet forward. In my mind, I see myself storming into the bedroom, jostling them all awake. Epap, David, Ben, Jacob, Sissy. Telling them that we must leave this very second, not only because I now know that the real Land of Milk and Honey, Fruit and Sunshine lies east of us, not only because I know that my father lives and breathes and awaits me there, but because I sense our time in the Mission has run out. That the last grains of sand have poured through, leaving only pools of awful emptiness and acid blackness. I already see us grabbing our bags, stealing into the dark woods as I pound my legs harder, trying to ignore the feeling that it is already too late.

I barge through the front door. I am about to sprint up the stairs—

—when something catches my eye. In the dining room. Firelight dances on the wall, small and flickering. But it is not the light that catches my attention.

It's David.

Except he is not facing me. He's standing in the corner facing the wall, hands cupped behind his back. As if standing at attention. Except he is trembling.

"David?"

I walk toward him, into the dining room.

"David?"

The light is flickering from a candle set on the dining table. Sitting directly behind the table, his face floodlit with light, is Epap. He's robotically stuffing soup into his mouth, so quickly and roughly that it is spilled all over the table and down the front of his shirt.

He looks up and his eyes are red and raw. He exhibits no surprise at my sudden presence, but his eyes emote desperation. Tears are streaking down his face, but all he does is keep shoveling one spoonful of soup after another.

In the corner behind Epap stands another person.

Back to me, head bent, body trembling.

"Jacob?" I say, and already my eyes are drifting to the other corner.

Ben stands there, body pressed into the corner, his body hitching uncontrollably. He is also facing the wall. His hair looks scruffy, as if pulled and roughly twisted in different directions.

My eyes snap down to Epap again. The spoon in his hand, as if dislodged by my gaze, falls, clatters on the table. His eyes are no longer fixed on mine, but have shifted past my shoulder . . .

Behind me, the floorboard creaks.

I feel the coolness of a sudden presence loom over me, swift and dark as a bat's wing at midnight. I turn around.

A bland face, spherical with rounded cheeks and protruding eyes, right over my shoulder.

Like the moon, like the full moon.

But his vacant eyes are bereft of light. He blinks, eyelids falling like guillotines in slow motion. I start to scream

But before I can, something heavy thumps the back of my head. My skull cracks, my brain squishes against the front of my cranium. Everything about me liquefies gray and black and I fall slack and insubstantial, seeing, hearing, feeling no more.

36

DARKNESS. VISCOUS AS tar, smeared in a thousand layers over my eyes. There's no difference whether I close my eyes or open them. It's all blackness.

Impossible to know how much time has passed. An inner instinct cautions me to hold still, to control even my breathing. Avoid panic-induced hyperventilation. Exhale, inhale with absolute silence. Gather what I can without moving, without speaking.

This I know: I'm not outside anymore. No raindrops falling on my face. No stars above, not the slightest feel of a breeze. Slowly, I place my hands palm-down on each side of me. Hard-packed dirt, dry, a grainy texture. I'm inside. An enclosure. Silent as a coffin.

Listen, Gene. Listen.

Nothing but the thumping of my heart.

I swallow saliva, and my Adam's apple bobs.

Stay calm. Don't panic. And again that inner instinct: *Don't move.*

And then, between the loud thumps of my heart, I hear something. Just a whispery sound, barely there. Then it's gone; perhaps I imagined it. But no: I hear it again, a faint rasping.

A breathing sound.

Somebody else is near me.

Stay quiet. Don't be detected.

I can't hear anymore. My heart, the blood gushing in my ears too loud. I force my breathing to steady. Slow, deep breaths, with mouth wide open to avoid making any inadvertent whistling sounds.

Where am I? Who's in here with me?

Slowly, I raise my arms above me, swing them in a slow arc. Nothing but cold air. My left arm, descending down, touches something cool, smooth, hard. Glass? A window? I turn my head, stare at where my hand is. I see nothing. Not my hand. Not the glass. Blackness. And still that inner voice: *stay quiet, stay calm, don't move.*

"Hello?"

Not my voice, somebody else's. To my right. The voice is a tendril of smoke, so faint it hardly seems there.

It's Sissy.

Don't move, don't speak, don't move, don't spea—

"Sissy?" I fight the temptation to sit up.

"Gene?" she whispers back.

Very slowly, inch by inch, I slide over toward her.

She does the same. Wordlessly. The same instinctive voice warning me to silence, also speaking to her. Our fingertips touch and our hands are immediately grappling one another, like separate entities tussling, wrestling to the ground. Our hands are ice cold; our grip ferocious and intense.

And like that we hold very, very still.

Because we both sense it. We are not alone.

She breathes; I breathe. Quietness.

And then: farther away, past her body, the sound of another person's breathing. Soft, light puffs past sleeping lips.

Sissy starts to move toward that sound. I grip her hand tighter, stopping her. She pauses. Then tugs my hand. I grip harder. *Don't move.*

But she's insistent. I crawl up until my body is pressed up next to hers, my mouth by her ear.

"Don't," I whisper.

Then she's moving, scuttling closer against me until her lips are grazing against my ear. "Where are we?" she whispers.

"Don't know. Dangerous." I feel something pressing up against the side of my leg, in my pocket. I reach down, take it out. A plastic tube. I examine the contours using my tactile senses. A GlowBurn, it has to be.

Sissy's arms move down, stopping at her boots. I hear the whisk of leather, then the short clink of metal. She's taken out the daggers she keeps hidden in her boots.

"I have a GlowBurn," I whisper. "It was in my pocket."

I hear a faint rustling of clothes, then Sissy says, "Me, too. What's going on?"

"We need to be quiet. And still." I feel her nod against my cheek.

"Don't use the GlowBurn," she says. "Not yet."

I squeeze her hand back.

We lie still for another minute. Again, I hear the breathing, louder now, disturbed, less rhythmic. Sissy starts moving ever so slightly. She's sweeping her legs, trying to figure out her surroundings.

What's going on?

Our eyes scan the blackness, urging shapes to emerge out of it.

Instead, there is a sound: a cough in the darkness, short, almost like a sneeze. Sissy's body tightens like a cord. Another cough, this one somehow transforming into a short snarl that fades gradually into silence again.

Then the recommencement of small puff-snores, more labored and frail now.

Sissy's hand grips around mine. I know her need; it is the same as mine. *Get out of here*. Wherever *here* may be.

Carefully, we stand up. We edge away from the faraway sound of breathing, our arms stretched out in front of us. We shuffle our feet slowly, careful not to trip over any object that might be lying unseen on the ground. My hand hits glass. A pause as Sissy's hand also touches glass. Then she gasps.

"Gene." It is the quietest, most whispery scream I have ever heard. "I know where we are."

She drops my hand, and just like that I'm alone in a sea of darkness. "Sissy?" It's absolutely silent. Not even the sound of faint snoring.

I spread my arms out to where Sissy was last. Empty air, as if she's vaporized. I edge forward, swinging my arms about, meeting only a vacuum. No sign of Sissy, no swirl of gray movement in the blackness.

A heinous snarl shatters the silence, salivary and slicing.

A shout—Sissy's—then a scurrying noise, followed quickly in succession by the scuttled sound of kicked-up sand hitting glass.

I snap the GlowBurn. A sickly green light blossoms around me.

I'm in the Vastnarium.

Inside the glass chamber.

Inside with the dusker.

A blur. Sprinting across the prism, right at Sissy. Its raven hair flowing back from its white face, fangs protruding out.

Sissy's hand is already flinging a dagger. A glint of reflected light as the dagger twirls toward the dusker girl.

Midflight, the dusker doubles over, crumpling to the ground and screaming a loud, high-pitched wail.

A *clink* as Sissy's thrown dagger smacks against glass. She missed.

I look back at the dusker. It's crouched and wailing, shielding its eyes. And then I realize. It's cowering from the green light. Strange: its reaction is more pronounced now compared to yesterday when more than a dozen GlowBurns were shining. Must be because the glass wall filtered out the more painful wavelengths. But now with no glass between it and the light, the dusker is fully exposed. This pale faint green is like razors in its eyes.

"Your GlowBurn, Sissy! Use it! The light blinds it!"

She whips it out, snaps it into operation. Green light fans out, illuminating even more of the chamber. The dusker screams.

I waste no time. I pivot, run to the glass. *The door, where is the door?* But the glass wall's smooth and unbroken surface offers no hint of a door. I bang on the glass in frustration. Diamond-hard, no give at all. And then I see it, right there in front of me, the outline of a door, faint, as if merely etched into the glass. My hands scamper all over it, trying to find a latch, a handle, anything.

But it's all a smooth nothingness. The handle is on the other side of the glass, the keypad on the other side, everything is on the other side. And that is when I see the elders. And Krugman. Sitting on the other side, gazing at us with excitement brimming out of their eyes. Faces lit up in the faint glow of green. They gave us the GlowBurns for their entertainment. To better view the spectacle of our deaths. I pound on the glass in anger.

"Gene!"

I spin around. The dusker is crouched, eyes crunched shut against the light, its pale skin greenish and splotchy.

"Don't speak, Sissy! You'll give away your position!"

And proving me right, the dusker propels off its hunched legs, leaping toward me, arms flung out, fingers with pointy black nails splayed out like poison-tipped arrows flying toward me. I fling my body to the side, ungracefully landing on the side of my face.

The dusker flies by me, its long hair gliding across my arm like a caress.

It smashes into the glass, its head whiplashed violently backward. For a split second, it's glued to the wall like a splattered frog before sliding down, limp. But even now, it is pushing off its arms, concussed eyes squinting to find me. It shrieks with a rabid, ear-splitting screech.

I roll over, jump to my feet. Sissy is grabbing me as we race to the other side.

"There's only one way out of this," she says with grim lips.

"It's coming back—"

"No, listen!" She wrenches my arm down, almost right out of the socket. "There's only one play. Let it come to me. I'll hold onto it as long as I can. While it's distracted, you slice its neck from behind with this," she says, handing over the dagger.

I try to pull my arm away even as I feel the cool handle slide into my palm. "No—"

"There's no other way! Rip it true and deep—"

"—*I'll* grab it then! *You* slice it, you're better with the dagger."

"Just listen, listen, *listen*! Don't fight with me. Only one of us is surviving this. You know that!"

"Then you—"

"Don't let Gene die!" she shouts just as the dusker hurdles toward us with wet bloodlust.

Instinctively, I throw the dagger; at the same instant, Sissy throws her GlowBurn. The dagger strikes the GlowBurn right in front of the dusker's face. The GlowBurn explodes in a spray of glowing green, splattering right onto the dusker's face. *Into* the face, burrowing deep like spits of molten lava into a sheet of ice.

A hellacious scream screeches along the glass walls. The dusker lands between us, balled in pain, its hands scrabbling, crawling at its eyes. A pungent smell rises, burning and corrosive. The dusker will want to, will need to, wash off that burning liquid.

My eyes immediately shift to a flat, mirrorlike plane of water. At the far end of the chamber. It's the opening to the U-shaped well through which it receives food delivered from the other side of the glass chamber. Where, just yesterday, the teacher had pushed through the sack of meat. Down one vertical shaft, across a short horizontal bridge at the bottom, and up the other shaft.

The dusker starts crawling toward the water.

And suddenly, I realize: that's our way out. It's so obvious, fear must have cramped my brain. It's our *only* way out. And we have to get there before it. We have to get there now, already, done, finished.

I grab Sissy's arm, pull her. No time to explain.

But she's trying to get to the dagger on the ground, thinking this an opportunity to kill the dusker. I pull her against me, half carry her to the other side.

"What are you doing?" she yells. "This is our chance—"

"I'm saving *us*!" I say. We're at the well now, less wide than I thought it'd be. Looks to be just wide enough, for her. For me, we'll have to see.

"Remember this well opening? U-shaped, goes ten meters down, curls around at the bottom, then up the other side."

But she's already shaking her head. "We won't fit, it's too tight, too deep, we'll drown."

The dusker is crawling toward us now, arms outstretched and swaying along the ground. It hears our voices, hisses venomously. The light from the GlowBurns is fading. And with it, time; with it, our lives.

Sissy sees this. "You first," she whispers.

"No."

"Gene."

"I'm not leaving until you get in there."

"No. *Don't let Gene die,*" she says, her eyes fierce with determination.

"And Gene is not going down until you do," I answer, every bit her equal in resolve.

"Damn you," she hisses, then grabs me around the neck, her

smooth cheek pressing against mine. Then she pushes off and slides over to the cusp of the slot. Taking a deep breath, she submerges herself headfirst. The last I see of her body is her feet, then her toes, submerging underwater, down the well.

For a second, I'm confused. Why is she going down headfirst?

Then it occurs to me. But of course. Of course she'd have to go down headfirst. Had she gone in feet first, the U-curve at the bottom of the well would prove to be far too narrow to curl around. Only swimming down headfirst would enable her to inwardly curl her body around the bend at the bottom before coming up headfirst on the other side.

It's also an all-or-nothing plunge. There's no possibility of back-tracking now, of coming back up for air, of second-guessing yourself.

A snarl from behind, claws and nails scuffing dirt. Then a silence that can mean only one thing: the dusker is airborne.

I know better than to waste time glancing back. I throw myself to the right, rolling hard even as the dusker hits the ground next to me. I spin my body, unhooking my right arm that's caught behind my back, fling out my arm. The one still holding the GlowBurn.

The stick is barely glowing, a dying ember that's barely casting light. But it has enough juice to illuminate the dusker: its face startlingly close to mine, its right eye puffy with white discharge pouring out, but its other eye clear and hungry as it glares at me.

I have one more card. I ram the stick into my mouth and clamp down on it. Then I twist my face away, ripping off the tip. Liquid gushes into my mouth, gooey and sticky and vinegary. I hold it in there.

The dusker leaps at me—

—is on me, straddling me, pinning my arms down, its one good eye shining with victory, saliva sputtering out of its mouth like boiling water out of the kettle spout.

It has me.

And in that split second—as its head drops swiftly down toward my neck, its fangs bared—I'm spitting out the GlowBurn fluid, shot-gunning it out of my mouth. Wads of glowing green fluid splatter onto the dusker's face.

It screams, leaps back, hands covering its face. The sound of something crackling the air, a raw sizzle.

I'm already scrambling for the well's opening. Can't find it, not in the darkness. There! A few steps away, where its gray surface ripples ever so slightly. My fingers break through the water's surface, and I waste no time. I plunge myself in, water—biting cold—rushing past head, jawline, my neck, my shoulders.

And just like that, I'm in. I'm underwater.

The icy embrace of water is a shock to my system, cold fists clenching my lungs, shriveling up the air carried within. The sudden change in environment madly dizzying.

And it's a tight squeeze. The well barely wider than my shoulders. A panic threatens to overtake my mind even as I try to ignore the terrifying disorientation of being upside down, underwater, inside out with fear. At least I had the presence of mind to go in with my arms stretched out in front of me. If I'd gone in with my head leading, my arms would right now be pinned against my side. I'd be trapped.

Small comfort, though. And certainly no time to be patting myself on the back. Because I'm still hemmed in. My lower (upper now?) body is still above water, my legs kicking air, futilely trying to find purchase. They feel like separate entities, twirling about like tentacles, a thousand miles above me. I envy them, for their access to air. I want to inhale through them like they're straws.

I hear the snarl of desire, muted, but frightening. Even underwater, I feel the rumble of its intensity rippling through the ice water. It is coming for me. For my legs, anyway. For a moment, I feel an irrational sense of relief. That I'm safe behind my legs, for the buffer they will offer me. The dusker can have at them, so long as it doesn't get to me.

My brain. My thoughts. Scattered. Not thinking straight.

I start to thrash from side to side. I need air. In my panic, I'd forgotten to take deep breaths before diving in. I'm short of air. Already. I'm only scratching the surface—almost literally—of the distance I have to cover underwater, and I'm already sucking on emptiness.

I twist and turn, trying to dislodge my trapped body, now thinking that I should have stripped out of my bulky, cumbersome clothing before plunging in. I jiggle, squirm. Somehow it works: the twisty motion causes me to slide down a few feet. My palms slide over the smooth, enclosing metal, searching for a grip. I find something, the smallest protrusion: nothing more than a nail incompletely screwed in. But it's enough, just enough leverage for my finger to pull against and sliver my body down another few feet.

Inch by inch, I pull myself down, until my whole body is underwater. But this is too slow, it's no good. My eyes open, seeing nothing but blackness, the icy cold like a thousand pins pricking the skin of my body, void of air, this was all a mistake, I have to backtrack somehow, have to resurface, get air, precious air—

From above, something grabs my foot.

I scream. The last remnants of air bubble out of me, like a release of a half-inflated balloon.

My shoe is yanked off, my foot almost ripped off along with it. I kick out, shrieking now into the black wet, urging my body downward.

Something gives. Somehow. My body slides down a couple of feet. I start pulling, my fingers searching along the walls for traction, my shoulders hunched and narrowed as much as possible—

A sharp fingernail grazes the exposed sole of my foot.

My mouth snaps open to scream. Nothing escapes it. There's no more air, no more sound.

Don't swallow water! Don't! A drop of water into my air pipe will set off a fatal spasm. I kick out with my foot. It finds skin, rounded bone—the dusker's cheekbone?—as I jerk my leg away, I feel strands of its hair caressing around my ankle, sliding down my foot.

Panic ripples along the length of my body. I grapple against the slippery sides, desperate for traction. Then, a miracle: the slot suddenly widens. Just an inch or so on each side, certainly not enough to turn around, but it feels wide as a canyon. My body drops another two feet, then two meters, my arms pushing against the sides and pulling down, my legs kicking above me in shortened kicks. I've traveled down what feels like a galactic five meters. I feel the sharp ache of water pressure in my ears.

Out of reach of the dusker. It will not venture down any farther.

And then I feel its clawed hand like a pincer around my ankle. Its grip is sure and unflinching. I scream, bubbles gushing out. I kick out, but this only seems to incite it further. Its grip tightens. I kick out again, and this time my heel catches on something solid and large, like a head.

It is underwater. Head submerged. As if itself suddenly realizing, it begins to thrash. I feel the release of its grip on my ankle, but its hand is caught inside the leg of my pants. With its movement confined by both the narrowness of the well and the tight pants leg, it is only able to partially slash through the pants material. It tears my pants into a webbed mesh inside of which its fingers become inextricably caught. Panic seizes the dusker as I pull it farther down the well; its scream, muted in the water, is accompanied by the sharp snaps of its fingers as they get disjointed, bent out of shape. I feel one final violent spasm, then nothing at all. The dusker has stilled. It has drowned.

My eyes fling open, trying to see the bottom. But it's all blackness. All I can do now is keep pulling myself farther down into the abyss, yard by yard. Then a chilling thought. What if instead of touching the bottom, I touch Sissy? Her drowned body, blocking the way, her clothes billowing around her, her face turgid and expressionless in death as her hair swirls about in slow motion?

I squeeze my eyes, as if to shut off the image in my head, as if to banish the thoughts, and now I'm scrabbling downward, the temperature dropping around me, the sound of blood rushing in my ears—

I'm not going to make it. I have nothing more in me.

Air. None. A shrieking delirium takes over my mind, razor-sharp claws slashing at my chest. I want nothing more than the end of these spasms, for this final stage of drowning to pass and the repose of death to take over.

Then my fingers touch something. Not the soft give of skin, but blissfully hard metal. The bottom of the well. I flail at the sides, trying to locate the opening where the chute curls around to the other side of the wall. I can't find it. Only when I push my body farther down and my head hits bottom do I see the opening. It's right in front of my face.

It's horrifically small.

My shoulders will barely squeeze through. Maybe. Or not. I reach in with my arms. There's nothing left but to drown trying.

It's not long, this horizontal stretch. In fact, it's short enough for my hands to cup around the edge on the other side. Grabbing that edge, I pull hard with my outstretched arms like a sideways pull-up, ramming my head and shoulders through. My head slides through, until it's pulled even with my hands, and I'm looking up the other vertical shaft. The shaft on this side is much wider. All I need is to pull my body through, then kick up. Seconds away. Air is seconds away.

But I'm stuck. Something is impeding my progress. It's the dusker. Though drowned, its hand is still caught in the ripped shreds of my pants. It's being dragged along by me, dead weight wedged somewhere in the well.

I pull harder, feel a little give. I'm able now to pull most of my body out of the horizontal chute, and into the wider vertical shaft. But again, I feel my progress impeded. Its hand, dead and still, is still anchored into my pants, and no matter how much I kick at it, I cannot dislodge it. I'm stuck. Even drowned, the dusker has become a ball and chain of death.

And so this is the end. Alone in a cold watery grave, the world rendered black. The distillation of my life, the loneliness, the discomfiture, the desperation, concaving into this narrow coffin. My body now unwinding, tension easing out of it. A spasm, then nothing; my muscles relax. Even the rush of blood in my ears, slowing, fading. My fingers slowly unclench, and when my arms float up, they are like twin trails of smoke above a funeral pyre.

It is not so bad, death. It has taken so long to get here, that's all. All these years.

An angel appears above me, a gray silhouette. Hair pulled back as it descends on me, eyes wide, floating down like two doves. I am ready for her as she reaches down with her long arms, smooth as clay. She pulls at me, once, twice. I'm stuck; her body inches downward.

Something dislodges from my leg, and the angel tugs me out, the release distant and inconsequential. I feel the press of her warm body against my back, soft and assuring. A slow drift upward, her arms under my armpits and clasped across my chest, the black walls sliding past us as we float up, out the well, past the ceiling of the Vastnarium, past the clouds, past the stars, to the heavens above, except there are no stars up here, no singing angels, no streets of gold, no milk, no honey, no fruit, no sunshine, but only blackness and darkness and then everything is no more.

37

I AM BROUGHT back to consciousness by rough, insistent heaves that painfully, rhythmically pound against my rib cage. A lull of nothingness follows; I'm slipping back into the gray.

Then velvet lips on mine, dewy and sweet. Soft on soft, the lips alive and encompassing. Then becoming fiercer, the grip ironclad.

Air gushes into my mouth, gliding down my windpipe. The rush of oxygen singes, an acidic whiteness splashing across my brain. Then I am choking, rank water gushing out my mouth, foul and tepid as if it has rotted in me for years. I gasp in air, the rich purity of oxygen bringing a blazing clarity.

"Turn to your side," Sissy says, helping me. "Cough it all out."

Water spurts out of me, more than I'd thought possible. With such force, it feels like chunks of my liver, my stomach, kidney are being vomited out. I remain on my side, too tired to move, for a minute. Sissy sits me up. Her fingers are pulling up my shirt, her hands exploring my body, across my chest, dipping into the grooves of my abdominals.

"Sissy?" I sputter her name, water flicking off my lips.

"Are you scratched? Cut? Are you bitten? Did it get you anywhere?"

"I don't know."

"Did it get you, Gene?! Tell me!" Her eyes are cauldrons of alarm.

And suddenly I'm afraid, all over again, this new fear smacking alertness into my mind. Sissy's right: if either of us has been so much as scratched by the dusker, we'll start turning. The symptoms of this gruesome disintegration always show immediately, although the actual process can take hours to complete. She studies me with alarm, her hair pressed against her vase-pale face, water droplets spilling down her face like sweat.

And we're standing up, together, her hands grabbing at my shirt and pulling it off, my fingers undoing the buttons of her blouse pressed against her skin like barnacles. Under the glow of dying green light, our eyes roam over each other's skin. My fingers glide across the soft span of her body, searching for punctures, scratches, cuts.

Her hands drift down my right leg, to my ankle. She flinches.

"What is it?" I ask.

"Gene," she says, her voice husked with fear, "your pants are all torn up down here."

In the longest two seconds of my life, she peels up the ripped material. Her mouth drops in horror. At the long gashes scratched across my skin, mostly whitish lines where fingernails grazed. But there is one long bloody gash. Where its claws broke skin and cleaved an opening for its contagious saliva to enter me.

Our eyes meet. Then I'm kicking away from her.

"Get away from me!" I shout. "Sissy, run!"

But she doesn't move, only stares intensely like she's trying to inject a cure into me by her very gaze.

"Sissy! You have to leave. Before I turn!"

"Gene! Are you?"

"What?"

"Are you turning? I don't think you are."

And it's like I'm struck dumb by her question. I grab my chest as if an answer lies there. But she's right. I'm not experiencing any of the symptoms of turning that my father drilled into my head all those years ago. No shaking. No sense of my internal organs ripping apart. My skin isn't burning feverish hot.

"You told us the symptoms always appear within a minute at most. But it's been well past a minute, and you seem fine." Her eyes sweep across my body. She stands up, walks over to the front row where I'd seen the spectating elders. The row is empty now, only a few GlowBurns left behind as they'd beat a hasty exit. She picks up a GlowBurn, snaps it.

Green light blazes out.

I don't flinch or squint. I don't even blink. The light doesn't hurt me in the slightest. The opposite, in fact: it is the most radiant, beautiful color I've ever not flinched at. The color blurs, and I realize I'm tearing.

I hear the crack of plastic, then liquid is splashed on my face.

"Hey," I say, "cut that out." Bright glowing green spots splatter about my face and clothes.

"Sorry," Sissy says, suppressing a glad smile, "I just had to make sure." She reaches up, wipes a few glowing beads from my face. Her finger wipes lightly over my cheekbones, resting there for one long second.

"Gene," she whispers, "you really are the Origin. You were cut, you should've turned. But look at you now." Her eyes glisten with marvel.

All I can do is gaze back, momentarily speechless. The dusker was slavered in its own saliva, its hands and nails covered in drool when it first plunged into the well after me. But perhaps by the time it cut me, water had washed away the saliva. "I don't know, Sissy."

"It's really true," she whispers as if she hasn't heard a word. "You're the one. The Origin."

I shake my head doubtfully. "Its saliva might have washed away by the time it cut my foot. I mean, that's a lot of water in that well. If it cut me with fingernails washed clean of any droplets of saliva, then I wouldn't have been infected. And that could be the reason why I'm not turning. That could be all."

But she's still looking at me with wonderment.

"I need to check you," I say, quickly. "Turn around." She does, slowly, bringing the wet sheen of her back into the pale green light. My fingers lightly trail over her protruding shoulder blades, drift down the valley of her spine. Her back, curved and smooth like the inside of a shell. My fingers come to rest in the small of her back. I hold still, sensing a shift in her. Her rib cage starts to expand and contract, faster, deeper. She turns her head, regards me from the corners of her eyes over her shoulder.

"You're okay," I say, softly. "No scratches." I pick up her shirt, and she puts it on. "You breathed air into me. How did you know what to do?"

"The Scientist described it to us," she says. "He was always afraid we'd drown in the pond back at the Dome." She falls silent; she's looking at the doors. They're rimmed with the morning light outside. "It's not safe out there," she says. "Nowhere is safe anymore."

"They were in here," I say. "A group of elders. Spectating our deaths."

She nods. "I saw them, too. Why would they do this to us? Why would they want to kill us? I thought the Civilization's Order would have shielded us from being . . . killed."

I pick up my shirt, start wringing it. "We stepped over a line at the station platform. In front of the whole village. We physically attacked the elders, even if it was in self-defense. They couldn't let that go. Not with all the girls watching. They had to make an example of us, Order be damned."

"We've got to get the boys," she says, buttoning her shirt quickly. "Then we run into the woods, as far from here as possible. Forget about waiting for the bridge to lower for now. Let's go."

I put a hand on her arm. "I need to tell you something. It's huge." I recap everything Clair told me. I speak quickly, all the time feeling the urgent need to get back to the cottage, to the boys.

"East of here?" Sissy says, gobsmacked. "The Scientist's still alive?"

"It's a lot to digest, I know. But what we need to do now is *flee*. We can digest and understand later. But now we run, we descend the mountain to where the river flows out and follow it east."

But Sissy's no longer listening. Or looking at me. Her eyes are latched onto something just outside the chamber. Skin blanching, she points at the well opening.

The dusker—facedown and unmoving—has floated up to the surface, a lifeless blob. Its black hair is splayed across the surface of the water like cracks in glass. Its talons were caught in my pants, and I'd dragged it through the bottom tunnel and over to the other well. Where it had floated slowly and lifelessly upward.

Sissy moves toward it.

"It's dead, Sissy."

"Gotta make sure," she says, and reaches down. The dusker is waterlogged and too heavy. Sissy drops it on the rim of the opening, and its upper body hangs out like a black, diseased tongue.

With my foot, I nudge its head until its side profile comes into view. Its eyes are closed, mouth open like a gaping maw, the tips of its incisors pressed against its lower lip.

It moans.

Sissy and I leap backward.

Its face begins to give off smoke, thin gray tendrils. It begins to whimper, fingers trembling. It's the light from the GlowBurn: not bright enough to kill it, but more than enough to excruciate a slow burn on it.

"We need to end it. Destroy it. I'm taking it outside into the sunlight."

"Sissy, let's not risk it. Or waste time."

"I'll never rest easy knowing there's a dusker in the mountains."

"Sissy," I say, my voice urgent and questioning. "It's too dangerous. It'll revive."

But she ignores me. She bends down and links her arms under the dusker's armpits. She hoists it out of the slot, then drags it backward, its heels dragging along the ground. But the waterlogged dusker is too heavy. After only a few steps, Sissy loses her grip on it, and it drops to the ground. It grunts lowly.

I pick the dusker off the ground, hoist it over my shoulder. Its head flops against my shoulder blade, its fangs unnervingly close. Wanting to keep its fangs in sight, I flip the dusker around until I'm cradling it. Its face holds an unexpected fragility. Long black eyelashes, in harsh relief against the white face. More smoke rises from its skin, the raw stench of burning flesh filling my nostrils.

We stand before the exit door. Daylight rims in through the edges.

"It might come to. From the pain. Be careful, watch its mouth, its teeth."

Sissy positions herself next to me, her body pressed against my side.

"I've got its arms pinned against me," I say. "You watch its mouth, its fangs—"

"Got it," she says.

I grip the dusker tightly against my chest and sprint toward the double doors.

On impact, the doors smack open, banging loudly against the

outside wall. Sunlight blinds us, smacking into us like a wall. But we don't stop; our legs keep pounding the ground even as the dusker starts flopping in my arms, even as its skin starts to sizzle with the singeing glare of the sun. We run as fast and as far as possible from the Vastnarium, from the darkened inside in which the dusker might yet seek refuge.

Bathed in early morning sunlight, the dusker gives a bone-chilling scream. Its jaws start snapping, the sound of marble cracking.

I trip. I don't know how, if it was over a rock or my own panicking feet, but I'm suddenly in the air. I plummet to the ground, knocking Sissy over, and the hard wintry ground sucker punches me in the gut. I curl up, gasping for air, hardly aware that the dusker has escaped my grasp.

"Gene!"

Incisors fly past me, gritted and grinning. A blur as its sleek body leaps over me, then it is bounding away.

I leap up a half second later and give chase. The dusker is fast, but compromised: already weakened by the near-drowning, it is pummeled by the devastating effect of sunlight. Its speed drops precipitously; then it stumbles, its legs soft as butter in a hot pan, its bones turning to gelatin. The body droops, definition fading quickly as muscle and skeleton carbonize away.

I leap at it, tackling it to the ground. All fight has gone out of it. Dragged by my momentum, it sheds warm lumps of skin and fat on the ground as we skid across. Coming to a stop and lying astride its body, I pin its head down, clamping the slowly snapping teeth away from me. My hands sink into the decaying skull, soft as a boiled egg now.

And then the dusker is all weakness. Not a muscle left to move its limbs, not the desire to live or to eat. Its chest, rising and falling weak as a rabbit's sigh. It shrivels before me, only its thick raven hair undamaged by the sunlight. It is over.

And yet still it whispers, still it murmurs.

Sissy moves in, kneeling next to me. The dusker continues to melt away, yellow effluvium pooling around us. A raw pungent smell of flesh burning fills the air.

"Watch its fangs!" Sissy warns.

"It's okay, it's okay, it's done in."

The dusker's mouth suddenly opens wide as if yawning, exposing a row of sharp incisors. Its jaw shudders, vibrates, as if shivering. A faint sounds scratches out.

"S-S-Saw . . ." it whispers, mouthing a word.

Sissy and I share a confused, horrified look.

"Saw-saw . . ." it murmurs, barely audible.

I lower my ear to its mouth.

"No, Gene. It's a ruse . . ."

I push her hand away. "It's okay," I whisper, but not to Sissy. To the dusker. "It's okay. It's over now." And I lean forward until my ear is down to its lips.

It sucks in one last breath, eyes gaping wide like a pair of gasping mouths. And that's when I notice its arm, what's left of it, anyway. Five branding marks, disintegrating in the sunlight.

And finally it utters its last word. I lean in closer.

"Sorry," it says.

And then it closes its eyes.

We don't say anything. I put my hand in the dusker's black hair and, with hesitation at first, gently stroke the silky lengths. My fingers comb through the still-damp hair, over and over, until the dusker is silent, until the dusker is gone, until nothing is left of her but hair.

38

WE SPRINT THROUGH the village. Morning has swung into full momentum and village girls are now pouring out into the streets. Sissy and I drop all hopes of remaining undetected and make a beeline right down the main road. Girls turn to look at us, their heads swiveling around as we pass.

We enter my cottage quietly and take in the silence of the interior, the emptiness of the dining room. Avoiding the creaky steps, we ascend the staircase. The bedroom door is slightly ajar, and I carefully peek inside. All the boys are on the bed, their wrists tied to separate bedposts. Only David sees me; his eyes widen. I raise a finger to my lips. Blinking hard, he points with his chin toward an unseen corner of the room.

They've posted one sentry.

A large one, but, more importantly, a sleeping one. A finished bottle of wine lies on its side, pressed up against a chair leg. The elder's mouth is wide open, a snore gurgling in his throat but not quite making it out of his mouth. They obviously weren't expecting any resistance or rescue.

Sissy slides into the room behind me, dagger in hand, and starts cutting the ropes. The boys, all wide-eyed now, know better than to say a word. I stand facing the elder, the wine bottle now in my hand. At the first sign of waking up, I will smash the bottle into his face.

Within a minute, the boys are all cut loose. The bags we'd packed earlier are still stacked by the door, and we grab them as we tiptoe out of the room, closing the door behind us, leaving the drunk elder none the wiser.

Outside, we fly down the path. We have the advantage now. Out in the open, we can easily evade their potbellies and lotus feet. Our escape is all but assured. We run past groups of girls who gape and stare. We sprint off the cobblestone street, onto a dirt path. Girls are washing laundry on the deck by the river, and they stop to observe us as we run past. I see one of them stand, take a few urgent paces toward us. It's the girl with freckles and she raises an outstretched arm, beckoning us to stop. But there is no time, and we blow past her, cross the river, sprint into the woods. There might as well be a hundred miles between us and them, there's no way they can catch us now.

We don't stop running for a full fifteen minutes. A bubbling stream gives us the excuse to stop; we fill our canteens, glad for the chance to catch our breath. Sissy checks on Ben's head where he'd been earlier struck by an elder. There's a small bump but he seems none the worse for wear. Epap has a few bruises and scrapes on his face and arms. He says he delivered a few good punches before they'd overpowered him.

He clutches his jacket suddenly, then stumbles behind a tree. We hear him retching, then dry coughing. He comes back, his breath sour, his face pale. He kneels beside the river, splashes water on his face.

"Better now?" Sissy asks.

"Still a little groggy. From that soup they made me drink. They forced me to drink it on threat to the other boys. Said they'd bring you back if I finished it." He grimaces, shakes his head. "The only thing it brought was a fainting spell. But the cold water's helped. So has running, breaking into a sweat." He stands up. "Whoa, too fast. Still dizzy. Give me a few."

We do. I use that time recounting to them everything I learned from Clair: the Mission, my father, the need to travel east. They nod somberly as I speak, their eyes casting warily in the direction of the Mission.

Only Jacob is conflicted. He picks up his bag slowly, drops it back down to the ground. "So we're really on our own now."

Sissy turns to him. "We can make it, Jacob. We stay together, we'll survive."

He kicks a small rock into the stream. "So we just follow the river."

"Until we get to the Land of Milk and Honey."

"And how long is the journey? A few days? Weeks? Months? A year?"

"I don't know, Jacob."

His face wobbles with emotion.

"What is it, Jacob?" Epap asks.

"Why don't we head west?" He looks at all of us. "Where the Civilization is. We follow the train tracks. At least we know there's a destination. Even if it takes us weeks, at least we know there's light at the end of the tunnel. A place where we know has cows and chicken and food and supplies. And people. Civilization."

"But it's not where we should go," I say. "It's not the Land of Milk and Honey, Fruit and Sunshine."

"Says who?" Jacob says. "That weird girl? Maybe she's wrong. Maybe she's lying. Why believe her?"

"And you want to instead believe the elders? Excuse me, but aren't these the very elders who just tried to kill Sissy and me? Who just tied you up and were going to force you onto the train?"

Jacob's cheeks burn red, but with embarrassment and not anger. I feel a stab of remorse for yelling at him. "I just want to make it to the Promised Land," he says, staring down glumly at his feet. "Where the Scientist promised he'd lead us. That's all."

I speak, softer now. "And it lies east, Jacob. I'll get you there. I promise."

He looks up at me with wet eyes. He nods, a quick motion; but in that movement I sense he is handing something valuable and fragile over to me, entrusting me with it.

"Okay," Sissy says. "Let's keep moving. I want to make it to the log cabin before nightfall." And then we're running through the woods again, toward the rising sun, east.

It's hard going. Within minutes, we slow our pace to a brisk walk, mindful of Ben's short stride and tender age. He's trying his best, his hair sweaty beneath his winter hat, his cheeks rosy with exertion. Gradually, the floor of the woods, cushioned with pine needles, gives way to barren land, until the last of the trees are behind us and our boots are smacking on the hard compact surface of mountain rock. The sun reflects off the unbroken miles of gently undulating granite, its glare as blinding as it is intense.

We take another break perched on the edge of a steep drop. The same cabled ladder we'd used to ascend days ago hangs down the face. It's a heart-stopping, strength-debilitating descent, and Sissy wants to make sure we're fully rested before climbing down. We sit on the hard surface, our legs splayed in front of us, leaning back on our bags. A brutal wind gusts across the domes, whistling between ravines.

Sissy digs into her backpack, takes out a pair of binoculars. From where we are, we have a near-panoramic view. She surveys the land sprawled beneath us, rumpled like a blanket. On our left, the thin silver thread of the Nede River glistens under the bright sun. Sissy points the binoculars east. If she's hoping to see something on the horizon, anything that might hint of the Promised Land, she's not saying.

"Can I get a look?" Epap asks.

Sissy ignores him, scans to her left.

"How much farther?" Ben asks.

Epap answers. "I'd say we're halfway. So another four hours or so to reach the cabin. Hey Sissy, give me a go on those binoculars will you?"

But it's as if she doesn't hear him. She's completely engrossed: her index finger maneuvers the focus wheel, rotating it back and forth in smaller and smaller gradations. Arched over the binoculars, frown lines deepen across her forehead. Her back suddenly stiffens.

"Is everything okay?" I say.

Her mouth falls open, wide as the two circular binocular lenses. She pulls the binoculars away, gazes out with naked eyes. There's alarm, bewilderment in them.

She stands up. We all stand with her. I think perhaps she's seen a group of elders coming down the mountain. But the binoculars were pointing away from the mountain, at the land far below us.

"No way," she utters. The wind whips away her voice, shredding it into a frightened whisper.

Epap takes the binoculars from her hands. He doesn't see anything at first. But then his eyebrows fling up his forehead like kites gusted into the sky. He jolts backward, almost dropping the binoculars.

"What is it?" David says. He's gazing out in the same direction.

Epap shakes his head as if to clear it. "I don't know . . . it can't be."

"What is it?"

"It's just my mind playing tricks, it's—"

"Boats," Sissy says. "Floating down the river."

I snatch the binoculars out of Epap's hands. It takes a few seconds to locate the river, and even then all I see is the glisten of water. The river is a thin curling strip filled with bright, sun-reflected orbs, very disorienting, and I begin to think that perhaps Epap and Sissy are imagining things not there.

But then I see it.

A circular ship, in the shape of a dome, light gleaming dully off the metal chrome plates encasing it. It is spinning and bobbing in the fierce current, at the river's mercy. Thin lines of rope dangle from around its circumference, like the legs of an insect. At the end of each line is a little balled shape. I zoom in.

These balled shapes are submerged horses, lifeless and flaccid, dragging in the river on ropes like hung criminals. Early on, these horses must have steered the boat during the daytime while the duskers sheltered inside the dome. Three horses on each bank, each tied to the boat, guiding it down the length of the river. When the river current picked up, the horses must have been forced to break into a canter, then a gallop; and finally, no longer able to keep apace, they collapsed and were dragged into the river.

"What is it?" I hear Ben's voice, sounding a million miles away.

I move the binoculars up the river. There are more boats. All domed, all dragging drowned horses at the end of rope lines.

"Do you see a dusker?" Ben asks, his voice rising hysterically.

I maneuver the focus with a trembling finger. Yet more boats come into focus, a whole fleet of them stretching down the length of the river. The current is pushing them toward the mountain cave. Toward us. I lower the binoculars.

Ben is staring at me. "It is, isn't it? It's a party of hunters," he says, his voice whittling the air.

I shake my head. "Not just a party. There's a whole army of them."

Sissy bends over, hands on knees, as if punched in the gut. "Remember when we were attacked on the river? With the grappling hooks? I said they were getting shrewder and stronger." She shakes her head. "I had no idea."

"How is this even possible?" Epap asks. "How did they build these boats so quickly?" He turns to me as if I should know.

"Maybe they . . . I don't know," I say.

"A fleet of so many boats . . . you don't build them in a few days," Epap says. "It takes months, years. You're the one who lived with them. Didn't you hear anything about the construction of a fleet of boats?"

"No, nothing."

"Let's focus on what we do know," Sissy says. Her voice grapples for steadiness. "We know the duskers are a couple of hours from entering the cave. The waterfall will kill a fair number of them, I should think, but many will survive. And it's dark in the cave; those that survive will hunker down in it until nightfall."

"And then what?" Ben asks.

"And then they come for us," David says. He looks so small, his thin arms trembling against his sides.

"No," I say. "They won't."

They all turn to look at me.

"Look at this wind. It's gusting west-east."

"Meaning?" Ben asks.

"Meaning they'll smell the Mission first. So long as we keep heading east, staying downwind. The Mission population numbers in the hundreds. We're only six. The Mission is a volcanic eruption of odors while we're barely a wisp. So long as we put quick distance between us and the Mission, so long as we stay downwind, we'll be fine. We keep running. We keep surviving. To the Promised Land."

"They'll follow us."

I shake my head. "They'll be so gorged on human flesh at the Mission, so inundated with human odors swirling around them, they won't smell the faint riff of us dozens of miles away." I look at the river. Even without the binoculars I can now see the black specks that are the boats. "But we have to move. This is the make-or-break time when we have to make speed."

I grab my bag, swing it onto my back. I'm the first to the cable ladder, the boys right behind me. Epap volunteers to head down first, and straps Ben's bag around him. "Don't look down," I tell the younger boys. "Keep your eyes focused on the rungs in front of you. Slow and steady, all right?"

Epap is grabbing hold of the post, planting his foot on the top rung when he stops. "Sissy?" he says.

She hasn't moved. She's still standing in the same spot, her face wrought with conflict.

"C'mon, Sissy!" I yell. "We have to hurry."

Then her face becomes smooth, her inner battle resolved. She looks at me with eyes that are steady but moist.

"Hey!" I shout. "Let's go!"

"It's not that simple," she says.

"What's not that simple?" I say.

"Running away."

"What?"

"We have to go back."

"To the Mission? Are you out of your mind?"

"We need to warn them about the dusker boats."

I walk back to her. "We go back, we die. We leave now, we live," I say. "It is *that* simple. If we leave now, we make it to the Promised Land. We see my father again. It doesn't get any simpler than that."

"I'm going back to the Mission."

I stare at her. "To what end, Sissy? They're dead anyway. Even if we do warn them, how far do you think they're going to get with those feet?"

"I can't do this, Gene. I can't just leave them to be ravaged."

I turn to Epap. "You talk some sense into her, will you?"

But he only looks at Sissy with wavering, uncertain eyes.

"Oh, c'mon, not you, too, Epap!"

Sissy stares out to the river. "The Scientist told us we never leave our own. If we simply walk away knowing what we know, we'd be betraying everything he's taught us."

I point east with an angry finger. "The Scientist wants us to head east. The Scientist wants us to go to the Land of Milk and Honey, Fruit and Sunshine. The Scientist is waiting for us there. We go east. That's what the Scientist wants! So don't go telling me about what you *think* the Scientist wants!"

Sissy's voice is quiet next to my berating tone. "If we leave, it's their blood on our hands. The village girls, the babies. Hundreds of them. I won't be able to live with that."

"Oh, c'mon Sissy, they brought it on themselves."

"No!" she says, her voice rising. "We brought it to them! Don't you get that?" Her eyes search mine. "It's because of *us* they're now in danger. If we never came, the boats would never have come out this far. But for us, the duskers would never have discovered the Mission."

The wind whistles across the granite domes. Long strands of hair blow across her face, but she does not pull them away. "I'm going back," she says. "It's the only thing I know to do. I will tell them about the duskers. I will convince them all to get on the train, to leave immediately. It'll be a tight squeeze, but we'll manage."

"Are you out of your mind? Sissy, we don't know where the train leads! That's why we left the Mission in the first place."

"And that's exactly why we'll get on. Because we don't know. It *might* lead to deliverance. But if they don't get on the train, it's *certain* death." Her voice is steeled and resolute. "Their lives have been hard enough. I can't leave them to be torn apart by duskers if I can help it. I won't be able to live with myself knowing I abandoned them."

I glare at her. "Sissy, don't do this."

She ignores me, turns to the others. "You all go with Gene. Help him find the Scientist. Don't worry about me, I'll be fine."

"No." Epap blinks hard, his face pale. He steps toward Sissy. "I'm with you, Sissy. It's the right thing to do."

"Me, too," David says, brushing tears from his eyes. "Let's go back to the Mission."

"And me," Jacob joins in, his voice shaking, a small, brave smile breaking out on his lips. "I'm with you, too."

And then Ben is running to Sissy, hugging her tightly around the waist. She ruffles the hair tufting out from the bottom of his winter hat. She looks at me.

I break my eyes away. The wind blows, and though it is no stronger than the previous gusts, it cuts through me as if I've been emptied out, all substance sucked out of me. I kick a rock over the edge.

"This is what you want then?" I say. "To be chased, to be hunted? To be their prey your whole life? Born prey, die prey?" I look at them in turn. "This is our chance to be more than prey. To escape all this. But instead you're choosing to go back to it, like an escaped animal right back into the cage."

Nobody answers. In the distance, the clot of dots on the river thickens.

"We can be free!" My voice cracks. I thrust my arms toward the eastern horizon. "That's where we need to go. East. Where my father is."

I'm suddenly dizzy and light-headed, the ground insubstantial beneath me. I bend over, wait for the world to stop spinning. "Don't do this, guys," I say, and my voice, whittled by the wind, has lost all strength. It is barely a whisper. "Don't leave me by myself."

For a moment, they don't speak. They stand perfectly stationary. Only their hair, blown by the wind, ripples in this tapestry of stillness. Then David moves toward me, and though it is but a single step, it seems as if he's closed the whole distance between us.

"Come with us, Gene," he says. "Please?" And it is that last word that breaks me a little inside.

I turn my head, gaze at the eastern horizon. The wide expanse, empty and barren.

"Gene," and now it is Jacob who is speaking. "Come with us. You're part of us now. You're with us. I really feel that. You fit so perfectly. We're family. We won't let you leave!"

Nobody has ever begged or pleaded for me. For a few moments, I don't say anything, only feel a strange molten warmth fill pockets inside me where I've only ever felt emptiness. I turn to face them again. Ben gazes at me with eyes wide with hope and expectation. He sees written on my face the decision I'm barely aware of making, and he breaks into a wide smile. He tugs on Sissy's arm with excitement. "He's coming! He's coming with us!"

Epap nods at me, his eyes warm. "We should get a move on," he says. "It's a ways back to the Mission. You take the lead, Gene. I'll take the rear, what do you say?"

I see myself stepping forward, into their midst. I can almost feel their hands patting me on the back, the light dancing in their eyes, the surge of energy in my legs as I lead them back to the Mission.

But I haven't moved. I'm rooted to the spot. Once again, I stare at the eastern horizon. I feel the pull of a million hands tugging me in two different directions.

"I get to walk behind Gene!" Jacob says, picking up his backpack.

And yet still, I have not moved.

And then Sissy, quiet for so long, speaks. But unlike the others, there is no excitement in her voice. "Gene." That is all she says, just my name, quietly. Her voice is filled with an unbearable sadness that devastates me. She shakes her head as she looks at me, and in that small movement a thousand hidden words of realization and understanding pass between us.

The boys turn to her, confusion etched into their faces.

"Sissy?" Ben asks. "What's the matter—"

"Gene won't be coming with us," Sissy says, her eyes never leaving mine.

"What? What do you mean?"

Her voice is calm. "East is his destination. It's the path the Scientist determined for him."

"No," David says, his voice thick with emotion. "He's one of us, he stays with us—"

"He's the Origin," she says. "His path is different from ours."

"Sissy," Ben says, "he wants to come with us and—"

"*Don't let Gene die,*" she says. "Gene is the Origin. He is the cure. He needs to stay alive. He needs to head east. Nothing is more important."

The boys' faces turn pale. But their wide eyes and silent quivering lips betray the unwanted acknowledgment that Sissy is right.

"He needs to find the Scientist," she continues with a determined calmness. "It's what the Scientist wants, it's what he designed from the very beginning. We can't let our personal feelings"—her face hardens like flint—"get in the way." She gazes at me from the corners of her eyes, and for the first time her voice trembles with conflict and anguish. "And deep down it's what Gene also wants."

The boys look at me. And Ben now sees something else on my face, a different expression that causes his lower lip to wobble, his eyes to tear up. "Gene?" he asks, and his question hangs in the air, dangling in the wind.

Sissy moves toward me, her face rigid. "He wants his father. Nothing—and nobody—matters more to him. We can't deny him that. We have to let him go." And now she is standing right in front of me, so close I see the cracks in her hardened expression, the soft crevices of ache. "You'd walk to the ends of the earth to find him, right, Gene?"

Behind her, the boys are gazing at me. The sky is a vivid deep blue above them, not a cloud in sight. Ben starts to sob and Epap puts a comforting arm around his shoulders.

"I won't leave you," I say.

"You must," Sissy says. "I won't let you stay."

"I'm done with deserting—"

She places her finger on my lips, quieting me.

The sunlight reflecting off the granite dome draws out the deep pools of her irises. I remember the first time I saw those brown eyes, on my deskscreen at school. It was when she picked out the lottery numbers for the Heper Hunt. So many days ago, yet I still remember the qualities those eyes held, even through the digitalized pixels of the screen, of strength and softness both.

And that is how her hand feels on my face. Strength and softness.

"Gene," she whispers, and her voice at last betrays her. She swallows hard. "Go." For a moment, her resolute eyes break into shards of hesitation. She pauses, as if to give me a chance to speak. But I say nothing. She closes her eyes and turns back to the boys.

I don't move. Then, in a movement that seems to take hours, I step toward the cable ladder. Nothing has substance, not the granite beneath me, not my legs, not my body. It feels as if I might get swept up in the next gust of wind, not so much blown away as quickly whittled, bone by bone, into nothingness. I plant my boot on the first rung.

"Gene!" David shouts. "We'll see you again. One day, okay?"

I nod. He smiles back and I feel my owns lips naturally curl and part in a smile. I did not know this, that smiles could be fashioned out of sorrow. Then I do something my father always cautioned me not to do. I lift up my hand and wave it slowly. They wave back, all of them, with damp eyes.

As if pulled down by the weight of my heavy heart, I step down to the next rung and the next. The sight of Sissy and the boys is replaced by the hard granite wall rushing up before me as I descend down the cable ladder. My foot finds the next rung down and the next and the next, and then I am all alone in the world again.

39

I HIKE HARD and fast. It is better this way, to keep my heart pumping with vigor, lungs sucking for air, mind focused on what lies ahead and not what I've left behind. I am a tiny dot gliding across an immense, forgotten land emptied of memory, stuck in a stasis that will never shift.

As the sun begins to descend, my boots strike not hard granite but the soft floor of the forest. It's colder in the woods, and darker, as if dusk has stolen prematurely into its midst. I keep up the brisk pace, eager to put miles under me.

But the densely spaced trees, and their similarities in appearance, disorient me, spin me around. I look to the sky for guidance, but the tall redwood trees, packed tightly together, reveal only splintered patches of sky and obscure the position of the sun. I don't even know which way is east. The hue of the sky worries me, its tone no longer blue, but spilled with the bloodred tint of dusk.

Nightfall has begun.

I'm a city boy, unused to navigating the wilderness. I press on, panic cupping the back of my eyes. Ten minutes later, I'm forced to accept what I've been denying for over an hour. I'm lost, my inner compass gone kaput. I no longer know if I'm walking toward or away from the Mission. I've lost precious time.

With alarm, I note that a few stars are already peeking out in the twilight sky. Night is pouring into the world. Under my feet, right now, in the cavity of the mountain, hundreds of duskers are waiting for the day to recede to full darkness. The thought completely unnerves me. Shortly, the duskers will start scaling the walls of the cave, clinging to vines and other plants, and filter out of the openings through which sun columns beam down in the daytime. They will stream out in countless streams, cloaking the mountain like rising black oil as they race toward the Mission.

I hope Sissy and the boys made good time and are safely back in the Mission. I hope they will be able to convince the girls to get on the train, that they'll be able to leave before the duskers arrive. As I walk, a growing sense of guilt begins to weigh on me. That I have deserted them. In the same way I abandoned Ashley June, I have betrayed them. I walk harder and faster, needing tiredness to rid me of thought.

A half hour later, I lean back on a tree trunk, breathing hard, eyes wide in the dark woods. I should be on the other side of the mountain by now, miles away, safely out of their path and downwind. Not lost and afraid in the darkness and silence of the woods. Days ago, with Clair leading us, the forest was teeming with wildlife. But now, there is only an eerie silence. As if all the forest dwellers have sensed the arrival of the duskers and have already fled.

When my ragged breathing quiets, I hear the faint sounds of a stream. I shuffle my way toward it, not because I'm thirsty and in need of water but because I remember a stream passes only fifty meters or so from the log cabin. Perhaps it is the same one.

It is a gurgling, fast-flowing brook. I bend down, splash water on my face. The ice water snaps me out of my cloud of fatigue and into the clear expanse of alertness.

An idea formulates in my head. Of a way out. It's not perfect; far from it actually. But as the temperature plummets around me, the cold creeping down the nape of my neck, I realize that not only is this a viable method of escape, it is the only one. I hitch up the backpack, tighten the straps, and run alongside the river. Eyes peeled for the cabin.

Because inside the cabin is my father's hang glider.

I almost run right by the cabin. A single wail is what saves me. It is flung up into the night sky, unnervingly close. It stops me in my tracks. And that's when I see it. Not the log cabin, not at first, only a clearing. Within seconds I'm sprinting across the clearing and onto the front porch of the cabin.

As I turn the knob, a chorus of other cries, masculine and feline, rises into the sky, a pitched yearning to their joined voices. Thin cloud lines, dyed red from the setting sun, take on the appearance of deep bloody gashes. I stare at the woods encircling the clearing. No movement. East of me, the clearing falls away into a sudden cliff, a sheer drop. A dark wind blows across it. That's where my father took off with the hang glider. Right off the cliff, into the skies, soaring above the Vast. And that's where I'll need to take off.

It's dark inside the cabin. I take out a GlowBurn from my bag, snap it. The hang glider is right where I remember it, hung up on the bedroom wall. Now that I know I need to fly it, it seems both flimsier and more cumbersome at the same time. I examine it, trying to make out a method behind the madness of straps and bars. None of it makes any sense at all. There has to be something else. And then I remember. I open the chest of clothes, take out the odd-looking vest I'd seen days earlier. I unzip it, try to decipher the metallic hooks and cords and carabiners dangling from it. I put on the vest, fitting my legs through harnesses. Now the hang glider makes more sense: hooks attach to counter hooks, carabiners match up with same-colored carabiners.

A scream outside rattles the windows.

The window is a sheet of black now. Night has saturated the skies.

As if to officially usher night in, screams fly across the mountainside. But louder now, scraping against the cabin windows like fingernails across a sheet of ice. I hear faint cracking sounds, like toothpicks snapped—it takes a minute before I realize these are the distant sounds of trees being felled, trunks pulverized by the horde of duskers. The heper odors drifting across the mountain ranges are driving them into a frenzy.

I drop the hang glider onto the bed and run outside. From the front porch, I see the progress of their stampede. Tall trees in the distance shaking.

They're coming. They're coming. By accident or by design, the cabin is in their direct path.

I run inside. I consider closing the shutters, fortressing myself in the cabin. But I shunt that idea aside immediately—the cabin stands as much chance resisting the duskers as a matchbox in a fire. They'd rip this log cabin into shreds within seconds.

I pick up the hang glider, walk sideways down the hallway with it and out the front door. Cold wind gusts manically around me, the echoes of howls swirling in them.

It's now or never, ready or not. I choose *now,* I hope for *ready*.

I latch a hook to a corresponding hook on the hang glider. I start walking toward the cliff edge even as I lock carabiners into place, slide cords through loops, all guesswork and no conviction at all in what I'm doing. I can only hope they're going where they're supposed to.

The ground begins to rumble under me.

Shrieks loft out of the forest behind and beside me. These are different in tone, rapturous, the cries of pleasant surprises, of unexpected discoveries.

I run. Dangling, still-unhooked carabiners bounce against my body like the nudges of a needy child—*fix me fix me fix me*—but it is too late for that. All I feel is the razor edge of their screams, slashing not only my eardrums, but the skin on the back of my neck, the skin on the back of my heels, reaching out toward me like claws on outstretched fingers. I pull the metal handlebar of the hang glider over my head, making sure I don't trip as I run. A single stumble now will be a fatal mistake.

A pool of darkness begins to enfold around me.

Don't look back. Don't look to the side. Just keep your eyes on the edge. Run for the edge, run run run.

And then it is there, the cliff edge racing toward me, the mouth of nothingness gaping wide beyond it. I don't know what I'm supposed to do with the hang glider but it is too late for second-guessing now. Ground rumbling, the air pierced with a thousand cries of lust, I fling myself over the edge, into the yawning chasm of bottomless black.

And just as I do, I hear a shout, a single word verbalized from behind. *Gene!*

I am plummeting, my feet scrabbling empty air as the cliff face screeches past. There's no wind. The hang glider flaps like a wounded bird, wings rattling with hysteria. A sick, panicky feeling settles into the pit of my stomach.

A terrific wind gusts out of nowhere. The glider latches on to it with an almost audible click. The night air—once so vacuous—suddenly gains the solidity of a palatial carpet under me, lifting me into the night sky.

Throat in mouth, clasping the bar with a white-knuckled grip, I glance down. Duskers are spilling off the cliff edge, dropping into the black abyss. The glider wobbles. I snap my eyes to the handle, focus on the heady task at hand. I lean my body this way and that, test out the flight mechanics in careful gradations. I'm a quick study at most things, and soon enough get a feel for flying the glider. Everything done slowly and smoothly, no rough jerks or sudden maneuvers. It's not too difficult, once the initial fear is overcome.

In fact, it's exhilarating. The sensation of soaring through the airy expanse, the surprisingly gentle, refreshing breeze on my face. Far below, emerging out of the mountain in a titanic waterfall, the Nede River flows out of the mountain. It shines beneath like a magnesium strip, a directional arrow pointing east. To the Promised Land. To my father. If this easterly wind keeps up, I will make good time.

I take one last look back at the mountain. The moon is now pouring its milky light on the mountainside, and I can see a blanket of silver and black dots streaming up like a cloak. Wave upon wave of duskers pouring out of the mountain's innards. They will be upon the Mission before too long.

I have tried not to think of them, but my thoughts involuntarily swing to Sissy and the boys. They will have made it back to the Mission by now. For a second, an emptiness vaster than the night sky echoes in me.

I stare dead ahead. East. Somewhere out there, beyond the scope of my eyes, is my father.

I wonder how many girls Sissy has convinced to leave by train.

My father will be tanned, I think, no longer having to stay out of the sun. And perhaps fuller around the waist, with all the food and drink he will have consumed.

I wonder if Sissy and the boys are on the train now. If the village girls are piling in with them as the train engine revs up.

My father will have a beard, or a moustache, or perhaps a scruffy shadow. He will have hair on his arms, on his legs. The bags under his eyes will be reduced, or altogether gone, removed by months and years of deep, restful sleep. He will look different, my father, but, free from the masks he has worn his whole life, he will be his true, unveiled self.

I wonder if Sissy and the boys are fine. I wonder if they know they must leave immediately. I wonder if they know the sheer volume of duskers storming toward them.

I will, for the first time in my life, see my father really smile. I will see that purest of emotions he had learned to stifle. I will see his lips curl back, his teeth shine bright with a now-practiced naturalness, a brightness touch his eyes. His arms will remain at his side, no longer feeling the need to faux scratch his wrists. And that is what he will do when he sees me. He will smile. He will smile in the sunshine and not feel compelled to move into the shadows.

I wonder if Ben is not too tired from hiking all day. If David knows he'll need gloves and a scarf because the wind whipping through the open cages of the train will be harsh and biting. I wonder if Sissy's arm is better, if the brand has staved off infection. I wonder if they are thinking of me as I am them. I wonder if Sissy is needing to be with me. As I her.

Stars blink into existence above and around me, seemingly within arm's length. As if I might reach up and dislodge them, and watch them drift down like snowflakes to the earth.

I stare east. See my father in the warm glow of sunshine, glowing and blurred like a fantasy. See him diminishing, fading, as all dreams, in the harsh light of morning, inevitably do.

I grip the bar tighter. Then angle my legs to one side, canting my body. The stars spin around me as I turn the hang glider, the moon swinging like a ball on a string. The silvered river rotates under me. And then the mountain is in front of me, its silhouetted peak leaning to the side, like a head cocked in surprise and confusion.

I'm flying west.

Back to the Mission.

40

THE MISSION IS nestled between two ridges in the mountain, and I miss it the first go-around. It's the bridge—its two halves raised like bookends—that proves to be an invaluable reference point. I circle around, see a few specks of light flickering in the dark breast of the mountain. I fly closer until the Mission fully emerges out of the darkness, and I see the soft, illumined cottages. From up here, the village's smallness and quaintness catches me by surprise.

My landing, I've already concluded—sadly, with resignation, and not a little trepidation—is going to be ugly, probably painful, potentially fatal, and dependent on gobs of beginner's luck. I've had a lot of time to think about it—the fifteen minutes or so it's taken to fly back—and have already decided that my best option is to land in the glacial lake on the far end of the Mission. But what seemed like such a good idea is in actuality incredibly difficult to achieve. From up here, the lake is the size of a small coin—a ridiculously small landing pad surrounded by cratered granite and thick coniferous forests with trees jutting up like knives.

Landing in the lake feels like crashing into a wall of ice. No give in the bracken waters. My legs, then body, are run against a metal shredder as I skid along the surface. The glider suddenly spears into the depths, coldness and bubbles and darkness flipping my world upside down and inside out. Completely disoriented, I unbuckle and wrest myself free of the vest, and kick away the sinking glider. *Watch the bubbles, follow them up, watch the bubbles.* I break surface and the wide open dome of the night sky spreads above me, filled with oxygen.

I swim to the lake's edge, drag out my dripping mangled body. Cold. Need to hurry, limbs shaking like branches in a gale, mind already splintering into disjointed, haphazard thoughts. Stumbling along on unsteady legs, my jaw jackhammering away, I shuffle toward the nearest cottage, my arms wrapped around my chest, hands tucked under armpits. Frozen hand barely able to mold fingers around the doorknob. Dark inside. Throw open the chest, tear off the wet clothes, put on dry ones.

It's then I realize I haven't seen a single person.

I run out to the street, my teeth chattering.

My eyes scan the village square; nothing moves, no one is around. Just as I'm thinking that Sissy was able to convince everyone to leave, I see a group of girls. Their eyes, lidded and half-asleep, widen with surprise when they see me.

"Where are my friends?" I say. My first spoken words in hours come out shrill and jittery.

The girls only stare at me warily.

"Did you hear me? My friends: Sissy, Epap, the boys. Did they make it back here? Have you seen them?"

But they stare back vacantly, unaffected by the urgency in my voice. Except for one. She looks petrified.

"They made it back?" I ask her.

She nods.

"Where are they?" I say.

"At the train station," she says quietly. "Most of them."

"What do you mean *most* of them?"

She clenches her skirt, balling the material in her hand.

"What's going on?" I demand. Alarm rises in my heart.

"I can't say any more. I can't," she says, her body going rigid.

"What's going on around here?" I demand. And when no one answers, when no one even meets my eyes, I start running for the train station.

"Get to the train now!" I yell back at them over my shoulder. "If you want to live, you need to get on the train!"

The train station bursts with activity. Seemingly half the village is here, unloading the train cars. *Still* unloading the cars.

"Sissy!" I shout.

Faces turn, round face after round sleepy face. But no sign of Sissy or the boys.

"Epap! David!"

Everyone stops moving, turning to look at me. Surprise flits across their faces, but nobody speaks.

And then, on the far side of the train, I hear her. Sissy shouting, "Over here, Gene! Over here. Hurry—" She's cut off by the sound of a smack.

That sets my feet afire. I race down the platform, pushing aside containers and generators, leaping over hoses left curled on the platform floor. A group of elders is congregated down at that end, bunched up in a tight group.

I stop in front of them, breathing hard, sucking in gulps of wispy air. The elders spread out, blossoming like a Venus flytrap, encircling me. That's when I see them. They're all tied up inside a train car. Sissy and the boys. Almost all the boys.

"Where's Ben?" I say.

"Krugman's got Ben in his office," Sissy says. Her face is bruised on one side. Her hands, chafed and raw, are tied above her head, and looped around one of the metal bars. "They wouldn't listen to us. They grabbed us, forced us onto this train."

Next to her, David is shaking, almost in tears. Jacob is tied on the other side of the train. I can see the knotted ropes tying them to the bars. Epap looks to be in the worst shape. Alone in the corner, his eyes are purpled and swollen shut. He's slumped over to the side, barely conscious, arms tied behind his back. And I see someone else tied in the other corner. A girl, her eyes blazing with renewed life. Clair.

I turn to the elders. They're grinning, leering at me. "Okay, okay," I say. "You got us. We give up. We'll get on the train. We'll leave now."

Their faces frown. They're expecting pushback, not surrender.

"Just get Ben. Then you can send us on our way."

"Fine," says one of the elders. "Get on the train now."

"Once you bring Ben here," I say. "Then I'll get on."

The elder's face breaks into a warm smile, laugh lines rippling out. "Oh, okay," he says. "Whatever you say. But it might take, oh, maybe an hour or two to bring him here. Give or take three hours."

The circle of men breaks out in guffaws.

I look at Sissy. She shakes her head. *It's not going to work*, her eyes tell me.

I try a different tack. "Listen to me very clearly," I say. "Let me spell it out for you. We have to leave now."

"How do you figure that?" the elder says.

"They're coming."

"Who?"

"The duskers."

The elder smiles. He points at Sissy. "That's what she claimed. Ohhh . . . we're so scared. Ohh . . . the duskers are floating down the river on pretty little boats."

"You should be scared." I stare at their smiling faces until their smirks disappear. "Because I've seen them. They're on the mountain now. Sprinting toward us as we speak, blanketing the face of this mountain like an avalanche of black desire. They'll be on us in minutes."

For a second, two, three, they're silent. A silence that is broken up by uproarious laughter.

"Oh, well played, sir, well played," the elder booms out. "I have to admit you nearly had us there for a moment." Then he stops laughing, his tone turning on a dime. "But not good enough, not nearly by half." His face hardens. "Now get on the train."

"First bring Ben. In the meantime, the girls should start getting on the train."

"What do you mean?" one of the girls asks. It's the girl with freckles. Her voice is timid and afraid, distrusting even herself. She ignores the elders glaring at her. "Tell me."

The elders turn to glare at her. "You be quiet—"

"We all have to leave," I shout, now directing my attention to the girls. "The train is the way you survive. The *only* way." I see the girls listening intensely, leaning forward. "You think the dusker in the Vastnarium was scary? Imagine dozens of them. Imagine hundreds of them tearing through this village!" I shout, and she flinches back. "Now imagine them grabbing you, eating you. As they surely will within the next fifteen minutes."

A short girl standing close to us, no older than seven, starts crying. The freckled girl puts a comforting arm around her shoulders, but it is pale and trembling.

"Don't listen to him!" an elder shouts. "Don't listen to these barefaced lies!"

"Listen to me!" I shout over him. "Start the train engine. Start lowering the bridge. We have to leave now!"

Nobody moves.

And then: the only thing that would have worked.

A full-throated scream howls across the night sky.

It is not the sound of a wolf or an animal, nor is it the bay of loneliness. It is the sound of pining and a deranged impulse. It is soulful but not human. A second later, and it is joined by another wail, then another, until an explosion of bestial howls is flinging across the darkening skies.

The elders' faces drain pale, their eyes widening with the realization of a lifelong nightmare. Then they do something strange. They do not order the girls onto the train. They do not themselves get on the train. They simply turn around and silently shuffle away like performers booed off the stage, their faces shell-shocked. The elders trundle back toward the village, through the black grassy meadows. Toward the howls.

"What are they doing?" Clair asks. "Where are they going?"

None of this makes sense. The village girls, initially following the elders off the platform, stop and gaze quizzically at one another. Their faces are pictures of conflict: a struggle between their base instinct for survival and their conditioned submission to the elders.

Another scream. Not a dusker howl, but a human cry. The scream's distance from us—the farms on the far side of the Mission—does little to diffuse the raw terror in it. Full of horror, squeals that pierce the fabric of night. In my mind, I see the farm girls fleeing into the butchery, grabbing hold of cleavers and choppers to ward off the duskers. They do not realize the futility of defense, do not realize that the sight and scent of blood in the butchery—even if only that of an animal's—will only serve to incense the duskers even further.

"If you want to live, get on the train right now!" I shout. The freckled girl steps forward. Voice shaking badly, she tells the girls to get on the train. They need no further prodding; they move as one into the train cars with surprising quiet, only an isolated sob or muted cry escaping their mouths.

A girl picks something off the floor of the train car. It's the girl with pigtails, and in her hand now is Sissy's dagger belt. She kneels down next to Sissy, unsheathes a dagger. A second later, she's cut through Sissy's ropes. Sissy stands, rubbing her wrists. She gives the girl an appreciative look, then unsheathes another dagger from the belt. Together, they start cutting away at the other ropes restraining the boys and Clair.

"How do we get this train moving?" I ask the freckled girl.

"There's a control panel at the end of the platform," she says. "It controls everything. A sequence of buttons that sets the train on autopilot. From there, it takes fifteen minutes to rev up, then all doors to the train lock, brakes are released, the train sets off, the bridge is lowered. The process cannot be reversed. Not until it reaches the destination, the Civilization."

"Do you know how to work the panel?" I ask her.

She nods, her eyes steady on mine. Unexpected strength there. "I've watched the elders work it many times," she says. "It's all very simple, everything color-coded and labeled pictorially."

From the village come more howls, louder now, interspersed with screams of pain. Bloodletting has begun. I may not be able to smell it, but I can feel it in the air. The night's blackness is doused with death.

"Go now," I say to her. "Start the engines." She scampers off toward the panel, fast as her lotus feet can take her.

I see David whispering to Jacob, urgently. They spin around, readying to take off.

"Where do you think you're going?" I ask, grabbing them by their jackets.

"To get Ben," David says, punching my arm away.

"No way. You both stay here."

"We're not leaving him behind, Gene."

"I know," I say, clenching my jaw. "That's why I'm going for him."

"You and me both," Sissy says.

"I work better alone," I say.

"Not this time. It's Ben we're talking about." She turns to David and Jacob. "You two stay here with Epap, make sure he's okay. Those two girls"—she points to the girl with pigtails and the one with freckles—"are capable. Get behind them."

And then Sissy is leaping off the platform, cinching her dagger belt around her waist. Moments later, I'm right there with her, sprinting down the meadow. More screams sound from the village. Terror has been unleashed in the streets, in the cottages, full-blown. And we're running headlong into it.

"Why did Krugman take Ben?" I say.

She shakes her head, eyes filled with fear. "I don't know." Her feet pound the ground faster, harder.

Halfway there, I throw a quick look back at the station. A loud mechanical click explodes in the air, followed by a burst of light gray smoke snorting out the engine car. The train's revving up. Fifteen minutes. That's all the time we have. Assuming we even make it back alive.

At the first cottage on the village periphery, we lean up against the wall, peek around the corner. The street is empty. From behind, the sound of someone running toward us. It's Clair.

"Going any farther is suicide," she says, panting hard. "Listen to the screams! Come back to the train."

"We're going for Ben, in Krugman's office," Sissy says. "I'm not leaving without him."

The two girls stare at each other. Clair spits to the ground. "In that case, I'm coming. I can help. I know the quickest way there. And back."

"Clair—" I say.

"C'mon then," Clair says. "There's no time to waste." She races off, knowing we'll follow, dashing in and out of the alleyways, slipping in narrow spaces between cottages. Agile and nimble, she quick-cuts around tight corners, sprints through cottages, leaps over fences. Every so often, we bump into a group of girls fleeing down the streets, screaming, going as fast their lotus feet can take them. "Go to the train station!" I order them. But even as I see them hobble off, I know they have no chance of outracing the duskers.

Who are everywhere and nowhere. I have yet to see a single one even though their howls pierce every corner of the village. By the gathering volume of their cries, I know they are still pouring in, an endless stream of them. They are incited by the coppery scent of our blood as they race through the streets, through the cottages, through our clothes, through our skin, through our muscles and fat and internal organs and blood vessels.

"This way!" Clair urges, her voice hushed, and we race faster down the street.

Two cottages ahead of us, a girl rushes out the front door. The screams have panicked her out of her hiding place inside. She's confused and uncertain as she turns toward us. She never sees—

—the black wind that takes her. In the blink of an eye, an indiscernible black shape swoops in from the side, swiping her off her feet and back into the house, the door smashing into smithereens. The girl's screams intermix with the duskers' howls, an eerie, interlacing intimacy.

I grab Clair's hand, pull her away. Her arm is limp, her feet dragging with shock.

"Krugman's office, that's all you think about, okay, Clair? Take us there!"

She nods, but her body is betraying her. She starts to shake, her eyes darting from side to side, trying to make sense of a world gone dark and black and bloody. She pulls off her scarf, wraps it around her head.

"What are you doing?" I ask.

"My white hair, it's giving our position away in the dark."

"No. It's the smell of blood that'll draw them," I say, removing her scarf, wrapping it around her neck again. "And that's our advantage right now. We know exactly where they are. Wherever there's screaming, there's blood, and that's where they are. We stay away from the screams."

She nods frantically, her lower jaw juddering.

"You stay with me, Clair, and you're fine. Because I know these things, I've survived their attacks before. I know how they move, where, when, why. Look at me, Clair, look into my eyes!"

She does, and I pour all my resolve into her eyes, into those pools of fear. I can almost hear the blood rushing through her veins. She nods, slowly, takes a deep breath.

"This way," she says. "We're almost there." When she takes off, she's found her legs again. Screams—sometimes solitary, often in groups—scald the night sky and we're forced to circle or backtrack around them.

Hazy dark shapes dart through the village, disconcertingly close. Two girls, trying to escape out of a cottage by squeezing through a window, scream for help, their eyes beseeching. They are wedged in the window frame, and their arms lash against the outside wall. Their bodies suddenly arch straight and taut, their mouths screaming silent cries, their eyelids disappearing behind their eyeballs, exposing the whites of agony. Then their bodies collapse, dangling limp from the window like hung laundry, before being whipped back inside.

We don't dawdle. We sprint across an alcove, in and out of smaller alleyways. "This way," Clair says, and we're suddenly in the wide open, running across the meadows toward the fortress walls. Above us, like a directional arrow, is the long power cable running from the center of town to Krugman's office in the corner tower. Light pours out his panoramic windows, glowing like a halo.

41

We race up the spiral staircase, feet thumping on the stairs, hands pulling on the steep, curling handrail. It is eerily empty and quiet. Halfway up, Clair grabs my arm, stopping us. The soft sound of singing lilts from above.

From the deadly sword deliver me;
rescue me from the hands of outsiders
whose mouths are full of fangs,
whose hands are clawed with nails

We look at each other, then start climbing again. Our steps slower, quieter. We stop; it's Ben's voice, trembling with fright.

Then our sons in their youth
may be as fortress walls,
and our daughters like polished pillars
of a fortified palace.
Our cottages will be filled
affording all matter of store.

At the top of the stairs, we follow Ben's voice. Down the hallway to Krugman's office. His door is ajar, and through the narrow gap, we see Ben, holding a sheet of music in trembling hands.

The office is illuminated with the soft glow of lamps. A faint drone of electricity—from the cable line—hums in the air. The office seems softened, the contours smoother compared to the previous time when the harsh glare of daylight had lent a sharpness to the interior. Krugman sits with his back to us, gazing out the floor-to-ceiling window on that side of the office. He is subdued, holding an emptied whisky tumbler as if toasting the night, seemingly oblivious to the screams and howls that threaten to crack the window.

Ben stands in front of a set of bookshelves lining the wall. His face is pallid and wan as I signal him to come, finger pressed against my lips. He glances back at Krugman, then tiptoes toward us. His hand slides into Sissy's.

"Where do you think you're going?" Krugman says with a subdued tone. There is not a hint of threat or urgency in his voice. As if he has all the time in the world, as if a wave of duskers is not sweeping over his village. "Why don't you come in? All of you?"

We start retreating down the hallway.

"Because I surely hope you're not trying to escape on the train," Krugman says.

I pause. Sissy pulls at my arm, but something in Krugman's tone . . .

"Because that would be jumping from the frying pan into the fire," he says. "In fact," he continues, somehow knowing he has my undivided attention, "*into a volcanic pit of burning lava* would be more apropos." He snickers to himself.

"What do you mean?" I ask.

"Gene!" Sissy says.

"No, wait," I say. Raising my voice, I say, "We're leaving now."

"That's your choice," Krugman says, as weary as ever. "You'll only be delaying the inevitable."

Again Sissy tugs my arm. And again, I resist. I turn to Krugman. "You're too old and fat to make it to the train; you don't want us to get away. You're just trying to delay us."

"And yet you stay, and yet you stay." He swivels around slowly on his chair, his eyes watery and bloodshot. He smiles sadly, stroking his protruding stomach. "I wasn't always this heavy," he says lethargically, as if too tired to push words out.

It's his resignation, his surrender to fate that alarms me. Because such men are not out to stall or set traps. If he's delaying us, it's because he wants to confess something.

The thought chills me.

"You think the train is certain death," I say. "Tell me why."

"Gene! Let's go!" Sissy's voice is ringed with urgency.

"Tell me why the train is certain death!" I insist.

Krugman taps his palms down on the armrests as if affectionately patting the heads of two toddlers. "Really, do you have to scream? Isn't there enough screaming going on outside?"

"Okay, we're leaving," I say, turning around.

"It is not the train that's certain death," Krugman says, and his words flick out with such icy clarity, it is as if he has, for a moment, regained sobriety. "It's the *destination*." His voice then disintegrates into a wet mumble. "Much death and screaming there. Much. Muchly."

"Tell us what's in the Civilization."

He giggles. "It will take time to explain. Much time. Muchly."

"Gene, don't fall for it! He just wants to—"

"—keep you from getting on the train?" Krugman says. "Then go, go I say. Off you go now, smack on the bottom, tussle of your hair, peck on your lips, off you go now, little darlings. Don't let me keep you. Don't miss your school bus on account of me."

I walk over to Krugman, smack the tumbler out of his hand. It flies across the office, shattering against the wall. The sound jolts him; clarity shines in his eyes before a glassy fog clouds them again. He walks over to the window, the darkness outside framing him. A scream rips out from somewhere on the grounds below us, at the fortress wall. Its volume and proximity are terrifying.

"Gene!" Sissy says.

I ignore her. I need to know. "It's the Ruler's Palace, isn't it?" I shout. "The train leads to nothing more than heper pens. I'm right, aren't I?"

Krugman starts giggling. "Give the boy a cookie, please. Give the little detective a smiley face." He wipes away a line of tears. "That's only the tip of it," he says. "You think you're so smart, you think you've got this all figured out. You want the truth?"

Clair screams. A dusker, pale and glowing like the moon, slivers across the glass window like a leech. It can't see through the one-way glass; it pauses, its face directly in front of the unmoving Krugman, its nostrils flaring. Then it skimmers away. Outside, a black wave of duskers is pouring over the fortress walls.

Krugman wipes his nose with the back of his hand. "The truth, now," he says with a shaky voice. "Unvarnished for your consumption. Steady yourselves, little children." He turns from the window towards us. "We're all alone. Mankind was wiped out generations ago. The duskers took over the world. And we never took it back. We never found an antidote, a cure, a poison. We never found anything but death. The Civilization never existed."

Sissy stops pulling me. She turns slowly, reluctantly, to face Krugman.

"After the dust settled, only several thousand humans survived. We eked out a horrendous existence. In the bowels of the Ruler's Palace, imprisoned and force-bred. Our sole purpose in life was to live and die to satisfy the Ruler's appetite. And it was insatiable. He tried to slow down, pace himself, but he couldn't resist the temptation. We were too proximally close. And that was the same for each successive Ruler. None had self-control. The captive human population began dwindling at an alarming, unsustainable rate.

"One night, many, many generations ago, the Ruler at the time had a brainchild. A brilliant plan. He came to us and struck a deal."

"With *who*?"

"With us. The humans. The Ruler agreed to release a couple hundred of us to form a commune here in the mountains. Hundreds of miles away, the journey too far for duskers to travel because it entailed—even by train—exposure to daylight. The humans agreed—as if we had a choice—and set off.

"This plan was all very secretive, of course, only the top brass knew. And for decades, the succession of Rulers has supplied all our needs and wants. It's a secret that's held up longer than anyone expected, down the line of Rulers. But I suppose all secrets, especially this one, will eventually leak out."

He strokes the strands of his mole hair. "Of late, we'd gotten a whiff of rumors. About dissension within the Palatial ranks, about certain factions getting wind of the Mission. Even rumors of sun-protected boats being constructed, a whole armada. We discounted these rumors out of hand." He stares into the blackened skies. "That was a mistake. We'd been lulled into a false sense of security. They always fulfilled their end of the deal."

"Tell me about this deal. Tell me everything," I say.

"We breed for them," Krugman whispers. "That's the purpose of this Mission. A breeding farm. We trickle in hepers to the Palace at a sustained pace like drips through an IV. We're far enough removed from them that they can't gorge on us, throw us into extinction in one uncontrollable binge session. In return, they supply us everything we need to survive and yes, even thrive. Food, medicine, materials. Tit for tat. It's a beautiful symbiotic relationship in many ways. Not quite roasting marshmallows and singing 'Kumbaya' around the campfire with them, but you get the picture."

"You've been sending children to them as food," I say.

His voice lowers. "Save your judgmental tone, lad. I'll tell you what I've done. I've propagated our species. I am the sole reason why we're not extinct right now. I'm the reason why *you* even exist at all. So if I were you, I'd bite my tongue."

"All those boys you sent. All the older girls . . ." says Clair.

Krugman turns to Clair, and his look is tender, his eyes moist with affection. "I've given you happy years. That's what I've done. Music, smiles, sunshine, food, warmth. You've known not the tyranny of fear, imprisonment in cold wet cells, surrounded by death and violence, hearing the wretched sounds of a dusker eating a loved one. You've never had to live in fear of having your number drawn, of iron claws gripping around your limbs, pulling you away. Instead, you and all the other village children have lived in a paradise here, a veritable Eden. So what if I've had to fabricate some tales, make up stories about the Civilization? Ignorance is bliss, and bliss is what I've given all of you."

"You've given them nothing but a death sentence," I say.

"Oh, don't we all have one!" he yells, spinning around to glare at me. "Don't we all have a death sentence! The very second we're born, aren't we all sentenced to death? But come, see. I've only made death row manageable for them. No, more than that, I've made it happy, idyllic. Filled with laughter, singing, food. Look at the paintings on this bookshelf. Do you not see the childhood whimsy in them, the dreamlike bliss?" The folds of fat on his face tremble violently. "You. Just like the Scientist with your judgmental tone. You sound just like him after he returned to the Mission. He came back too good for this place."

"Gene," Sissy pleads, urging me to leave.

"That's why there're so many pregnant girls here," I whisper, the truth becoming hideously apparent. "It's how the Mission survives. How it . . . supplies the Palace. In order to keep receiving food, medicine, supplies, it needs to replenish . . ." I can't finish the sentence.

"Tit for tat," Krugman whispers. "Tit for tat."

"And you send away the boys when they're mere toddlers—why?"

Krugman's eyes turn black.

"You send them away before they grow to be a physical threat," I say, realizing. "Right? Because boys have no place here."

Krugman stares outside. "No reproductive place." And after a long pause, in a strained whisper, he says, "The elders take care of that end." He does not look at me, only continues to stare outside at the darkness that shrouds the massacre on the streets.

"How long . . ." I begin to ask.

"Centuries. We've been here for centuries," he says. A long pause. The faintest hint of remorse touches his brow, the quickening of a long-dormant conscience. "And yes, there have been birth defects over the years. Inbreeding will do that over the long term. A sad but unavoidable consequence. Which we're always quick to remove. Out of sight, out of mind."

A cold chill pours down my back. I remember now. The hooded person carrying a newborn two nights ago, scurrying toward the Vastnarium.

Krugman pours himself a refill, the whisky spilling over the tumbler and splashing his fingers. He continues to pour, not caring. "Why don't you just wipe that judgmental expression off your face? You'd do the same. You have no idea the pressures we've faced. When we don't meet our quota," he says with sour, drooping lips, "they withhold food, supplies. Once, during a particularly dry spell, they decided to make a point. So they sprang a surprise on us. Among all the food delivered to us was an apple. So ordinary looking on the outside, but secreted within was a tiny razor blade that was contaminated with dusker saliva. It infected one of the girls when she bit into it. She turned." He giggles. "And we finally realized why the Palace had made us construct the Vastnarium months before."

His eyes meet mine in the glass.

"That was a warning to us. To keep us in line. After that, we tightened the screws around here. We increased . . . production. Girls' feet were 'beautified' to keep them from wandering, leaving. Boys were sent off younger and younger. We learned to hose down the train's shipments. Make sure everything was free and clear of . . . contaminants."

Two milky-pale bodies skimmer across the glass. They scamper off as quickly as they'd appeared, leaving behind thin sticky trails in their wake.

Sissy walks up to me, turns my face to hers. "Gene," she says. Her face looks like it's aged ten years. "Let's go. Let's just go."

"Or you can stay." Krugman's eyes look horrifically young, as if a little boy were peering out of a cage of fat and wrinkles and facial hair and dark circles and regret and fear. "Please stay. It's over now. And I've accepted it. I just don't want to die alone."

I feel no sympathy for him. He has the blood of countless children on his hands. He did nothing to break the cycle of blood and death, but instead benefited from the horrific exchange. He sold out his own people for what? Food and drink and the freedom to slake his lust on a town of innocent girls.

"Let me tell you how things will end for you," I say, walking to the door. "You will think you've prepared yourself for this moment but when they pour in like black water through a broken dam, you will scream. And you will be all alone. Do you understand? In a crowd of feasting pale bodies, you will be alone in a way you've never known loneliness."

We turn to leave.

"Please," he whimpers, "just leave the boy. That's all I'm asking—"

"Let's go," Sissy spits.

"—he reminds me of . . . me. When I was young. When I was innocent. Please! We're all dead, anyway. I just want to hear him sing. Please leave the boy . . ."

We walk out, Sissy's arm around Ben. The door swings shut, cutting off the sound of Krugman's voice.

42

AT THE TOP of the spiral staircase, Clair grabs me.

"No, Gene! Not that way!"

"Where then?" Howls reverberate up the metal stairs, vibrating the handrail.

"The fortress walls have been compromised!" Clair says. "The Mission's completely swarmed."

"We need to get to the train!"

"Forget the train!" she says, her face knotted in fear. "Didn't you hear anything Krugman said? The train leads only to more duskers!"

"We don't have any other choice. Staying here guarantees death. The train at least gives us a chance—"

Clair spins me around. She looks at me, a resolve burning in her eyes. "There's one way out of here. We can still get to the hang glider. You fly out. To where your father wanted you to go." She pulls me along. "You and Sissy can double up on the training hang glider for two."

"No way!" Sissy says. "I'm not leaving the boys, they're on the train—"

"Leave them be! They can't be saved."

"What about Ben?" I shout. "What about you?"

She shakes her head. "This is what your father wanted. For you to fly east. There're machinations at work you can't even begin to imagine, Gene. You and Sissy have to fly east. It was always meant to be the two of you."

"What did you say?"

"You have to go east—"

"What do you mean, *it was always meant to be the two of you*?"

For a moment, a wave of regret washes over her face. "I'm sorry. I really am. I lied before. That hang glider was for you and Sissy. Not me. Your father was insistent that you and 'the girl' were to fly east. Together." Her eyes tear up. "I was never 'the girl.' "

"I thought originally *you* were going with me. Isn't that what you said?"

Her eyes shoot down, weighted with regret and shame. "You're not the only one who wants to go to the Promised Land. I'm sorry. I let my own dreams get in the way of what your father wanted." She shakes her head. "It was always supposed to be you and Sissy."

A loud crash from below. Silence. Then screams unfurl up the stairwell.

"This way!" Clair says, knowing we have no choice but to follow. She turns left, tears down another hallway. The clamoring echoes of our boots race ahead, into the cold shadows. From behind, I hear the nattering *click-clicks* of claws against the floor.

Clair throws open a door and we rush into a room, faintly familiar. Clair is kicking away boxes and containers, then she's opening another door and pushing us all through. The door slams shut behind us, and I hear Clair moving in the complete darkness, her hand patting the wall. Then a snap, and the corridor breaks into a green glow.

Hang gliders emerge out of the darkness, hanging high above us like mammoth moths. Ben stares at them wide-eyed.

Clair is already grabbing the training model for two. It's surprisingly light, and Clair has no trouble carrying it herself.

Something pounds the door. Nails start clawing on the other side, nails breaking. Clair ignores the sounds, grabs equipment, GlowBurns, gloves. Another deafening blow that almost takes the door off its hinges.

"We need two more hang gliders!" I shout. "Clair, we—"

"We don't have time to find the operable ones! Almost all of these are in disrepair and—"

Another loud boom rocks the door.

"Not going to hold much longer," I yell. "We have to go now! *Now!*"

"Go first, I'll catch up with you!" she yells, picking up pairs of goggles, bags. "Down the corridor, out the door!"

"No! We leave now!" Behind us, the door thumps again, then continuously, bodies pounding against it like rain falling. Then the groan of bending metal.

"Clair!" I yell. And now we're all tearing down the hallway, dropping bags, losing equipment, but no longer caring. Only the hang glider matters.

The door explodes inward and duskers shoot in like pellets out of a gun. They surge toward us on the floor, walls, and ceiling, their screams deafening.

Clair flings open the door at the end of the corridor, and we throw ourselves through. I kick the door shut as I fall, and Sissy is already there, slamming down the latch. Duskers pummel the door from the other side, denting it with thunderous blasts. We gather ourselves, blood racing through our veins, and run up a flight of stairs and through another set of doors.

We're outside, the air cool and sweet. I stare down the length of the fortress wall—the takeoff strip. It's empty, not a dusker in sight.

But not for long. We've been spotted by duskers roaming the meadows, by duskers sitting like hawks along the fortress wall a stone's throw over. They're racing toward us on all fours, legs and arms bounding in a pale blur.

Clair starts trying to buckle me into the duo hang glider.

"No, Clair. Ben goes. With Sissy."

"No way," Clair answers. "It's supposed to be *you* and Sissy."

"I'm not going to waste time arguing," I shout. I pull my face close to hers, leveling our eyes. "I'm staying. Ben and Sissy are getting on."

"Let me tell you what Sissy's going to do," Sissy says. "Sissy's going back to the train. I'm not abandoning the boys."

The fortress wall begins to tremor. A wave of duskers screams from the meadows.

"Gene has to go!" Clair shouts. "The Scientist said—"

A *ding* of metal. Sissy's unsheathed a dagger and is pressing it into Clair's neck. "Strap yourself in."

Clair realizes there's no point resisting. She latches herself in, Sissy watching closely.

Sissy sheathes the dagger, grabs Ben.

"Sissy!" he cries.

"Ben," she says, strapping him in, zipping up his jacket. "We'll find you." She connects a pair of carabiners. "You're in good hands; Clair'll fly you to the Promised Land."

"Don't leave me," Ben says, lips trembling, tears beginning to pour down his cheeks.

A hum rumbles along the fortress wall. "Go now!" I shout. "They're almost on top of us."

Sissy gives Ben a quick hug. His tears smear on her face as she pulls away. "Go!" she shouts to Clair.

And then they're off, charging down the length of the wall, their legs kicking round and round. At the end of the strip, they throw their bodies through a gap in the wall. They plummet out of sight then resurface a second later, soaring into the night sky, the hang glider slanting up and away from the mountain. I see Ben's hair blowing in the wind, his arms rigid with fear. And then they're sailing away, smoothly, Clair firmly in control, heading east.

"We've got to get to the train," I say, looking for an escape.

The howls of the duskers screech closer. Across the meadows they pounce, slithering up the fortress walls.

Sissy turns to me, unhurried and deliberate. Something in her eyes slows everything down, and for the first time since I've returned to the Mission, we really look at each other. Her eyes pool with wetness even as a sad, brave smile touches her lips.

"I think we both know, Gene. This is the end."

Duskers—pale and naked as newborn rats—crest the sides of the wall. We're surrounded. The Hunt, begun so many days ago, is nearly over for them.

Sissy unsheathes two daggers, holds one out to me. "Fight to the finish?" she says.

I take the dagger. "Always."

Glass shatters behind us. It's Krugman's office. Naked duskers are scaling the walls, pouring into his office through the broken window. Like rotten milk down a sink. I can't hear Krugman screaming above the squall of the duskers, but I don't need to.

The light haloing out of the office is suddenly snuffed out, lightbulbs inside smashed, throwing everything into an even deeper darkness around us. The power is still running—I see sparks leaping inside the darkened office.

An idea turns on in my head.

My eyes snap to the top of the corner tower. There: the long power cable connecting the office tower to the main generator in the village. It crosses high above the meadows, over the swarms of incoming duskers.

Heart pumping furiously, I grab Sissy's hand, pull her along. No time to explain.

Behind us, as if enflamed by our attempt to flee, the duskers wail with fury.

We sprint. Our eyeballs bounce wildly in their sockets, mercifully blurring the sight of pale bodies emerging on both sides of the wall, like waves smashing up against the fortress walls. The duskers perch, eyes swiveling around to locate us; as we whisk by they jump onto the strip and bound after us.

"Your dagger belt," I shout at Sissy.

She hands me the belt as we reach the power line. I loop the belt over the cable, holding one end as the other end swings around. I tug down on the belt. It'll hold. It has to.

Facing me, Sissy drapes her arms around my shoulders, then leaps onto me, cinching her legs around my waist. I feel her head nod against mine, her lips pressed against my temple.

I leap. Into the night air, the ends of the belt looped around my wrists, Sissy clinging around my shoulders. The jolt of gravity as the belt takes the full brunt of our weight almost rips my arms out of their sockets. We bounce, once, twice, and the double impact causes Sissy to lose her grip; but her legs squeeze tighter around my hips, and she's able to link her arms around my shoulders again.

And then we're zip-lining down the cable with greater speed than leather on metal would seem to warrant. Sparks are shooting off like crazy from the belt, and only when I look up do I see why: a dagger is pinched between the belt and metal cable. It's metal on metal. We're flying. And sparking.

Far beneath us, duskers sprinting toward the wall stop in their tracks. Their upturned faces glare at us in surprise and fury. We soar safely over their outstretched, leaping arms.

Sissy, facing behind us, gasps. I turn my head to look. A dusker is chasing us down *on* the cable. Perfectly maintaining its balance on the high-wire, it's trotting along with surprising speed, its legs and arms working in careful, balanced synchrony, as sure-footed as a stallion on the widest, flattest green meadow.

It is horribly disfigured. Perhaps, desperate to gain an edge over the hundreds of other duskers, it had left the darkness of the caves prematurely and been exposed to lingering dusk light. Whatever the reason, it now has the appearance of a hairless cat on a balance beam. Half its face has melted, giving it a lopsided lunacy. It opens its mouth, jaws separating well beyond the point of dislocation, and screams. And still it widens its mouth, until the corners tear into its cheeks, splitting the skin like stretched cheese and exposing lines of fangs and teeth.

This brutish creature, with cheeks gone and incisors exposed, appears to be smiling at me in wonderment.

A flash of silver light. Sissy's removed a dagger from the belt and thrown it. At the dusker.

It's a direct hit. The dagger sinks into the hunter's chest cavity. Disappears.

Then splatters out the other side of its chest, having met little resistance.

The dusker stops momentarily. It—almost literally—doesn't know what just hit it. It seems only briefly surprised, as one might be by a sudden, embarrassing burp. And as unaffected. It fixes its eyes on me, continues its pursuit.

Another flash of light, another dagger thrown. This time at the hunter's face, at its eyes, a throw meant to deface and eviscerate.

But the dusker sees the throw. It slants its head at an angle; the dagger whizzes past. But the movement throws it off balance. It teeters for a second, trying to regain its balance. And in that second, Sissy throws another dagger. It slices right through the dusker's leg, at the ankle. The dusker blinks, once, twice, then loses its balance. Its arms spiral wildly as it plummets, its scream silenced when it splatters on the meadow floor.

Sissy and I glide into the village a minute later. By then, the power line is running low and almost parallel to the ground, and it's an easy landing. And not a second too soon. My arms are about to fall off.

The attacks in the village have only intensified. Screams come loud from darkened corners of the village, and from nearby cottages, wet sounds slip out of the shadows.

"The train's leaving any second now," Sissy whispers. "We have to hurry."

"Hug the walls," I say. "Keep your arms by your sides and as stationary as possible. Duskers are drawn by swinging motions."

Screams funnel toward us. We move in a ragged line, staying off main paths where we'd be more exposed, and sidle along narrow gaps between cottages. Sissy suddenly stops.

"What's wrong?" I ask.

She's gazing around the corner of a cottage, eyes sweeping across the village square. "We can skirt along on this side of the street, then cross about a hundred meters up where the street's much narrower. Or we can just race across now. But we'll be a lot more visible and exposed."

"There's no time," I say. "The train's about to leave. We cross now. Stay low."

We slide across, crouching. Halfway across, Sissy freezes. She's staring down the street, her eyes transfixed.

I turn my head slowly to look. Up the street, no more than a mere speckle, is a person. Clothed in white and bathed in the whitewash of moonlight, it stands like a marble statue before me. Even before I can make out its face, I know who it is.

It's Ashley June.

43

THE ORANGE-RED OF her hair drapes down her white body in a fiery curtain. Her eyes, twin specks of green diamond, pierce deep into me. She starts moving toward us, slowly. On all fours.

Sissy grabs my hand, tugs me forward. But I stand fast. It's too late for that.

"You go," I whisper to Sissy.

"No." She stays next to me, her hand still in mine.

"Go."

"No." She grips my hand tighter.

Ashley June saunters toward us, her shoulder blades jutting out her back with each stride. Her form is relaxed, like a zoo cheetah lazily pacing inside its cage on a hot summer night. Yet her eyes are raw and intense with desire. A small pouch bag is strapped tightly against her back.

Thirty meters away, she hisses; her hind legs bunch, and she is suddenly all coiled muscle and charged energy. Her arms shoot out as she bounds forward, grabbing the ground under her, thrusting her long sleek body upward and forward. Her eyes spear into mine with as much obsession as desperation.

"It's me!" I shout. "It's me!"

Not a flicker of recognition. Not a hint of a slowdown. She races toward me, her lips now snarling to reveal the bottom of her fangs.

Sissy reaches down instinctively for a dagger on her belt. But it is too late for that.

Ashley June comes, her legs and arms a blur under her loping body. Ten more bounding strides, and she will be at my throat.

"Ashley June!" I shout.

A flicker of recognition in her eyes. She snaps her head violently. Her eyes meet mine again, but there is a sliver of confliction now. She slows to a stop. Saliva dangles from each corner of her mouth, ropy and gelatinous, almost touching the cobblestone. Her head half cocks to the side. She frowns.

"It's me, it's Gene," I say.

She examines my face as if trying to place me. Something flits across her eyes, softens their gaze. Her lips tremble. She's beginning to recall.

"Ashley June." Despite my fear, I speak with tenderness. And with guilt.

A low growl rumbles from her throat. Her feet kick at the ground but she does not close the distance between us. Light suddenly blazes in her eyes, jolting her. She remembers me. Suddenly self-conscious, she wipes at the drools of saliva.

"Gene?" she whispers. The sound flutters out, girlish and shy.

I flinch back. The clash between her savage body and the gentle utterance of my name is almost too much. I turn my eyes away. Now she stands, rising off her arms and hands until she is upright on two legs. As if trying to reclaim her humanity. Yet a battle rages; every fiber in her wants to pounce me cheetah-like. I can see it in the saliva dripping off her still-exposed fangs, in her quivering thigh muscles. She wipes at her mouth again. And then her eyes latch onto something.

My hand. Holding Sissy's hand. Ashley June's eyes snake up the length of Sissy's arm and when her eyes lock onto Sissy's, it is as if she has noticed her for the first time.

Ashley June suddenly drops down to all fours again. A hardness coarsens her body, marbles her eyes. She shakes her head, sending ropes of saliva looping around her head, splattering in her hair. She crouches down, quivering with building energy, caving in to animalistic urges. Then explodes toward Sissy.

She is a blur, a dart flung with force. Thin, tight muscles bulge out of her arms, waves of muscle ripple across her thighs. And then she is springing herself.

At Sissy.

She rips Sissy away, flinging then pouncing on her fallen body. I'm knocked to the ground. By the time I've picked myself up, Ashley June is pinning Sissy down, her mouth clamped around Sissy's neck. Her teeth, her fangs, sunk deep, only her red-stained gums showing. Her eyes gaze languidly at me as she sucks and sucks and sucks.

Sissy is trying to squirm out but her arms are pinned. Her legs kick uselessly, strength draining out. She writhes futilely underneath. Ashley June's flaming red hair is splayed all across Sissy's prostrate body, like fingers spread wide, possessing and claiming her.

"NOOO!" I shout, and charge at Ashley June, throwing myself with all the force I can muster.

She smacks me away. I feel nails gash the side of my head but no pain. The pain will come later. I go flying, over ground that spins wildly beneath me. The impact smacks the air out of my lungs. I rise unsteadily, fall down. Start crawling toward Sissy.

Ashley June's eyes flick past me, over my shoulder.

Another dusker has emerged out of the dark shadows of a cottage. Its eyes are rapt with desire as it places me in its crosshairs. It crouches low and scuttles forward, crab-like, its legs and arms stabbing the ground like pincers.

Ashley June lifts her head from Sissy's neck, blood dripping down her chin. She growls at the other dusker.

In a split second, the dusker goes from crab-shuffle to puma-sprint. At me.

As it leaps past the unconscious Sissy, Ashley June snaps her hand out and grabs its long flowing hair. I hear the tear of hair roots ripped out of scalp skin. The dusker's legs fling out and it flips over, crashes to the ground. Ashley June is upon it before it can regain its footing. Crouched atop the dusker's body, she lowers her face until her nose is almost touching the dusker's. She snarls, her jaw widening to expose the long sabres of her razor-sharp teeth. The dusker snarls back, its eyebrows pulled together in fury. But also fear. It snaps at Ashley June.

Ashley June pulls her head back to avoid the clash of teeth. Then, in one fluid, powerful motion, she flings the dusker across the square. The dusker spins ungracefully through the air. Its upper torso smashes through a cottage window, its legs smacking into the siding. It hangs draped and twitching, half in, half out the window.

Ashley June turns to me. Her chest is heaving in and out. Her emerald eyes, clear and fierce, yet somehow also softened, contain a questioning, yearning glimmer. The pouch bag strapped on her back is ripped half open now; the cover of a book pokes out.

I take a step backward.

She is suddenly pummeled from behind by the other dusker, shards of glass sticking out of it. They fall away in a tangled ball of fangs and claws, hissing and attacking one another.

I use the precious few seconds to run to Sissy. Her eyes are closed; she's murmuring incomprehensibly. I pick her up in my arms, start sprinting. I ignore the sound of Ashley June fighting with the other dusker behind. I ignore the tiredness in my legs as I race across the meadows on the other side of the village, ignore even the sight of the train beginning to pull out of the station. Ignore the thunderous stampede I know is closing in on me, the horde from Krugman's office catching up with me. And most of all, ignore the heat humming off Sissy, the sweat pouring down her face, the ashen paleness in her face. Ignore the fact that she's begun turning. Right in my arms, she's turning.

I cry out sounds that have grown hidden and unseen in me for years, for my whole life, gurgled, strangled sounds of anguish. They pour out of me like a tide of fury, and they are more than the tears gushing down my face, more than the lactic acid rocking my legs.

The ground softens and undulates beneath my feet, and I can't locate solidity, can't find traction. And then I am collapsing because I have no strength left, because I cannot go on for one more stride, because the running and constant fleeing has wrung out the last drop of strength. I fall on the grass. Enough. Enough. I cradle Sissy's fevered head on my chest, gaze at the stars above. Feel the ground shaking under me. I hear their approach, so close now. Pounding of feet, hollers, high-pitched, hysterical voices.

Then hands grabbing at me, my legs, arms, pulling me apart.

No, not apart. Pulling me *up,* hands in my armpits, hoisting.

"Gene! Get up! Get up!"

Above me loom the faces of David and Jacob. They're already picking up Sissy, dragging her away. More footsteps approaching. It's Epap, and he pulls my arm over his shoulder. "Gene, you've got to help me. I can't carry you all by myself. Run, damn it! The train's pulling out!"

I do. As fast as I can, but I'm exhausted. I reach the platform, can barely climb the stairs. The train is halfway down the platform, pulling away. I see David and Jacob climb into the nearest train car, lower

Sissy to the floor. The train is already picking up speed. Epap and I are going to have to run for it. From behind us, a cry of anger. I steal a quick look back. There're about a dozen duskers way ahead of the pack. They'll be on us in less than ten seconds.

Jacob jumps out of the last car, sprints back to Epap and me. He pulls my arm over his shoulder, drags me. "C'mon Gene, come on, help us."

"Drop me," I say. "There's no time." I'm right, and they know it. We'll never make it to the train, not with me weighing them down; the duskers will get to us before then.

Jacob suddenly lets go of me, starts sprinting ahead. "Keep going, don't stop, get into the train!" he yells. And he bends over, picks up a hose from the platform. As we push past him, he flicks the ON button of the generator. It hums to life. Water shoots out, a strong propulsive force.

The duskers bound up the steps onto the platform. As they do, Jacob turns the hose on them. The jet of water smashes into their misshapen bodies. Their flesh—partially melted and made pliable by earlier exposure to the sun—is hosed off their bones in seconds, splattering off in a wet explosion of chunks. Not even their skeletal structure is spared. The jet of water obliterates their bones, sending fragments and chips flying into the air. The duskers disappear in a mist of bone and flesh. Jacob drops the hose, races to catch up with us.

And then he trips over another hose. Goes sprawling onto the platform floor.

A trio of duskers leap up the stairs. In seconds, they are upon him.

"NO!" Epap shouts. He drops me to the platform floor. Even as he vaults over a large container and picks up a nearby hose, the three duskers are already hunched over Jacob's body, fangs sunk into his neck and thigh, eyelids fluttering with rapture. Epap turns on the hose. In seconds, the duskers are obliterated. He runs to

Jacob, picks him up, slings him over his shoulder. Doesn't look to see the damage he knows has been inflicted.

I've gathered strength in the meantime, enough to scramble to my feet and kick aside hoses on the platform that might trip the approaching Epap. He draws even with me, and together we run for the train.

I can feel the heat pouring off Jacob in droves. Even without looking down, I know he's turning, and rapidly. Bitten and infected by *three* duskers, his turning will be exponentially swift.

"Faster! The train's pulling away!" David shouts, hanging out of the last train car.

Fear injects both Epap and me with adrenaline. We explode forward in a burst of speed. As we draw even with the train, David sticks his arm out of the still-open door. He pulls in Epap and Jacob, then me, and we go crashing onto the train floor. Sissy is lying next to us, still unconscious, surrounded by a group of kneeling village girls. The girl with freckles looks at me, then casts a panicky look back at the duskers giving chase.

"No, no, no!" Jacob says. He's beginning to shiver, sweat beads pouring out. I see his punctured neck, not just two tidy holes, but a slew of fang marks polka-dotting his neck. He's turning with exponentially accelerated speed.

He knows it, too. He looks at Epap with frightened eyes.

"You're going to be all right, Jacob!" Epap says, stroking back Jacob's hair. "Everything's going to be just fine."

Outside, we hear the manic cries of the duskers as they charge toward the train. It's gradually picking up speed but the doors are still open.

"Where's Ben?" David screams, looking back.

Jacob spasms, a film of sweat glimmering over his cold body.

"How much more speed?" I shout to the girl with freckles. "Before the doors close?"

"Soon!" she answers. "I think we've almost hit the critical speed."

And then, sure enough, there's a mechanical click, and the door begins to slide shut.

At the sound, Jacob turns to see. A haunted, terrible expression crosses his ashen face. "I'm turning," he says. He stares at the closing door. And he realizes what none of us have yet to fully grasp. If the door locks shut and he turns inside, everyone in this train car is dead.

Jacob springs to his feet. A second later, I realize what he's about to do. My hand shoots out to stop him, to tackle him to the floor. But I freeze. And in that hesitation, he takes three strides and is leaping through the closing gap. And then he is gone. The door clicks shut.

"NO!" David cries out, and he is already at the door, trying to pull it open. But it is locked and will be, until we reach the destination. "JACOB!" he shouts, "Jacob, Jacob!"

And Jacob has picked himself up, his face shuddering with fear and shock. He is out there in the world all alone for the first and only time in his life. It is more than he can stand, and he runs alongside us, if only to tenuously be with us a few seconds longer. David stretches out his arm between the bars, and for a moment, Jacob is able to sprint fast enough to catch up and hold his hand. His hair is flopping up and down, his cheeks are bouncing, his eyes are full of tears, this boy who dreamed of carousels full of galloping horses and leaping frogs and flying dolphins. He looks so small out there. He is alone and there is nothing we can do about it now.

The train picks up speed and Jacob can no longer keep up. Their hands begin to separate.

"Jacob!"

Their hands part.

And still he sprints as fast as he can, his arms swinging wildly, his legs a blur beneath him. He doesn't want to be alone, he doesn't want to fall away into the night, he doesn't want to lose sight of the only family he has known. But he is losing ground, the train now accelerating.

And then he trips and falls. I can barely look. He is a pale pebble on a beach of darkness. A tide comes from behind, swallowing him up.

The metal bars of the car start to vibrate. Not vigorously, more like a hum thrumming up and down the bars. But it increases, until the bars are shaking in my hands as if they're coming to life. And then it's not just the bars; the whole train starts pitching side to side.

A hard drumming noise fills the night, the sound of a thousand horses galloping. But these are no horses outside, gaining on us. Horses do not emit a pale fleshly gleam off their skin, do not hiss and spit and drool, do not howl and wail, do not emerge from darkness with the whites of their eyes glowing like demented moons.

A scream. A dusker has leaped onto the car, catching a small girl—who'd been leaning against the bars—by surprise. It rips her out through the bars, more or less in one piece, bones broken, joints pulled out of sockets. On the ground outside, it balls around her, silencing her screams.

"Move away from the sides!" I yell. The freckled girl starts throwing girls from the side into the center of the car. A dusker suddenly flies out of the darkness, splats onto the side, hands wrapping around bars with the dexterity of an ape, then reaches in, its arm slashing through the air.

"Duck down, stay down!" the freckled girl shouts, and a moment later, a dusker lands on the roof. We cower, flattening ourselves against the floor, just as its arm swings from above like a poisonous vine. It hisses in frustration, gobs of saliva dripping down onto us. I leap to Sissy, still lying unconscious, covering her neck bites from the dripping saliva, tucking in her arms and legs, making sure none of her limbs stray within reach of a dusker arm. Her skin is cold as ice, her arms jerking spasmodically.

Yet another dusker smacks against the side of the car, then another, rattling the car like a birdcage. And still they fall upon us, covering the exterior of the car until their collective pale skin drapes over the entire caged car. The translucent, membranous blanket of skin is a vision of hell. Dotted intermittently in this unbroken cover of skin, like a teat on a dog's underbelly, is a dusker face, hissing and snapping, eyes wide and gaping.

The train rattles on, speeding toward the bridge.

Under me, Sissy murmurs, her lips struggling to speak, her eyes closed. As if uttering a prayer. Or ministering last rites. To me. For now I feel the pain on the side of my head, and when I gingerly touch it, my fingers come away with blood. Where Ashley June had clawed me, had opened me up. With nails dripping in her own saliva.

The train rumbles forward, the duskers scream their strange howls at us, and the only thing I find myself capable of doing is tucking in the strands of Sissy's hair, carefully, obsessively, behind her ears.

The tracks start to rattle with a different tempo. We're crossing the bridge. *Throok-throok. Throok-throok.* The clacking of the rail tracks, passing underneath. And then we've crossed the valley and are heading down a steep decline, picking up earnest speed now. *Throok-throok, throok-throok-throok, throok-throok-throok-throok.*

I gaze back at the bridge through thin gaps between hanging duskers. On the other side of the bridge, I see swarms of duskers bottlenecking at the entrance to the bridge, dozens pushed and spilling over into the canyon.

And we pull farther away, gathering more speed, until we curve a bend, and the bridge, and the Mission, are no more.

44

THE JOURNEY THROUGH the night feels endless. We huddle together at first from the duskers who, refusing to let go, remain strapped onto the cage. Then later, we huddle for warmth against the bitter cold. We move boxes of supplies around us, cocooning ourselves within the tight perimeter. Nobody sleeps, nobody can, not with the gobs of deadly saliva dripping down on us, not with the intermittent screeches of anger and desperation from the duskers.

Sissy is burning hot, sweating profusely. Spasms shake her every so often. She is turning slowly—and I do not understand why it is so slow—but in a day or two, the disintegration will be complete. We cannot allow her to turn in here. When her turning progresses too far, we will be forced to do the unthinkable. We will have to move her to the side of the train car where, within reach of the duskers still draped on the bars, they will do what we cannot. No one mentions this but it weighs unspoken on all of us. On Epap most of all. He has not slept all night, has only stroked Sissy's hair again and again, his face taut with grief and worry, his other arm over David.

Sometime in the dark of the night, I slide over to her. She is burning furiously hot now. I unsheathe a dagger from her belt. Epap awakens, jolts at the sight of the dagger. He looks at me, thinks I am about to do a mercy killing.

"Not yet," he says. "She might still—"

"It's not what you think," I say. I place the dagger into my palm then slice; blood oozes out, pooling in my hand. The duskers are sent into a frenzy. I part Sissy's lips and drip the blood from my hand into her mouth.

"In case it's true. That I'm the Origin. That I'm the cure. Maybe it's in my blood."

But Epap is shaking his head, his eyes sad and withdrawn.

"It's our last resort," I say. "There's nothing to lose."

He can barely look at me as he speaks. "Gene," he says, pointing at the gash on the side of my head. Where Ashley June had cut me. "You're turning, too."

He's right. He's seen what I have been denying, the paleness of my skin, the sweat glistening off my face, the fact that my shivering is not from the freezing wind, but from something deeper and sicker, the start of convulsions.

"You're not the Origin," he says, lying back down, closing his eyes. "You're not the cure."

Dawn arrives. The duskers fling themselves off the train, with reluctance, with anger, some of them swiping away one last time in hopes of catching someone off guard. Only a few remain; then, in a collective howl, they leap off, scampering into the dense woods. With the sheet of duskers gone, the wind blows unabated through the birdcage-like train car.

Only one dusker remains. But only because it has no choice. It had leapt headfirst at the train car, and its head had rammed right through between two bars. It could not extricate itself, not even after hours of pulling, not even after dislocating its shoulders and breaking its jawbone in five places.

Sunrise arrives, and our ears are filled with the cries of that dusker until, sufficiently melted and softened like butter, it drops off, a pus-filled sac that splats wetly on the tracks. The train runs over it; yellow fluid is spun around wheels and spit up like a spinning firecracker. Gooey drops splatter down on us like thick yellow rain.

But it is morning, at last, and the rays of the sun offer a reprieve from the terrors of the night. No one speaks; we still sit huddled together despite the warmth of the sun, despite the absence of duskers.

A pale girl lifts her face to the sun, her eyes squinting. There is shock written all over her body, in her clutched hands, her tightly curled legs. But there is also a glint of hope in her eyes, an anticipation of what lies ahead. *The Civilization*, the shine in her eyes seems to suggest, *the Civilization*. Her eyes flick to me, hold my gaze for a second or two. The bars of the cage cast slanted shadows across her face.

Perhaps I should tell her the truth. Everything Krugman told me. But even now, in my feverish state, I'm beginning to question that truth. Because something doesn't quite add up. But I say nothing, only tear my eyes away from her, tuck my head down. The sunlight, like acid to my turning eyes. Its rays slip through the pores of my skin, into my bones, jangling harshly against nerve endings I never knew existed in my marrow. Epap is right. I'm turning. I shake. I shiver.

45

In the afternoon, we open the boxes of supplies. There's a lot of warm clothes we no longer need now that we're entering warmer low-lying terrain. We find paper, stationery, medical supplies. And, to cries of relief, a chest filled with canned peaches. A baker's dozen, to be exact, which coincidentally matches the number of us in the train car. For now. By nightfall, there might be two fewer. The freckled girl distributes the cans. After a moment's consideration, she places one next to the still-unconscious Sissy. She warns us to consume it judiciously. Nobody knows for sure how long the trip will last. It might be several days.

Epap scribbles individual names on each can. A good way to learn new names, he says. He is trying to be brave, trying to be strong. He writes Sissy's name on her can. He is refusing to acknowledge the undeniable: in a few hours he will have to do the unthinkable. First to her, then to me. He scribbles my name on a can, as if to make a point.

I stare at the cans of peaches, standing side by side. My name, Sissy's name, scrawled in block letters. Like names on our tombstones.

Nighttime. I spasm awake, feeling the chill of the desert night clinging to my bones. Even the light of the moon has become an assault on my eyes. The turning is nearing completion. A cool breeze whistles through the train car, tinged with the scent of smoke. I sit up, glance up. A column of thick smoke rises from the lead car's smokestack. The engine must have automatically kicked in after we'd lost our downhill momentum. It will stay at this speed, in all likelihood, all the way to the Palace, never slowing down. Everything automated.

Like my turning.

I shiver, my whole body racked with tremors. My heart racing, my shirt sticky with the cold condensation of sweat. The slowness of the turning, an agony all its own. Moonlight splashes through the cage; the shadows of the metal bars bend and curve across the topography of our bodies. Now and then, a girl cries out, lost in her nightmare. I sit up, feel the crackle of dried, crusty bone. David sleeps fitfully next to me, anguished words murmuring out of his lips. I pull the blanket over him. His arm is draped across the empty space on his other side. Where Jacob would be sleeping.

The land lumbers by, miles and miles of nothingness. Sissy lies at my feet, her head nestled in Epap's lap. The daggers sheathed in her belt glint in the moonlight, beckoning me. My fingers touch the rough leather of her belt. I unhook the strap, draw a dagger out. It is time.

Epap will not do it. But I can. I must. First her, then me.

I place the dagger against her neck. The blade sinks into her soft flesh; I see the ripple of her pulse beating just above the blade.

It is pulsing out with a slow steadiness, not rapid hammering. With a frown, I touch her skin.

It is dry. It is warm.

I place my hand over her heart. The heartbeat is steady and slow.

She's not turning anymore. She's *un*turning.

I stare at her calm, rested face, not understanding. A wind blows through the bars, and I shiver with the heated delirium of the turning.

"Sissy?"

Her eyelids flutter slightly. She is coming to. Her arm slips out from under the blanket, knocks against the peach cans by her head. Mine and hers, side by side.

I think I see something, and my heart, for reasons not immediately apparent, starts to hammer away even faster.

And then I hear something, the voice of my father, his voice startlingly clear even after so many years: *You're looking but not seeing. Sometimes the answer is right under your nose.*

Sissy starts to stir awake. Her tongue laps out, dry and white, moistening her cracked lips. Her eyelids begin to open, not with the jittery flutter from earlier in the day, but with a sureness about it.

In a few moments, she will come to, sit up, look at me.

But not yet. My eyes fall on the cans again, standing side by side. At the letters scrawled, the names Epap had written on them.

Gene. Sissy.

But not quite. Because her name, with so many letters, is only partially visible. Just the first three letters are visible, the last two letters disappearing behind the curvature of the can.

Sis.

The name the Scientist christened her with.

And suddenly, I am thinking of the hang glider. *It was always meant to be the two of you.* I am thinking of Krugman, his insistence that the Origin was something typographical. Of Epap, saying my father always gave names for a specific reason. Of my blood, in her, conjoining with hers.

I keep staring at the names, and I am a blind man who suddenly gains sight.

Gene. Sis.

Gene. Sis.

Genesis.

She starts opening her eyes, eyes that I will never look at again in the same way.

Her eyes open, locking onto mine. She does not flinch, does not blink against the moonlight splashing down on her face. She will think my eyes widen because of gladness, because of surprise, on seeing her revive.

But they widen only because of realization; because of the truth that has been staring me in the face all this time. Right under my nose.

Genesis. The beginning.

The *Origin*.

Not me. Not her. But both of us.

Together, we are the cure.

Don't miss the final book
in the Hunt trilogy

The Trap

Available November 2013

Acknowledgments

Catherine Drayton has continued to be an agent par excellence. I am thankful to have in my corner someone so dependable, whose insights and business acumen I have come to both rely upon and take for granted. Thank you also to the übertalented people at InkWell Management, especially Richard Pine, Lyndsey Blessing, Charlie Olsen, and Kristan Palmer.

I am especially indebted to Rose Hilliard, my editor at St. Martin's Press. I have a deep appreciation for her wizardly editorial skills, warm encouragement, and elegant guidance. This book breathes clarity, depth, and life because of her. Many thanks also to Matthew Shear, Anne Marie Tallberg, Joseph Goldschein, Loren Jaggers, Paul Hochman, Jeffrey Dodes, and NaNá V. Stoelzle.

Thank you to Ingrid Selberg, Venetia Gosling, Kathryn McKenna, and the rest of the team at Simon & Schuster UK for embracing this series with such tireless dedication.

For their generosity with time and words, I am forever indebted to Andrea Cremer, Becca Fitzpatrick, Richelle Mead, and Alyson Noël. Your early support meant—and has continued to mean—the world to me. Thank you so much.

Thank you to Monsters Calling Home for inspiring me.

And finally, to Ching-Lee and the boys, for love and support and laughs and rest and hope and fun and excitement and joy and sanctuary and inspiration and a hundred thousand other reasons.

CPSIA information can be obtained
at www.ICGtesting.com
Printed in the USA
LVHW090040220821
695820LV00015B/1399